"*O Little Town* serves up three d[...] [...]rs who have perfected the art of cr[...] [...]ll want to grab a mug of hot coc[...] [...]es of healing, budding romance, [...] [...]nt cover-up, all set in the picturesque, wintry backdrop of small-town Mapleview, Michigan. The endearing characters found within these pages will leave you savoring each story to the last drop."

AMANDA COX, author of the 2021 Christy Book of the Year, *The Edge of Belonging*

"In this heartwarming compilation, three talented authors bring us the perfect blend of small-town nostalgia and holiday warmth. Spanning over a century, these stories capture the hopes and heartaches of three couples as they approach the holidays and remind us of the deeper meanings found within the Christmas season. As timeless as the notes of a favorite carol and as softly luminous as lights twinkling on an evergreen tree, this anthology is destined to become a much-beloved addition to your festive reading list."

AMANDA BARRATT, Christy Award–winning author of *The White Rose Resists*

"I'm in love with Mapleview, Michigan, and the people who call it home—past and present. With heartwarming journeys and characters that grab hold of your heart, *O Little Town* is a perfect holiday read—that can be read anytime!"

TAMERA ALEXANDER, *USA Today* best-selling author of *Colors of Truth* and *With This Pledge*

"Recipe: Take one charming schoolhouse in a small town in Michigan, blend in novellas from three different decades, add a teaspoon of history, a pinch of mystery, a tablespoon of faith, and a heaping cup of swoon-worthy romance. Result: *O Little Town* is the perfect book to savor this December, hot chocolate in hand."

ELIZABETH MUSSER, award-winning author of *The Swan House*, *The Promised Land*, and *By Way of the Moonlight*

"A charming tale of love and joy. Raney's voice shines in this sweet romance."

RACHEL HAUCK, *New York Times* best-selling author of *The Wedding Dress*

"*O Little Town* is an absolutely delightful collection of three charming stories from three talented authors. This book is filled with tender romance, hope, redemption, and even a little mystery that is sure to warm the hearts of readers on the coldest of winter nights. A lovely read!"

HEIDI CHIAVAROLI, Carol Award–winning author of *Freedom's Ring* and *The Orchard House*

"At turns charming and thrilling! Mapleview at Christmas brings out the best in all these characters, especially those reluctant to be there! This collection brims with a sense of community and family. Heartwarming romances set across the decades, all leading to Home."

ERICA VETSCH, author of the Thorndike & Swann Regency Mysteries series

———— ❊ ————

Find more Christmas cheer in

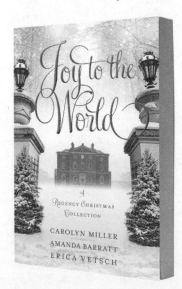

A
ROMANCE CHRISTMAS
COLLECTION

O Little Town

AMANDA WEN

JANYRE TROMP

DEBORAH RANEY

KREGEL
PUBLICATIONS

Published by Kregel Publications, a division of Kregel Inc., 2450 Oak Industrial Dr. NE, Grand Rapids, MI 49505. www.kregel.com.

"While Mortals Sleep" by Janyre Tromp published in association with William K. Jensen Literary Agency, 119 Bampton Court, Eugene, OR 97404.

The persons and events portrayed in these works are the creations of the authors, and any resemblance to persons living or dead is purely coincidental.

Scripture quotations are from the ESV® Bible (The Holy Bible, English Standard Version®), copyright © 2001 by Crossway, a publishing ministry of Good News Publishers. Used by permission. All rights reserved.

Library of Congress Cataloging-in-Publication Data
Names: Wen, Amanda, 1979- Hopes and fears. | Tromp, Janyre. While mortals sleep. | Raney, Deborah. Wondrous gift.
Title: O little town : a romance Christmas collection / Amanda Wen, Janyre Tromp, Deborah Raney.
Description: Grand Rapids, MI : Kregel Publications, [2022]
Identifiers: LCCN 2022011595 (print) | LCCN 2022011596 (ebook) | ISBN 9780825447488 (paperback) | ISBN 9780825469602 (kindle edition) | ISBN 9780825478642 (epub)
Subjects: LCSH: Christmas stories, American. | Romance fiction, American. | LCGFT: Christmas fiction. | Romance fiction. | Novellas.
Classification: LCC PS648.C45 O15 2022 (print) | LCC PS648.C45 (ebook) | DDC 813/.08508334--dc23/eng/20220314
LC record available at https://lccn.loc.gov/2022011595
LC ebook record available at https://lccn.loc.gov/2022011596

ISBN 978-0-8254-4748-8, print
ISBN 978-0-8254-7864-2, epub
ISBN 978-0-8254-6960-2, Kindle

Printed in the United States of America
22 23 24 25 26 27 28 29 30 31 / 5 4 3 2 1

Hopes and Fears

AMANDA WEN

CHAPTER ONE

Mapleview, Michigan
November 1912

"Have a wonderful weekend," Emma Trowbridge called to the last of her departing students as they clambered down the steps of the redbrick schoolhouse into a crisp, cloudy afternoon. "Make wise choices and honor the Lord. I love each and every one of you."

Her pupils—twenty in all, plus the older ones from the upstairs classroom—responded with murmurs of "Thank you, Miss Trowbridge," as they headed toward the stable out back to retrieve their horses or traipsed down Twenty-Fifth Avenue, lunch pails in hand.

"I love you, too, Miss Trowbridge." This from Janie Seiler, a precocious, freckle-faced blond. At six, she was Emma's youngest student.

Emma pulled the little girl close for a quick embrace. "Off with you, now. Best get home before it really starts coming down." Snowflakes had drifted from the sky since lunchtime, highlighting barren branches. They swirled thicker now, brilliant white accumulating between the street's deep maroon bricks.

"Don't worry, Miss Trowbridge! I'm fast like a horse. See?" Janie scampered down the lane, braids bouncing behind her.

Emma watched until the little girl disappeared around the corner, then turned back to her classroom, where she began cleaning the blackboard. As usual at the end of the day, her brain was full of both evaluation of today's lessons and preparation for tomorrow's.

At the top of her list? The Christmas pageant.

Though the school's traditional holiday offering was a series of short recitations and songs, this year a new play tugged at her heartstrings. She'd seen a performance of *Met in Thee Tonight* two years prior and was instantly inspired by its fresh approach to the familiar story. Her previous school had been too small to make it practical, but here at Visser School, the students were numerous enough—and talented enough—that it just might work.

In past years, she'd have simply purchased the script herself, since, in a one-room school, there was no one else with whom to coordinate. No supervisor to ask. But her recent move to the larger town of Mapleview meant a two-room schoolhouse, complete with a principal, Mr. Rudolf de Haven, who also taught the upper grades in the upstairs classroom. Working closely with another teacher had taken some getting used to, but there was no denying the superiority of the two-room approach when it came to individual attention and age-appropriate instruction. And since he valued ability over credentials, Mr. de Haven certainly didn't mind that her certification came from County Normal rather than some fancy four-year teacher's college.

Emma brushed chalk from her hands, smoothed her skirt, and headed upstairs for her daily check-in with Mr. de Haven. She'd grown fond of these afternoon meetings with a colleague and mentor who'd also become a close friend.

"Afternoon, Miss Trowbridge." Mr. de Haven's salt-and-pepper head was bent over a stack of papers, his pen dancing across a line of composition. "I trust your day was productive and inspiring as always?"

"Even more so." Enthusiasm bubbled within. "Jesse Meijer's recitation this morning was the finest he's given. He really seems to be turning a corner, that one. Which brings me to the annual Christmas pageant." She paced in front of his desk, woolen skirt swishing around her ankles. "Now, I know our current format is quite traditional, but two years back I saw a newer pageant—a play, really—one that would involve the whole school in various roles in a unique retelling of the biblical . . ." Her colleague's drawn expression put a stop to both her pacing and the babbling brook of ideas. "Mr. de Haven?"

"I'm afraid the Christmas play will be something you'll need to discuss with my replacement, Miss Trowbridge."

"Your replacement?" Emma's heart lurched. "Sir, I don't understand."

His hazel eyes were sad and faraway. "I've had a letter from my mother."

"Oh no. Is it your father?" The elder Mr. de Haven had been in poor health the last several months with an illness he couldn't quite shake. Something similar to what had taken Emma's mother several years ago.

Her colleague nodded. "Mother can no longer shoulder the burden of his care alone. I've informed the district I'll be unable to fulfill my contract for the remainder of the term, effective immediately. Lord willing, I'll return in the fall."

The words that hung heavy between them—*after he's passed*—filled Emma's eyes with tears. "I'm so sorry, Mr. de Haven. I'll be praying for your father. For all of you."

He cleared his throat. "Much appreciated, my dear Miss Trowbridge."

"You'll keep in touch? When you can?"

"Of course." A glint of amusement flickered amidst the sorrowful strain. "I'll want detailed reports of how you and young Mr. Oberstein are getting along in my absence."

Emma's brows shot to her hairline. "Not . . . *Frederick* Oberstein, is it?"

"The same. He's been in an administrative role for three years or so, but he has teaching experience in the upper grades and comes highly recommended. And he was one of the first four-year graduates from Michigan State Normal College."

Emma stifled the urge to roll her eyes. "Of course he was." Her childhood nemesis always had to have the best. To *be* the best. He came from furniture money, never once hesitating to point out the Oberstein Furnishings stamp on the bottom of their desks. Smart as a whip—and fully aware of the fact—he frequently stood at the head of the class during their school days.

He rarely stood alone, though. Despite being two years his junior and bereft of many of the advantages into which he'd been born, Emma still frequently held the spot right beside Frederick. Most of the time, he ranked at the top, but on rare occasions, she bested him. Not once did he let her win, so her hard-earned victories remained among her most cherished memories.

But then, toward the end of their shared school days and to her infinite horror, her traitorous heart had softened toward him. Begun to want things she shouldn't want with someone so obnoxious, so merciless in his desire to win. He was arrogant. Domineering. Everything wrong with the male species, wrapped up into a single package . . . and yet, she'd fancied him. So much so that—her stomach lurched at the memory—she'd poured out her fevered, fourteen-year-old feelings in an impassioned letter, which she thrust into his hand at the train station moments before he left for Ypsilanti.

He never wrote back, thank the Lord in heaven. And she'd hoped and prayed her past would never come back to haunt her.

But the heavy tread on the stairs told her those prayers had been in vain.

"Do you know him, Miss Trowbridge?" Mr. de Haven's voice penetrated only the periphery of her awareness.

A second later, Frederick appeared. Coffee-brown hair sparkling with snowflakes. Warm dark eyes. Straight nose, square jaw, and that slight scar above his left eyebrow, the mark of a tumble from a tree at age ten. Lanky limbs had gained muscle, and his countenance held a bit more wisdom and experience than when she last saw him . . . but he was still the very same Frederick Jedediah Oberstein she remembered from childhood.

"Mr. de Haven, I . . ." The salutation died as his keen gaze swept over her. His brow furrowed. "Emma?"

And then the tilt of the head. The glint in the eyes.

That *smirk*—the one that had infuriated and infatuated her in equal measure.

"I did know him. Once. A long time ago." Her gaze snapped from him to Mr. de Haven. "Please excuse me." Then, cheeks aflame, she swept past him and clattered down the stairs to the safety of her own classroom.

For a single instant, the life his younger self had dreamed of lay before him.

Neat rows of desks. A bright American flag. The trademark smells of woodsmoke and wet wraps, chalk dust and musty books. The canvas upon which he, the young idealist armed with impressive credentials and undeniable passion, could change the world.

It would be hard to walk into a school to teach again. He'd braced himself from the moment the county board informed him he'd have to leave the cocoon of administration and return to the classroom.

But Emma Trowbridge standing at the front of that classroom? That he hadn't prepared for.

Mr. de Haven looked up from the stack of papers on his desk. "Best get that ironed out, Mr. Oberstein."

"Forgive me, sir, but I think it best if you and I start—"

"We will. But these essays won't grade themselves. I can almost guarantee I'll still be here when you're finished with Miss Trowbridge."

Wry amusement tugged Frederick's lips. "You've clearly never tangled with Emma Trowbridge."

"Apparently not in the same way you have." With a mischievous gleam in his eyes, de Haven jerked his chin toward the staircase. "Go."

Steeling himself for a return to their old rivalry, Frederick descended the wooden stairs and rounded the corner into the back of her classroom.

Emma had always dreamed of being a teacher, and she'd set up the downstairs classroom precisely the way he'd pictured she might. A large, scripted copy of the Golden Rule stretched across the wall above the blackboard. The Stars and Stripes stood at attention between photos of Washington and Lincoln, and alongside them hung portraits of dignitaries ranging from Shakespeare to Clara Barton.

Emma stood with her back to him, broom swishing across the wood-planked floor with decisive strokes. Her chestnut hair—in braids the last time he'd seen her—was swept up into a more adult style, though a couple of wayward curls had escaped to dance around her cheek. Always on the small side, she'd added a few inches here and there—but what a womanly difference those inches made.

He shuffled his feet, the floor creaking beneath them.

Emma flicked a glance at him over her shoulder. "It's going to be rather awkward working together if you don't speak to me, Mr. Oberstein."

"Forgive me, Em—Miss Trow—Em—Miss Trowbridge." *Oh, good heavens.* "I simply didn't expect to see you here."

How could he, when he never expected to be here himself?

She turned, challenge sparking in brilliant blue eyes. "You're surprised I became a teacher?"

"Not in the least. You always managed to achieve anything you set your mind to."

"Unless you got in my way." At least, that's what it sounded like she muttered as she stashed the broom in the corner. But when she turned to face him, a no-nonsense, highly professional expression was firmly in place. "Now. Welcome. I realize I should give you a chance to settle in to your new post, but time is of the essence, and we really can't wait any longer."

"Longer for what?"

"The Christmas play. I tried to speak with Mr. de Haven earlier, but he says the decision falls to you."

Christmas. Frederick stiffened against the two-syllable blow.

"The students have been performing the same pageant since before I came to Visser, and they find it trite and uninspiring." She clasped her hands in front of her, lips flickering in a self-deprecating smile. "All right. *I* find it trite and uninspiring. Although when I broached the subject yesterday, the students also responded with a palpable lack of enthusiasm."

Hmm. Perhaps he and the students already had common ground.

"There's a new play I've got my eye on that would be much better suited to our students' abilities and interests, and more worthy of the momentous event of our Savior's birth."

His chest tightened. "A play?"

"Yes. *Met in Thee Tonight* by William Mueller. I saw it performed two years ago and found it deeply moving. I've located a bookshop in Grand Rapids that carries the necessary copies, but we'll also need costumes, sets—perhaps see if one of the nearby farms can provide live animals, and—"

"No." His voice sliced through Emma's pink-cheeked enthusiasm. This time of year already threatened to undo him. A play like that would guarantee it.

"No?" The sparkles in her eyes turned to sparks.

"I've received instruction from the school board not to approve any unnecessary expenditures." It was true, thank God. A providential excuse that nearly made him sink to his knees in gratitude.

She tilted her head. "It sounds as though the school board warned you about me."

Oh, they had. But they hadn't needed to. "The furniture workers' strike has had ripple effects across the whole of West Michigan. Governor Osborn's cut school funding to eliminate the deficit."

"I'm not a child, Frederick." Hurt flashed in her eyes. "I understand the straits we're in. But this play, with its literary depth, scriptural accuracy, and sheer memorability, will have a ripple effect far beyond this generation. If you'd seen the look in the eyes of the girl who played the angel, or how tall the boy walked as the shepherd Malachi, or heard stories of the impact God made on the students through this play . . . How can you put a price tag on a connection between learning and life? One that may well change eternity? The Frederick Oberstein I remember would've jumped at this sort of chance. Especially for Christmas."

The Frederick Oberstein you remember is dead and gone. Silenced in a savage instant by a spooked horse and a shattered sleigh.

He swallowed hard. "People grow up. They assume adult

responsibilities. And part of my responsibility as principal of Visser School—"

"—*Interim* principal—"

"—is to ensure the basics of education are achieved before any frippery."

"*Frippery.*" She flung the word in his face like a snowball.

He gritted his teeth and met her gaze. "Were it up to me, I'd cancel the pageant altogether. But I fear the good citizens of Mapleview would come after me with torches and pitchforks."

"Justifiably."

"So the pageant may proceed as scheduled, using the present script and costumes and the like." The words contained a bit more anger than he'd have wished, and he pulled in a breath. "Now, if there's nothing further, I have some things to discuss with Mr. de Haven before he departs."

Emma's expression churned like the sky on a stormy day. She turned on her heel, crossed the room toward the door, then paused, hand on the knob. "We're not schoolchildren anymore, Frederick. And this is no petty rivalry. You might have that fancy four-year degree, and you might have more experience than I do, but you don't know this town. You don't know these children, and you have no idea what's best for them. I do. And I'll fight for these students, no matter the cost."

And then she was gone, slipping into the cloakroom like a mist, but the *creak-slam* moments later reassured him she was very much real.

No matter the cost. He might've said those words himself not long ago. He'd been so like her once, full of fire and drive, stopping at nothing to secure the best for his students. But she had no idea how steep the cost could be.

Neither had he.

His feet like lead, Frederick trudged up the stairs to the second-floor classroom, his prison cell for the rest of the term.

Cost?

Ha.

It had cost him everything.

Chapter Two

The freshly lit fire reached tentative fingers of warmth into the chilled Monday morning classroom as Emma sat down at her desk to review her lesson plans for the day. Her first full day with Frederick Oberstein in the upstairs classroom, an unpleasantry upon which she refused to dwell.

Another unpleasantry sat at the corner of her desk, left of the globe: a stack of papers outlining the traditional Christmas pageant. With a sigh that puffed clouds of vapor up around her face, Emma retrieved the stack and leafed through it. Short, mediocre poems and simpering songs for the younger students. Brief, uninteresting sketches for the older ones. The same old thing, year after year. Nothing challenging. Nothing to inspire her students to give their very best. Nothing that would truly connect them to the Christmas story.

It just didn't feel right, especially this year. Jesse Meijer had finally overcome his struggles with reading aloud and needed something to sink his teeth into. The once-shy Viola Taylor had begun to display a flair for the dramatic. These two in particular needed more to do than stand in place and stare beatifically at the swaddled gourd that would play the infant Jesus. They needed a challenge.

And the reason they couldn't experience one? Frederick Oberstein.

Oh, Lord, quiet my spirit. Quench this bitterness, this rebellion. Frederick is my superior—for the moment anyway—and if he says no, then it needs to be no. If this pageant is your plan for yet another year, then please

15

provide the enthusiasm we need to do the old one to the best of our abilities. But, Lord, if there's any other way . . .

"*Goedemorgen*, Miss Trowbridge." Though many of her students' families spoke at least some Dutch, the full-throated, half-sung baritone greeting that accompanied the knock at her door could belong only to one person.

With a smile, Emma leaped to her feet and opened the door to the elderly yet still spry Jan Voorhees. "Goedemorgen to you too." The once-surprising sight of the white-haired man with his wheelbarrow full of books had become most welcome over the last few years, especially for the area farmers and pastors who depended on Jan and his mobile bookshop to stock their own libraries.

"You're on my circuit today. I knew I'd have to get here before those little troublemakers started flooding in." Jan's smile bloomed beneath his neatly trimmed white mustache as he stood at the bottom of the steps. "Got any good stories for me?"

"Always." For the next few minutes, Emma regaled her bookseller friend with tales of her students' latest escapades, delighting in his merry laughter.

"And how is your *vader*?" he asked.

"He has his ups and downs." Emma rubbed her hands together to ward off the biting cold. "Christmas is always difficult since Mother passed, but each year gets easier."

"Earth has no sorrow that heaven can't heal, after all." Jan adjusted his grip on the wheelbarrow. "I'd best be off, but I'd be derelict in my duty if I didn't inquire as to your interest in a few new books for your classroom."

"Not today, my friend." Emma tamped down the rising bitterness at the knife-sharp swiftness of Frederick's denial the day before. "I've been told we can't afford any new purchases at the moment."

"Then I'll do my best not to tempt you, painful though it may be." With a grin, Jan started the wheelbarrow in motion. The piles of books within shifted, and there, in a patch of pale morning sunlight—

Was that?

It was!

William Mueller's *Four New Plays for Churches or Schools*.

"One moment, Mr. Voorhees!" She skipped down the steps and slid the slender leather-bound volume from his wheelbarrow. Leafed through it. Breathed fresh ink and crisp paper.

And there it was. *Met in Thee Tonight*. The script bore a few scribbled notes, some modified staging instructions, but was otherwise pristine.

"Where did this come from?" she asked.

"A church over in Byron Township," Jan replied. "A bit of a surprise, since it's but a few years old. I suppose it wasn't to that congregation's taste. In any event, it's yours if you're interested."

She closed the book, chilled fingertips caressing the smooth cover. "I can't." Frederick was her principal. Interim principal . . . but still. He'd said no. So she couldn't just . . .

Unless . . .

"How much?" Frederick's objection had been to the expenditure of district funds. But perhaps, if it wasn't too dear, she could pay for it with her own pocket money.

Jan quoted a price, and she gulped. It would cost most of her meager savings, leaving little for the purchase of Christmas gifts for her family. Ah, well, she could always make the gifts. Surely her loved ones could use new knitted scarves or mittens.

However, Jan only had one copy. How would she distribute it to the students? Father had gifted her a typewriter when she began her teaching career, but how many late nights would she have to spent hunched over it to produce sufficient copies?

By the same token, though, how could she stand by and watch Jan Voorhees wheel a golden opportunity off into the snowy Michigan sunrise?

"I'll take it." She held the book out to Jan. "I'm afraid I don't have any money on me at the moment, but if you come back tomorrow, I'll—"

"Consider it a Christmas gift, Miss Trowbridge."

Emma froze. "Are you certain?"

Jan waved away any objections she was gathering. "I'm just happy to see it find a new home and watch it take the next steps on God's path."

Her eyes stung. "Oh, thank you, Mr. Voorhees. Thank you. A thousand times, thank you."

The old bookseller touched the brim of his hat, then hefted the wheelbarrow and walked on, footsteps crunching through the freshly fallen snow.

Hugging the volume to her chest, Emma retreated to the warmth of the schoolroom. *Met in Thee Tonight* was hers. *Hers.* Whatever long hours, whatever late nights lay ahead would be worth the students' sparkling eyes and eager enthusiasm.

And she'd pulled it off without spending a penny of district money.

Take that, Frederick Oberstein. She allowed a small, triumphant smile as she stood at the head of the class. Of all her victories over her old rival, this one had the potential to be the sweetest.

Frederick trudged through the snow, stomach twisting, palms damp inside his mittens. A man pushing a wheelbarrow full of books bade him a cheerful good morning, a greeting Frederick returned with only the most economical of waves.

And now here he stood, taking in the two-story schoolhouse, its red bricks interwoven with cheerful yellow ones in the Dutch style typical of the area. A festive green wreath hung on the snow-capped entrance, and greenery was draped around the windows. Emma must've been industrious over the weekend.

Once upon a time, he'd have been just as devoted to sharing the joy of the season. Christmas used to be his favorite time of year.

Now he hated it.

Because everything, everywhere, reminded him of Maria.

Especially this schoolhouse. Guilt and grief battled for supremacy as he stared up at the stately brick structure.

How ironic that a school building would be so tied up with Maria, given that it was the last place his little sister ever wanted to be. She tolerated the hours of learning only because school was where her countless numbers of friends could be found.

But as a teacher, he'd practically lived there. With their parents away on extended holiday that year and Maria in his care, she'd spent nearly as much time at the school as he did.

And in his care was the last place she should have been.

After pulling in a breath of frigid air, he forced one foot in front of the other and climbed the small staircase to the entrance. Perseverance. Wasn't that part of the scriptural progression? Suffering to perseverance to character to hope? By now he was well-versed in suffering. Perhaps perseverance was next.

Character and hope? Those felt a long way off.

He stomped snow from his boots on the threshold, then pulled the door open, doffed his hat, and hung it on the rack. A gentle lilting hum from Emma's classroom signaled she was already there and hard at work.

The tune stopped at his heavy tread on the floor by her doorway. Emma turned from the board, chalk still in hand, a chestnut curl springing free from its neatly pinned style. "Mr. Oberstein. Good morning." Her brow furrowed. "Are you all right?"

He fixed his attention on a bit of snow clinging to the toe of his right boot. Doubtless she'd seen evidence of his nearly sleepless night. She never did miss a detail. "First day nerves, I suppose."

"You? Nerves?" With a quiet laugh, she turned back to the board. "Never thought I'd see the day when the great Frederick Oberstein admitted to a case of the jitters."

Her comment drew a small grin. "The great Frederick Oberstein hasn't been in the classroom for quite a while."

"Climbing the administrative ladder, no doubt." The swish of chalk on the board underpinned her remark.

"Something like that."

"Well, you're tremendously talented and you've worked hard. That combination should bring it all right back to you."

His head snapped up. That sounded dangerously close to a compliment. From *Emma*.

"We're stuck together, Mr. Oberstein." She set the chalk in the tray and turned to face him, pink lips curved in a bright, if slightly forced, smile. "It's in everyone's interest for us to make the best of it."

If she kept talking, the words bounced off his awareness, thanks to the little leather book on her desk. *Four New Plays for Churches or Schools.*

"What's the meaning of this?" He crossed the room and picked up the offending book. She called this making the best of it? "I thought I made myself clear on Friday."

"You did." Emma folded her arms across her chest. "But before you get all grumpy about it, you should know it didn't cost the district a penny."

"The cost to the district was only part of my objection, Emma." He tossed the book back onto her desk. It landed with a slap, but she didn't so much as flinch. "And my position as interim principal—and therefore your superior—does give me the authority to make a unilateral decision."

"If you're my superior, then you can't call me Emma."

She had him there. "Very well, Miss Trowbridge."

Her eyes lit. "What if we let the students decide? We live in a democracy, after all—"

"Technically a constitutional republic, not a true democracy."

"A representative democracy, then, at the very least."

"Which is essentially the same, thus proving my point."

"Semantics." She rolled her eyes. "Nonetheless, voting is still an important right and responsibility that the boys—and God willing, the girls too—will need to take seriously."

"So you want them to practice on a Christmas play."

She lifted her chin. "Why not?"

Why not indeed. As her principal, he could shut down the play in a heartbeat. And as a desperately wounded man, he should shut it down for so many reasons. His own sanity most of all.

But making a dictatorial decision would doubtless start his tenure off poorly, and for the sake of his time here—and his career as a whole—he needed to maintain a decent working relationship with Emma.

Ahem. Miss Trowbridge.

"Fine. I'll allow for an election in the day's schedule."

She gave a half-hearted curtsy. "How very magnanimous of you, Mr. Oberstein."

The door at his back opened before he could reply. A trio of boys, stair-stepped in height and bundled in winterwear, spilled into the cloakroom, laughing and carrying on with the boundless energy of youth. A pair of girls followed at their heels, lunch pails in hand, hair in braids.

Emma—*Miss Trowbridge*—greeted each of them with a warm smile. She brushed their shoulders with caring fingertips, stooped to look the smaller students in the eyes, asked a girl named Janie about her weekend and a little boy—Sammy, if he'd caught the name right—about a new cow named Norma Jean.

Her obvious love and care for the students both warmed and pricked his heart. He'd been that way once. Like Emma, he'd thought nothing of coming in early and staying late. Giving his very best for the students—for the season—at any cost. But he'd let his passion for his job eclipse his responsibilities to his family.

In the end, it had cost him both.

Setting his jaw, he started for the stairs.

"Mr. Oberstein?" Emma again.

No. *Not* Emma. Miss Trowbri—

Ach. He gave up with an inward sigh. She seemed to have no problem with the formality of their new roles, but he'd known her since she was a precocious little snip of a thing, with hair in braids and a freckled, slightly upturned nose. Clearly he was never going to think of her as Miss Trowbridge.

He turned to find her behind him in the stairwell, leaning in, voice low and close to his ear. "Do you think perhaps we should address the students regarding Mr. de Haven's extended absence? Some of them have grown quite close to him, and it may be best to allow them time to process the change."

"The best thing for the students is business as usual."

Challenge sparked in her eyes. "How can you be so sure?"

"Because I have a four-year degree. Two additional years in the classroom. I know students, Miss Trowbridge." *Aha*. Finally, he'd gotten it right.

"But I know *these* students." She punctuated her declaration with emphatic gestures. "I know who's closest to Mr. de Haven. Who'll struggle the most with him gone. I may not have read the same textbooks you did, and I may not have the same degree. But I know these children, and many of them will need time to adjust before *business as usual*."

She was correct, of course.

But time to adjust meant emotions. And student emotions—even for a dramatically different reason—might well peel the flimsy cover from his own.

"Has it occurred to you that some wounds are too deep to discuss, much less in a public setting surrounded by peers who might mock any sign of weakness? Perhaps the message we need to send is when difficult times strike, each of us must keep putting one foot in front of the other." He bit off the last word, breathing suddenly difficult, and balled trembling hands into fists. *No. Not now.*

Instead of a fiery retort, Emma remained silent. She tilted her head and studied him, eyes slightly narrowed, as though pondering a difficult equation or sussing out the meaning of a Shakespearean sonnet.

He resisted the urge to tug his jacket around himself. To hide from Emma's penetrating blue gaze. To turn and run and never look back.

"I stand corrected, Mr. Oberstein," she said softly. "I hadn't thought through that side of it, but you're absolutely right. In fact, some of the students may benefit more from business as usual."

As total a surrender as he'd ever received from Emma, but the victory seemed hollow.

"Perhaps a compromise is in order." She tapped her chin with a fingertip. "Take the first few moments of the day as a unified school, then we split into our assigned classes and go about the day like normal, with the caveat that anyone who has questions or wants to talk with me—or you"—she tossed in as an obvious afterthought—"can do so over the lunch hour."

He swallowed hard. Feet. His feet were on the floor. The blackboard was in front of him. The cloakrooms to his back. He smelled wet wool and woodsmoke. He was at work. Grief, mourning, self-flagellation, regret . . . he ordered them all into silence and rebuilt the walls around his heart that a single glance from Emma had so easily breached.

"That's very sensible, Miss Trowbridge," he said.

She nodded. "Thank you." A brief hesitation, where it appeared she wanted to say something else, but a young student approached, and Emma turned, the moment lost.

That was just as well. He couldn't let himself feel anything. Not for the students. Not for Emma. Definitely not about Maria. He had to freeze his heart. Feel nothing.

It was his only hope of surviving this assignment.

CHAPTER THREE

EMMA PICKED UP the handheld bell from the corner of her desk and rang it, the metallic *clang* piercing the din of student arrivals. "My class, take your seats, please. And if you're in Mr. de Haven's class . . . try to find a space along the back wall."

This would prove easier said than done. Visser School had once been small enough that all grades fit in this room. Even with the recently added second story for the upper grades, Vanderburgh County's rapid growth meant the school would likely burst at the seams before too many years passed.

She returned the bell to her desk as the younger students scrambled to their desks and the older ones lined the back and sides of the classroom. After the Pledge of Allegiance and the prayer, Emma fixed her charges with a bright smile. "Good morning, everyone. By now I'm sure you're all aware that Mr. de Haven has taken leave to care for his ailing father, and we will, of course, remember them both in our prayers for the rest of the term. This"—she motioned to Frederick—"is Mr. Oberstein. He'll be filling in until Mr. de Haven can return to us."

Dozens of skeptical eyes turned toward her new colleague, who himself looked as though he'd just drunk a cup of vinegar.

"It's an honor to be entrusted with all of you." He greeted the students with a half-hearted wave.

"Change is never easy, so I wanted to take a few minutes to open the floor and address any questions you may have, either for me or for Mr. Oberstein."

Viola Taylor, standing near the cloakrooms, raised her hand. "Will Mr. de Haven be back next term?"

Emma regarded the thirteen-year-old with a kind smile. "That's his plan, but only the Lord knows for sure."

Ten-year-old Michael McCormack raised his hand next, and Emma's heart went out to him. Still reeling from his own father's death the previous summer, he'd grown close to Mr. de Haven this fall. He was one of the pupils she'd been most concerned about.

"What do we do in the meantime, Miss Trowbridge?" he asked, brown eyes large and overlaid with tears.

"Well, Michael . . . we simply do the next thing God has put before us, even when it doesn't make sense. And then we do the next thing he shows us, and the next thing, and the next. And with each moment, with each step we take, we trust that God will give us the strength and courage to do what he's prepared for us."

Michael swiped his sleeve under his nose and fixed his attention on the wooden surface of his desk.

Behind him, Jesse Meijer's hand shot into the air. "What about the Christmas pageant?" the energetic twelve-year-old inquired.

"Excellent question, Jesse, and one that segues nicely into the next item on my agenda."

"Are we going to do the same pageant as last year, Miss Trowbridge?" Janie Seiler asked.

"It's been . . . highly recommended to me"—Emma glanced toward Frederick, whose gaze was fastened on the wood-planked floor—"that we produce the usual pageant this year rather than stage anything new."

The students seemed to be making an attempt at stoicism, but a couple of groans slipped out anyway, and with that, all the air was sucked from the room.

"However," she said, and the sea of faces before her brightened. "There's a new piece, recently published, that I think would present a suitable challenge for us all. Rather than a series of short vignettes,

Met in Thee Tonight is a full play, a retelling of the Christmas story from the perspective of the Angel of the Lord and a shepherd boy named Malachi." She tried to stay neutral, to simply describe the play rather than betray her enthusiasm, but oh, it was difficult.

Viola's eyes brightened. "Would there be costumes?"

"Yes," Emma replied.

"Scenery?" Sammy piped up from the back row.

"We'll do as much as we can with the space we have."

Excitement buzzed around the room, seeming to touch everyone but Frederick, who stepped forward and cleared his throat. "What Miss Trowbridge hasn't told you is that this pageant will cost significantly more than the traditional one in terms of time, effort, and resources."

"And producing a familiar pageant might be more comfortable for some of you," Emma forced herself to admit. "For those reasons, I— *we've*—decided to put it to a vote."

A smile spread across Viola's face. "Even the girls?"

Emma met her gaze. "Even the girls."

The room buzzed again, louder than before, and Emma quickly clapped her hands to regain control. "If we're to have an election, it must proceed in an orderly fashion, yes?"

The students quieted, eyes toward the front.

"That's much better. Now. All who want to do the new play, *Met in Thee Tonight*, please raise your hands."

The vast majority of the students raised their hands, most with great enthusiasm.

"Thank you, you may lower your hands." Excitement surged, as the next vote wasn't necessary for anything but protocol. "All in favor of the traditional pageant?"

A few students raised tentative hands, but it was clear from the skeptical expressions on their faces that they wouldn't be too heartbroken by the result.

"Very well." She glanced toward Frederick, trying to keep the triumph out of her smile. "It seems the majority has spoken, Mr. Oberstein."

"Indeed they have," he allowed.

When she'd bested Frederick before, especially as they'd grown older, respect had always shone in his eyes. But this time, as they stood together at the head of the class, he looked genuinely distraught. The eager flame of optimism had been snuffed, the old shine replaced by a dull hardness. A granite set of the jaw, a stony flatness of the eyes.

What had happened to change him so? What had extinguished his spark?

"If there's nothing else?" he asked in a tone that suggested there'd better not be.

"No. Nothing else." *For now.*

"Then, my class, if you'll follow me, please." Frederick started up the stairs, and the older students left their spots at the back wall and followed him.

"And if anyone needs to speak further with me about Mr. de Haven, or the pageant, or anything at all," Emma said over the din of scraping chairs and shuffling feet, "I'll make myself available at lunchtime."

As the older students traipsed upstairs and the room quieted, Emma proceeded to her desk to retrieve Dickens's *A Christmas Carol*, the novel she'd just begun reading to her students.

She'd gotten her way. The students had voted and *Met in Thee Tonight* had won by a landslide. She'd beaten Frederick. She had won.

So why did it feel instead as though she'd lost?

--------❖--------

The stairs creaked beneath the shoes of the last of the students, and Frederick plopped into his wooden desk chair with a weary sigh. His first day back in the classroom in nearly three years had been even more exhausting than he'd anticipated. But, as Emma had advised that morning, he'd done the next thing God had put before him. And then the next thing. And the next. He'd made it through the day one hour, one minute, at a time. Now the students were gone, and he was alone and finally—*finally*—he could take a deep breath.

Perhaps, in time, he could focus on doing his job well. On revisiting his training and giving the students his utmost efforts.

For today, it was enough to have simply made it through.

The stairs creaked again, with footsteps approaching rather than retreating, and Frederick suppressed a groan. He didn't want to see anyone until tomorrow morning at the absolute earliest. And definitely not Emma Trowbridge, rosy-cheeked and peeking around the corner into his classroom, still looking as fresh as a morning daisy.

"Well? How was it?" She stepped into the room, a grin tugging at her lips.

"Tolerable" was the best he could come up with.

"Tolerable?" Laughter bubbled in her voice. "I dare say it went better than that. How did Viola Taylor do with her recitation?"

Viola Taylor . . . Viola Taylor . . . The name drew a blank.

"Red hair? A bit on the shy side? When I arrived, she struggled so, but she was so good to stay in during lunch or after school occasionally, and toward the end of last year it all seemed to click." Emma wove between the desks, drawing ever closer, and Frederick shrank back.

He couldn't deal with her and her sunshine. Not when his soul was nothing but shadows.

"Which is why I'm so delighted we're doing *Met in Thee Tonight.*" She chatted on, seemingly oblivious to his discomfort. ". . . Because she'll simply shine. Oh, and Patrick McGowan. How did he do with—?"

"He was fine." Frederick tried to keep the sharpness out of his voice but failed miserably. "The day was fine."

Black pointy-toed shoes paused before his desk. The right one tapped quietly, back and forth, as it always did when Emma was pondering something. Funny how some things remained the same, even from childhood.

"Of course," she declared, with a snap of her fingers. "You're tired. Who wouldn't be when it's this close to the end of the term? To Christmas?"

You, apparently. He managed to keep that comment from slipping out, though not without supreme effort. "Yes. Tired." He hoped the words didn't ring as false to Emma's ears as they did to his own.

She smiled, merry and bright. "A few days under your belt, and you'll be right as rain."

"If only it were that simple." That comment, he couldn't suppress. He focused his attention on shoving a pile of half-finished lesson plans into his satchel, a project for the evening whilst seated before a roaring fire and nursing a hot drink of some sort.

"What happened to you?" she asked quietly. "The Frederick Oberstein I remember would've loved nothing more than to sit back and discuss how the day went. To laugh and share stories and make plans and start working on the play and decorating the school and—"

"The Frederick you remember is dead, Emma."

Wounded blue eyes blinked, and he looked away.

"What killed him?" she asked at length.

"Maria." It was one of the few times he'd allowed himself to speak her name aloud.

"Your sister?" Emma's hand flew to her mouth. "Oh, that's right. I heard she passed. An accident of some sort, was it?"

"Yes." He willed away the lump that always formed in his throat when this topic of conversation came up.

"I'm so very sorry, Frederick."

He nodded his thanks. "The accident was right before Christmas, and ever since, it's been . . . difficult to get in the spirit of the season."

"Of course it would be difficult." Emma's hands fluttered through the air. "The first Christmas without my mother was terribly painful."

But your mother had been ill for two years, he wanted to argue. *For her, death was sweet relief. She wasn't in the bloom of youth, with her whole life in front of her.*

And you didn't as good as kill her.

But then Emma placed her hand on top of his, quieting his thoughts and stopping his breath. She hadn't touched him since she thrust a letter into his hand at the train station the day he left for Ypsilanti. The day he was full of life and energy and enthusiasm, blissfully unaware of how ascending that platform and taking his seat would set in motion a chain of events that couldn't be undone, that would irreversibly and irredeemably alter who he was.

I think—despite everything—that I've fallen in love with you, Frederick Oberstein.

He still had that letter at home in a drawer. He'd read it and reread it so many times the folds in the paper were worn almost to the point of falling apart. Though she'd dominated his thoughts for as long as he could remember, he'd had no inkling she felt the same. And the timing couldn't have been worse. On the cusp of starting his brand-new life, his old one had popped up to say *that*?

And though he'd felt the same, he'd never written back. He wanted to present himself to her whole and complete, degree in hand and career firmly established. He'd wanted to be perfect for her. That was what she deserved.

What a fool he'd been. Because now even his old, imperfect self was an unattainable goal.

For at least the thousandth time, he wished to go back to that fateful December night. An hour. Only an hour.

If he could just have that single hour back, everything about his life would be different.

Sliding his fingers from beneath Emma's, he cleared his throat and studied the scarred oaken surface of Rudolf de Haven's desk. "Anyhow. If I'm less enthusiastic about the Christmas pageant than you remember, that's why."

"We don't have to do *Met in Thee Tonight*, Frederick," she offered quietly. "If it's too painful for you, then—"

"No." His voice was gruffer than he meant it to be. "Produce the new play. Please."

"But—"

"Emma." At last he dared look into those clear blue eyes. "You yourself said we needed to put one foot in front of the other. Do what God has put before us, even when it doesn't make sense. He put me here, back in the classroom, in this school, doing this play, with you, and . . . and I can't help but think there must be some kind of reason for it." At this moment, punishment was the only purpose he could think of.

If he served his sentence, though, perhaps God would have mercy on him.

"But you're the principal," she said. "You truly could have put your foot down. Said no. It would've been well within your rights. Why didn't you?"

"Because I know you," he replied, with a smile that came far more easily than he'd expected. "And I know that whatever objections I might raise are no match for your determination."

Amusement sparkled in her eyes.

"Am I wrong?" he asked.

"Frequently, yes. But on this occasion, no."

"All right then." He stood and retrieved his satchel from the desk.

Emma started toward the classroom door, then turned back, delicate brow furrowed. "You'll let me know if it gets to be too much for you?"

Oh, sweet Emma. Teaching again. Christmas. The play. Being in her presence, tantalized and tortured by the one thing he'd always wanted but had never been good enough for.

It was already too much, and then some.

He forced assurance into his voice. "I'm confident it will all be just fine."

It wouldn't. Not for him.

But for Emma? For the students?

He could only hope.

CHAPTER FOUR

"You're doing a wonderful job with this, Viola." Frederick's voice
drifted down the stairwell as Emma climbed the wooden steps after
school on a chilly Tuesday. Viola, playing the part of the Angel of the
Lord, had regularly stayed after class to work with Frederick one-on-
one for the last two weeks, and her efforts were paying off. The whole
cast had read through the script earlier that day, and it had gone far
better than Emma expected.

"Thank you, Mr. Oberstein."

Emma entered the classroom to see Viola making a note in her
script. "Mr. Oberstein's right, you know. Every time you read that part,
you embody the angel more and more." Emma smiled at the girl, who
glanced up and brushed a stray copper-colored curl behind her ear.

"Thank you," Viola replied, then bade them farewell and brushed
past Emma on her way down the stairs.

A quiet chuckle from Frederick drew Emma's gaze. "What?"

He flashed a wry grin. "You said I was right."

"It's been known to happen on occasion. *Rare* occasion," she
amended, with a raised index finger.

"Perhaps I should mark it on my calendar, then." He grabbed a pen
from its holder on his desk and pantomimed scribbling on the blotter.
"Emma . . . Trowbridge . . . said . . . I . . . was *right*. There." Grinning,
he replaced the pen. "It's in ink now. No taking it back."

Emma approached his desk with a laugh. She hadn't quite known what to expect from her old rival and new colleague, especially given how difficult the Christmas season was for him. But after their heart-to-heart on his first day, he seemed to have filed away his unpleasant emotions and approached his new job with the sort of vigor she'd expected of him. Having never seen him teach, she was impressed at his knowledge and skill. And though they'd competed with one another as children, now, with a common goal—doing their best for the students in their care—they quickly fell into a rhythm as colleagues. In fact, reluctant though she was to admit it, working with Frederick Oberstein was . . . *enjoyable.*

An assessment she'd never in a million years have thought she'd make.

She tilted her head. "Seems like you had a good day."

"I've definitely had worse." He fastened his satchel and looked up at her. "Are you ready to leave, or did you need to stay longer?"

"I decided to take all my grading home with me this evening." A glance out the window confirmed the wisdom of her decision. Snow had fallen since late morning, covering the ground with several fluffy inches, and the storm showed no sign of letting up. "Seems sensible."

Frederick headed down the stairs, Emma behind him.

She quickly gathered her things from the desk, and the two bundled up in the separate cloakrooms, shielding themselves against the elements for what would assuredly be a chilly afternoon walk.

Since Frederick learned shortly after his arrival that the two boarded a mere three blocks from one another and in the same direction, he'd insisted on walking her home. She'd bristled at first—she'd made the journey alone hundreds of times—and had been dangerously close to arguing that point. But his hollow expression, the depthless dark of his eyes, had told her this wasn't about her, necessarily. It was about him. About Maria, perhaps. And so Emma had swallowed her objections and allowed him to be a gentleman.

Now, several days into the new arrangement, to her reluctant astonishment, she found these walks with Frederick to be quite pleasant. In fact, these twenty minutes were sometimes the best twenty minutes of her day.

"What a beautiful afternoon." Emma stepped into snow-covered crispness. Childish though it might be, she never stopped marveling at how a mere few inches of snow transformed Mapleview's familiar landscape into a winter wonderland. Brick buildings wore caps of fluffy white, smoke puffed into the air, and barren tree branches shone with crystalline highlights.

Still more snow tumbled from the sky, as though shaken from a large wooden barrel over the streets of Mapleview. The snow was heavy. Wet. Perfect for snowman construction, which she and Frederick had done as children. Once, on sudden impulse during an afternoon recess, she and Frederick had asked their fellow students to vote on whose snow creation was superior. She'd won, as was typical when artistic endeavors were involved. Similarly, Frederick had dominated toboggan races, as well as skating competitions on the frozen lakes of their hometown. But where they truly battled was in snowball fights. Those always ended with both of them soaked, shivering, and embroiled in a vehement argument about who'd truly emerged victorious.

Nostalgia blanketed her heart with a warmth that chased away winter's chill. That nostalgia made her pause just a few paces into the shortcut through the woods to study a particularly appealing pile of snow next to the path.

Then she did more than consider. Setting her satchel at the base of a nearby maple, she bent and scooped snow into her gloved hands. It was the perfect consistency for a snowball. The perfect size. Perfect shape. A glorious sphere of wintry beauty.

It would be most undignified, what she planned. Teachers were to behave with the utmost circumspection and propriety. But no one else was here in these woods. No parents. No students. No one except Frederick, several strides ahead of her, seemingly lost in thought and clearly unaware that she was no longer beside him.

That did it. He might be her colleague—her interim principal—but he was also Frederick Jedediah Oberstein. Never had it been more tempting to let fly with the world's most perfect snowball than it was right now.

As though summoned by her thoughts, he paused. "Emma?" He turned, a slight frown creasing his brow, and she fired.

Her perfect snowball sailed straight and true, and nailed its target: Frederick's right cheek.

His square jaw unhinged. Dark eyes blinked rapidly. His satchel fell to the snow-covered ground.

Mischief gave way to anxious regret. Perhaps she and Frederick had reached a level of professional collaboration, but they weren't childhood chums anymore. They were teachers. He was her supervisor.

How big of a mistake had she just made?

But then his eyes lit with that old competitive spark, and she knew. She was in for the snowball fight of her life.

With a grin, he bent and quickly scooped a handful of snow, but his haste was his undoing. His snowball was decidedly messier than hers had been and sailed wide, at least six inches to her left.

"Someone's a bit out of practice." She quickly formed another snowball and heaved it at him from behind the safety of a thick-trunked maple.

"Seems I'm not the only one," he retorted as her latest offering piffed into the snow beside his boots.

"We'll see about that." Teeth gritted, Emma crouched and assembled a whole arsenal of snowballs.

Her next attempt failed when a laughing Frederick ducked behind a tree, but as minutes progressed and years melted away, more and more snowballs hit their target. Not just hers, unfortunately. But for the first time ever, she didn't care who won. She found herself curiously disarmed by the way his hearty laugh—deeper than she remembered—pierced the forest's snowy hush. By his eyes, warm and shining and bright. By the flush of his cheeks from cold and exertion. This was the Frederick she remembered. Passionate and full of life and determined to succeed, no matter the cost.

But if this was indeed the Frederick she remembered, then he'd stop at nothing to defeat her. She flung the last snowball in her stockpile at his left ear, but he ducked, chortling, and the snowball smacked harmlessly into a tree at his back.

Chagrined, she retreated behind the safety of the maple once more and crouched to craft more wintry projectiles, churning them out as fast as her numbed hands could form them.

The barrage of snowballs from Frederick stopped.

She glanced up at the eerily silent forest. Had Frederick grown tired of their game? Was he declaring a truce?

She stood and peered around the tree, snowball in hand. "Frederi—" The final syllable of his name dissolved into a quiet grunt as his arms locked around her waist.

"Gotcha."

She could feel his grin against her cheek.

And then the snow. Handfuls of cold down the collar of her coat, shocking the warm skin beneath and drawing a shriek from her throat. She fought against him, shoving her last snowball into his face, but he was strong. Much stronger than he'd been as a child. Or maybe her laughter had weakened her.

Or . . . maybe it wasn't that at all. Maybe it was the look in Frederick's eyes. A hundred emotions, none of them named, but all of them swirling and churning and focusing on her. Could he feel her heart pounding through the layers of her clothes? Was his hammering just as hard?

"Truce?" she asked, breathless. Whether her gasp was from the snowball fight or the unexpected onslaught of emotions that penetrating gaze produced, she couldn't be certain.

Another chuckle rumbled through his chest, low and deep and vibrating against her. "Never did I think I'd see the day when Emma Trowbridge asked for a truce. Not once did you when we were children."

The richness of his voice shot straight through to her toes. As did the strength of the arms around her. The shadow of dark stubble on his jaw. The scent of him—coal and cold and something slightly musky.

"We're not children anymore." Her voice sounded odd. Distant.

"No." His intense expression pinned her in place. "We most certainly are not."

Time hung suspended like the clouds of their breath, mingling between them. His eyes pierced the vapor, near ebony in the fading light.

Then he stepped back.

His gloved hands left her arms, and the chill of the snow he'd dumped down her neck edged her awareness.

"Thank you." He cleared his throat. "It's been . . . quite some time since I had that much fun."

"Of course." Her reply was a reflex, as he'd already turned his back to her and retreated down the path to gather his hastily discarded belongings.

What—what *was* that? What had just happened? Her crush on Frederick at fourteen had been humiliating, but mercifully brief. A bump in the road, a moment of poor judgment, a blot on her otherwise stellar record of independence.

Or had it?

Because one unguarded moment, one breath-stealing gaze and fierce embrace, and she was fourteen years old again. Entertaining feelings for the person who'd lord it over her if he knew.

Except he'd grown up. Far beyond his height and strength and other physical traits she dared not allow herself to entertain, life had dealt him a vicious blow. Even earlier, when he'd teased her about agreeing with him, he'd done so gently. Affectionately. Not to claim a victory, but to share one.

And if she weren't mistaken, he shared something else with her. That look in his eyes . . . no man had ever looked at her that way before. As though she was highly desired, but too treasured for him to act on that yearning.

With a shaky breath, she retrieved her satchel and allowed the cool air to restore a bit of her composure. She'd have to. Because she and Frederick still had ten minutes left of their walk.

And if the previous ten minutes had been any indication, she wasn't nearly as over her feelings for Frederick Oberstein as she'd once thought.

Chapter Five

When Frederick arrived just before dawn the next morning, smoke already billowed from the schoolhouse chimney. Nearly three weeks into his assignment at Visser, and he had yet to arrive before Emma did. If he didn't walk her home each night, he'd have wondered if she slept in the classroom.

Ach, the walks home. Especially yesterday's. Memories of that walk, the snowball fight, and the moments afterward had occupied him most of the night, and entering the schoolroom and seeing Emma did nothing to help matters.

She sat at her desk, bent over a pile of paperwork, a single chestnut curl already dancing around her cheek. He knew the sweet scent of her hair now.

Her chin rested on her hand. He'd felt that hand swatting playfully at him yesterday afternoon when, in a moment of uncharacteristic impulsiveness, he'd captured her and poured snow down her neck.

She wore a blue dress, the one that brought out all the varying hues in her eyes and fit her slender form so perfectly. And he knew exactly how she felt in his arms now.

She felt right. Perfect, in fact.

And he'd never, ever wanted to let her go.

"We need a lamb," she said.

"I'm sorry?" In a hundred years, Frederick would never have guessed that to be the first sentence Emma would speak to him this morning.

Emma blinked, her gaze locked on him, but seeming to look through him rather than at him. "It's too bad the spring lambs are so big now."

He set his satchel down and unwound the scarf from around his neck. "Perhaps I'm a bit dense this early in the morning"—or in Emma's presence—"but what, pray tell, brings about this pressing need for a lamb?"

"Malachi's lamb," she said, in reference to the lead character of the play. "It's a huge part of the plot. Surely you'd considered what we might do for it."

"A pile of white fabric in a basket. Done."

She stashed her pen and stood. "A lamb wouldn't ride around in a basket, Frederick."

"Then have the students craft something out of wire and cotton."

"We're already behind as it is. And no one would believe it's a real sheep."

He stepped between the rows of desks. "Doubtless the good citizens of Mapleview could use their imaginations, couldn't they?"

But Emma's mind apparently had gone off on another tangent, because her eyes widened and she clapped her hands. "Oh, of *course*. Why didn't I think of it before?"

Those sparkling eyes and flushed cheeks alarmed him for multiple reasons. "Think of what?"

"The Meijers's runt sheep, Snowball. Jesse was just telling me about him the other day. He's larger than a newborn lamb would be, but still small enough to be believable. There, you see?" She fixed that appealing grin on him. "Why force people to use their imaginations when we have the perfect reality right under our noses?"

Surely she couldn't be serious. "And what happens when the real sheep runs wild through the aisles? Or drowns out the lines? Or—or does any of the myriad other things an animal might do at an inopportune moment?"

She dismissed his concerns with a wave of her hand. "If it's Jesse's own lamb, his familiarity with it would make that less likely."

"Unless the animal is frightened by the unfamiliar setting and the commotion."

"Jesse would be able to control it."

"I think remembering his lines is enough of a challenge for Jesse, even without the added difficulty of baas and bleats." He shook his head. "I'm sorry, Emma, but I have to put my foot down on this. No live animals in the schoolhouse."

She pursed her lips. "What if we had the play outside? We could spread out, have a few more animals. Perhaps Sammy's new cow could wear a hump and play a camel . . ."

"Outside? Now you're adding the unpredictability of Michigan weather to our list of needless complications?"

"Needless complications?" She folded her arms across her chest. "An outdoor play would solve many of your concerns about using the live lamb. And a clear, cold night would be an added touch of authenticity."

"But if there's a lamb in the play, then the play supposes Jesus was born in the spring. Which might not be inaccurate, given other historical evidence. If it is true that Jesus was born another time of year, then that's yet another reason why all the fluff and feathers around Christmastime is unnecessary and unwarranted."

Emma's brows shot up. "You might think it 'unnecessary and unwarranted,' but plenty of people around here don't."

"Yet those who find it unnecessary have good reasons."

"Frederick." She took a step closer to him and rested her delicate hand on the sleeve of his coat. "I understand this time of year is painful for you. I can't imagine what it must be like, having the anniversary of a loved one's death fall so close to the holiday. However, I need to know that you're making these decisions not for personal reasons, but because you feel they're truly in the best interest of the school."

He pulled in a breath and faced her. "Emma. I admire your creativity and your commitment to making the play as impressive as possible. Once upon a time, I'd have done the same thing. But I've learned that it's best to keep things simple. Uncomplicated. Not just for the students, but for you too." He smiled. "How early do you arrive each morning? Are you getting enough sleep?"

She stepped back. "I sleep plenty."

The circles beneath her eyes begged to differ, but he didn't need to belabor the point. "Caring for yourself as a teacher—caring for those closest to you—is even more important than caring for the students." He swallowed hard against an all-too-familiar thickness in his throat. "It's a lesson I learned the hard way. I don't want to see you do the same."

"All right." She nodded, her gaze locked on his. "If it's best for the school, then I'll consent to an entirely unbelievable artificial sheep. And an indoor performance."

"And no camel-cows."

"And no camel-cows," she agreed, with a self-deprecating smile.

He lifted a brow and tilted his head. "No loopholes either."

"What on earth makes you think I'd find a loophole, Frederick Oberstein?"

Grinning, he nodded toward the script on the desk. "Call it a hunch."

"All right, fine, I suppose there is some precedent."

"A touch." Had he spoken aloud? He couldn't be sure, because she'd turned and walked back toward the board, leaving in her wake a trace of the sweet fragrance he'd received in full force yesterday, when she was in his arms.

He'd held her close to his heart, and that was part of why saying no to her was so difficult.

But saying no to her was the only way to preserve what little remained of his sanity.

That said, he was even more determined than ever before to arrive early enough the next morning that she'd find a crackling fire when she walked in.

CHAPTER SIX

"IF I'D HAD a sled like this one all those years ago, I'd have beaten you fair and square, Frederick Oberstein." Emma's cheeks stung with cold, and her toes numbed inside her shoes as she and Frederick tramped down the snowy wooded path. The day was frigid, but their errand was a pleasant one: selecting the perfect schoolhouse Christmas tree.

"Whatever you need to tell yourself." Frederick grinned over at her, the toboggan he pulled behind him quietly swishing through the snow.

"I would have." Laughter underpinned her words. "You only beat me by a second as it was."

"A second? Try *two* seconds, at the very least."

Emma shoved Frederick's shoulder, knocking him slightly off-balance. He was laughing, though, so that might have been what caused him to stumble.

No. It was the shove. Had to be.

Whatever she needed to tell herself.

Truth be told, there wasn't much she needed to tell herself these recent lighthearted days. *Met in Thee Tonight* was coming along about as smoothly as could be expected. Jesse Meijer was doing wonderfully as Malachi, the shepherd boy, provided he remembered his lines, which wasn't yet happening as often as Emma would've liked. Viola performed the role of the angel beautifully, and her singing was

42

exquisite . . . until the moment she stood before her peers, when stage fright seized her and she became quiet as a mouse. And they'd have an infant Jesus, so long as Caroline Seiler's newest arrival, who she'd graciously offered to allow them to swaddle, didn't squall too much at the prospect.

But all those concerns were for another day. Another time. Cold and cloudy as it was, the afternoon was still beautiful, the trees wearing jaunty caps of snow, and cardinals perching on the rails of Mr. de Haven's farm fence. Her colleague normally brought in the tree himself, but as he was still upstate, Emma would have to take care of it this year. Thank goodness Frederick had been willing to accompany her.

"What about this one?" Frederick stopped before a muted-green fir, hacksaw at the ready.

Emma shook her head. "No. Too scraggly."

"Very well, milady." Frederick backed away from the tree with a gallant bow, then gestured to another nearby fir. "And this one?"

She considered it. It was full enough, but the bend at the top simply wouldn't do. "It's a funny shape."

"Aren't we all?" He motioned to another tree. "Perhaps this is more to your liking."

"No. It's too skinny."

"I was warned once about the indecisiveness of the female species, and now I see it in all its glory." Frederick's dimple deepened, and Emma threw him a mock glare.

"All I want is the perfect Christmas tree for our classroom, and I'll know that tree when I see it."

He chuckled, low and rich.

She placed her hands on her hips. "What?"

"Nothing." His laughter gentled, then hushed. "It's just . . . I love how much you care about something so inconsequential as a Christmas tree."

"It's the teacher's responsibility to provide the tree for the schoolhouse. To set the tone for the season. To provide an evergreen reminder of God's love, guidance, and provision, and how faithful he is to grow us as well. It's not inconsequential at all."

"You're absolutely right. Forgive me." Frederick's voice was quiet yet intense, and his gaze was even more so. Eyes dark as midnight glittered in the snowy afternoon, then dropped to her lips.

Her breath caught. Was he . . . ? Were they . . . ?

The chatter of a squirrel shattered the moment, and branches rustled with rodent activity. A second later the fluffy gray creature bounced right between them, snowflakes clinging to its bushy tail.

Backing away from Frederick, lips curved in amusement, she followed the animal's tracks, and—

"Oh. There. Frederick. Look." She rushed up to a gorgeous spruce, resplendent with fresh snow, its full boughs the ideal shade of deep green. "Isn't it beautiful?"

"Don't you think it's a bit big for the space?" Frederick asked at her elbow, brow creased as he evaluated the tree.

"Nonsense. It's perfect."

"Emma, it'll scrape the ceiling." He moved a few paces to the right and motioned with his saw. "What about this one?"

She tilted her head. The tree was almost as tall. Almost as full. Almost as beautiful. But . . .

"It's not the one, is it?"

"I'm sorry, Frederick." She turned pleading eyes on him. "But no. It isn't."

"Very well. What the lady wants, the lady shall receive." With a lopsided grin that made her heart flip, Frederick tugged the toboggan beneath the tree, then crouched in the snow, saw at the ready.

"I'll help." Emma took a position on the opposite side of Frederick, and as the scrape of the saw cut through the silent forest, she grasped the tree and pulled it away from the cut.

The sawing intensified, along with some quiet grunts from Frederick—as well as a couple of German words she didn't recognize and might not want to know the meaning of—and then, with a gentle crack, the tree gave way.

"Oof." Prickly weight landed on her, its load more than she expected, but she righted herself just in time for Frederick to hoist the trunk.

The two of them together maneuvered the tree onto the toboggan and tied its fragrant boughs with twine.

"Oh, Frederick." She clasped her hands together and studied their handiwork. "Thank you. Thank you a thousand times. This tree will be so beautiful in the classroom. The students will adore it, and I simply can't thank you enough for . . ." She trailed off at his response.

Or lack thereof. He was only staring at her in that all-seeing way of his, those dark-brown eyes drilling deep into her soul.

"What?" she asked.

"Emma." His voice sounded hoarse. "I've known you since I was a boy. And I can't count the number of times your beauty took my breath away."

Her own breath hung suspended in the wintry air.

Beautiful.

Frederick thought she was beautiful.

He stepped closer, his gloved thumb brushing across her cheek. "But never, in all the years I've known you, have you been more beautiful than you are right now."

And then he was kissing her.

Frederick Oberstein. Was kissing her.

She was kissing him too. Kissing. Frederick. And . . . merciful heavens . . . enjoying every moment. The gentle pressure of his lips. The soft scratch of stubble against her chin. The cold tickle of gloved fingertips trailing from her temple to behind her left ear. The scent of snow and pine sap and *him*.

He pulled back a long yet too-short moment later, their breath puffing up in clouds around their faces. Tingling lips tried to form his name, a word, anything at all, but nothing came out in the face of another one of those dark-eyed, intense looks.

"Emma, you make me forget everything I want to forget. And you make me remember everything I want to remember." He turned slowly, expression tender, and grabbed the rope of the toboggan.

She stood in a stupor for a moment, every fiber alive with the memory of his touch, moving only when he started back toward the schoolhouse.

They walked in silence, her feet barely skimming the surface of the snow, the tree-laden sled swishing behind them.

He'd kissed her.

Like *that*.

Had she been cold on the way here?

After a kiss like that, she'd never be cold again.

------------>+<------------

The steady popping of popcorn and its savory aroma mingled with the scent of woodsmoke and the fresh pine of the Christmas tree that filled the corner of the downstairs classroom. The tree had indeed been too tall; Frederick had been forced to saw off a few inches, and the wood-planked floor still bore needles from their brief struggle to wedge the tree through the classroom doorway. But it was up now, the mood was festive, and Emma was happy.

He was too. Happier, in fact, than he'd been in years. He'd meant what he told her in those snowy woods, right after he kissed her. She did make him forget. And remember. And feel all sorts of things all at once. Things he'd felt since he was a boy. Things that would always and forever be associated with Emma Trowbridge and no one else.

She sat opposite him, perched on the edge of her desk, stringing a popcorn chain with fluffy white kernels from the bowl that contained their most recent batch. He was attempting the same, though he was far less adept at the task than she. Blaming it on the kiss would be simple enough, but it wouldn't explain the fact that popcorn chains had always befuddled him.

"There." Emma flitted to her feet, skirts swishing around her ankles, and hung the popcorn chain among the boughs of the evergreen. "A couple more of these, a few candles, and we'll have a proper tree."

He grinned. "What, no tinsel?"

"You have tinsel?"

"Sorry, but no." He'd scour the ends of the earth for some, though, if it meant she'd keep looking at him like that. If it meant he could kiss her again.

"No matter." She waved a hand. "The tree is beautiful as is, don't you think?"

He nodded, his focus returning to the lackluster popcorn chain in his hand. As he wedged the needle through a kernel, a quiet crunching mingled with the popping of corn and settling of firewood. He looked up just as Emma stuffed a handful of kernels into her mouth. Grinning, he arched a brow. "I thought that was supposed to go on the tree."

"It is." Her eyes gleamed. "Most of it, anyway. I made extra." She popped in another handful as if to prove her point. "Try some. It's delicious."

"I'm sure I'll find more success eating it than stringing it." He set the chain aside and reached for a handful of the snack.

"Are you admitting defeat?" She indicated his paltry half-finished string.

"Will you mock me relentlessly if I am?"

"Always. Give me that." Emma reached for the chain and deftly threaded a few more kernels onto it. "I'll string, you hang?"

"Best idea you've had all night." Relieved to abandon the maddening task, he got to his feet and took the chain from Emma's outstretched hand, then wedged it between the prickly boughs with careful attention. Though he might be terrible at making popcorn chains, he'd drape them as beautifully as he could.

But then Emma hummed "Deck the Halls," and his world tilted on its axis. His pulse roared in his ears. His vision dimmed, and in an instant he was back in another school. Another classroom. With another soft soprano humming that same cheery Christmas tune.

"There. Done." Maria had eyed the trimmed classroom tree with a satisfied smile, hands on hips, her new, smart black shoes peeking out from beneath a crimson skirt. "Shall we?"

"Not yet, *schwesterchen*." He'd barely noticed the tree, his thoughts already a hundred tasks ahead. "Now that the decorations are in place, I can finalize the standing arrangements for the pageant. Oh, and the essays for the eighth and ninth graders. Those have to be graded tonight, so I can—"

"Can't you do that at home?" Maria's voice was threaded with irritation. "Greta's mother is making pfeffernuesse this evening, and she promised I could help."

"One more hour, and I'll be finished." Turning his back on Maria, he rubbed his chin and considered the schoolhouse's small stage. With the tree taking up most of the near corner, they'd have to shift everyone a few paces to the left, but there should still be enough room. Except . . . no, the manger. What had he been thinking? They must leave room for that.

"Only an hour?" Maria's voice penetrated his thoughts.

"Perhaps a bit more. I'm sure you'll find some way to amuse yourself."

"*No*, Frederick." Maria punctuated her vehement response with a stamp of her foot, far too childish for her fourteen years. "I've waited here in this dull, sinfully boring schoolhouse every night for the past two weeks, and I'm *tired* of it."

"Tired?" Frederick rolled his eyes. "In addition to my teaching responsibilities—which are far more numerous than you realize—I've been responsible for putting on the Christmas pageant and caring for you while Mutti and Papa are on holiday. Please, spare me your talk of being tired."

"Caring for me? You don't truly care for me. All you care for is your dumb job and your ridiculous students—"

"—Of which you are one, let's not forget." He finally glanced her way. "Now calm down. The longer you fuss, the longer we'll have to stay here."

"Fine." It came out more shriek than actual word. "But if you're not finished in one hour, I'm taking the sleigh and going home by myself."

"Fine, Maria. Fine," he snapped. "Do whatever you want. I'll be able to concentrate more easily if it's quiet anyhow."

And quiet it became. So quiet, in fact, that when Frederick at last finished his tasks and glanced at his pocket watch, he was shocked to see that more than two hours had elapsed.

"Maria?" he'd called.

But it was still quiet.

"Maria?" Through the cloakrooms. Around the school grounds. A knock at the door of the privy.

Nothing but quiet.

And then he spied the tracks in the snow. The vacant spot where the sleigh had once been. The horse shed empty but for hay.

That little . . . she'd truly gone through with it, hadn't she?

Teeth gritted, he'd gathered his things and braced himself for a long, frigid walk home. With every step, every lung-searing breath, every indication of horse hooves and sled tracks on the snowy lane, he'd called her every insult he could think of. How dare she just light off for home? What was she thinking? What in the world had possessed her to—

But then the tracks veered to the right into a stand of trees.

The sleigh lay on its side. The horse was nowhere to be seen.

And Maria . . .

A black shoe in the ditch.

A flash of crimson against the snow.

"Frederick?" The voice sounded as though it came from a great distance. "Frederick?"

He blinked.

Emma.

Not Maria. *Emma.*

He was here. Not there.

But it had happened. It happened, and no matter how fervently he wished, no matter how hard he prayed, he couldn't reverse time, go back to that awful night, and take Maria home when she'd asked.

"Are you all right?" Emma asked.

What a question. He'd have laughed aloud, if laughter was something he was capable of at the moment.

He could run all he liked. He could try to move on. Attempt to be happy.

But even at his happiest, even when the woman he'd always loved had kissed him that very afternoon, December presented a mountain he couldn't scale, a wall he had no hope of running through.

Emma deserved better. She deserved someone who was whole and healed, not someone who'd spend the rest of his days avoiding Christmas and begging an unseen God for the chance to trade all the quiet in the world if he could just see his baby sister one more time.

CHAPTER SEVEN

IT WAS THREE days before the performance, and nervous anticipation thrummed through Emma's veins during this late-morning rehearsal. Regular classes had been condensed temporarily, with the majority of the mornings given over to making certain the play was the best it could be. The tree they'd fetched filled the corner with fragrance and festivity. Flickering candles gave the tree a warm, cozy glow and bestowed upon the whole room a cheery air.

Or at least it would, if Frederick weren't being such a bear.

"The line is 'Unto you is born this day *in the City of David* a Savior,'" he told Viola, then exhaled noisily and ran a hand through his hair. "The location is rather important, yes?"

Viola nodded and clutched her script closer to her chest. "I'm sorry, Mr. Oberstein. I keep forgetting."

Perhaps if you'd give the girl a moment to breathe. Emma bit back the words. He was her principal. Well, interim principal. But still, she couldn't correct him in front of the students. Much as she'd have loved to do exactly that.

"It's *Scripture*, Miss Taylor," he snapped. "The very Word of God. You cannot forget."

Viola mumbled another apology, cheeks pink, and circled the line in her well-thumbed script.

Teeth clenched, Emma breathed a silent prayer. *He means well, Lord. Help her know that. He means well.*

"Again," Frederick barked. "From the top."

His shout frayed her already-thinning restraint. "Mr. Oberstein? A moment?"

"Not now." He dismissed her with a wave. "We're making progress."

"Are we really?" A bit impertinent, perhaps, but irritation was dangerously close to crowding out professional propriety.

Frederick gave no indication of having heard her. "Again. From the angel's line."

Viola glanced down at the script once more, then hesitantly raised her chin and took a shaky breath. "Fear not—"

"Energy!" Frederick clenched a fist.

"Fear not," Viola repeated, the tremble in her voice an ironic under-pinning to the line. "For behold, I bring you glad tidings—"

"*Good* tidings, Miss Taylor."

"Good tidings. Of great joy. For unto you this day in the City of David—"

"No!" Frederick smacked the desk, causing half the cast to jump. "Not yet."

"I'm *sorry*, Mr. Oberstein." Viola's voice was thick with tears. "I've tried and I've tried, and I've studied the script—honest I have—and I just can't remember—"

"It's a simple verse, Maria."

Emma swooped between Viola and Frederick and pulled up short, facing him. She sought Frederick's gaze, but those depthless orbs gave no indication he knew she was there. Knew any of them were there.

Where was he? He wasn't here. Not today. He was in some past, pain-filled place. And God alone knew what would happen if she left him there.

Anger fading and melting into heartache, she crossed to her desk and picked up the little brass bell. "Thank you, everyone." Her crisp voice mingled with the bell's high-pitched clangs. "That's enough for the morning. We'll have a few extra minutes for lunch today."

Surprised excitement whispered through the younger children, and the older students bolted for the cloakroom, content not to look a gift horse in the mouth. All except for Viola, who scribbled a few more notes in her script, lips pressed tight, green eyes bright with tears.

Emma closed the gap between them and wrapped an arm around Viola's shoulders. "Don't let this shake your confidence, Viola. You're doing a wonderful job."

"Oh, I am not."

"Yes. You are." Emma sought her student's gaze. "The role of the angel is one of the most difficult and most important in the whole play. It's why we chose you to fill it. It's challenging, but you're doing beautifully."

Viola sighed. "Thank you. I just—I can't remember the order of that verse. I don't know why. I've heard it every Christmas my whole life, but there's simply something in my brain that won't hold onto those words."

Emma pursed her lips. What could help? A mnemonic, perhaps, or—"I've got it." She beamed at Viola. "The alphabet. *Born* this day, in the *City* of *David*." She underlined each word midair as she spoke. "*B, C, D*. The phrase is alphabetical."

"*Born* this day in the *City* of *David*. Born this day in the City of David. B—C—D. Born this day in the City of David." Viola's eyes lit and her dimples deepened.

There. There it was. The moment of understanding. That locking-in of knowledge, that second when the external moved inward. As a teacher, Emma lived for that moment.

"I've got it, Miss Trowbridge!" Viola scribbled the letters in her script, then turned toward the cloakroom to swim upstream against the tide of students who chattered excitedly on their way outside or settled into their desks, lunch pails in hand.

"Oh, and Viola?"

"Yes?" She turned back.

Emma glanced toward the stairs, where Frederick was already retreating to his classroom. "Do you think you might be able to supervise the lunch period for a few minutes?"

Viola blinked, then beamed. "Of course, Miss Trowbridge. Thank you."

"Thank *you*. If you need anything at all, we'll be just upstairs." As she moved toward the stairs, her cheery disposition faded to annoyance. Not anger, as it would be if she didn't know for absolute certain Frederick's cantankerous behavior was coming from a place of pain. But annoyance nonetheless.

"I know." Frederick greeted her from behind his desk before she even reached the top step. "You think I'm being too hard on them."

"They're children, Frederick. And they're learning a very challenging play." With a brief exhale, she gentled her tone. "But that's not why I'm up here."

"It isn't?" He eyed her, head tilted, jaw set.

"You called her Maria."

His brow knit. "Who?"

"Viola. Just now. You called her Maria."

"Slip of the tongue." Rattling filled the room as Frederick dug through a desk drawer, his gaze firmly locked on his task.

"Perhaps." Emma shifted her weight, hand on one hip. "Or perhaps an indicator of why you're not yourself right now."

Frederick paused in his rummaging, then slid the drawer shut. With a sigh that seemed to come from deep in his soul, he leaned his head on his hands, as though the weight of holding it up one second longer was simply too much to bear.

"Viola is a bit like her, I suppose." Emma leaned against the edge of the desk, memories of Frederick's baby sister dancing through her head. Maria Oberstein had been nine years Frederick's junior, seven years Emma's, so though they inhabited the same school for a time, they frequently occupied separate realms.

"Some," Frederick answered, voice thick. "Maria was far more of a flibbertigibbet than Viola, though."

"And Viola wants to be a teacher, whereas Maria seemed happiest just about anywhere besides the schoolroom, as I recall."

Something flashed in his eyes.

Emma bit her lip. Had she said something wrong? Poked at a point of pain?

"That didn't change as she grew up," he said at length. "And I should've listened to her, Emma. Especially that night."

The sheen in his eyes brought a lump to her throat. She waited in silence, offering space for him to say more if he so chose.

"Our parents were on holiday. She was my responsibility." White-knuckled hands grabbed fistfuls of dark hair. "But I had so many other responsibilities too—the play, the students, trying to prove myself as a teacher—and Maria slipped through the cracks. Every night we stayed past dark. She got impatient with me, and rightly so. She wanted to bake pfeffernuesse with a friend, and I should've stopped what I was doing and taken her home. But I had work to do, so we quarreled, and the next thing I knew, she'd disappeared. Taken the sleigh and started home. But she didn't make it."

"Frederick." Emma squeezed his shoulder, and he gripped her wrist as though it were a lifeline.

"She was the light of our family, and with her went everything good about Christmas. Now all I can do during the month of December is grit my teeth and wait for it to be over. And I thought I could handle this play, Emma. Truly, I did." His voice broke, and he looked up at her, eyes bright with unshed tears. "But this play, this season, this time of year, it's just . . . I don't think I can."

"You know her death wasn't your fault, don't you?" Emma's other hand, warm despite the chill in the room, rested lightly on top of Frederick's. A loving touch amid the shrieking chorus of self-recrimination and regret, the aching agony of wanting more than anything to travel back in time and make a different choice.

"Tell that to my parents." He let out a bitter chuckle. "To this day, they still say if I'd just taken Maria home when she asked the first time, if I'd just put my family ahead of my work for once, she'd still be with us."

"How awful of them," Emma quavered.

"Which is ironic, I think, given that Oberstein Furnishings wouldn't exist without my father working six days a week at the very least, and seven more often than not." He picked up a small clock from his desk and turned it over in his hands. A gift from Maria, the last Christmas she'd been alive to celebrate. "And now, work is my only choice. After her death, my parents willed their entire fortune to the church. My inheritance has vanished, and teaching is all I have. So the thing that cost Maria her life, the reason I couldn't be there for her, the reason I as good as killed her . . . now that's the only way to keep a roof over my head."

Emma gave a sad smile. "Despite all that, I think you might still love it. At least a little."

"I do." The reply resonated in the depths of him. "In spite of it all, I still love this work. Most days, there's not a thing in the world I'd rather do. I tried to hide on the administration side of things, but there's something about being in front of a class that's brought me to life these last few weeks." He shook his head. "Not today. Today is a horrid example. But most days."

"Then perhaps that's exactly the thing God has for you, Frederick. Perhaps he wants you to embrace teaching, not run from it."

"But how can I fully embrace it when it's the reason my sister is dead?" That was it. The existential question. The one that had haunted him for nearly three years.

"Because you didn't die with her." Emma leaned down, her sweet fragrance teasing his nose, her blue eyes clear and bright. "Perhaps that sleigh would've crashed even if you were the one driving. Perhaps your staying at school that night was the very thing God used to preserve and protect you. Perhaps it's a miracle you're still here."

A miracle. He'd never thought of it that way.

"It is a very natural thing, I think, to question the Almighty. To not understand why he does what he does. And I believe it's even all right to be angry with him, on occasion. I hope it is, anyway, because when Mother was sick, I was plenty angry." Emma gave a self-deprecating smile, yet the pain behind it was obvious. "But even in the midst of it, God showed me reasons to be grateful. I know they're difficult to see, especially when you're so deep in grief. But I can see one, because while God chose to take Maria home that night, he also chose to leave you here. And for that I am very grateful indeed."

Three years. Nearly three years since the accident, and he'd never heard those sentiments. Certainly not from his parents. But not from anyone else either. Was anyone besides Emma grateful he'd lived? Was he grateful?

Certainly not if living looked like this.

But the way Emma watched him now, he felt like a diamond harvested from the roughest of coal. Her fingertips trailed over his jawbone as though discovering him for the very first time. Her eyes shone with both tears for the past and light for the future. A light that penetrated to the deepest part of his wounded soul and washed over it like rain on a sun-parched field.

For the first time in three years, there was hope. And he had Emma Trowbridge to thank for it.

She drew back then, delicate brow knit. "Frederick, do you smell that?"

"Smell what?" All he could smell was sweetness and hope and Emma.

"Smoke."

He chuckled. "It's freezing outside. We've had two fires going all day."

She shook her head. "No, this is diff—"

A shriek from the first floor cut off her words, and Emma bolted for the stairs.

He followed immediately and met a panicked Viola Taylor halfway.

"Miss Trowbridge! Mr. Oberstein! The Christmas tree—it's on fire!"

CHAPTER EIGHT

"WHAT HAPPENED?" EMMA raced down the stairs behind Viola into a cloud of thick gray smoke. Her eyes stung before she even got to the first floor.

"I don't know, Miss Trowbridge. Honest." Viola's voice shook. "Some of the bigger boys ate their lunches outside, but the little ones wanted to eat in here. And then Mattie Lou Stephens needed help putting on her wrap, so I went into the cloakroom to help her, and everyone else went outside, and when I came back into the classroom the tree was on fire. It must've been the candles."

"Oh, my . . ."

The black skeleton of the trunk and branches sharply contrasted with blazing orange and yellow. And the ravenous flames hadn't stopped at the tree. They licked at the bottoms of her portrait of Clara Barton. Abraham Lincoln. The blackboard's wooden frame.

Emma raced for the cloakroom. "Viola, get out of the building."

"But—"

"*Now!* Go outside, gather the students, and make sure everyone is accounted for."

Viola rushed through the cloakroom and out the door, bringing a brief but welcome blast of cold, fresh air in her wake. After grabbing her wraps, Emma turned and ran to the front of the classroom, where she climbed atop her desk and beat at the flames around the blackboard.

Frederick grabbed the bucket from near the stove and tossed water onto the flaming remnants of her perfect Christmas tree, but it merely hissed futile clouds of smoky steam. "It's no use, Emma." His voice sounded tight. "We can't put it out."

Her frantic pulse roared in her ears. "We have to try. Otherwise the whole school will burn up!"

Flames leaped to the top frame of the blackboard.

With a quiet cry, she squeezed her eyes shut against the smoke and heat, turned her head, and beat blindly at the fire, her movements growing more frenzied despite the ache in her arms.

"The smoke is too thick, Emma. We have to get outside." The bucket clattered to the floor.

Emma wanted to argue, but a coughing fit seized her, and she doubled over. Thus proving Frederick's point, although the inferno made her too miserable to care.

"The brick exterior will likely slow the flames enough to save the structure." Barely visible through the smoke, Frederick reached his arms out to her.

Eyes streaming, choking back a sob, she fell into his embrace, and he helped her down from the desk, through the classroom, and to the clear, snowy outdoors.

Still coughing, she struggled into her smoke-singed wraps and wiped her eyes with her wrist. Children milled about everywhere. The younger students huddled together, some crying, others seemingly oblivious, while a group of the older boys filled their lunch pails with snow and charged for the schoolhouse.

Frederick intercepted them, his hands on the arms of the first boy to reach him. "It's too late for that, men," he told them. "We'll need the fire brigade."

"I'm on my way." Jesse Meijer tore off down the street, legs and arms pumping, and his two best friends chased after him.

Emma turned to Viola, who had herded the younger students beneath a maple tree set well back from the school. "Thank you, Viola," she croaked. "Do we have everyone?"

"I think so." Wide-eyed, Viola nodded.

Emma counted heads. Viola had ten in her circle, but where were the Becker sisters? Oh, just there, in the shed, comforting their horse. That made twelve . . . The Duyet boys stood near the privy. Sixteen . . . eighteen . . . twenty. All her younger students were accounted for, thank the Lord. And sixteen older students circled around Frederick. Jacob, Jesse, and Sean were fetching the fire brigade, so that made nineteen.

Emma's stomach lurched. Only nineteen.

One of Frederick's students was missing.

"Elisabeth?" Frederick called.

"Coming, Mr. Oberstein." The dark-haired girl pulled away from the circle beneath the maple tree and sprinted through the snow toward her classmates. Always a bit on the small side, Elisabeth Fellows must've stayed close to her sister and blended in with the younger students.

But Emma's relief was short-lived. Because now all Frederick's students were accounted for, which meant the missing student was— *oh, dear Lord*—one of hers.

"Miss Trowbridge, I can't find Janie," a breathless Viola blurted to Emma's right.

Emma's heart dropped to her shoes.

Janie Seiler. Sure enough, those blond braids were nowhere to be seen.

"Janie!" she shouted, her throat searing. "Janie!"

Viola returned to the glut of students. "Have you seen Janie? Does anyone know where Janie is?"

"Who's missing?" Frederick appeared at her elbow.

"Janie Seiler. She's six, and she's probably terrified, and—"

Glass shattered behind her.

Emma turned to see smoke pouring from the front window of the schoolhouse. "We have to go back in there."

"*What?*"

She pushed past him. "Janie hides when she's scared. The cloakroom is her favorite place. She's probably there, and I didn't think to check. Janie!"

Frederick grasped her arms. "Wait for the fire brigade."

She whirled to face him. "She'll never last that long! I'll go in myself."

"You'll do nothing of the sort."

"But she's my student. My responsibility."

"You're *all* my responsibility. Every last one of you is my responsibility, and I will *not* have a teacher risk her life to run back into a burning building."

"So you'll lose a student, then? Are you prepared to live with that on your conscience? Because I'm not."

His face darkened to a thundercloud. "I'm not prepared to lose anyone. Not again. I'm going in myself, and that's final."

"You absolutely are not." Without waiting for a reply, she sprinted through the snow toward the steps. Her heart pounded in her throat with the rhythm of her mission. *Janie. Janie. Ja—*

An arm closed around her waist and then she was on her knees, sunken in a snowdrift while Frederick raced past her.

"Frederick!"

"She's my responsibility, Emma," he tossed over his shoulder, eyes wild. "*My responsibility.*" Then he disappeared into the smoking schoolhouse.

The inferno inside was even worse than Frederick had feared. The tree was long gone, as was everything else that had been at the front of the primary classroom. Emma's desk was engulfed, and greedy flames licked at a couple of the nearby students' desks. But, thank the Lord, the fire was still confined to the front of the building.

Heart pounding, pulling his scarf around his mouth to ward off the worst of the acrid smoke, he hurried into the girls' cloakroom. "Janie?" He tore through the few wraps that remained on the pegs and bent to peer under the small bench.

Nothing.

"Janie? Are you here?" He moved to the boys' cloakroom. The

smoke was thicker here, and his eyes streamed. Coughing despite the scarf, he shoved aside the scant remaining belongings and felt around for anything that might be a terrified little girl.

She wasn't here either.

He pulled as much air into his struggling lungs as he could, then burst around the corner and shouted up the stairs. "Janie?"

A shaft of light and a burst of cold pierced the smoke, and Emma's silhouette appeared in the doorway.

"Emma, for the love of all things holy, get *out*." Smoke strained his voice, and a cough punctuated his command.

"Not until we find Janie." She ducked into the girls' cloakroom.

"I already looked there."

But she ignored him, brushing aside lunch pails and wraps and wasting precious seconds. "Did you check the boys' cloakroom too?"

"Yes. Emma, she's not here."

But Emma was already gone, dashing around the smoky corner to the boys' side of things. "Janie?"

"If you insist on wasting time checking places I've already looked, then I'm heading upstairs to see if she may be hiding there." Smoke seared his throat, making him cough again.

He'd barely started up the stairs when the door burst open once more, spilling clear bright light and welcome cold into the flaming classroom.

"I found her," Viola shouted. "Janie. I found her. She's outside."

"Oh, thank God." Emma tore out the door.

Struggling through the smoke, choking and gasping, Frederick followed.

Air. Sweet, fresh air. Had air ever tasted so good? Smelled so wonderful? For a moment, he rested his hands on his thighs and gulped air between coughs. Tears froze on his cheeks.

"Janie." Her voice choked, Emma fell to her knees in the snow to his left and wrapped the pint-sized girl in her arms. "Janie. Where were you?"

"I was in the privy, Miss Trowbridge." Janie pulled back, eyes wide. "And while I was in there, everyone started running around and screaming and saying the school was on fire, so I just stayed where I was. I'm sorry I scared you."

"No, no, sweetheart, no. You did exactly the right thing. You stayed safe. I'm just so very glad you're all right." Emma pulled the little girl close.

Frederick's legs wobbled, then gave out, and he knelt in the snow, weak and dizzy with relief.

Safe.

Everyone was safe.

The building was in flames at his back—he could feel the heat of it—but everyone was safe. The students. Janie. Emma.

A fresh wave of tears stung his eyes. The woman he loved most in the entire world, the woman who'd scribbled her name across his heart in indelible ink, was out of the building. Right in front of him. Safe and alive and whole.

Emma was safe.

How differently it could've all ended. So very easily too. Another few seconds, and this moment of relief could've been but an ache of a wish. He could be mourning a student. A colleague. The love of his life. A simple twist of fate, and all of them could be gone.

Just like Maria, they could all be gone.

He couldn't win, could he? Then, he'd been too focused on the responsibilities of his job, and Maria had paid the price. Now, he'd tried to make Emma happy—to see her eyes sparkle at the sight of the perfect Christmas tree—and it had nearly cost him the woman he loved. Was this who he was, then? Bringing tragedy at every turn?

Emma must've thought so, looking for Janie in places he'd already checked. Didn't she trust him?

She didn't. And why should she? He'd failed in his responsibility to Maria, and he'd failed in his responsibility to Emma and the students. The results this time weren't as tragic, but his failures were no less severe.

He was a menace to anything he touched. Anything he loved.

There was only one thing to be done, then. Only one way to protect those he loved most.

He had to say goodbye.

CHAPTER NINE

DUSK PAINTED THE snow in shadows of mauve as Emma rounded the corner from Church Street. The children had all either left for home or been retrieved by shaken parents, many of whom had thanked her for her efforts in keeping them safe.

They were safe. That was the main thing. All her students were safe.

A heavy smoke smell lingered in the air, soot striping the yellow-painted bricks on the east end of the school, but the structure itself still stood. *Thank you, Lord.* She'd heard the fire brigade had been able to save most of the building, and indeed it appeared so. Extensive repairs would doubtless be required. The building would be unusable for the rest of the school year, perhaps longer. The church had already offered its space. She appreciated the gesture. Or at least she would once the shock wore off.

She pulled open the door of the schoolhouse and stepped inside, bracing herself for the gut punch.

It was somehow both better than she'd hoped and worse than she'd feared.

The back half of the schoolroom, save for the smoke, was largely untouched. All but a few of the students' desks seemed fine. A bit of water damage, some smoke stains here and there, but most should be salvageable. Perhaps after a good cleaning, they could even be moved to the church.

But the front third . . . Lord have mercy. Ravenous flames from the Christmas tree had charred a whole corner of the classroom, as well as a third of the wall and a good half of her desk. The stack of students' poems she'd meant to grade during lunch was nothing but soot and ash.

And her script. Where was the script? That precious leather-bound gift from Jan Voorhees that had started this whole thing? She'd tossed it on the desk, hadn't she? Gingerly, she sorted through the soaked, sooty rubble, her fingertips quickly turning black. If it had been there, no trace of it remained now.

At least the students still had their scripts. That would be enough.

The door opened, and a shaft of weak late-afternoon light shadowed Frederick.

Frederick.

Once her rival. Then her colleague. Her friend. And now much more than that. Today he became the man who'd risked his life to save Janie.

She'd barely seen him since they both escaped the schoolhouse, so focused was she on corralling her students and checking over Janie and making sure everyone was safe. By the time she'd thought to look for him, to thank him, to make certain he was none the worse for wear, he'd disappeared, and no one seemed to know where he'd gone. Now here he was, unscathed, and her knees went weak with relief.

"Frederick. Thank goodness you're all right."

But was he? He took slow, measured steps toward the center aisle, his face still streaked with ash, his nose red from cold.

She wanted to embrace him, but something in his haunted expression stopped her.

He paused a few feet away from her, gaze raking her from head to toe. "You could have died today."

"You could have as well." Slowly, cautiously, she closed the gap between them.

He clutched an envelope in his right hand, which fluttered with a slight tremor. He tucked the paper into his jacket pocket, then reached up to trail cold, tentative fingers down her cheek. Whispering her name, he continued down her shoulder, his caress strengthening from featherlight to almost desperate. "You could have died today."

He looked so distraught that she longed to comfort him. "I was never in any danger. Not really. Not to the extent that you—"

"You ran into a burning building, Emma." His hand left her shoulder to grip a handful of his disheveled hair.

She blinked. "So did you. A student was unaccounted for during a life-threatening situation. It was our responsibility as teachers to do whatever was necessary to make certain she was safe."

"You could have *died* today, Emma." His voice ricocheted off the damaged walls. "You. Could have died. Today. Because of this—this ridiculous Christmas tree." He gestured toward the charred corner of the classroom. "This giant Christmas tree that barely fit in the room, but 'tis the season, and deck the halls, and *fa la la la la*, and you had to have it. So there it was."

Emma recoiled, stung. "That fire could've been caused by any number of things, at any time of year. Someone could knock over a lamp. A spark could escape from the stove. And the cause of the fire is beside the point. The point is that all the students are safe. You and I . . . we're all right. Things can be replaced. The school can be rebuilt."

"But at what expense?" He gestured around at the damage. "Emma, do you realize the cuts the district will have to make? The damage that has to be repaired? I'm not even sure the building is salvageable."

"But the bones of it are still good. The foundation is strong." Their eyes met, and the conversation took on another layer of meaning. "Isn't it?"

"I don't know. I'm not an architect. I'm a teacher. An administrator. Someone tasked with supervising those under my care. Ensuring their education, yes, but also their safety. I didn't fulfill that responsibility."

"The blame isn't yours alone, Frederick." She sought his gaze, imploring him to come back from the mouth of the dark cave where he teetered. "I left Viola in charge. You and I needed a moment, and I took it."

"You and I needed a moment. *You and I.* Needed a moment." He paced the back of the classroom.

The silence stretched so long, so thin, she worried for him. "Frederick?"

He whirled to face her. "You and I needed a moment, and it became far more than a moment, and look what happened. Look what it became. Imagine what a tragedy it could have been. Everything I touch, Emma—especially around Christmas—everything I touch is a disaster."

Her heart ached at his words. How untrue they were. "I'm not a disaster."

But he seemed not to have heard her. "I was too wrapped up in work to care for my family, and Maria died because of it. And now, it's the opposite. I was too wrapped up in you to do my job, and this is the result."

"Seems like you've given yourself no way to win, then."

"There *is* no way to win, Emma. Because no matter what course of action I take, no matter how hard I try, I always fail. I'm a danger to anything and anyone I love. This fire happened because I was too wrapped up in you to say no to over-the-top Christmas frippery, too wrapped up in loving you to even think of—"

"Loving me?" His words struck at her core.

"Yes, Emma. Loving you." His voice grew soft. Rough. "Being unable to concentrate on anything but you. Being near you. Having you in my arms. Making you laugh. Encouraging you. Watching that dimple in your cheek come out when you smile. That little sprig of hair that always falls down by the side of your face."

Eyes wide, she reached up. Sure enough, a curl had escaped its chignon.

He stepped toward her, lips tight, cheeks flushed. "Emma, I've loved you from the first moment we stood at the head of the class together as children."

Nothing he could've said would have surprised her more. "You certainly had an odd way of showing it."

His gaze fell to the floor, a parody of a smile twisting his features. "I was trying to impress you. To be good enough for you."

All those times he'd beaten her. Lorded his achievements over her. He'd been trying to impress her? Because he loved her?

He gave a bitter laugh. "And now I'd give anything to be who I was back then. Because who I am now . . ."

She stepped toward him, praying her words would land. "Who you are now is bold and brave. Kind. Caring. A man who'll stop at nothing to protect those you love."

"Protect them?" He drew back. "I'd love nothing more than to protect them. But instead, no matter how hard I try, no matter what course of action I take, I hurt those I love most. I'm a menace, Emma. I'm a menace to everything I touch and everyone I love. So the most loving thing I can do right now, the best way to protect everyone I care about, is to walk out this door and never come back."

Panic surged. "Frederick, no. That's ridiculous."

"Is it? Is it really?" He looked around the burned-out classroom, eyes wild. "Another Christmas. Another disaster. It's just . . . too much."

Whatever reply she might've formed stuck in her throat, and he took another step back, withdrawing the envelope from his pocket.

"I'm on my way to speak with the board." He tapped the envelope on a student's desk. "You'll manage just fine without me, since there are only three days left in the term."

The room tilted.

Without me. Frederick was leaving.

"But . . . Mr. de Haven's not back yet." Her heart in freefall, she grasped at anything resembling logic. Reason. "And in the last letter I received, he wasn't certain when he would be."

"Then they've got all Christmas break to find someone. But it can't be me. For a thousand different reasons, it can't be me." He walked toward the door.

"Suppose I told you I love you too?" She stepped into the aisle. "Would that make a difference?"

He turned, expression tormented. After closing the space between them in a single large step, he cupped the back of her neck and leaned his forehead against hers. His mouth hovered mere inches away. "Oh, sweet Emma."

The words tickled her lips.

"That makes it even worse." Then he released her, and his footsteps echoed through the empty classroom and out the door.

Hours. Mere hours, and everything she'd worked for lay charred at her feet. Her classroom. The play. Frederick. Everything lay in smoldering ruins.

What would God have her do now?

The setting sun illuminated a nearby student's desk, on which lay a leather-bound volume.

Her breath caught. Could it be? She crossed the room and picked it up.

Yes, it was her script. It hadn't burned up after all. The edges were scorched, but the words—her notes—the stage directions . . . all were mostly legible.

The sight brought a sting to her eyes. God had seen her. He hadn't forgotten. And he'd sent her a reminder of his presence in the way she needed most right now. The plot of her life might be soot and ash, but the Lord wasn't finished writing her story quite yet.

Renewed hope settled around her shoulders like a warm blanket. The play wouldn't be the grand production she'd envisioned. It wouldn't be at the school, as she'd always pictured. Some of the sets, the props, the decorations would have to either be replaced or done without. And she'd have to do everything alone. Without Frederick.

No. She wasn't going to think about him just now. She'd have plenty of time to be brokenhearted about him after the play was over.

She couldn't fix him. She couldn't fix the school.

But God had shown her, in his own inimitable way, that she could salvage the pageant. She could still put on a production of the play whose story had simmered in her heart since the moment she first experienced it.

Her next steps clear, Emma squared her shoulders. She would focus on the guidance she'd so clearly received. She'd concentrate on her students. The play. The meaning of the season.

Even if it didn't look the way she'd pictured, she was determined to make this production of *Met in Thee Tonight* the best, most meaningful Christmas play the citizens of Mapleview had ever seen.

CHAPTER TEN

FREDERICK'S FEET CRUNCHED through the snow-muffled silence of the woods, his satchel full of the last load of his belongings from the schoolhouse. His breath puffed up around his face to cloud the crystal clear, starbright night. After two days of hiding out in his rented room at the boardinghouse, tonight would be his final night in Mapleview, after which he'd return to the county seat of Vanderburgh Center for reassignment to an administrative role.

This certainly wasn't how he'd expected to spend the night of the Christmas play.

He'd expected to be enveloped in the energetic buzz of excited students, providing emergency costume assistance or last-minute reminders of long-learned lines. He'd even, once or twice, imagined himself placing a hand on the shoulder of an anxious Emma to reassure her that their hard work would pay off, that the play was going to be just fine. Or—more likely—he would align with the force of nature that was Emma on a mission and do whatever tasks she assigned him in order to make the play a success.

Instead, it seemed the best way for him to ensure the play's success was not to go anywhere near it. Not to go anywhere near Emma.

The quiet *clip-clop* of horseshoes shattered the frozen silence. Behind him, a dapple-gray horse trotted purposefully through the woods, its breath puffing in clouds.

The horse bore no rider. No sign of anyone coming from behind either.

Anxiety clawed at Frederick's chest as he looked this way and that. He retraced his last few paces, scanning the dark woods for any sign of recent catastrophe. But there was no evidence of mayhem. No crumpled form beside a tree. Not this time.

Pulling in a breath, he ordered his chaotic thoughts. A disaster of that magnitude would've left some evidence. Shattered the stillness of the woods. Instead, it seemed this beautiful gray horse with the star-shaped white patch between long-lashed eyes had simply gone for a jaunt on its own.

Wait. He knew that horse. It was Felix, the constant companion of ninth-grader Sean O'Grady. The horse had been known to wander off on occasion, and the set of tracks in the snow came directly from the south.

From the church.

"What happened, Felix? Did you slip the hitching post again?" Gently rubbing the horse's nose with one gloved hand, Frederick grasped the reins in the other.

Felix nickered and nudged closer.

Well. It wasn't far to the church. Might as well lead Felix back and re-hitch him. Surely this small act of kindness, his swan song in Mapleview, couldn't lead to too much harm.

A few short, chilly minutes later, Frederick and Felix arrived at the church. Its redbrick exterior was framed in evergreen and garland and capped with snow, and light from within bathed the whole west end of Church Street with golden warmth.

Quickly, Frederick retied Felix at the hitching post with his equine brethren. "There you go, my good fellow. Not quite sure where they are in the proceedings, but I wouldn't think you'll have to wait too much longer." He patted the horse's neck.

But Felix gave him a look, one of those all-knowing horse expressions that saw through any pretense, and Frederick sighed.

"Oh, all right," he said to the horse. Then he moved toward the large window near the rear of the church and wiped away the frost. "One quick look."

His breath caught as he took in the scene. In only three days,

Emma had managed to secure an alternate location, reimagine the stage setup, and put the finishing touches on the students' performance. And now, here they all were at the front of the church, performing *Met in Thee Tonight* as though nothing had happened at all.

There was Viola, resplendent in her white angel costume and gilt halo. The Seilers' newest addition lay swaddled in a wooden manger, downy head peeking up over the blankets. And there was Jesse, with—was that—? Yes, sure enough, a live lamb cradled in his arms. Small for its age, but still an armload.

Frederick had to chuckle. The replica lamb upon which he'd insisted had been a casualty of the fire, and rather than try to create a new one, Emma had simply allowed Jesse to bring Snowball. A practical decision, given the time constraints. But he strongly suspected she'd also reveled in the opportunity to override Frederick's objections to live animals.

Bittersweet adoration enveloped his heart. She'd done it, bless her. She'd taken this ambitious play and this hodgepodge bunch of students and combined them to create a true work of art. Of all the times he'd watched her triumph in the schoolroom over the years, he'd never been more proud of her.

Or more in love. She sat in the front row of the church, clad in a gorgeous dress of deep green. The script was open on her lap, and that wayward chestnut curl had escaped to dance beside her neck.

A single glimpse, and he could remember the warmth of her in his arms. The sweet scent of her skin. The softness of her hair. The wonder of her kiss.

The heartbreak in her eyes when he walked away.

He should walk away again. Right now. He should turn around and walk away before he did any further damage. Not for her protection this time, or for the students', but for his own. Because standing here outside the window, so close to Emma yet so far away, was sheer torture.

But he couldn't leave. Not yet. Not when the play was nearing the critical scene.

It was only natural, this curiosity of his. He had invested in this production, after all, and no one could fault him for wanting to see the fruits of their labor.

Perhaps he could sneak in the back. There was a spot in the corner pew, just inside the door. If he crept in quietly enough, and slipped out the moment the applause began, no one would notice him.

Jesse's sheep let out a loud bleat then, causing a murmur of quiet laughter to ripple through the audience. Before he could talk himself out of it, Frederick took advantage of the momentary distraction, hurried around the corner, and tugged open the church door. He slipped into the welcome warmth as the audience's chuckles died down, then stole into the corner and sank into the empty rear pew.

He spied the silver hair of Rudolf de Haven a mere two rows in front of him, and Frederick's heart jumped into his throat. The man whose shoes he'd filled so ineffectually? That was someone he couldn't face right now. A few seats away sat three members of the school board. The men to whom he'd just delivered his resignation three days prior. He didn't care to face them either.

And the students. All eager-faced and scrubbed clean, looking to Emma for guidance or to their parents in the audience for reassurance. None of them seemed to have spotted him yet, thankfully. But what on God's green earth would he do if they did?

Maybe this had been a mistake. Maybe he should just go back the way he came. Maybe Emma's greatest triumph would be best served if he walked away right now.

"Don't you see, little lamb?" Jesse's voice permeated the remaining murmurs, his right hand firmly planted in his sheep's thick snowy wool, his left around a hastily carved crook. He knelt beside the manger in reverence, the perfect picture of Malachi, the shepherd boy. "This is the one we've been waiting for. The one you and all your kind have pointed us to since the very beginning. This baby, wrapped in swaddling clothes and lying in a manger . . . this is who the angel told us about. This is the true Lamb. The Lamb of God."

Teacher's pride surged in Frederick's heart. Jesse's delivery of the line—one of the most crucial in the whole play—had been utter perfection.

"And all the sins I've committed in the past, all the ones I will commit in the future, no matter how grievous my error . . . this baby, this Lamb, means there's always hope. There's always forgiveness. There's always another chance." Jesse caressed the surprisingly calm young sheep in his arms. "You were a sign pointing the way, little lamb. But this baby, he *is* the way. The only way to forgiveness and restoration and peace with God." Smiling, Jesse turned back to the manger and trailed a reverent finger over the newborn's cheek. "The hopes and fears of all the years truly are met in thee tonight."

The words knifed directly into Frederick's heart, and his throat thickened. Peace with God. He'd known what that felt like. Once. Long ago. Before Maria.

But since her death, that peace had eluded him. Forgiveness? He may as well be tasked with building a ladder to the moon.

Yet here, before the manger, with a shepherd boy cradling one lamb and worshiping another, for the first time in three years, peace seemed possible.

No amount of money could pay for this peace. This forgiveness. This wiping clean of the slate. It couldn't be attained. No matter how hard he tried, no matter what he did, he couldn't be worthy of it. Not just because of his role in Maria's death, but because of everything he'd done. Every careless word, every thoughtless deed, every willful act of rebellion. No one could achieve peace with God.

But God offered it freely. As a gift.

The baby in the manger, the true Lamb of God, was proof.

Warmth radiated from the center of his heart outward, chasing away not just the chill of winter, but the chill of the last three years. The isolation. The guilt. The unbearable burden he'd carried. There in the quiet of the church, with the organ softly playing "O Little Town of Bethlehem" and Viola Taylor's angelic soprano soaring to the rafters, it all melted away.

He had surrendered. He was forgiven. He would be restored.

Jesus offered hope. And that hope meant that the season which had caused Frederick the most pain—the season he'd dreaded and run from and avoided—became the season he most needed to embrace. Not the tinsel or candles or mistletoe, but the barn. The dirt floor. The braying animals. The very humblest of circumstances. The divine meeting mankind where he was and offering a priceless gift.

Jesus had met Frederick in his darkest fear and deepest pain, taken them, and offered instead a hope Frederick didn't deserve and couldn't achieve on his own.

What a priceless gift. What a precious season.

What peace now flowed through his soul.

⸭

"Viola, my dear, you were absolutely outstanding." Emma wrapped her costumed student in a fierce embrace. "I am so very proud of you."

"Thank you, Miss Trowbridge." Viola's glowing cheeks and sunny smile perfectly reflected Emma's inner triumph and, truth be told, no small amount of relief.

They'd done it. Against all odds, despite the obstacles thrown at them the last few weeks, *Met in Thee Tonight* was in the history books.

It wasn't perfect, of course. What performance was? But the students remembered their cues, and those few who forgot their lines quickly recovered. Excepting one memorable moment toward the beginning when Snowball the sheep got loose and butted one of the other shepherds, Jesse had kept his lamb under control.

Thank the Lord.

"A fine Christmas pageant, Miss Trowbridge." A deep baritone spoke behind her, and when she turned, Rudolf de Haven smiled down at her. "A very fine pageant indeed."

"Mr. de Haven." She greeted her colleague with a friendly embrace. "I didn't expect to see you here tonight."

"I knew you'd make this something special. This play truly brought out the best in all these students. And in you. I'm just thrilled I could be here to see it."

"Thank you." His praise warmed her cheeks. "Have you seen the school yet?"

He waved a hand. "I heard the damage wasn't nearly as bad as it could've been. Haven't seen it for myself yet, but I'll stop by while I'm in town."

"I feel just awful," she said.

But her older colleague looked on her with kindness. "Nothing occurred that's beyond the ability of God's grace and man's gifts to set to rights. And, in the meantime, you and I can happily teach together here at the church for the spring term."

Emma's eyes widened. "The spring term? You're coming back? Does that mean . . .?"

"My father's health has stabilized. The medical treatments seem to be working well enough. And my mother—God bless her—she's had to put up with me being utterly miserable without teaching. She finally talked me into returning to my profession and convinced my sister to come for the winter. All in all, my presence there is no longer as urgent as it seemed earlier this fall."

"That's wonderful. I'm so very glad to hear it." And she was. Truly. Working with Frederick had been eye-opening, to say the least, but now she was getting her former colleague back. Her mentor. It was for the best. Really. It was.

He cleared his throat. "Apparently my presence is far more needed here in Mapleview."

"What makes you say that?" She shifted uncomfortably under her colleague's penetrating gaze.

"The look on your face." Mr. de Haven's silvered eyebrows drew together. "Things between you and Mr. Oberstein seem not to have gone as well as I'd hoped."

"Oh, they did go well." Her voice sounded bright as fool's gold. "Quite well, in fact."

Until they didn't.

"It's a shame he's leaving, then." Mr. de Haven's statement hung in the air, part question, mostly invitation.

"It is. Quite a shame." For a moment she didn't trust herself to speak, so strong was the squeeze of sadness around her heart. "I understand it, though. I believe he blames himself for the fire at the schoolhouse. Not that it was his fault, of course, but he carries around guilt for some other things in his past, things which also happened around Christmas, and I just . . . I wish he wouldn't." Her eyes stung. "I wish he could see past it and know that the Lord forgives, and I don't know how to—"

"You can't fix him, Emma," her mentor said quietly.

She gave a sad nod as the truth settled in her soul. "I know. I can't. He's too far gone for that." Metaphorically, certainly. Perhaps even literally. She hadn't seen him since the day of the fire. He'd likely already left Mapleview.

"He's not too far gone to be healed." Mr. de Haven leaned in. "But you can't be the one to do it. Now, I know that's not in your nature. You set your mind to becoming a teacher, and you've become a wonderful one. You see each student's potential, and you leave no stone unturned to help them get there. You pulled those children from cinder and ash and put on a Christmas play for the ages. But Emma, my dear, much as you might want to, you cannot change a heart. Only the Lord can do that."

Her gaze fell on the wooden trough near the altar of the church, its straw still bearing the slight imprint of baby Jonah Seiler. "And the manger is a sign."

"Exactly." Mr. de Haven's hazel eyes shone. "If God sent his own Son to fix the problem of our sin, then there's nothing in the world he cannot repair and restore. But sometimes it proves necessary for us to step aside and let him do exactly that."

Emma nodded.

"Again, wonderful job, my dear." He patted her shoulder. "I look forward to working with you again next term."

Then he melted into the crowd, leaving Emma standing there pondering his words. *Step aside. Let God work.* She didn't have much choice in the matter now that Frederick was gone. Whether it was in her nature or not, she couldn't do a thing to help him now. He was entirely in God's hands.

But really, that was where Frederick had been all along.

Chapter Eleven

IN CLOSING, I'D like to reiterate how proud I am of you, how dramatically the Lord worked in my heart, and how deeply I regret not seeing my commitment through to the end. I make no excuses, only apologies, and I pray someday you'll find it in your heart to forgive me.

Frederick's pen scratched across the paper on the scarred oaken desk in the frigid upstairs classroom, the light from the lantern flickering across the lines and casting a glow into the room's darkness. He'd never expected to inhabit this space again, but he needed a quiet place. An alone place. And what better place to seek solitude, to scribble out his farewells, than a smoky schoolhouse on a night when everyone else was still at the church, congratulating one another on a play well-performed?

His heart had ached to commend the students in person, but he couldn't face them. Not after leaving the way he had.

And Emma? The way he'd left her. God would forgive him, but could she? And even if she did find it in her heart to forgive him, there'd be a blizzard in July before she'd give him another chance to break her heart.

That's why he was penning this letter. Was it for the students? Emma? He wasn't certain yet.

Footsteps thumped on the stairs, and he looked up with a start. No one was supposed to be here. That's exactly why he'd chosen this spot. His heartbeat sped. Was it a student? Was it Emma?

Rudolf de Haven creaked his way up the steps, silhouetted against the back wall in the soft lantern light. "Apologies, Mr. Oberstein," the older man said as he reached the top of the staircase. "I didn't think anyone would be here at this hour. Least of all you."

A wry smile tugged the right corner of Frederick's mouth. "Fair enough. I was just finishing a few last things."

"And I wanted to assess the damage," de Haven replied.

Frederick stashed the pen in the inkwell, the half-finished letter fluttering with the slight breeze de Haven's movement created. "The fire was mercifully contained. The building won't be usable for quite some time, of course, but structurally it's still sound."

"Good." de Haven nodded. "However, I wasn't speaking merely of the fire damage."

Frederick arched a brow.

"I saw Emma earlier."

The two syllables of her name hit Frederick in the chest.

"And now I've seen you."

Perhaps the dim lamplight would hide the raw emotion he was certain showed on his face. But by his colleague's gentle tsking, that hope was dashed. Frederick rested his forehead in his hands, his gaze on the writing in front of him.

"Why are you leaving, Frederick? Really?" The question was gentle yet probing.

"Because no matter how hard I try, everything I touch is a failure of epic proportions."

"Tonight wasn't."

Frederick chuckled. "Whatever success met tonight's play was in spite of me, not because of me. Everything good about that play was Emma's doing. I merely functioned as an obstacle for her to work around."

"At first, perhaps. But Emma and I have corresponded quite regularly this term. She's told me how you helped coax Viola Taylor out of her shell. How you assisted Jesse Meijer with his lines. How devastated she was when you gave notice you weren't coming back." He chuckled. "Well, perhaps she didn't have time to write me that letter. But when the board informed me you'd resigned, I suspected as much."

"Of course she was upset," he retorted. "I left her with an entire schoolhouse full of students right after fire destroyed half the building, and three days before a play that required a tremendous amount of work to put together. She has every right in the world to be upset."

"It wasn't just the play, you addlepated twit."

Frederick blinked at the insult.

Mr. de Haven leveled him with a steely gaze over the wire rims of his spectacles. "In fact, she didn't even mention the play when I spoke with her this evening."

"She didn't?"

"Not a word. That woman has all the symptoms of a classic case of broken heart, and I came here to investigate why, only to find you're in even worse shape than she is."

"Another mistake, then." His fist clenched. "Even when I mean well, I hurt someone I love."

"Then thank the good Lord for the grace of the manger." The older man arched a brow. "I'm assuming you saw that scene, since you sneaked in the back right before it started."

The look on Frederick's face must've been amusing, for de Haven gave a deep, gentle chuckle.

"What Emma needs most is for you to love her. To walk the path of life with her. Yes, you'll make mistakes. She'll make mistakes too. But the two of you need each other, that's as clear to me as the nose on my face."

Nothing but truth rang in the man's words, at least from Frederick's perspective. And if Emma was as brokenhearted as his colleague claimed, then perhaps there was hope here too.

An idea lit in his soul, one that seemed to warm and brighten the room. He rose from his desk. It was completely insane, this idea of his, but it just might work.

"Then perhaps, my good fellow," he said to de Haven, "I could prevail upon you to provide a bit of last-minute assistance."

Straw scratched Emma's neck, and the wooden manger trough dug into her arms as she more or less blindly found her way up the front stairs of the schoolhouse. Sean's family, the O'Gradys, had built this manger specifically for *Met in Thee Tonight*, which made one less prop to assemble for next year's production.

Or perhaps not. Perhaps she'd need to find a different play, since memories of producing this one with Frederick might prove too painful to endure.

Ah, well. Whatever she decided for next year, they'd need a manger. The schoolhouse would provide excellent storage, since it wouldn't be used for quite some time and space at the church would be at a premium.

After reaching the top of the steps, she stashed the manger in a corner of the upstairs classroom. Freed from her heavy, itchy burden, she glanced around the empty room, then wished she hadn't. An empty classroom was so dull. So devoid of life.

Or perhaps it was Frederick's absence, itself a near-physical presence. The desk chair pushed back as though he'd vacated it briefly and planned to return. The slight woodsy scent in the air, one she always associated with him. His handwriting, rapid but neat, scrawled across the blackboard at the front of the room, a remnant of his last lesson taught. A lesson that seemed a lifetime ago.

But his desk was missing the stacks of papers that normally covered its surface. The pen was stashed neatly in the inkwell, not tossed haphazardly to the side. And his worn leather satchel was nowhere to be seen.

He truly was gone.

So, too, was her desire to be there. She skimmed down the steps, avoiding even a glimpse into her former classroom. Its burnt shell would break what was left of her spirit. Even the lingering smell of stale smoke was nearly too much.

But beneath the smoke, a different scent. Fresh. Clean. Outdoorsy.

If she didn't know better, she'd think it was the pine of a Christmas tree.

A ridiculous notion, and evidence she was beyond exhaustion and needed to sleep for the better part of a week. But the scent was so strong she finally retrieved a lantern, lit it, and stared.

For the second time in as many weeks, a freshly cut Christmas tree inhabited her classroom. It was a small one; much smaller than the one she and Frederick had cut down together. With soil and roots bulbed in burlap, it stood proudly on what was left of her desk, its deep-green needles a stark contrast to the charred blackness all around it.

She blinked, absorbing the sight. There was a Christmas tree. On her desk. In the classroom.

Why?

The door behind her opened, and Frederick appeared, arms laden with tinsel and baubles. He must've heard her quiet gasp, because he hurried past her and deposited the things on the floor beside the desk.

"You weren't scheduled to arrive until after this was finished," he said cheerfully. "Ah, well. It's but a minor detail."

Emma took in the tree, the decorations, and Frederick himself, whose smile was even brighter than the strands of tinsel.

"What are you doing?"

"Decorating." His voice was even, as though decorating a Christmas tree past dark in a shell of a schoolhouse was the most usual thing in all the world. He picked up a few of the decorations.

"A bit late for that, don't you think?" Fatigue and heartbreak made her voice sharper than she'd intended it to be. "The term has ended. The play is over. Not that you would know."

"I do know, as a matter of fact." His voice came from behind the tree.

"You came?" Hope and heartbreak butted heads.

"Couldn't stay away."

"You certainly managed to since the fire."

Frederick emerged from behind the tree, gold bulb in hand. "And for that I offer my humblest and sincerest apologies. Truly, Emma. I abandoned you—abandoned all of you—in your time of need."

"It didn't matter." She lifted her chin. "We did fine without you."

"I knew you would." His voice softened. "Emma, that play was sensational. I can't remember ever being more moved by any production of any kind, ever. It was a thing of beauty. Truly."

His praise melted some of the ice around her heart. "Thank you."

He hung the bulb on a central branch.

Curiosity overcame her pride. "Why on earth are you decorating a Christmas tree? Here? Now?"

He gave a smile that almost seemed shy. "I know you won't be teaching in here for a while. I know the term is over. But I wanted you to know that your play touched my soul. God used that production to reassure me of the forgiveness we all freely receive. That I freely receive from him, despite my many and grievous errors. So this tree—small though it is—it's simply my way of thanking you for that reassurance. And asking your forgiveness as well. Because Christmas isn't the cause of my pain, Emma. It's the cure. This play caused me to see that." He handed her a slim, paper-wrapped package.

She arched a brow. "There's more?"

"Not much. Certainly not an adequate thank-you."

She tore off the paper and pulled up short. A brand-new, unscorched, leather-bound copy of Mueller's *Four New Plays for Churches or Schools*.

"Frederick," she breathed.

"Fortunately for me, a bookshop in Grand Rapids had one copy remaining."

Eyes stinging, she set the book on her desk. "Thank you, Frederick. Truly. You didn't have to do this."

"I wanted to."

"I appreciate that. Really, I do." She glanced briefly at her shoes, then met his gaze. "But it's going to take more than a Christmas tree and a book of plays to make me happy, Frederick. I need you. All of you. Even your broken parts. Your damage. You have to stop running away and hiding when things get too difficult. You have to face it."

He stepped toward her. "With you by my side, I think I could. With God, I know I could. And if I'm so lucky as to have both of you, then nothing in the world could stop me."

"By your side is exactly where I want to be." She closed the distance between them, and they stood at the head of the class, just as they had all those years ago. "Not ahead of you. Not behind. Not winning against you. Not losing to you. With you. Together. Haven't you seen what we've been able to accomplish, working together?"

"Ironic that we won't be working together anymore, then. Although, perhaps that's for the best."

"Why?"

"Because I'm fairly certain the board of education would frown on what I'm about to do." His gaze fell to her lips, his intention crystal clear. "Especially in the classroom. Especially when one of us is the principal."

"Interim principal." Her voice sounded odd.

"Recently resigned interim principal, to be scrupulously accurate."

Joy bubbled in her heart. "Then you're in no way, shape, or form my superior."

His soft laughter tickled her lips. "I have never been your superior, Emma Trowbridge, nor will I ever be. In my deepest self, I'm that obnoxious half-wit from way back when, just hoping the most beautiful girl I've ever seen will notice me."

She smiled. "I did more than notice."

And then he kissed her, warm and sweet as a cup of hot cocoa. "I love you, Emma." He stroked the fallen curl beside her face, eyes shining with adoration. "Thank you for redeeming this season."

"I think God's the one who's redeemed it." She wound her arms around his neck. "But I'm overjoyed he chose me to help."

A ruckus from outside made her turn, and there, kicking up white clouds of snow, was Jesse Meijer's lamb. Moments later, the boy himself, high-stepping it through knee-deep snow, shouting the sheep's name. "Perhaps a live sheep does have its challenges," Emma conceded with a laugh.

"But it truly was a needed touch of authenticity." Frederick pulled her close. "That sheep—that Lamb—changed my heart."

"And the fact that he did is why this will forever be my favorite time of year, even if it's not yours."

Frederick tilted his head. "This season will always bring an ache, I think. But not the fear it once did. Fear has, at long last, given way to love. To joy. And to hope." His lips found hers once more.

Hope. The very thing Christmas was always meant to bring.

Epilogue

One Year Later

THE POPPING SOUNDS from within the heavy iron pan had slowed, and Emma cautiously lifted the lid and welcomed the warm, fragrant steam of a fresh batch of popcorn. In a few minutes, the white kernels would be cool enough to string onto a chain and add to the classroom Christmas tree. She might even sneak a few handfuls as a snack before Mr. de Haven returned with another load of wood for the fire.

After removing the pan from the stove, she set it down to cool in her newly refurbished classroom. The people of Mapleview had rallied around the school over the last year, pitching in and lending their skills to repair the damage from the fire. And, thanks to a generous donation from Hans and Marta Oberstein—Frederick's parents, with whom he'd reconciled shortly after the new year—they'd been able not only to expand the downstairs classroom, but also to add a small stage to the front. Due to the large audience expected, this year's production of *Met in Thee Tonight* would still take place at the church, but the schoolhouse stage had proven perfect for rehearsal purposes.

Oh, that popcorn smelled too delicious to wait any longer. She grabbed a couple of experimental kernels and tossed them into her mouth. Cool enough to eat, but just barely.

Scooping up a handful of popcorn, she blew on it just as the rear door opened.

"Oh. I didn't expect you back so soon." She stuffed the handful into her mouth and turned toward the door.

It wasn't Rudolf de Haven who greeted her, though, but Frederick, his arms full of firewood. "I wasn't aware you were expecting me at all." He greeted Emma with a kiss to her temple and a glance at the popcorn. "Make sure you save some of that for the tree."

Emma shot him a half-hearted glare and reached for another handful.

It wasn't uncommon for Frederick to appear for an after-school visit these days, although it took him a bit longer to show up than when he'd taught at Visser. Though she missed his presence in the upstairs classroom, it wouldn't be proper for him to be her supervisor given the decidedly unprofessional status of their relationship. Thus, he'd taken a position as principal and upper grades teacher at Voorhees School, a new facility farther out in the county on a plot of land donated by the venerable roving bookseller, and Frederick was as happy as she'd ever seen him. As the Christmas season approached this year, she'd worried for him. There were moments when he grieved the loss of his sister, but he was mercifully free of the recrimination and regret that had plagued him last year. For that, she was thankful.

Frederick stashed the firewood and turned back to her, pulling a folded piece of paper from his pocket, deep dimples carved into his cheeks. "I was going through some things last night and happened upon this. I'd forgotten what I did with it."

Frowning, Emma took the paper from his chilled hand and unfolded it. And—oh. Oh, *no.* Her faded fourteen-year-old penmanship stared up at her, the lines of her childish adoration there in living color.

I think—despite everything—that I've fallen in love with you, Frederick Oberstein.

"Oh, my goodness." Her cheeks flamed.

"I told you I still had it."

"And have it you did." Emma refolded the letter and tapped the shoulder of Frederick's coat. "But my fourteen-year-old self was right. Despite everything, I have fallen in love with you."

"Your fourteen-year-old self had excellent taste." Frederick grinned and slipped the paper back into his pocket. "Your current self has excellent taste too."

Emma rolled her eyes and reached for the bale of thread for the popcorn chain. She expected Frederick to join her, but when she glanced up, the expression on his face was suddenly serious. Her brow furrowed. "Are you all right?"

He shuffled his feet and cleared his throat, looking suddenly like a student before the blackboard faced with an equation he couldn't quite solve. "I've tried to decide how to best say this to you, and I think the ideal course of action is to simply be honest."

Possibilities tumbled in her head, from the wonderful to the awful, and she arched a brow. "Exactly what is it you wish to say to me?"

"Emma, I love you. Deeply. Enormously. And I want to ask you to marry me."

Emma's breath stilled. Marry him. *Marry* him.

"I've wanted to ask for quite some time. Because I've known since I was a schoolboy that you were the one I wanted to spend the rest of my life with." He let out a breath. "But I don't want to force you to give up your career. Emma, you are a remarkable teacher. You come alive when you're in front of a classroom. And I don't want marriage to take that away from you."

Frederick. Wanted to marry her. But he also wanted her to continue teaching.

"Well." Hands shaking slightly, she poked the needle through a popcorn kernel. "It just so happens that—forward though it may be—I've been thinking about that very issue a great deal, and I may have a solution."

Frederick handed her another kernel. "Somehow this doesn't surprise me, although I am indeed quite curious."

"As much as I love teaching younger students, I feel a distinct pull toward the older ones. Students like Viola Taylor, who have the potential to be truly excellent teachers but lack the resources to attend a four-year college."

"Students like you were." His fond gaze caressed her.

She smiled, affection for both Frederick and Viola warming her spirit. "I do see a good deal of myself in Viola. And as grateful as I am for all County Normal provided, there was so much more I wanted to learn. So I'd like to start my own teacher's college."

Frederick blinked. "Your own college?"

"Yes, specifically one for young women, with its level between a County Normal and a four-year university."

"This sounds like a wonderful idea."

"I'm glad you think so. Because with my degree from Normal, the nature of the instruction would also require someone a bit more senior. Someone with a four-year degree, perhaps, and a few years' experience as both a teacher and an administrator, who could impart his wisdom on these impressionable young minds."

"I see. Did you have anyone under consideration?"

"Well." Mischief tugged at her lips. "Until I find someone more qualified, you'll do."

"Aha. And how do you plan to fund this school?"

Emma resisted the urge to roll her eyes. It all came back to finances with him, didn't it? "Fortunately, I have a solution for that. I've spoken with a pair of wealthy benefactors who are passionate about education and also eager to continue making amends with their son."

His brows shot up. "My parents? You've talked with my parents?"

"I have." Her needle pierced another kernel. "It turns out I'm quite persuasive."

"You've really thought of everything, haven't you?"

"Would you expect anything less?"

He passed her another piece of popcorn. "I would not."

"Well, then. Now we can get married, and I can still teach." She studied his expression. "What do you think?"

He took the popcorn chain from her and set it on a nearby desk, then covered her hand with his own. "I think, Emma Trowbridge, that you are a remarkable and brilliant woman, and I am truly fortunate to know you."

Anticipation surged. "And to marry me too, yes?"

"Of course." Frederick paused, brow furrowed. "Wait. No. One moment. Did you just propose to me?"

Had she? Oh. Goodness. "It appears I may have."

He frowned. "No, no. That can't be. I'm the one who broached the subject of marriage."

Love welled in her heart. "Ah, but you said you *wanted* to ask me. You never actually asked."

"All that was a preamble to my asking."

"Which you never did, because I asked you first."

He looked at her left hand, his movement exaggerated. "I see no ring."

"A ring is unnecessary for an engagement," she argued. "Merely a promise."

He cleared his throat. "For you, perhaps, it's not a requirement. But for me, a ring is indeed quite necessary." Before she could move or react or even blink, Frederick reached into his pocket again and pulled out a small, shimmering ring, its brilliant diamond surrounded by intricate gold filigree.

"All right, Frederick Oberstein." Her voice wobbled. "You win."

He slipped the ring onto her finger. "I think, if you agree to marry me, then we both win."

"Then yes, Frederick. Of course, yes."

Victory was, after all, sweetest when it was shared.

Author Notes

⟶⋅⟨⟶

Writing a novella has presented some unique challenges to this author of split-time fiction, chief among them sticking to a single timeline. However, the challenges of writing a new era, a new setting, and an entirely historical story all as a novella have grown both my writing and my faith. In addition, it's been a wonderful opportunity for me to reflect on God's gracious gift for several months, not just during December.

It has been great fun to research school settings from a century past, particularly since my other job as a choral accompanist sends me into our local public schools on a daily basis. I've both seen and experienced just how much teachers and staff grow to love their students, and a few of the characters in this book are either named for or inspired by some of my amazing choir kiddos. (A special shout-out to Taylor Vogt, who will no doubt recognize more Easter eggs than perhaps anyone else who reads this novella.)

Our roving bookseller, Jan Voorhees, is inspired by none other than Louis Kregel, founder of Kregel Publications. A Dutch immigrant to the Grand Rapids, Michigan, area in the early 1900s, Mr. Kregel quickly saw a market for religious books among his fellow Dutch settlers. Over the next few years, he established a presence as a purveyor of books in both Dutch and English, frequently purchasing used texts from seminary professors and ministers, and selling them at a discounted price. And yes, just like Jan Voorhees, Louis Kregel really did go from farm to farm with a wheelbarrow full of books! I am immensely grateful for Mr. Kregel and his son, Robert, whose influence led to the wonderful publishing company I'm honored to write for today.

This novella has not been an easy one to write, and at times I've sat at my computer with a blank page on the screen and a prayer that was basically, "Okay, God, I've got nothin'." Which is, I think, exactly where he wants me to be sometimes. Any and all glory from this book is due directly to him.

In closing, I'd like to thank my wonderful coauthors, Janyre Tromp and Deborah Raney, for being amazing writers and even better friends. It has been so much fun to write with you! Special thanks to Janyre for hatching the idea for this collection, to the folks at Kregel for trusting me to contribute to it, and for the amazing editorial and marketing teams who've helped shape it into the best story it can be.

My deepest gratitude is also due to my wonderful critique partners, Theresa Romain and Linda Fletcher; my fabulous agent, Tamela Hancock Murray; my rock star husband, Cheech; my three hilarious (and very understanding) Wenlets; my parents (perhaps my biggest fans), Jim and Deanna Peterson; all my readers who've been eager for another story from me; and to my fabulous friends (both writers and normal people) who've prayed for me, supported me, and graciously listened to me rant about people who exist only in my head.

Last, but most certainly not least, a heartfelt thank you to my friend and colleague Riley King, without whom I'd have never met Frederick Oberstein.

While Mortals Sleep

JANYRE TROMP

CHAPTER ONE

Lennie

JUST LIKE EVERY other day in the smoke-filled newsroom of the *San Diego Times*, I banged away at my typewriter, starting with the boring but precise slug—*12-06-1944 / 14 Injured in Dock Collision / Lennie Sweers*. The date, subject, masculine pen name as my byline. Eleanor Catherine Sweers would never be accepted by the male-dominated newspaper readers, not to mention that the woman known by that name had disappeared a long time ago. I hit return, racing the clock to press time, and the ding of the bell chimed in companionable harmony with the clacking of other typewriters.

"What?" The single word belted from the editor's office, along with the slam of a fist on a desk.

I jolted enough that my fingers stumbled. My last line now ended in *the stevedore sai;lkj*. "Phooey."

Around me, the newsroom transformed from merry tunes into grumbles and the rasp of offending paper yanked from hapless typewriters. I hadn't been the only one startled.

"No!"

This time we all expected the exclamation and turned, in near perfect unison.

Our editor, Phil, a grizzled man of fifty with wild white hair, shouted into his phone, "You're kidding me!"

He met my eye and blinked, shocked stupid. In the decade he'd been my mentor and only real friend on the West Coast, I'd never seen Phil off-kilter. It was his routine to blithely command reporters during an earthquake or freak Santa Ana–induced firestorm.

The ring of my telephone—the call transferred from Phil— interjected into the quiet, and I never finished the story of the cargo ship colliding with the dock. The life I'd buried long ago in Mapleview slammed into my resurrected life, leaving Lennie Sweers crumbling under the weight of Eleanor's past.

Part of me wished I'd never answered that call. But then I wouldn't have known about Peg or the fire.

I owed it to my sister to investigate. So I called in every favor I'd ever collected, hopped on a B-17 metal albatross, and flew to Michigan.

Thirty-some hours later, I slumped in a musty taxi, gripping the strap of my purse like a shield. The engine of the parked taxi ticked as loudly and insistently as my older sister's impatient nails against a table. I stared out the fogged window at the split-rail fence skipping along my younger sister's front yard. It was like her, like Peg— welcoming anyone to her home, a poetic rhythm of warmth, stark against a cold, white world. I caught myself waiting for her to burst out the door barefoot, too excited to see me to bother with shoes.

I cracked open the window, gasping for air, and the fantasy fractured against the subzero breeze.

With his head buried in the trunk, the cabbie was blessedly muffled as he chattered about his daughters. One was still home and the other, if she could believe it, ran off to join the war effort. Girls should stay home, where it was safe, was his definitive conclusion.

But, for my sister, home had been anything but safe.

Not that the cabbie, my father, or even my brothers would see the truth for what it was.

The rotund cabbie slammed the lid, then thunked my travel-worn suitcase onto the damp road, erasing my last excuse to hunker in the warm taxi. There was no going back now. I could probably make my way back to the Detroit airport, but I was a stranger to the Women Air Service Pilots here in Michigan. And the San Diego–based crew I'd written a national story on—"Women Pilots, Avenger

Girls"—wouldn't return until after Christmas. Three eternal weeks away.

I shoved the car door open and wound my scarf tighter.

The cabbie chuckled and held the door against the wintry blast. "Wind's not so strong in California, is it?"

It wasn't the strength of the wind—the Santa Ana could blow a house over—but the bite of it. I'd spent eighteen of my thirty years living a few streets over, and I didn't ever remember feeling as though I'd been dipped in ice water and then buffeted by an arctic wind.

Not that I would make the mistake of telling the cabbie anything more about myself.

After I'd informed him I was in town for a family emergency, he took me under his wing as one of his long-lost daughters and copious unrequested wisdom sprang forth.

Not that I minded much. The man's forty-five-minute monologue from the bus station spared me from having to make small talk and gave me space to tease apart the words of my sister's lawyer.

"There's more," Mr. Braum had said during the call. "But I don't want to talk about it on the phone. Censors and all. We'll talk when you get here."

Why would the censors care about my sister's death in a fire on my parents' farm?

"Blood gets thin when you live in the warm." The driver's words snapped me into the moment, and he leaned an ample hip on the taxi's dented fender to impart another dose of fatherly wisdom. "It won't take long to toughen up."

In lieu of a retort to his lavishly uninformed thoughts, I passed the cabbie the money I owed him, then snapped my handbag closed before shoving it under my arm and hoisting my suitcase. I arranged my face into something like a grateful smile, but the cutting wind destroyed the effect and sent a quiver up my spine.

"If you want better winter gear, check at Herpolsheimer's in Grand Rapids." The cabbie stuffed the bills in his jacket pocket, and I nodded in numb acknowledgment of the department store I dreamed of visiting when I was a child.

For the first time in my life, I could afford to buy a brand-new winter coat. But there would be no point. No matter what the mystery behind the lawyer's words, I would resume my life in San Diego as soon as I could conceivably arrange it. As my editor was fond of saying, the news waits for no man . . . or woman.

The yellow taxi slid away from the curb and gave a jaunty toot as it disappeared around the corner.

"Well," I said to the expectant street, "I suppose this is it."

I tiptoed in my red kitten heels to the front door, ruing my choice to wear new shoes rather than my more practical oxfords. It would serve me right if the slushy snow ruined the leather. Pride cometh before the fall, and all. As if God himself heard me at that precise moment, the smooth soles of my shoes slid on the top step. My hand shot out and clutched Peg's rail, which stood firm.

My sister, still saving me from beyond the grave. Though there was no way Mapleview was out to repay me for the egotistical heresy of abandoning the town, the thought did cross my mind.

I found the key the lawyer had left under the mat as if a rug of woven grass was Fort Knox, and unlocked the front door. It opened with nary a squeak, and I was greeted with an unexpected radiating warmth. From the kitchen, the voice of Bing Crosby crooned his hit "I'll Be Home for Christmas," only to be followed by a clatter.

I swallowed an irrational stab of fear. This wasn't my one-room apartment huddled above the drugstore near the docks. At the worst, a housewife would drown me with tuna sandwiches. "Hello?" I called.

The oven clanked shut and the smell of cream-of-something soup confirmed one of the neighbors was cooking me dinner. In the mind of the local housewives, a well-made casserole was the cure for all that ails a person. Even the prodigal deserved to eat.

I unwound my scarf and divested myself of my wool coat, wholly unsuitable felt hat, and sweater, the static snapping and standing my straw-like hair on end. Peg would have managed to keep hers waved in perfect finger curls.

Heaven knows, I missed her. Though my father would say that if I missed her so much, I should have come home at some point in the last twelve years. I smoothed a palm over my hair, then down my skirt, determined to make a good impression. Or at least dispel any lingering rumors.

I rubbed the worn penny in my pocket. Heads, I would stay. Tails, I would—

"You're late." A deep male voice made me spin, and I squelched an unladylike squeal even as I tripped back, grasping for the door.

In the archway to the dining room loomed a bear of a man relatively close to my age. His bushy brows hovered menacing and low a moment before they seemed to remember themselves and shot up to match a belated grin, transforming the man's face into boyish excitement. When he thrust an oven-mitt-covered hand in my direction, I gaped at the garish purple lace, then at his sparkling brown eyes. "Oh dear." He yanked off the mitt and matching diminutive apron to reveal a perfectly tailored suit underneath.

Interesting. And intimidating, but not in an I'm-here-to-rob-you way.

"Mom sent me over with a tater tot casserole. She said it was your favorite when you were a child. Hopefully you still enjoy it, though we'll have to find that out later if we're to make it to the town hall in time to meet with your family . . . especially if you help me solve our conundrum first."

His words were careful and crisp, as if he might be one of Edward Murrow's boys. Was that why he wasn't in uniform? Was he a correspondent of some kind?

When I failed to move in response to the promised concoction of ground beef, sauce, and crispy potatoes, or the meeting at the town hall, he motioned toward the kitchen like a mother hen, and I followed hesitantly in his wake.

"Good heavens." The words burst from my mouth before I could control them. In complete contrast to me, my sister was always put-together, her space neat and tidy. But this, this was a disaster beyond even my capabilities. Egg shells puddled out of a bowl sitting atop butter wrappers, and flour snowed across the counter and merged with sparkling sugar.

The man swiped at the flour strewn across the counter, but only half made it into his palm. The other half drifted to the floor. A wastrel as well as a disastrous cook. Didn't he know anything about rationing?

I moved a crusted bowl into the sink and turned on the water.

"Since you weren't here yet, I thought I'd whip up some brownies." He motioned to the oven. "They'll be done in a jiffy. We can bring them with us. Might break the ice a little. And there are sandwiches to tide us over too."

The idea of eating anything while my sister lay cold and still in the funeral home's basement turned my stomach. My thought must have shown in my face because he blanched.

"Not that you have to, to eat them, I mean. But I . . . well, if I don't keep busy, I . . ." Nerves leached out of him, the smell of it leaking acid into the room and wearing away his crisp speech.

Why was he so jittery? I forced myself to be still. People revealed far more than they realized when they went sideways with nerves. Thoughts raced through his folding and refolding of a towel, and the way he wiped a palm across his square chin. What was he hiding?

"Anyway, they might make reading Peg's will easier."

My hands stilled in the scalding water. I blinked at the rainbows flowing across the curved bubbles. Peg's will.

"You're Mr. Braum, the lawyer?" I tried to place which of the sprawling Braum clans he belonged to.

The way he tilted his head, I wasn't sure if he heard me. He had the dark look of all the Mapleview Braums, and the looming size of most of the farming branch, but lacked the overconfident uplifted nose of the side who'd taken over the local government. And yet, there was the suit.

"Are you Mr. Braum, the lawyer?" I repeated into the viscous silence.

He shrugged. "Not really anymore. I mean"—he continued wiping the counter—"I mean, I'm still Mr. Braum. Just not really a practicing lawyer. Your sister—and most folks in Mapleview, really—treat me like the town lawyer, but I spend most of my time in the township office. Doing what needs doing, if you know what I mean." He studied me with an edge of high-and-mighty Braum judgment, as if I should have been the one to write Peg's will. But that was akin to asking a rooster to lay an egg.

Turning away from his inscrutable expression, I dropped the eggshells into the neatly lined garbage can. Egg dripped from my fingers, splashing into the can Peg no doubt had lined, that Peg had planned to fill with odds and ends no longer needed. Guilt seared through me. I'd failed to protect my sister as I'd promised when she was born. But how could I have known a freak fire would cause an explosion at the farm, of all places? It was still the strangest thing I'd ever heard.

"My mom always says chocolate is the best bandage a heart can have." His voice was as gentle as it was unnerving.

How had he known I was thinking about Peg?

"And you've always enjoyed them," he said into the lengthening pause.

My brain skittered to catch up. He remembered me? Definitely not from the normal political family branch then, despite his supervisor status. They wouldn't have known me from their Great Aunt Mildred. His expectation hovered in the air as I scrambled to bring his given name, or any remembrance of him, to the surface. Of course I could blame my sketchy memory on a lack of sleep, mourning for my sister, or even the decade I'd been gone. Still, I expected more of myself. Was I a journalist or that egg-laying rooster after all?

Mr. Braum studied me as he waited for a response, and my mouth flapped like a flightless rooster's wings.

The shrill *ding* of the kitchen timer interrupted, sparing me the need to form words.

The man did a little hop, spun, snatched the mitt, and opened the oven in one smooth motion. Surprisingly agile for his size, he curled himself over to lift out a pan, then settled it on the stove before shutting the oven door with his foot. "Voilá," he said with a flourish. "B-brownies with caramel."

When his tongue hitched slightly, a bolt of familiarity cracked through me. But time dragged a blackout curtain over my memory, and the flash escaped my grasp. I'd heard Harriet Braum's older brother had become a lawyer. Maybe she'd told him about me. What was his name?

The lawyer bustled about, jangling my nerves and shattering my hold on the memory as he slid the casserole into the fridge before wrapping the brownie pan in paper and string, and adding a knife and napkins to the stack. "I think we'll take these with us. Maybe it will help with . . ." He circled his hand in an encompassing gesture.

I filled in the missing words in my mind. Maybe it would help with seeing my entire family for the first time in twelve years. Maybe it would help with returning to a town that didn't want me. Maybe it would help with discussing the completely tragic and unnecessary events that led to my sister's accident.

"Until then"—he patted the package as if it held the secret to world peace—"we need to discuss some things."

Before I formulated a response, he turned and scrutinized me. "This won't do."

I examined my tweed skirt, indignation rising. It was one of the few outfits I owned that Phil had deemed fetching instead of utilitarian and severe. "What do my clothes have to do with discussing—?"

But Mr. Braum had already swung past me into the hallway.

I trailed after him, through my sister's living room, down the hall plastered with pictures of my sister smiling with her husband, Jack; smiling with an enormous belly; smiling with a tiny baby, Jack overlooking them both; smiling bravely with a little girl on her lap, Jack resplendent in uniform; and then a blank, gaping wall. I touched the simple wood frame of the last photograph. They were gone, save Enid. A girl of six I'd never met but felt I knew through my sister's letters.

"Where is Enid?" My voice echoed in the lonely hall, and I hesitated. Had he heard me, or should I risk being rude and repeat my question? Phil was forever telling me to "be patient, for Pete's sake."

Mr. Braum's excited *aha* interrupted my thoughts. He popped from one of the rooms holding a pair of overalls in front of him. "Here's a shirt and sweater too. And your sister left work boots by the mudroom door. I think . . ." He consulted his old-fashioned pocket watch. "Yes, we have time. We'll drive out to the east farm and call it important township business to cover the gas."

When I didn't move in response, he draped the overalls over my shoulder and swept an arm toward the bedroom. I'd have to ask him about Enid again later.

Peg's room was perfectly feminine, yet somehow masculine too. White lacy curtains counterpointed a stout chest of drawers sporting two serious fedoras, as if Jack might walk in at any moment.

A cluster of pine branches nestled beside the hats, and I brushed my fingers across the crisp needles. A note of pine lifted, and I smiled. The winter I turned thirteen, Peg and I had scurried out to the evergreens lining the woods, surreptitiously cut a few sprigs, and twined them in the rafters of our tiny shared attic room. The aroma of the boughs lifted the heavy smell of damp and girlish disappointment in what little celebration Christmas brought.

My little sister should waft into her room now and gather me in her arms. *It's been too long. I'm dying to tell you everything.* When was the last time I'd heard her voice?

After slithering out of my suit and slip, I pulled on the collared shirt, the overalls, the sweater. My image hung specter-like in the mirror. The clouded edge of the glass swallowed my ankles, my knees, and I could imagine it engulfing me entirely. Gone in a blink.

I had aged since I'd last been home, filled out, grown stronger in some ways and weaker in others. I was too weak to plow a row, but I knew how to live on my own, expect nothing, depend on no one but myself.

In the kitchen, Mr. Braum—who had changed into a pair of pressed jeans and a flannel shirt, donned his jacket, and strapped his feet into very practical boots—held my tattered jacket as though it were rat infested. "You need a new coat."

"Nothing made of wool gets much use in San Diego."

He ignored the rancor in my voice and nodded amicably, then, from the hall closet, unearthed a pair of old boots and Peg's cloche—spring green and full of my sister's ever-present hope.

I shrugged into the jacket and tugged the cap over my curls and my rambling thoughts. I reached for the brownie pan like a dutiful woman, but Mr. Braum snatched it from me and offered his elbow. The gesture stirred the veil of memory, and I nearly missed the flare of . . . Annoyance? Disappointment? . . . that crossed his face as I hesitated. I flipped the coin in my pocket. I didn't know the man, but Peg had trusted him with her will.

Just as he withdrew the offer, I pretended I'd been fiddling with my mitten and rested my hand in the crook of his surprisingly muscular arm. As we slid down the street, I was uncommonly grateful for his support. We turned west on Church Street, passing Mapleview Meats, Bob's Bakery, Vanderburgh's Floral. The sun peeked in and out of the steel-gray clouds, spreading and erasing our shadows under our feet.

Across the way, a gaggle of high school boys wound garland around the streetlights, and Peg's lawyer waved, drawing the attention of the group.

One of them let out a long wolf whistle. "Yowza, Mr. Braum. Where'd you find the girl? She's a tasty mix of Betty Grable and a hobo."

The young man on the ladder nearly fell from his rung as he turned to holler, "Whatcha got under that coat, honey? You a pinup under there?"

Angry heat stewed in my gut. "You ignorant—"

"Even cuter when you're mad."

"That's enough, b-boys." The lawyer pivoted, placing his frame as a wall between us.

While I would normally have railed at him for interfering, the moment rippled through time, reminding me of a decidedly more boyish back standing firm in front of me, protecting my childlike form curled at the base of a tree, weeping at the injustice of my brothers and the sting of the rock they'd thrown at my back.

"It was you." The words slipped from my lips. He'd changed from the rail-thin boy who'd hid behind his hair.

The lawyer hesitated until the young men resumed their work, then lumbered in a circle, a great bewildered bear. "I don't think . . ."

"On the playground. You're Gideon. Why didn't you say something?" I caught myself before saying, *"No wonder you couldn't hear me ask about Enid."* Severe infections stole his hearing in his right ear when he was a baby, and had left him with speech problems and the stutters that sounded so familiar.

Gideon heaved up one enormous shoulder, transforming from bearish to sheepish before my eyes.

My mind scrambled, piecing things together. "But you're not a Braum."

"My mother was. Grandad wouldn't help with law school expenses for a Baldwin. Dad was already gone and would have been the only one to have cared. So I had my name officially changed before I left for Princeton. My scholarship didn't cover—"

"You went to Princeton?" Suddenly his severe suit made sense. He was important, from out of town . . . and yet not. But then—"Why did you come back?"

Before I deciphered the kaleidoscope of emotions crossing his face, he swung along the street. Loping would be an apt description for his long-legged stride that left me scrambling to catch up. While I appreciated his optimism in my ability to match his efforts, there was only so far feminism and shortish legs on icy pavement could take a girl. When I finally managed to overtake him, he was talking as if I'd been there from the beginning.

". . . Needed to take over for my cousin as town supervisor. Besides, there aren't many lawyers in Mapleview."

"In Mapleview?" I plucked at his woolen sleeve like a schoolgirl trying to get the attention of a teacher in full lecture. I scolded myself for both the gobsmacked tone in my voice and the girlish gesture. He'd successfully put me off-kilter.

"Unless you're aware of something I'm not." His words were careful and clearly enunciated, and I recognized the effort to straighten his stilted tongue. "These days folks don't choose to stay in small towns, despite how much they're wanted or needed."

He said it without hostility toward me personally, but heat rose in me all the same. "Maybe they have good reason for leaving." *Stupid. Stupid. Stupid.* I crossed my arms and covertly pinched the soft skin of my underarm—a reminder to keep my mouth closed. It shouldn't have mattered if he thought I was selfish.

But instead of berating me for my defensiveness, Gideon nodded as though he understood not everyone could survive living in their hometown. He snuggled my hand back in his elbow, moseying now, touching the brim of his fedora at the few people braving the December chill as we passed the white clapboard church, its steeple stretching toward the gray, nearly blending in.

Beyond the First Reformed Church, a smattering of brick buildings marched down Church Street toward the horizon, oblivious to the snow collecting in muddy piles, churned up from the cars and ancient horse buggies navigating the one of four paved streets in town. Half the town lampposts were festooned with swirling garland and limp red bows, the other half awaiting the attention of the young men making their way through town. Store windows glittered with lights and ads full of smiling faces, telling passersby that Brillo Cream, Vernors, and every other product in the store could make the world a better place.

The hope of Christmas rose in me as it had when I was a girl. A wish for candlelit Christmas Eve services, Christmas break, and oh, to run free from my overbearing older siblings, to skate on the pond at the edge of town or sled on the hill behind school. Peg knew how to ply Dad with the right amount of pleading and sass so he would occasionally let his youngest children scamper away from chores. Gideon had always been there fixing someone's sled, retrieving a lost mitten, or sliding away, content as a summer's afternoon.

In the distance, children laughed and the chill air carried it echoing through town, filling the streets until the staid gong of the church bell broke through, announcing noon and easing me fully into the present.

"Almost there." Gideon's voice reminded me of where I was and why I was here, effectively slamming a cap on the fizz of joy. There would be no reliving Christmas Past. There was only the solid reality of my solitary life.

Still, I did not regret leaving. Peg had found her place. She had been happy, and so was I. Come what may.

Chapter Two

Gideon

I SHOULDN'T HAVE taken offense at the snap of surprise in Eleanor Sweers's enigmatic eyes, but hurt still twisted when she failed to recognize me. In fairness, I lived under a different name and I was far from the boy with stringy locks of hair who half pretended to not hear the boys call me *ij-j-jut* and the girls plead with them to be nice to the "slow" child.

Still, to be forgotten rankled.

Worse, it had taken mere minutes for her to cause my carefully trained tongue to tangle in stutters once again.

Beside me, Eleanor walked as stiff and unyielding as the icicles encasing the rooflines. If she took on any more pressure, she'd crack.

As if she heard my thoughts, she slipped her hand from my arm and jammed it into her pocket, the red thumb of her mitten showing through an enormous hole. Somehow I needed to find her a more winter-worthy coat. The last thing I wanted was to lose another friend due to my negligence. I rubbed at the ache squeezing my eyes, and stopped at the intersection, glancing for cars before crossing. When Eleanor continued, oblivious, I touched her elbow.

She jerked as if I'd attempted to steal her precious coin collection.

"My house is this way." I motioned to the alley sneaking off Twenty-Fourth Avenue.

Eleanor peered uncertainly down the narrow street.

Before I could say a word of encouragement, she strode across the street with the attitude of Ebenezer Scrooge being forced to visit an orphanage. Her blond locks unfurled from their pins, twisting in the slight breeze, like scampering children tethered to their stoic mother.

The men who'd harassed her weren't wrong, strictly speaking. Eleanor had an ethereal, otherworldly look that rivaled the pinups, but she'd always kept it buried under ill-fitting clothes, a thick layer of books, and an unparalleled fascination with odd coins she collected from the immigrants she and Peg befriended. She was a puzzle I itched to solve. What was going on inside that massive brain of hers? But as she navigated the slushy sidewalk without so much as a whimper, I knew there'd never be a chance for a small-town boy to be with an independent girl who'd found her larger-than-life dreams in the big city.

I trotted to catch her and pointed toward the winding street to my little house. It backed up to Mom's sweeping farmland, which allowed me to stop in regularly to help her and the field hands we hired every year.

"This is yours?" Eleanor blinked at the gingerbread trim, the cheerful green shutters, the wicker chairs tucked into the porch, the soaring white pine standing guard at the corner of the house.

I'd always been proud of my little home. But Eleanor was from San Diego, home to the mighty Pacific Ocean, the cultures of the world at its feet. My humble abode must appear provincial to her.

Instead she turned to me, her face full of wonder, her pink lips curving into a smile. "It's the kind of place where everyone would want to linger."

"You are welcome to come anytime."

If I could bottle the wistful expression she gave me, I would forever be a lucky man. But after I showed her what I had to show her, she might never speak to me again.

Lennie

Wrapped in my coat and Gideon's blanket, and bookended with Peg's winter boots and wool hat, I was at least semi-warm huddled in Gideon's twenty-year-old Ford truck. But I still had no desire to visit the east farm, no reason to see the site of the fire that had killed my sister. Gideon said we'd see Enid at the town hall later, but then refused to tell me why he was dragging me to see the site of the fire. He didn't want to "unfairly bias me"—a grubby plea to my reporter ethics that did little to assuage my questions. If anything, he'd poured gasoline on my sparking nerves.

The ride from town to the farm prickled with quiet, and bare trees scudded past the frozen window. Black Mill Creek pierced through the forest, and Gideon slowed to a snail's pace as we thumped over the narrow, wood-slat bridge.

On the other side, Gideon cooed to the old truck.

"You treat it like a child." The quarrelsome words slid from my mouth before I could properly filter them.

Gideon patted the dashboard and grinned. "The sheriff told me about this poor truck who'd landed in a junkyard. There was rust over the wheels, and the engine needed some tinkering and parts replaced. I did that easy enough, and now Henry is mostly good as new." Gideon waited a heartbeat, then lifted an eyebrow. "You don't get it?" He hesitated again, obviously waiting. "Henry Ford?"

I stared at him, scrambling to figure out the significance.

"The industrialist? He made transportation available for the common man. I like to think I'm supporting his ideas by resurrecting one of his earliest trucks."

"I see." But I didn't. Someone as famous as Ford didn't track where all his cars ended up, and likely didn't care much about the naming of one either. On the other hand, I very much liked the idea of someone caring enough about everyone and everything that he patiently endured finicky behavior until it turned itself around.

Mist rose from the waters and swallowed the moss-covered mill, its wheel turning at the invisible hand of the river. Under a blanket of snow, my family's muck field spread across the horizon, rolling west to east, away from Lake Michigan. Somewhere behind us were the higher, drier fields Dad used for corn.

Dad had wanted to be a preacher, but given his lack of education and exorbitant temper, he had the privilege of farming his father's land until he'd gone off the deep end enough that he settled into a semi-forced retirement.

A ragged fence blinked by as we twisted with the road, rising and dipping. I wished to run forever eastward until we ran past Detroit, through the Detroit-Windsor Tunnel, and into Canada.

The car engine ground lower, the gears changing, slowing, and I snapped my attention forward as Gideon guided the Ford to a stop. Above us a gnarled maple stretched over the wire fence that gashed through the snow-swept fields. The wind carried memories, whispers of girls running through the fields, laughing, tripping forward until their story crashed into the begging tears of the youngest's pleading not to be left behind.

I levered myself out of the truck, bolting from the haunting voices swirling in the cab, and dove into the relentless cold, passing flat-footed Gideon at the front bumper.

No doubt he'd been on his way to open the door for me, but there was a darkness in me that couldn't let him be kind. Couldn't let him see the gaping pit at my core, couldn't let him hear the buzzing inside my ears.

He hesitated behind me, clearing his throat.

With a horrible, sinking feeling I knew that in my savage desire to protect myself, I'd acted the cold narcissist my older sister Bitsy accused me of being. I flipped the coin in my pocket, a gift from Gideon himself. What penance could I pay for his forgiveness? My senses locked into his movements as he shuffled forward, patted the hood of the truck, then strode to join me on the berm.

The warmth of his arm touched the length of mine. It was a reminder of the places we'd been side by side before.

Wind groped across the open expanse, searching through the branches achingly bereft.

As I clenched my hands in the borrowed mittens, my nails pinched the tender flesh of my palms. Peg was gone.

"It's on the other side of the hill." Gideon's fingers touched my elbow as though he were the fading Ghost of Christmas Present, guiding me to claim the destruction of what I'd abandoned.

Then I ran, crashing across the ditch, hopping across the crusted ice, and clambering up the other side. Away and toward, twisting, sliding down the icy hill. Down. Down. Stumbling over a plowed divot before coming to a scrabbling halt at what was, presumably, the site of the fire.

But instead of the smoldering remains of a building, a patch of freshly turned earth spread in a wide swath.

I padded around the circle, confused. What had caught on fire? What was in the middle of nowhere that Peg was trying to save, as the report I'd been given claimed?

Gideon judiciously picked his way over the icy terrain toward me. He slid neatly down the last hummock, and the moment he took his gaze off his feet, shock bleached his face white. "This isn't . . . I don't understand. There w-was a crater here."

"A crater?" I turned again, surveying the scene. Hundreds of footprints marred the snowy landscape. I'd originally assumed they were from the medical team and such, but . . . I kicked at the meeting of the soil and snow. A charred metal cylinder broke free and rolled, breaking apart until it settled in the center of the dirt ring. I glanced up. Had Gideon noticed?

He was busy searching his pockets, mumbling about an explosion and having photographs to prove it.

But I wasn't a reporter for nothing. "I believe you." I lifted the bits of metal, turning them. Where had I seen them before? "This dirt's been moved recently. And I'm assuming there was no building out here. My sister didn't die trying to save anything."

I pivoted, surveying the landscape, letting Phil's advice slide through my conscious mind. *Look for the patterns and you'll uncover what doesn't belong.* The fence line followed the contours of the land, interrupted only when a hill dipped too low for me to see the continuation and . . . a tree reached above the horizon.

Leaving a muttering Gideon behind me, I skated across the landscape toward the windbreak, toward what my subconscious had noticed. A mass of cord tangled in the branches. There was no need for this much rope out here.

"Gideon?" I shouted.

He stopped his manic pacing and gaped at me as I shinnied up the tree to unravel the line. I could nearly see his mind churning through what I was doing. Bless the man, he was smart as anything, but not an investigator.

"W-what in heaven's name are you doing?" He trotted to the trunk and stood, fists on hips, looking for all the world like an avenging mother. "Get down."

"There's a tangle of rope up here."

"What?"

I pointed to the rat's nest of line above my head and repeated more clearly. "Rope."

"What's it doing up there?"

"Exactly," I said, with more acid in my tone than strictly necessary. I pushed up to standing and picked at the knotted cord.

"Hang on," Gideon said, obviously making lemonade with the citric acid I'd poured out. "I have a knife." He fairly bounced into the tree, and I gasped as the limb under me rebounded under his weight.

I clung to the branch above my head as he maneuvered to stand next to me. I was a tall woman, but Gideon loomed over me, his hat brushing the edges of the line that were barely in my reach.

"You must have superpowers to have seen this." His voice carried a note of awe.

"It's my job."

"No. It's more than that, Lennie. You don't give yourself enough credit."

He stood close enough that the warmth of his breath skimmed my face, and my neck heated with my desire to touch his dimpled cheek, to remember what it felt like to be protected. I shook away the thought. Nothing good came from depending on anyone.

Gideon

As usual, I bumbled my way into someone without entirely thinking about the consequences and ended up scrambling backward.

Lennie waved off my apology, her tone somewhere between businesslike and brusque—"If you cut here, I think." Her arm stretched to point, her body arching toward mine.

She smelled of the clove gum I'd introduced her to all those years ago. My gaze danced to her lower lip caught between her teeth, and I wrested my attention away, focusing instead on hacking at the rope.

"Wait." She grappled with the line, her shoulder tucking into my chest, my breath stirring a curl at the soft curve of her neck. Her girlish, upturned nose scrunched in concentration, and I was transported back to the two of us huddled over a spread of pages where we wove a story of a duo of friends saving Christmas. Twelve-year-old Eleanor acting out the story of defeating the evil Mouse King. Mom in the corner, snugly wrapped in blankets, laughed at our antics. I thought Lennie would always be there.

Lennie.

"Do you still go by Lennie?" The question popped out before I'd had time to consider. My family had christened the elfin girl with a name more fitting—less stoic and heavy than Eleanor. We were the only ones who called her Lennie, except for Peg.

But she didn't flinch at the name or any memories it carried, and continued unraveling the tangled line along with my composure. "It's my byline, and the reporters call me Lennie. Phil—he's my editor—said using a masculine pseudonym would make it easier for me to break in."

"Did it help? I m-mean . . . I know you're a journalist, but I don't read California newspapers."

She snorted, pressing closer, standing on tiptoes, one hand resting on my chest, the other directing me to cut another knot. "It helped a bit. Most folks out there think I'm an upstart even after twelve years. But Phil keeps assigning me work, and there are more female reporters now than ever. If I keep working hard, I'll get my shot at the bigger stories." She shrugged a single shoulder, eloquent in its dismissive despondence. Was the sadness in her because she was in Mapleview, because of her sister's death? Or did she always wear melancholy as a cloak, a symptom of the world shunning her for daring such brilliance?

The rope tumbled free, and she shouted in triumph, snapping our connection. The branch jarred under us, and I snatched for the sturdy trunk with one hand and Lennie's waist with the other.

Clutching my arm, her feet hovering over the abyss, eyes widening from the plunge open under her, she froze until I levered her onto the branch. Safe.

We stood there a breathless moment, Lennie gripping my lapels, face open, unraveled. I'd been tempted to kiss her trembling lips the day she left, almost pleaded with her to stay, but I let her fly, praying she'd return to me.

But, I reminded myself, she hadn't come back for me. Foolish, foolish man that I am.

My arm slid from her hip, and I scrambled away, ripped barren.

CHAPTER THREE

Lennie

I STOOD AS frozen as the wintry earth, while Gideon bolted down the tree and collected long lines of rope. His protection of me was obviously reflexive, born of his natural inclination to be a refuge. Little kids in the schoolyard had trotted after him like puppies after a loving mother. I shook off the desolation. I was no longer a child, no longer the discarded younger sister in want of a place to belong. Dad, Bitsy, and my brothers could say whatever they wished. I was a success. I had made it in the bigger world without them or anyone else.

I clambered down the tree and paced around the tangle of rope at the base.

Gideon stood stalwart with his back to me, coiling the line into a neat pile.

"There has to be a couple of hundred feet here." I lifted a length, weighing it, playing the icy rope through my palms until I reached the end. Instead of a broken, frayed edge, I found a scrap of material so soft it felt like kid leather.

"What in the world is that?"

Gideon's voice over my shoulder spooked me enough that I dropped the cord. For a large man, he moved with far too much stealth.

He retrieved the cloth, then turned it in his enormous grip. "Several people in town reported a huge balloon float from the sky."

My lungs deflated.

"Enid said she saw it from your mom's house, and Peg went to see what it was. Then something exploded. When I reported it, the military descended. Seeing as they have more experience in these kinds of things, I was glad to let them investigate. B-but they declared it a weather balloon and informed us your sister had died in an unrelated fire."

My head spun, and I sucked in air, trying to bring the world into focus. "I know about this." Sure as the Japanese had bombed Pearl Harbor, I knew exactly what had happened. I knew because I'd seen that circle of metal a mere month before. I knew, and I had let the military bury my story for the sake of national security. I let them continue, thinking it wouldn't do any harm. And now my sister was dead. Killed by my capitulation.

Gideon

The scrap of material dangled from my fingertips as though as bewildered as I. "What do you know?"

Lennie didn't answer. Instead, she circled the clearing, mumbling. She passed to my right and her voice jumbled in my damaged ear.

"What?" I asked.

She stopped but didn't turn. Her hand, stuffed in her pocket, moved as if turning something.

The penny.

She still had it, and even behind her brave facade, she was crumbling.

Abandoning the scrap of material, I stepped in Lennie's path. "Let's get out of here."

"No." Her face galvanized into iron—fierce and hard, a strength I'd never seen in her. "I won't let them get away with this. Do you have a safe deposit box where we can keep this stuff?" She paced before me. "No, they'll only search it. Better to keep it." She paused. "But I will need the name of the officer you contacted, and any other names you remember. Oh! And I must talk to the people who saw the balloon, heard the explosion, or witnessed anything out of place.

Do you know if Peg's telephone is still working? Better yet, can I use one at the town hall, or is there a telephone booth near there? I need to talk to Phil."

As I tried to process everything she had said, Lennie dropped the metal in her bag, then dug and retrieved a pad of paper and a pencil.

"Gideon?" She shuffled her feet, poised, ready to attack—the pen mightier than a sword.

The sound of a truck powering over the slick, isolated road had Lennie tossing her notepad into her bag. As I remained in place, she scrambled to wind the rope, shoving some at me, before she slipped her arm through mine and sauntered toward my car as if we were out for a Sunday stroll on a warm June afternoon.

"Hello?" A deep voice floated on the crisp air just before a large, square man appeared around the tiny grove of windbreak trees.

Though he was buried in a dark overcoat, the peaked captain's hat perched on his head told me that word of our visit to the site had already reached Captain Radcliffe VanderLaan.

"Gideon." He neared, nodding at me before turning an assessing gaze on Lennie. "Miss." He touched the brim of his hat, nearly dissecting the connection between Lennie and me, then appraising the coil of rope strung between us.

"Lennie, this is Captain Radcliffe VanderLaan. He's married to Bitsy, and he's the one who was kind enough to come and help figure out what happened to Peg."

Lennie's brother-in-law smiled like a conquering hero, thrusting out his hand as if he either wanted her to shake it or surrender the evidence she'd concealed inside her handbag.

If it were possible, Lennie's hold tightened further on my arm. "Is that so?"

Radcliffe could hardly mistake the skepticism in her voice, but his face didn't flicker and his hand didn't fall.

I untangled myself from her and the rope and shook the man's hand.

"What's with all the rope?" Radcliffe's voice was all polite curiosity, but I still felt the suspicion burrowing underneath.

"We're bringing it to Gideon's mom. She can use it on the farm." Lennie hefted more of the rope into her arms, smearing mud across the leg of the overalls.

"You came out here for that?"

"No." Lennie's expression matched Radcliffe's strained politeness, but her undercurrent snapped with volatile electricity. "That was a happy coincidence. We were here to reexamine the ground you failed to investigate thoroughly."

"Oh?" Radcliffe lifted a lazy eyebrow. "As for anything you think you found . . . well, I hardly think a lady is equipped to explore such a ghastly fire."

Good heavens, the man was starting a war. "Lennie's not a lady . . . I mean . . . She's a lady. She's just not . . ."

"I'm not a squeamish ninny. In fact, I'm with the *San Diego Times*."

"Oh! My wife loves the fashion reports of your colleagues at the *Mapleview Messenger*."

I could nearly hear Lennie's teeth grinding at his misrepresentation of her work. "As your wife would know if she bothered to find out anything about her sister, I'm an actual reporter. I've covered everything from white-collar crime to murder, all the way up the food chain to government cover-ups."

And just like that, Lennie dropped the proverbial bomb.

"Is that so?" The captain's eyes twinkled but warning crackled underneath. "Well, Eleanor, it's a good thing I'm here to make sure everyone stays safe and protected from the big bad government."

Lennie inhaled as if he'd slapped her.

"Well," I interjected, hauling on Lennie. "It's time w-we go. We'll see your family at the town hall in a few minutes. Will you be there?"

Radcliffe shook his head and vaguely referenced military business.

I tugged on Lennie again, and she tripped a bit to keep up. Trails of rope wriggled behind us, and I waved at the captain, trying to corral my tripping tongue. "It w-was good to see you again, Radcliffe."

Lennie ripped her hand free and stomped to the truck, the rope whipping after her. If it could, the heat of her anger would burn the good captain and me to a crisp. Lennie slammed Henry's door.

I contained the wince behind a shrug at the captain—*what are you going to do?*

He laughed and wished me luck.

"Merry Christmas." I touched the brim of my hat and slid onto Henry's bench seat.

"Seriously?" Lennie shoved the rope into the back seat, glaring at me as if I had attempted to make a peace accord with the Nazis.

"What was I supposed to do?" I cranked the truck over and eased onto the icy street. "You looked like you were going to assault the man, and that's the last thing we—"

"He's lying to my face and covering up what happened to Peg. I was quiet once. I will not be again."

"What do you mean that you've been quiet before?"

"The government is either testing weapons or we're under attack. That land was littered with pieces of a bomb trigger."

I stilled, letting the words settle into coherence. "A bomb?"

She studied me under hooded eyes as if assessing me.

I used the excuse of carefully stopping at an intersection to think. I wanted to believe her. But a bomb? Here? In all the years I'd known her, Lennie had never lied to me—to the point where she proudly admitted to stealing my cookies and, once, putting flakes of cow manure in Bitsy's soup.

As a kid, she'd been scared and smart, yet filled with bright hope. But this woman wasn't the Lennie I'd known. This woman was hard and sharp, like shattered glass. She pulled the metal pieces from her bag and cradled them in her palms. In her expression was determination, fear, and, yes, honesty. Glass, damaged or not, was still transparent.

"Catch me up. Why do you think this was a bomb?"

She rolled the components with a forefinger. "Because the last time I held pieces like this, an ordnance expert told me what these were. This isn't the only balloon bomb I've seen."

"This has happened before?"

"No one died then . . . at least that I know of. When the censor asked my editor to pull the story, he said the balloons couldn't hurt anyone. That with how they were constructed, they would set fires, not explode. But this"—she touched one piece—"this is a striker pin. This is a safety pin housing, the spring, and the pin. And this"—she placed a gnarled piece of metal on the dark wool covering her knee— "is shrapnel. It's not from an incendiary bomb like the others. It's antipersonnel, meant to maim and kill."

To maim and kill. I touched the deadly cylinders nestled in her palm. They were cold, and silhouettes of bright orange flamed across their surface. That they were in a fire was without question.

"Now you know why I very much don't like Bitsy's captain."

The rhythmic noise of the tires filled the cab as I tried to get my bearings. "If that is shrapnel, it would be a very bad thing. But this is the United States government. Why would they suppress bombs exploding in Mapleview? It'd be dangerous not to alert people."

"And yet they're not telling people. I didn't move away from Mapleview and become a reporter to let these kinds of things happen."

"They must have a reason to keep silent."

"A reason to allow unwitting American citizens to be killed by bombs a few weeks before Christmas without so much as a warning?"

She had me there. "So what do we do?"

A horn blared behind us, and Lennie clutched at the door, obviously preparing to make a dash for it.

I settled a hand on her tense arm and squinted into the rearview mirror.

Elizabeth VanderLaan frowned at me from behind the wheel of her pristine white Oldsmobile.

I frowned back. "It's your sister." Lennie's older sister had grown more sour with age, and I wasn't at all surprised when Lennie whispered the old nickname—Bitter Bitsy—under her breath. Radcliffe had obviously called his wife before he headed out to the fields. How those two ever managed not to annoy each other to death—

Bitsy honked again. This time loud and long, causing me to roll down the window and wave an I-see-you gesture. She used the opportunity to thunder up next to me and signal to her wristwatch.

"Lovely," I muttered. "We're going to be late to the town hall."

At least she hadn't tried to run us off the road.

Chapter Four

Lennie

Of course it had been Bitsy to drive up behind us. Bitsy to discover me and herd the negligent disappointment back in line. Not that I'd had much say in the delay. Worse, I was dressed in a getup worthy of mucking stalls. Fantastic.

Gideon had gone absolutely silent, driving white-knuckled through town as if the icy road might swallow his beloved Henry whole. Soft snow drifted through the steel-gray skies, catching on the corners of the windows, the flakes holding strong until the heat from the truck vents softened their frozen edges and the intricate, one-of-a-kind design puddled, then dribbled into the abyss of the door. Rather like what Mapleview did to those who dared protest the strictures of the expected.

I was the furthest thing from expected. I was born to explore, to be recognized and reckoned with, not settle for some boring man and keep his house. It was no surprise that my father paid for Bitsy's wedding dress and established my brothers in their trades, then refused to pay for my schooling. But I was wholly unprepared for him to order me to reject the scholarship I'd earned.

Although Gideon had been busy with a summer internship in the state legislature, he was the one who had believed in me enough to convince me to leave. And when I told him I had no way to get to the station, he borrowed his mother's Model T, put my suitcase in the trunk, and drove me to the Amtrak station in Grand Rapids, then sat with his arm across my shoulders to still my quaking.

But the sneaking was all for naught. When I boarded the train, I thought I'd neatly escaped. Then Dad strode down the platform, leading my gaggle of siblings, and pushed past Gideon as if he were merely a broken reed. I think if he'd seen me with Gideon and thought I was eloping, my father would have given me his blessing. Instead, he abandoned my siblings, muscled past the porter, and huffed up the narrow train aisle, towering over me while quoting verses about children obeying parents.

When I calmly quoted Scripture about parents not exasperating their children, he attempted to physically remove me from my seat. I stabbed his foot with the sharp tip of my umbrella, and the conductor, a burly man with a bristled mustache, escorted my un-ticketed father away. Fortunately, the porter had already stowed my battered box, otherwise Dad might have stolen what little I'd packed.

As the train chugged forward with painful slowness, Dad ranted on the platform, his rage smothering the rest of the crowd as they said goodbye to their respective friends and family.

I had yanked open the window and leaned out, shouting, "I wouldn't wish you on anyone . . . even my worst enemy. In fact, I don't want to see you ever again."

To this day I can still see the horror on Peg's face as she crumpled into Gideon, hear her wail, "Even me?"

I might have backpedaled for the two of them, but I'd already driven in the knife and carved myself out of the Sweers family. I wrote to Peg, addressing the letter to the general storekeeper who had been kind to me. And Peg had responded by writing that she would always stand beside me. She wished it were different. But she didn't want me to give up everything.

So we wrote letters, occasionally paid for a phone call when there was big news—my hiring at the paper, Gideon's going to college and dating some legislator's daughter, Peg's winning a national writing award, getting the highest score in her class on a math test, even Mama having to go to the nursing home. Twice I paid for Peg to ride the train to see me, and she left me in awe as she spoke with the immigrants on the docks, trying on languages the way I swapped out hats. I tried to convince her to become a translator for United Press and travel the world with me. But she fell in love, got married, had a baby—contented herself with the acceptable life that tied her to Mapleview and away from me.

And I couldn't exactly visit home. I'd not just burned that bridge, I'd obliterated it.

I swiped at the bit of moisture collecting on my lashes. Like so much fog rolling off the bay, Peg had been burned away by the glare of light. I thought there would be more time—after I was more established, when her little girl was older, when I proved that I'd made the right decision, when I was successful and happy with my byline in the *New York Times* so Dad could proudly point and say, "That's my daughter." Then I would be stitched into the family again.

Maybe if I found out what had really killed my sister, showed that what I was good at was good for the family, then they would see everything that happened at home wasn't my fault.

I turned the penny in my pocket, hearing Gideon's younger voice as we sat side by side on the hard wooden bench waiting for the train. "The thing about coins is that they're pretty much w-worthless unless you're in the country to which they belong. A British halfpenny is useless in the United States, unless it's a collector's piece from 1787, or—" He reached up, his fingers delicate on my cheek.

I stiffened, wondering at the one boy who saw me, solid and whole. I had half expected, half desired his lips on mine, his pleading for me to stay.

Instead, he'd pulled a coin from behind my ear. "Or it's magic."

I laughed, swatting at his hovering hand. But his gentle, sweet face remained serious, and he pressed the lowly penny into my open palm. "If you ever feel alone or ever n-need to know someone cares, pull this out and know I'm thinking of you, and that there is a God who loves you for being your brilliant self. But you need to go where you belong, where they appreciate the collector's piece you are."

At the time, I had no idea that the penny was a rare Indian Head from the early 1900s, or that it was indeed worth a bit of money. I had been tempted so many times to track Gideon down to beg him to rescue me, to admit that I wasn't a valuable halfpenny with John Wilkinson embossed on its face.

I pressed the magic coin between my fingers, felt the smooth edge of it against my thumb. I had no choice but to prove I was worth more than a ubiquitous newly printed penny. I would not let people get away with hiding the truth behind convenient lies.

Gideon turned the Ford around the corner and the old Visser School rose, red-bricked and menacing, from behind the new grocery store.

My fingers clenched reflexively on the door handle, and I cursed myself for not realizing. Of course they had turned the schoolhouse into the town hall. As if I didn't already have enough to deal with.

Though his face didn't betray my lapse, he reached for me in recognition.

I hated that he still saw me so clearly.

"Are you okay?" His voice lifted above the sound of the vehicle puttering down Twenty-Fifth Avenue, and he turned as if to catch my response in his good ear.

"Of course." I'd prepared myself to see my family again, but not in a place where my siblings had relished the free rein to torture me. And without Peg there to temper them? I squared my shoulders and sucked in a breath.

No one needed to know that a cold building made me quake more than a host of drunken sailors in a dark alley. After all, the sailors had hearts which could bleed and stop, but this building would haunt me forever.

Gideon

As we eased around the corner, tension tightened Lennie's shoulders. I'd become immune to the location of our mutual torture. But I should have thought to warn her that my office was on the second floor of the old Visser schoolhouse. The huge windows, bubbled with age, squinted like a short-sighted matron over what was now a little park. The outhouse was long gone, but I wondered if Lennie remembered hiding from her brothers behind it, the two of us pawing through coins I'd earned bagging at the general store or she'd gotten from one of the immigrants, pretending to be pirates and hoping to find a real treasure.

The smell of dry blackboard dust seemed to hover in the air, igniting memories of cruel laughter. But as town supervisor, even if it was interim, I ruled the schoolhouse now.

I parked Henry down the street and set the parking brake, then fussed with the keys, my wallet, and the sack with the brownies to give Lennie time to acclimate before jumping out. She barely touched my hand as I helped her from the car, and I folded her limp arm into my elbow in a show of solidarity.

When she caught sight of Bitsy striding from her car, Lennie snapped to consciousness and hauled me along with her. False bravado radiated from Lennie in her too-long stride, too-rigid spine. I wished I could tell her they could no longer hurt her, but I knew better. Despite my law degree from Princeton, despite the wall of photos of me smiling with dignitaries, in my own hometown I would always be the stuttering boy who was hard of hearing and unable to fight for his country.

Bitsy stomped into the building and let the wind slam the heavy door in our faces without so much as a howdy-do to her sister.

Lennie gave a rueful laugh. "She hasn't changed much."

"No, she has not. But she spared us the drudgery of making small talk with her."

"She meant it as a snub."

"I'm sure she did. Folks treated our good Lord much the same. I can't expect much better," I said, quoting one of mother's favorite sayings.

Lennie stiffened, and I wished I'd kept quiet. It was no secret that her we-never-miss-a-Sunday family had not been kind to her. One would think that such a religious family would be kinder to their own. But they were more apt to use a misapplied verse as a battering ram than anything else.

I nodded to my secretary, Mrs. Schmucker, at the front desk, in response to her quiet "They're upstairs waiting for you," and wove through the collection of secretarial desks to the stairwell angling to the old secondary school floor. I hesitated at the stairwell door to give Lennie and me a moment to steel ourselves.

The door swung open to a frowning Bitsy. "You're late," she said with more bite than a junkyard mutt.

"Actually, w-we're right on time." I resisted the urge to touch the small of Lennie's stiff back for support.

Lennie sailed past me to peer at her older sister like a hawk sizing up prey. "I believe you're incorrect." She raised her wrist so the tight semicircle of family on the far side of the room could see. "The watch given me by the base commander keeps perfect time, and it is just now two o'clock."

As if in confirmation, the church bell sounded two grave tones. "She's right," it seemed to say.

"Well." Bitsy fluttered about, fanning herself with a kerchief as though she might faint at the audacity of her younger sister to be correct. I barely held in my laughter as she plunked down next to her oldest brother, Walter. The folding chairs sat so tightly together it almost felt like a battle line had been drawn . . . until Walter scooted away just enough that it drew a wink from the next brother in the family. While the boys had been firebrands in the day, they'd settled down with marriage and children and responsibilities of their own. Whether that newfound graciousness extended to Lennie or not remained to be seen.

Lennie lifted the green hat from her head and fluffed out her profusion of curls before placing the hat and her coat on the already overflowing coatrack. "As wonderful as it is to chat"—her voice was as bright as an interrogation lamp—"I have important business back in California. If you don't mind?" She lifted a brow at me, smile fixed, eyes cold and dead.

"Of course." I shuffled past her, feeling old and irrelevant, discarded.

"Uncle Gideon." Little Enid leaped from her grandfather's lap and slung her arms around my neck, planting a damp kiss on my cheek. "I missed you." She frowned at her Aunt Bitsy as if the woman had purposefully kept her from seeing her father's best friend. For all I knew, Bitsy had. How I wished things were different, that I had some legal right to protect Peg's girl from the rancor that had driven Lennie away.

"I missed you too, Enid." I set her to the floor and knelt in front of her, noting that her black patent shoes were polished and her dress was clean, if sporting a few crumbs of what appeared to be a cookie. "This"—I pointed to Lennie—"is your Aunt Eleanor."

"Lennie?" Enid tested the name, a look of mischievous little-girl wonder growing. "*The* Lennie?"

From the corner of my vision, I caught Lennie's frantic expression, along with Walter's comedic attempt to hold back a laugh, but I simply nodded at Enid. I knew the stories her mother had told about her middle sister.

"Do I get to live with her instead of Aunt Bitsy?"

Bitsy's loud inhale proved that the girl's harsh whisper had carried to the other side of the room.

"Let's just see, shall we?" I stood. "In the meantime, your Aunty Lennie has a brownie for you."

Lennie stood stock-still, as if she expected an attack of bees. When I gestured to the pan she carried, she jolted into herky-jerky motion and slid a hacked-up brownie onto a napkin.

Enid fluttered her dark puppy-dog eyes at her aunt.

Lord knows I was sorry for everything that had happened to this child. But there was nothing I could do about the past, about my neglect of Peg or the abandonment of my high-powered path on the other side of the state.

Lennie, who'd been so self-assured just moments before, crumbled before her niece. Her ache at the sight of Peg's diminutive twin was plain as Lennie started a sentence, then abandoned it, shuffled the pan, the girl, the napkins.

Bitsy huffed, fist on hip, in preparation for a motherly intervention.

"Would anyone else like a brownie?" My voice echoed loud in the room, drawing hard looks from Bitsy and Mr. Sweers himself, and I immediately regretted stepping in.

"May we just read the will?" Lennie's voice strained high, and I wished I had warned her how similar Enid and Peg were in every way.

"Of course." I stepped behind my desk and gathered the needed papers.

Lennie sank to the chair in the protective shadow of my desk.

Enid surveyed the adults, shrugged, handed Lennie the brownie, and, before I realized what she was doing, opened a hole in the Sweers' defensive line by dragging her chair from Bitsy's left, screeching across the wood floors, to Lennie's side.

Lord help us. This was going to be complicated.

Lennie

Peg's daughter sidled next to me and clambered into her chair as though she hadn't just sent a traitorous shot across Bitsy's bow. No one chose me over Bitsy and lived to tell the tale. No one.

Gideon cleared his throat, and the noise drifted through the office like a shrouding coat of ash.

The girl, dressed in a frothy pink frock that screamed my elder sister's taste, sat in the wood chair, hands folded still and quiet while swinging her legs gently.

Bitsy gripped a no-longer-crisp hankie to her mouth, forgetting to portray the proper sadness and instead betraying her real nature with ice-blue eyes buzzing with anger. My father's squat fingers gripped the arms of his chair as though he were afraid the piece of furniture might attempt a strategic retreat from under his massive derriere. The younger brothers—James and Hank—glanced at our eldest brother, Walter, for direction. But he simply stared at Peg's daughter, a single thin brow winged high in curiosity, or perhaps humor. Maybe he really had mellowed.

The girl smoothed her dress in unhurried, unconcerned movements.

What was I supposed to do with her unruffled poise, with the cozy warmth of her body tucked uncomfortably close to mine?

When Enid leaned further into me, batting her mother's eyelashes at me, then winked with a mischievous twinkle, I couldn't help but think God was giving me another chance. She was Peg's child in every deviously innocent way.

I dropped an arm around the girl and together we focused our attention on Gideon.

"Well." He tapped the sheaf of paper on his desk before laying it out and squaring the corners one more time. "Well—"

"I think we can proceed now." Dad's voice made Gideon jump, and the papers bumped astray.

My father sighed in dramatic exasperation, but the sound seemed to drive steel through Gideon, and he lifted his chin and read Peg's will without a single stutter.

To our mother (still in the nursing home), father, the boys, their wives, and children, Peg left little bobbles and trifles. There was a bequest to the church, and one to the veteran's home in honor of her husband, who had perished in the Pacific some months before.

And then to me.

Gideon glanced at me, then my sister—"Eleanor Sweers is to receive the letter I left." Gideon slid a crisp envelope across the desk to me, and Bitsy smirked at the minuscule gift.

But it was precious beyond measure to me. A last word from my sister. I tore open the envelope, nearly missing Gideon's words.

"She is the executor of my will, making sure that the terms of this legal document are followed. I also appoint Eleanor as the guardian of my child, Enid Barrett."

The office was silent a moment, as a buzzing grew louder and louder in my head until the room erupted in a pandemonium of movement and raucous sound swirling around Enid and me. But the noise of Bitsy's caterwauling was swallowed under the numbing drone of blood pulsing through my ears.

I'd prepared myself for nearly every scenario, every word Bitsy or

Dad or Walter might say. But this? Becoming the guardian of Peg's daughter?

Bitsy knelt in front of Enid and the girl exploded into motion, scrambling away from my sister into my lap.

She wasn't a large child, but I was unused to anyone touching me, let alone filling the entirety of my space. I kicked out, catching Bitsy's arm as she attempted to follow Enid into my lap.

My sister fell in a heap of lace, aghast exclamations, and flailing appendages.

Gideon gaveled the paperweight on his desk. "That is quite enough." He towered over the debacle, glowering until everyone settled into their chairs.

Everyone but Enid. She simply rearranged herself on my lap as if I'd become a chaise lounge, complete with a soft pillow arm on which to lay her head.

This close, I could see the dark circles bruising the tender flesh under her questioning eyes, and I found myself vowing to protect Peg's child from the grasping, crushing woman on the other side of the room.

Gideon nodded at the subdued adults. "If we cannot contain ourselves, I will call the sheriff to assist in helping you remember yourselves. Am I quite clear?" He met the gaze of each and every family member besides the two of us.

Walter winked, a hand covering what appeared to be a smile. He at least seemed to glory in Bitsy's being put in her place.

Enid giggled and breathed into my ear, "He sounds like his sister, Miss Baldwin." When I lifted a questioning eyebrow, she clarified. "My teacher. She's ever so nice, but even the boys are afraid to cross her. She can outrun most of them and split logs better than my daddy."

"It sounds as if we could be friends," I whispered back conspiratorially, thinking of Gideon's older sister.

"Now then." Gideon tapped the sheets on his desk, mumbling to himself as he found his place again in the document. "If Eleanor is unable or unwilling to provide guardianship, I nominate"—Gideon paused, his Adam's apple bobbing a moment before continuing—"Enid's godfather, Gideon B-braum."

Bitsy drooped in a feigned collapse, but, thanks to Walter's restraining hand on her elbow, remained seated.

"Whoever claims guardianship is entitled to the remainder of my estate," Gideon concluded, then stacked the papers neatly on the desk again.

Bitsy shot to her feet, somehow managing to radiate both indignation and persecution in her stomp toward Gideon. "I will not let you ruin one more thing. You will be hearing from my lawyer." She flounced from the room.

My father trailed her, snatching both their coats, withholding even a glance in my direction. I was still invisible.

My brothers filed past me, each ruffling Enid's hair and pulling on their jackets before nodding goodbye to me, then Gideon.

Walter paused in the doorway and, after a moment, turned back. "I know a lot of water has passed under the bridge and all, but you'll let me know if you need anything?"

I wouldn't have been more surprised if an angel chorus broke out right there in Gideon's dark little office, but managed a mumble along the lines of "of course" before Walter shut the door quietly behind him.

Silence ticked with questions. Had this really happened?

Gideon collapsed into his armchair, and it swung in response to his momentum. He pushed his fingers through his mop of hair and grinned at Enid. "Are you okay, Sunshine?"

"Of course." Enid hopped carelessly from my lap as if she'd predicted everything that had just transpired. "Does that mean I get to go home with you two?"

I swallowed hard. "I don't—"

"For now," he interrupted. "I'm going to bring you and your aunt to your house, and she'll take care of you."

She twisted her mouth to the side in a perfect imitation of her mother trying to decide whether to cooperate without Gideon's presence.

"Gideon brought us a lovely dinner, and he'll stay, of course." I might have felt guilty for strong-arming Gideon into dinner without asking if I hadn't been so desperate. I had no idea what to do with this child—what she liked or didn't like, what her routines were. It had been half a lifetime ago that I'd cared for my sister at this age.

"I'll even help tuck you into bed before I go home. Sound good?" He was asking both of us.

And somehow it felt equal parts right and terrifying to slip into my coat and walk out with Enid linked between Gideon and me, like a proper family might.

CHAPTER FIVE

Gideon

TIDBITS OF LAUGHTER filtered through Peg's house and filled the spaces around the clacking of dishes as I stacked the simple white plates in the cupboard. After Jack had died, most of the town thought I'd give a proper amount of time to the grieving widow and then move into this cheery yellow kitchen as a second-rate substitute for my best friend. I'd been happy to help, of course. Mom had taught me that no one was too important to help others. But I wasn't Jack. And Peg wasn't her sister.

Eleanor had been a tiny thing when she'd first come to school. With an elfin, upturned nose and wispy white-blond curls, I half thought she'd sprang from another world. She was the youngest child traipsing to school, following a brace of brothers led by the oldest sister. Unfortunately for her, the eldest brother and the sister were often the bullies of the schoolyard.

Already I was the one the younger kids ran to when someone was teasing them. They'd hide behind my tall frame, and I'd be the wall between them and their tormentors, the taunts from the older boys of "you c-can't even s-speak" mostly bouncing off my chest. What I lacked in brawn, I made up for in scrawny height and scowling determination. They laughed, saying I probably couldn't hear them, then walked away, throwing a rag ball between them. I wished then that I truly had been deaf in both ears, and perhaps blind too.

But whoever I rescued would smile at me, slip their fragile hand in mine, and drag me to whatever game they were playing. I never minded being their climbing toy or swinging them into the trees where they pretended to be squirrels. They never questioned why I didn't speak or why I tilted my head at strange angles to listen.

Lennie took my protection for perhaps a week before she hid behind the outhouse. It earned her awful names that don't bear repeating. When the bullies didn't follow her, I figured she was the smartest of the bunch.

In those early days, she never so much as looked past my knees. But I could see the burn in her even then. One day she would make them rue the day they despised her.

The gurgle of the tub drain caught my attention, and I wiped the last crumb from the table. As I ambled down the hall, Lennie's low voice chattered, singing a nonsensical song about drying and dressing and the sandman. It wasn't anything I'd ever heard before . . . and neither was Enid's quiet compliance.

She hated getting out of the tub, hated getting on pajamas, and hated going to bed for fear of missing anything. She was certain the fairies came out to play, and the adults were hogging the fun. Either that, or evil dragon monsters might invade her room.

I grinned, thinking about how often she'd slunk out of her bedroom only to find her mother already asleep while I cleaned the kitchen. If Enid was searching for fairies, I helped her construct a fairy alarm system—tin cans on a rope strung across her bed. If it was fear of the dragons, I created a foolproof anti-monster spray from a bit of Peg's perfume diluted in water. After all, evil hated anything that smelled as good as a flower.

The bathroom door swung open, and Lennie fake-screeched while Enid giggled.

"See." Lennie curved over the girl, a soft curl draping in a protective curtain against the curve of Enid's cheek. "There are no monsters out here. Not when there's someone like Gideon around. Did I ever tell you how Gideon fought an entire army of evil warriors with only a flashlight?"

Lennie tucked the strand behind her ear, and my attention traced the delicate movement. "Go climb in bed." My voice careened higher than usual, and I cleared my throat. "I'll bring you some warm milk, and Lennie can tell you the story."

Enid skipped down the hall, leaped into her bed, and pulled a worn teddy bear into her chest. Satisfied she would stay, I wandered down the hall.

Already in the kitchen, Lennie poured a bit of warm milk from the saucepan into a mug.

"You are a miracle worker." I stood in the kitchen doorway. How were Lennie's movements so sure? To my knowledge, she'd never been to her sister's home, yet she seemed to know instinctively where everything was. Not only that, she had a tender way with Enid that belied Lennie's businesslike approach to nearly everyone and everything else.

Lennie's methodical confidence began to make me believe we could do what was best for Enid *and* figure out what in the world was happening at the same time. That desolate field bore little resemblance to the churned mess that had been there last . . . Radcliffe, strutting confident and sure, and yet obviously performing a sleight of hand to hide what had happened.

Could Lennie be right? A bomb and government cover-up?

"I don't know about a miracle worker." She ran fresh water into the pot. "But I took care of Peg until she was fourteen. I figured she would have similar routines with her daughter. I'm just glad it worked." After wrapping her palms around the mug, she meandered to Enid's room, then set the mug on the bedside table and snuggled next to her niece. "You don't know the story of Gideon versus the evil warriors?"

Enid glanced at me with unchecked adoration, and I leaned against the doorframe with a shrug. I had no idea what Lennie was talking about.

"One day when I was a little younger than you, my mama was feeling poorly, so I wanted to go pick her some blueberries. They were her favorite, and she loved them with fresh cream and sugar. When I got back, there was a dragon trying to steal away Grandma and your mama."

Suddenly the remembrance came to mind. Her father was overseas in Germany, her mother, pregnant with the twins Peg and Abner, was ill. Bitsy didn't let Lennie come with them to pick blueberries, saying Lennie was apt to make a mess of things.

I'd heard the screaming from the street. By the time I ran through the yard and up the steps, Mrs. Sweers had already delivered Peg, but the boy was purple. Bitsy came in cursing and spitting, blaming tiny Lennie for the boy born still as the grave.

"Gideon came and helped me fight off the dragon." Lennie's eyes found mine and softened at the edges in quiet gratitude. "Just as we banished the dragon, a line of evil warriors burst into our house, and he stood up to them. He proclaimed that I saved your mama's life. And when they didn't believe him and tried to banish me to the cave of forgotten memory, never to be remembered by anyone, he took out a flashlight and turned it on like a revealing beacon, and they all ran away from the truth he showed. Then he set me free and, while I was gone, he fended for your mama."

"And me!" Enid's voice piped in.

"And you." Lennie bopped Enid's little nose, so like her own.

"Uncle Gideon really saved you?"

Lennie nodded, making a show of tucking the blankets underneath Enid's body. "He and your mom were the only ones who believed in me." She kissed the top of her niece's head, then flicked on the night light, the glow joining the light from the hall, pushing the shadows into the corners.

"Would you like me to sing?" I shuffled into the room, and Lennie stood to make space.

"Auntie." Enid's demand was soft with sleep.

Lennie hovered inches from me. A ghost of the past, unsure, unsettled, wavering with uncertainty until she solidified, finding her choice.

The Enid-sized lump snuggled deeper under the quilt.

Lennie leaned into the bed, her profile silhouetted. Darkness disguised the passage of time. "O little town of Bethlehem, how still we see thee lie." Lennie's alto voice hovered slightly above a whisper, haunting.

Heat built in my chest. It had been the song Peg had sung to her daughter the night before she died. It had always been her favorite. The idea of such an innocuous place lighting the world lent her hope.

I had liked it such a short time ago. Now it was a reminder that I was no hero, had no ability to stop tragedy, and no sixth sense to know where I was really needed.

I had, in fact, been in Grand Rapids when Peg died. After a meeting with the WPA board, I was supposed to eat dinner at Peg's. I'd left the meeting feeling accomplished about gaining help from FDR's New Deal administration for several of our farms who were desperate for workers since most of their workforce had been drafted.

As I walked up Monroe, a woman cursed at me for dodging the draft—as if I hadn't already pleaded with the recruiters to accept a tongue-tied, half-deaf man. The woman spit on me, the slop of her spittle running slimy down my cheek. I hadn't even had a chance to respond before her young son spit on my scuffed loafers.

Instead of going home, I'd gone to a fourth draft board, hoping they would find something, anything, for me to do.

That delay meant I was late for dinner. That delay meant I wasn't there when a balloon floated into the field. That delay meant I wasn't there to stop Peg from exploring it, from a fire that left not only a crater in the farmyard but a motherless child screaming on the porch until the neighbor came to explore the reason behind the explosion. Peg had died in my town, on my watch, while I was trying to escape.

———— ⋇ ————

Lennie

Darkness dampened the last of the hopeful song which had been Peg's year-round favorite. Gideon's quiet contemplation mingled with Enid's blinking stare—what were they thinking?

Although I'd cared for Peg from the time she'd been an infant, I wasn't sure I could be who Enid needed me to be, let alone uncover what had really happened to my sister. It made sense to float a bomb on a balloon into a place like San Diego or Seattle, but Mapleview?

Besides, news like that was covered by national reporters. It had been my dream to report for United Press, but doubt niggled at the recesses of my mind. It was too easy to miss important pieces, and in Mapleview, I was far more a bungling Jughead than a conquering Wonder Woman.

"Aunt Lennie?" Enid's fingers touched my cheek, featherlight. "Are you going to stay?"

If there was ever a loaded question, that was it. Peg had left me everything dear to her, but did I want to give up my life? Move back to Mapleview? I didn't know how to be a mother. "I—"

"She'll be in your mama's room if you need her," Gideon answered.

Tension released in my gut. Enid was only asking about tonight. Of course.

Enid's mouth twisted, obviously trying to decide if he was side-stepping her. "Will you stay too?"

"I'm not sure that's a good idea."

"Please?"

Gideon shifted, and I shrugged.

The neighbors were far enough away that no one would know if we had a carnival inside. Not that anything untoward would ever happen. There wasn't an eligible man I knew who would be interested in the likes of me, and Gideon was infinitely eligible—sweet, handsome, educated, and the well-respected town supervisor.

"I'll be on the couch as usual, Sunshine."

Enid broke into a smile that proved her nickname, and beckoned Gideon with a flapping hand.

He snatched it from the air, kissed her palm, and tucked her fingers around it in a fist. "A kiss to hold while you sleep," he whispered into the girl's gossamer hair. "If you're lonely, you hold this to your cheek."

I'm sure I sighed right alongside Enid. She was, no doubt, content to be in her own bed, without Bitsy fluttering over her. What would it have been like to have a father like Gideon? Peg would have said that God was the perfect father, and I should trust him. But I had never once felt God as a strong tower, and there was no way I was running in the dark toward an unproven uncertainty.

I ducked between Gideon and the doorframe, the scent of leather and spice trailing me as he drifted behind me. Despite the mess we'd left in the kitchen earlier, Gideon had already set it to rights. Apparently he was less a disaster than I'd credited, and the brownies, if I were honest, had been so delicious I'd been tempted to throw away my aspirations and propose to the man then and there.

While Gideon dug in the hall closet, I loitered in the living room, moving a *Life* magazine from the end table to the coffee table and back again, then swiped at nonexistent dust, trying not to think about the fact that a handsome near-stranger would be sleeping on the couch.

He returned with a pile of blankets and a pillow topped with a pair of striped pajamas.

"Did you stay here often?" A jealous note sneaked into my voice, and I pasted on a whitewashed smile. It was no business of mine if Gideon had snuggled with my sister and niece around the fireplace.

He tilted his head as if he hadn't quite heard me, soft brown eyes searching mine, holding them so I couldn't run . . .

No, that wasn't right. They made me forget to be afraid, to want to crack open. I rolled the magazine into a tight curl.

"Whenever Peg needed help, I came. She was exhausted, and Enid still doesn't really understand that her dad died. How could she? I don't know how I'll explain Peg."

"Sounds like you love her." I released the magazine, smoothing the wrinkle running through Candidate Truman's aspiring face on the cover.

"Of course." His answer was quick, definitive.

I tossed the month-old magazine into the waste bin as if the fact that he'd loved my sister didn't rumple my thoughts, then cleared my throat. "Who wouldn't? I've never met anyone else like her." I cleared my throat again, trying to dislodge the slightly unhinged pitch.

Gideon fidgeted as though his feet weren't certain how to get from the closet to the couch with a half-crazy woman in between. "Enid is a great kid."

An unladylike snort burst from my mouth, and I covered it with an awkward cough. He loved his best friend's *daughter*, not his best friend's *widow*. It was a mighty good thing Gideon couldn't read my thoughts.

"What are we going to tell her?" I shifted topics, even as my mind pinged wildly. My sister had died. Why did I care who my niece's godfather loved? Yes, he was sweet and kind and his eyes sparkled with mischief, but I wasn't planning to stay. Was I?

Gideon settled the blankets on the armchair and wilted onto the floral couch, rubbing at the space between his dark brows.

The only place left to sit was on the cushion uncomfortably close to Gideon. I perched on the edge of the cushion, my overall-clad leg warming against his.

He slumped back, slinging his arm behind me as his body curved toward mine, compensating for the lack of hearing in the ear closest to me. "I mean, she knows her mom is in heaven. But what are we going to tell her about how she died?"

"We don't even know *why* she died."

"The military guys said it was a fire."

"I thought we established that it was a bomb." I swiveled away, pressing into the arm of the couch as I swallowed the inferno burning in my stomach. *Keep calm*, Phil's voice muttered in my mind.

"Well, we can't tell Enid that until it's proven."

I wanted to lambast his argument, pointing to the shrapnel, the rope, the witnesses, but he was right. We had to be smart, build the case. Putting a child in the middle of the debate was not only unfair, it was unwise. Even if the government wasn't behind Radcliffe VanderLaan, men like him did not stand for being questioned or crossed. "Then we don't tell her any more until we find out what really happened. Phil will at least hear me out on breaking the moratorium on the bombs. If we don't fight this, someone else might die."

Gideon stared into the fireplace, mouth in a grim line. "Have you read the letter she left you? She added it to the will a few days before she died, and it seemed pretty important."

The reminder of my sister's last words to me was too much of a lure to ignore. I tiptoed down the hall to retrieve the envelope from my purse, then sat next to Gideon to read it.

Mostly it was a list of Enid's routines, what food she liked or didn't, when bedtime was, her favorite parks . . . It was too ordinary, too obvious. Why had this been part of the will?

I held the letter to the light of the table lamp. Of course.

One thing few people knew about quiet, bookish Peg was that languages and codes had always fascinated her. She'd been the ripe old age of three when I successfully taught her to read, and five when she devised a code we used to pass messages without raising the suspicion of our nosy eldest sister. We'd write a banal note about what had happened in school or detailing some dream we had, then underline particular letters in pencil before erasing the lines and leaving a barely legible code behind. In this way, we told each other that Bitsy was a boogerhead.

But in this case, Peg had left for me to read *SOS. Ask Enid. Trust no one.*

Gideon reached for the page, and I let it fall into his hands. He hadn't known the code when we were kids.

Breath leaked out of me. *Trust no one.*

I was alone once again.

CHAPTER SIX

Lennie

THE NEXT MORNING I dressed carefully in a smart rose-colored suit. Gideon had arranged for me to meet the witnesses a little before noon and the suit was a perfect mash-up of Lois Lane and Nellie Bly—both feminine and professional.

As we locked up the house, I plotted how I would convince the people to open up without my revealing anything of myself. While I usually could convince the most rock-like human to talk to me, I was asking the witnesses to contradict authority, and that meant I had no margin for error if I wanted to find the truth. I trudged down the walkway, mind heavy with thoughts of how to approach these strangers, arrange for Enid's care, and get back to my job in one piece.

Enid, on the other hand, flitted from the house and down the sidewalk, her yellow dress flying behind her in careless abandon. She'd convinced me to let her wear a summer outfit with thick woolen tights despite the chilly air and snowflakes drifting from the sky. In perfect representation of her sunshine nickname, she claimed to be warm . . . while I was cold enough for both of us. "She's just like Peg." The words tumbled from my mouth in a puff of vapor.

Gideon's lips lifted in a contented half smile, and he guided my hand through the crook of his arm. From anyone else, it would have felt invasive and proprietary. But this was Gideon. The one who'd helped me fill out the college and scholarship applications and then sneaked me out of the house. I'd once thought he meant to marry me. Instead, he'd given me the space to fly. If I could trust anyone, it should be him.

"Look at me." Enid ran ahead of us. "I'm Snow White."

With her blond hair, she was missing part of the costume. But the rosy cheeks, childlike joy, and red lips were a spitting image of the Disney princess. How would I return to my life if it meant leaving her behind?

"Auntie Lennie?" My niece skated toward us, then careened into a snowbank at the corner of Church Street. At least I'd convinced her that Snow White wore boots, a jacket, and a hat.

Gideon guffawed at Enid's goofy grin, lifted her to his hip with one impossibly gentle hand, and brushed off the clinging flakes with the other. "Can the handsome prince wake the beauty from her frozen sleep?"

She clapped her ice-crusted mittens on either side of Gideon's face and smooshed her nose to his, and he folded her into a growling hug. Enid would thrive with this gentle teddy bear.

I thought of my apartment in San Diego. Four dingy walls with pathetic attempts at cheer—bright art prints tacked to the plaster, my collection of hand-thrown mugs interspersed with shells from the beaches, the binders of rare coins I'd searched out. It was decidedly warmer in California and filled with coppery sunshine, but it was so empty in comparison.

"Can we get a Christmas tree?" Enid grasped my shoulder and pulled me into Gideon.

I stumbled into him with an *oof.* My fingers splayed on his broad chest. My face, inches from Gideon's, heated with the proximity, his steadying arm on my hip, and the suggestive waggle of Enid's eyebrows. "A Christmas tree?" I managed, stirring enough that Gideon was no longer pressed against me in a tempting embrace. *Trust no one,* I reminded myself.

"You know." Enid gestured to the church parking lot spiked with evergreens for sale. "You put lights on it and bulbs. I know where Mama keeps her decorations. Please?"

We were early, as planned. But thoughts of my lonely apartment and my ghostly tangle of bewilderment and desire pricked at my carefully laid strategies. When was the last time I'd celebrated with a friend, or given anything of myself? "I guess it wouldn't hurt to look."

"Maybe they'll hold it for you." Gideon turned toward the church, opening a frigid space between us.

By the time Enid found a tree full enough and tall enough without being so big we'd never fit it in the house, fifteen minutes had passed, and I was so edgy that my sigh at the price tag had more than a hair of sharpness to it.

But the man tied a little *sold* ribbon on the tree and promised to hold it until we returned. The red fabric twirled happily in the wind, and Enid pirouetted one more dizzy time around her choice.

Finally on our way again, the happy tree out of sight, Enid's energy flagged. She was suddenly uncompromisingly hungry in the manner that belongs only to small children and ravenous bears coming out of hibernation.

"It's a good thing Russ' has burgers and malteds." Gideon winked at Enid, who perked right up and raced to the restaurant, whirling through the door with the merry jingling of bells.

Inside, two men and a woman hailed Gideon from a long booth near the end of the narrow aisle. I settled Enid on a red stool at the counter, where she happily swung her legs. The older waitress, who looked vaguely familiar, planted a cup of water and another of soda on the counter.

Without so much as glancing at the menu emblazoned with a Dutch boy and windmill, my niece ordered a meal large enough to feed that hibernating bear and chattered on.

The older woman hollered, "Enid's normal!" over her shoulder to the chef. Apparently Enid was a regular.

And I couldn't blame her. The place was cheerful and welcoming, humming with laughter and conversation between tables, all underscored with the voice of Judy Garland wishing us a Merry Christmas from the surprisingly modern jukebox. Everyone knew everyone, welcomed everyone . . . except me.

Gideon beckoned me to the booth, and I veered out of the social black hole and plunged into the false cheer reserved for meeting sources. Across from him, I recognized the narrow-set eyes and perky nose of the widow Judy Nesmith. And the twist on her face made it obvious she remembered her friend Bitsy's rebellious younger sister. Lovely.

I mumbled a greeting before turning to the men.

Ever the gentleman, Gideon introduced me to Judy's older brother, Oliver, and Howard, their neighbor. The men were grim but open, and I hoped I could turn their curiosity about the female big-town reporter into actual information about "poor Peg."

No sooner than I'd settled into the booth next to Gideon, he said, "Would you gentlemen tell Lennie what you saw?" He bumped my knee surreptitiously with his leg and gave me an encouraging nod.

I bristled at the intimation that I would quail under the pressure and forget how to do my job, but I pasted on a smile, mimicking Gideon's head bob as I pulled out my notepad and pencil. It was as good an opening as any.

"We were out on the pond ice fishing. Oliver saw the balloon first." Howard rubbed a pondering hand over his graying beard. "It was huge and, on account of storm clouds rolling in, we could see a bit of flame sparking around the edges. We packed up right quick to follow it. Didn't want anyone getting hurt without warning. You know?"

And I did know. Folks here watched out for one another. It was a trait that made Mapleview a good place to live. But if someone was on the wrong side of that focus, it could also make a person feel as claustrophobic as a feral cat trapped in a cage. I pushed down the thought and mm-hmmed encouragement, my pencil flying across the page in a series of shorthand hieroglyphics.

"The balloon disappeared over the trees." Oliver took up the story. "We figured the snow would put out the flame, but then there was a huge flash of light and an explosion."

"That's when we dropped our gear and ran. Our houses are near where we saw it go down. But there wasn't much left of anything when we got there. Just a hole."

My scratching across the page stopped. Gideon hadn't been lying. There had been a crater . . . unless he'd manufactured all this too.

"I didn't see the balloon." Judy interrupted my pondering. "Just saw Peg hustling through the field from your folks' place and then, a while later, the explosion. Don't know what she was doing out there." The woman folded the paper napkin, making sure the edges touched perfectly, before unfolding it, and folding it again. She tucked a sparse strand of hair behind her ear, then her nervous gaze flashed at me and away. "I was the one who found her. Looked liked she'd been . . ."

Oliver patted Judy's hand, then turned to me, tears shimmering in blue depths. "It wasn't pretty. She'd been banged up pretty good."

From the counter, the sound of Enid's fork clanging against the pie plate reminded me the clock was ticking, but I couldn't make my mind move beyond the image of my sister lying in a pit with hundreds of pieces of shrapnel riddling her body. She should have been safe here.

Trust no one.

She'd known danger was coming. I clasped my hands in my lap, nails biting the tender skin of my palms even as the edges of my vision sparked.

"I know he's your brother-in-law and all." Judy studied me, her gaze steady, determined.

I sucked in a breath, piecing together my composure.

"But I don't care what Radcliffe VanderLaan says. That wasn't a freak fire. Gideon says we can trust you to figure it out. So you tell us what you need doing, and we'll do it. Peg always cared for everyone. Tutored my Jenny when she was too sick to go to school, even taught her French so she could talk like a proper lady. You use those big-city connections and get justice for our girl."

The bell above the door jangled, and we all swiveled like children caught with our hands in the cookie jar.

When Bitsy appeared around the aisle of booths dressed in a powder-blue suit and sour mouth, Enid bolted from her stool and hid under the counter, and I found myself resisting much the same urge.

If I'd hoped that my sister had come in for a slice of pie, I was sadly mistaken. She beelined straight to our table, glowering at me from atop her lofty ego. "I trust you aren't partaking in the local gossip, Eleanor. These uneducated people can be so tiresome with their myth and lore."

"You shouldn't be so hard on yourself," I answered sweetly. "Just because you didn't finish school before getting married doesn't make you uneducated or tiresome."

Bitsy blinked for a few moments, brooding over my words until the barb struck and she reared back with a swooning "I never" and flounced out the door, the bell protesting the force of my sister's departure.

While both Judy and Enid tittered, my stomach churned. I knew better than to snipe at my older sister.

An angry Bitsy only shot back, and she never played fair.

"Well." Gideon scrutinized my sister as she stalked past the windows. The downward pull of his lips revealed that he sensed it too. He counted out a few bills and calmly laid them on the table. But his hand shook when he held it out to help me from my seat. "We appreciate your honesty. We'll be in touch if we have questions."

"And call me if you think of or hear anything else. Rumor always has roots in truth." I wanted to say more, to dig more, but Enid slipped her hand in mine, and I knew she needed me more than the story of her mother's odd demise. I had no idea how to be the sole caregiver for a little girl, let alone be the receptacle for her grief. But I supposed we'd muddle through for now.

Outside the diner, Gideon swung my niece onto his shoulders.

She giggled and stretched to touch the fabric bells hanging from a lamppost. "Look at me! I'm flying."

And she was. Up in the sky, her arms spread wide in exalted motion, her hair trailing out behind her.

"Just like a Christmas angel." I whispered the words, heart breaking at the memory of Peg at the same age riding piggyback on me. Back then we were each other's good in the ugly. Adult responsibilities, pain, and death weren't concepts we even considered. The only things that could get between us—chores, school, and Bitsy—were temporary and always surmountable.

How I longed to reverse time to those Christmases when I'd believed family and ambition weren't mutually exclusive. When I still believed I could change the minds of the people around me. When I thought God promised an easy life.

"Let's go get our tree." Gideon winked, including me in the holiday spirit spreading across his face. "Then we can put this angel on top."

Enid clapped, fully game for climbing to the tip of a tree and perching there in her sundress.

I let Gideon grab my hand and haul me into the fantasy that Christmas Future didn't have to be a lonely one standing over a gaping grave.

Gideon

I wasn't sure where Lennie's attention had gone when we left Russ', but Enid's enthusiasm for Christmas beguiled her into at least playing along as I sifted through the attic and emerged with box after box of decor. Lennie changed from her suit into Katharine Hepburn–like wide slacks and a silky shirt. When I found my gaze lingering on the enigmatic sparkle in Lennie's hazel eyes, I leaped from the pile of boxes and crowned Enid the Sugar Plum Fairy in charge of all decorating decisions. She reigned, paper crown, fire-poker scepter and all, from the couch cushions, keeping my mind where it belonged as she busily subjected her aunt and me to her holiday trimming whims. *Put the nativity over there* (presiding over the mantel), *the giant wooden snowman inside* (crowding Enid's room instead of the porch), *and the little Santa music box on that* (hanging from the lamp over the kitchen table).

We stopped only when the fairy princess declared she was far too hungry to continue. Lennie dug out a jar of Peg's homemade tomato soup, while I slapped together grilled cheese sandwiches for dinner. Enid chattered happily, and I imagined this was my family, my home.

But that would require Lennie to stay. And I would never ask her to surrender her dreams.

"That was almost as yummy as mommy's. It's just missing the crunchy sprinkles on top." Enid poked at the last bit of crust on her plate.

Lennie's spoon clanged in her bowl, and she stared at the ceiling, pretending the moisture gathering on her lashes was nothing.

"I know, Sunshine." I draped an arm around her fragile shoulders. "I know."

She slipped out of her chair and wandered to the living room, swiping the paper crown off her curls as she went.

Lennie sniffled, then stood and cleared the food in an obvious attempt to disguise her tears.

"It's okay to be sad." I eased the plates from her grip.

The muscle in her jaw ticked. "Being sad doesn't prove what happened, and it doesn't make everything magically work out. And before you tell me that God works out everything for good, I don't understand a God that lets Hitler live and my sister die." She flung a napkin on the counter and stumbled from the kitchen.

A bedroom door slammed, and I flinched. I hadn't meant to be condescending.

Enid glanced at me through the archway with a what-do-we-do expression. Well, heaven knew I had no idea. I set the dishes in the sink, figuring they were less important than comforting Enid or Lennie and crossed to where Enid sat on the floor, thumbing through the records, studying each cover as if it held some kind of code.

"Would you like to listen to one?" I picked a Glenn Miller album from the stack.

Enid bobbed her head and clambered onto the sofa, snuggling in with a dark-green cushion against her belly. Behind her, ornaments sparkled between the sparse branches of the evergreen. I wished I'd brought some of my Christmas albums from home. But then again "I'll Be Home for Christmas" wouldn't be the most appropriate choice for the moment. Poor kiddo.

I fit "Moonlight Serenade" on the Victrola, then wound it.

"You want to talk about it?"

She shook her head.

Well, so much for being good at this kind of thing.

But the moment I sank beside her, Enid nestled into my side, the smell of Johnson & Johnson soap hovering around her. "Mama's in heaven. Right?"

"Of course she is. She loved Jesus very much. And you too."

Enid studied the nativity on the mantle in front of us as if the baby in the manger was hiding Peg. "I still want my mama."

I tucked her in closer. At my father's graveside, I'd learned there were no good answers. At least not answers that would help in the moment of crisis. Sometimes—I leaned my head against the couch—sometimes, I wished God would swoop in and take us all to heaven. But somehow, someway, I had to trust that the one who set the world spinning wouldn't abandon the people he'd so lovingly crafted.

A trail of tears cascaded down Enid's rounded cheek, and I wiped the moisture with my hankie before kissing her wrinkled forehead. If I could be God for just a moment, I would reverse the earth on its axis and stop Peg from leaving the house. But then where would I stop? Where would I decide that I'd done enough? And if I fixed all my darkness, what about everyone else's? No, there were no good answers, only trusting God was good enough and strong enough to save a broken world drowning in chaos and misery.

As Enid and I listened to the music, my arm grew heavy under her sweating neck. I wasn't sure how much time had passed, but her steady breathing told me she might have drifted to sleep.

"That's one of my favorite songs." Lennie's tear-roughened voice lifted from the hall.

Enid raised her head and gazed at her aunt.

Lennie's eyes were red, but there was a spark of mischief to them. "You both look comfy. May I join you?"

When Enid motioned to the space on the other side of me, I swallowed. The couch wasn't small, certainly, but Enid's legs stretched over half the length.

Lennie hesitated only a moment before wedging herself in next to me.

Enid's hand slipped into her aunt's, and Lennie allowed the girl to pull her I-don't-need-anyone arm across my lap in a kind of family hug.

Lennie's breath hitched right along with mine, and I went rigid, not sure what to do.

But Lennie settled against my side and stared into the tree, which was all bright lights in the darkening room. Her breath settled into rhythm with mine, her lashes splaying content across the apple of her cheek. Lennie's eyes lifted to mine, and her mouth quirked in a smile. "I think the tree is lacking a little."

Enid sat bolt upright in glaring offense.

Rubbing her chin, Lennie waggled her brows, a hint of playfulness sneaking out. "Your mama always wanted a popcorn chain, but I can't handle it by myself. Think you both could help?"

And just like that, I knew Lennie had shaken off whatever fear had snatched her. If only she could banish it forever.

———— ✳ ————

Lennie

In the kitchen, Gideon hummed and clunked a pot on the stove to make popcorn.

It wasn't a lie that Peg had loved a popcorn chain on the tree. But it was less about the festivity of the tree and more that she and I would sneak down at night and have a snack straight off the evergreen boughs.

Bitsy was always beside herself, thinking some critter had come in and stolen the kernels. Served her right for skimping on our portions of dinner.

But mostly I needed to keep Gideon busy so I could talk to Enid alone. While I wanted to believe that the boy who'd rescued me time and again would help, Peg's words haunted me. *Trust no one.* She was the only person I had ever trusted implicitly, and I wouldn't ignore her now.

The problem was that I didn't know what to say. If Enid had been an adult, I would have shown her the code and asked her what she knew.

But she was six. What could she possibly know?

The Victrola scratched to a stop, and I lifted the needle, beckoning Enid to me. "What would you like to listen to next?"

She plopped in front of Peg's precious box and flipped through the sleeves. Her hands dimpled at the knuckles, holding just enough softness to prove that she was still a child. So soft for such a hard life.

"This one." Enid grinned at me, passing me a Victor record.

"Take the 'A' Train."

Not exactly chatting music.

"Good choice." I slotted the album on the spindle and lowered the arm.

The trilling saxes and blaring brass established themselves into the piano groove, and Enid pulled me from my knees into a happy romping dance across the floor. Her dark hair fluttered around her rounded cheeks pinking with exertion, so much like her mother that it scalded my lungs.

I sat, gasping, until she yanked on my arms to join her wiggling 'round to the scatting of Betty Roché's vocals.

Just as the song ended, the popcorn kernels erupted, banging furiously in the kitchen. I only had a few moments. I lifted the needle again, scrambling for a way to ask Enid about the code.

"You dance like Mama." Enid leaned into my leg.

I was an idiot, trying to figure out how to pump a child for information when she was hurting and in desperate need of someone to love her.

But I was the last person she should depend on. All I ever did was bungle things. Starting with being responsible for the death of her mother's twin brother. It didn't matter that I'd been younger than Enid herself when Mama's time came. Didn't matter that I'd helped deliver the one baby safe and sound—pink and slimy, like a baby ought to be. Didn't matter that the second baby was born already purple. I couldn't stop staring at his perfect little blueberry toes long enough to unwind the slimy cord wrapped around his neck.

I could still see the horror in Bitsy's expression when she told me Mama's last boy died because I couldn't do anything right. And that meant Mama, who to this day lived in her wild, lost mind, was my fault too.

"Auntie Lennie? You listening?" Enid's pudgy hands surrounded my face, forcing me to stare into her sky-blue eyes. "Can I show you something? Mama said you were the only one to tell. That you'd taught her."

And that's how I found out that my niece knew the code too.

Chapter Seven

Gideon

I WOKE TO the not-so-quiet tiptoeing of a six-year-old. Movement flickered in the tiny hall light, and I hoped she'd use the facilities and head right back to bed. My sluggish body said it couldn't be morning. Of course, with the blackout shades covering the front windows, it might have been anywhere from midnight to nine. I rolled to my side, blocking the glow with the blanket.

The smell of popcorn and the sound of laughter lingered in the air, and I sighed contentedly. Enid and Lennie had eaten as much popcorn as they'd strung, but considering how the two seemed to bond over the bowl, I was happy to make more.

Shuffling stole down the hall, pausing on the other side of the couch. Maybe Enid needed water, after all that popcorn salt.

"Hi there, Sunshine." My voice sleep-cracked at the edges.

The rambling noises died and the living room dropped into looming silence.

A trick of my nearly deaf left ear threw the sounds of breathing around the room. "Enid?"

Scrambling footsteps pounded through the living room.

I jerked upright and dashed behind the decidedly adult-sized form through the kitchen, bursting through the open door into the moonlit night. I pumped my arms, ignoring the burn of frozen sidewalk on my bare feet, then veered onto the gravel driveway, tiny rocks skidding under my toes.

The man's coat flapped behind him as he leaped into a waiting dark Pontiac, which screeched away before the door even closed. Sprinting after the car, I squinted at where the license plate should have been. The brake lights flickered and the car turned away from town, gravel pinging against the bumper as it accelerated out of sight. It was hopeless. I stumbled to a stop and leaned over, panting, trying to catch my racing thoughts along with my breath.

Lennie's quavering voice lifted barely above a whisper behind me. "What's going on?"

"There was someone in the house."

"In the house?" She tightened the tattered dressing gown around her slender waist. Wisps of her hair lifted in the wind as if she were falling backward. Down. Away from my grasp.

If I hadn't been there . . .

"What were they doing?" Her breath crystallized in the air, forming a transitory mist that obscured her face.

"I don't know. When he realized I was awake, he ran."

"Did you get a license plate number?"

"There was no plate." My words dropped like heavy stones between us, the ripples of what this meant growing into a tidal wave.

"That was no robbery."

I turned, dragged her into the relative warmth of the house, then shut the kitchen door and, as an afterthought, shoved kitchen chairs under the handle of both the front and back doors.

"You think they'll come back." Lennie pointed to the chairs, not as a fearful question but as the beginning of a battle plan.

"Yes." There was no use withholding information from someone who reported on criminals. I trotted down the hall to check on Enid, who'd slept through it all, and returned to the kitchen to find Lennie hunched over the table examining her shorn nails. "She's still sleeping like a log." I shoved my frozen toes into a pair of Jack's old slippers. "I'll call the sheriff in the morning."

"There isn't much he can do. Radcliffe's men are professionals. There won't be anything a local will find."

"Then what do we do?"

Lennie's eyes snapped to mine, surprise flitting through.

I shrugged. "I'll protect you with my life, but I'm no detective."

"First, we make sure they didn't find the pieces of the bomb or the rigging." She spun and dug through the freezer before lifting out the metal pieces with a triumphant snort.

"We best bring those with us wherever we go." I held out my hand, but she ignored it. Instead, she dropped the pieces in a handbag hanging on the coatrack.

"Next, we decode these." She pointed to the set of Pictured Knowledge encyclopedias stacked on the coffee table.

"Decode?" I gaped at Lennie, then the stack of at least a dozen hefty books. Had she lost her mind?

Lennie

"Yes, decode." If someone had broken into the house, they—whoever they were—knew there was more to discover than just the pieces of a bomb they'd left behind. We had to decipher fourteen massive books. If I wanted to finish before next year, I needed more than Enid's help. I had to take the risk that if Peg trusted Gideon with her will and her daughter, then I could trust him with this.

"Peg left a code in the letter she left me. It's one we used as kids." I lowered myself to the edge of the couch, unfolded Peg's letter, and showed him the dim lines on the page. "She was warning me. Something was going on, Gideon. Something Peg was afraid of."

I stared at the curl of Peg's script, not daring to let Gideon read my face. At his nod, I clamped my shaking hands between my knees. "Earlier, Enid showed me the same code in the encyclopedias. As soon as we translate it, we can figure out what Peg knew. Then I can bring the story to Phil. If anyone can get this published, it's him. No one can ignore that a bomb went off in Mapleview after that."

My heart pounded. Yes, there was an edge of fear. But there was a spark too. This was the kind of story that launched a journalist's career. And I had a solid plan no one could object to.

"What about Enid?"

Gideon's question stopped me in my tracks. In my single-minded focus to solve the mystery and win a Pulitzer, I had nearly forgotten about my niece.

It was Sunday. She'd be home and needed someone to feed and babysit her. What if I'd been in San Diego and Gideon hadn't been here? What if I'd actually left her alone, and those men had come back? What if—?

Then Bitsy would swoop in and take the last piece of Peg and grind away the girl's laughter and spunk until she resembled Bitter Bitsy in every way.

"Being responsible for her is new. You'll get used to it."

I swallowed. How had Gideon read my thoughts so easily? "I hadn't forgotten," I lied. "But we can start writing out the list of letters while she sleeps."

"What happens when she wakes up?"

"Then she can help." Exasperation boiled in my voice, and I pasted on a stilted smile.

Gideon sat implacable on the far side of the couch. If he had been any other witness, I would have used a magic trick to make him comfortable, a joke to make him laugh, a commonality to convince him to trust me. But the sadness in Gideon's eyes stilled my tongue. He would see through any manipulation and that would only make it worse.

I slammed open the first encyclopedia, extinguishing the scorch of guilt in my gut. "It was a game Enid and Peg played. She'll be fine for at least a while."

I'd just proven I had no business caring for a child, even if she was perfectly feisty and the last piece of my sister here on earth. Trusting people, letting them in, only led to hurt. She'd be better off with Gideon. They could comfort each other when I left.

Gideon pushed to his feet and slogged to the kitchen.

How had I messed up so badly with one of the few people who had encouraged me to be myself? After a moment's hesitation, I trailed after him.

He pawed through the cabinets and arranged ingredients on the counter—flour, baking soda, eggs, honey, vanilla. "I'll make eggs and pancakes," Gideon said without facing me. "We'll need fuel."

Cooking. It's what Peg always did when working on a problem, what she did when she was teaching herself yet another language. It was an idiosyncrasy I missed, a hole in my takeout-filled world. "Thank you." My words were quiet, remorseful, as I studied the scuffed white tile under my bare toes.

Suddenly Gideon's slipper-clad feet were in front of mine.

I dragged my gaze up, trying to find enough indignance to shrug off his disappointment in my cold egotism. Instead of displeasure, the gold in his deep-brown eyes flashed—a warning? Desire?

My clammy hand uncurled of its own volition and settled on his steady chest. My ears rang with adrenaline, my heart pounding with longing. "Gideon, I can't . . ."

He lifted a single ironic brow, and all my words leaked out as my body arced into his magnetic calm. "You can't what?" His voice was deep and untroubled, rumbling through my splayed fingers.

"I can't . . ." I slammed my lips closed over the words, refusing to hurt Gideon more.

But he was waiting, forcing me to continue.

"I don't know if I can go to church today," I said, transparent as the viscous fog rolling off the San Diego Bay.

"Have you ever considered that maybe you aren't close to people because you push them away?"

"What?" I uncurled, yanking myself away from his spell, but he caught my shoulder, his fingers outstretched, wide and gentle.

"We're meant to be together."

My heart stuttered, and I gaped at him, the sides of my mind clashing in a brutal civil war—the desire to be wanted, loved, and held versus the overwhelming fear of losing myself inside someone else.

Gideon's eyes widened, cheeks coloring under the dark stubble on his cheeks. "No, that's not . . . I mean . . . maybe someday, but . . ."

I pressed my lips together to stifle a giggle.

Gideon pushed away from the wall. "Why do you make this so hard?" He tugged the purple apron from the hook behind my shoulder. "What I mean is that humans are created to be together. You push everyone away, then feel lonely *because* you're supposed to be with people."

The arrow pierced and stuck deep, bile rushing into the hole. "Maybe you're meant to be with other people." The bitter words slithered low from my mouth. "Maybe everyone else is. But my life is one example after another proving that I'm different. I try to help. I do. But it's always a disaster. It's better for everyone if I figure out what Peg knew so you and Enid will be safe, and then leave."

"Better?" His voice raised a touch into a harsh whisper. "Better for whom? For me? For Enid? She already worships you, and I . . . I've loved you since high school." He advanced, towering over me as the heat of his words shimmered between us.

Hunger boiled behind my chest bone. But I could never be what he needed. "Perhaps it isn't entirely what I want, but I am a force to be reckoned with now. And for a woman, that means making her own way. Alone."

"You used to hope and believe in so much more."

"Fairy tales aren't real, and I learned the hard way to live solidly planted in reality."

"I'm not real enough for you?" His thumb stirred the hair brushing my clavicle, distracting my rational mind until I snatched at his hand.

I had to think of something, anything, to work my way out of this tempting corner. My hand skimmed to his shoulder, stalling on my sister's ridiculous apron. "If you're going stay"—I plucked at the frilly fabric, my body thrumming at his nearness—"we need to get you a different apron."

He growled and snapped away, a chasm widening, dreadful under my feet.

My hand shot to his arm, trying to bridge the gap, to find a steady place to stand.

"I won't beg, Eleanor. I have enough pride not to do that."

"I didn't . . ."

"I know. And I won't hold you back." Gideon slid the apron over his head and brushed a beefy hand over the purple flowers. "For the record, you're right about the apron. I'll be sure to send it with you when you leave."

The idea of being stuck in a kitchen my whole life, the years stretching blandly into the forever future sent me retreating from the room. Gideon was a good friend. Saw me as an equal for now. But no man wanted a wife gallivanting across the country, forgetting her responsibilities of hearth and home.

Gideon

I beat the pancake batter, taking out my frustration on the tan, glutinous stuff. Lennie had finally been telling me what was on her mind, flirting even, and then . . . Then I'd gone and opened my big mouth.

I've loved you since high school. "Gah." Slapping the wooden spoon in the spoon rest, I sucked in a steadying breath. The pancakes would be a rubbery disaster if I kept whacking away. I stared at the black-and-white checkerboard floor. I'd helped Jack lay it the month before he deployed. We'd misplanned and wound up stranded together in a corner while the glue dried. That's when he'd extracted my promise to stop trying to get a draft board to accept me and, instead, take care of his family. Somewhere deep inside, I knew the war would grind on without me.

Of course it was the same curse that had won me my current job. The only young man blessed enough to be passed over who wasn't responsible for a farm. But, like the Israelites, what was on the other side of the Passover was miles and miles of desert. Maybe someday I'd stumble into the promised land.

I lit the stove and slid the pan over the flames. Mom had taught me how to cook, and it had come in handy as I worked my way through college. The best paying job with the most flexibility had been a short-order cook. And it worked well. I taped lists of terms and legal cases above the stove at the O'Brien Family Restaurant so I could study and practice enunciating while I flipped burgers and dunked fries. Even though my tuition was covered by my scholarship, and the O'Briens took me in as a sixth—albeit much older—child under their roof, working was the only way to pay for the board and books Grandad's small stipend didn't cover.

I poured oil into the pan and waited until it spattered in response to a drop of water. Rather like Lennie's response to me. I used a measuring cup to drop dollops of batter into the hot pan, and the dough sputtered and bubbled. Despite the fact that baking seemed a bit like magic—put soupy goop into an oven and pull out a cake—it was one thing that always made sense to me. If a cook followed the recipe, he got the right results.

I flipped a pancake, then stopped, hovering over the perfectly browned surface. There'd been a sound, a low moan. Was that—?

A scream erupted.

In one quick motion, I switched off the stove, then spun, spatula flying from my grasp, and sprinted down the hall.

I nearly ran Lennie over as she bolted across the hall into Enid's room. The bedroom door slammed against the wall and bounced back, smashing my arm.

Enid sat bolt upright, hair wild, mouth wide in a rising scream, eyes gaping unseeing across the room.

Lennie collected the terrified girl in her arms and eased onto the bed, shushing and humming nonsensical tones.

Enid's body remained stiff until Lennie grasped the girl's cheeks and raised her voice above the child's own. The girl's gaze snapped to her aunt, recognition sliding through her expression a moment before she flung herself against Lennie's chest, the tension draining as she whispered into her aunt's shoulder.

Lennie smoothed her hand across the light plane of Enid's hair, and the girl twisted her fist in Lennie's thin dressing gown, exposing the smooth skin beneath Lennie's earlobe.

My cheeks heated, and I mumbled an excuse about rescuing the pancakes. As I left, Lennie asked Enid what her favorite outfit was and if she would show Lennie her favorite places in town and would Enid like to help her choose what she should wear? She didn't have anything nearly as pretty as Peg, but maybe Enid could help.

I scraped the burned pancakes onto a plate to cool, then wiped the black bits from the pan and started over. The chatter in the background was soothing and familiar. Somehow, despite Lennie's insistence otherwise, she was a natural, stepping unconsciously into a routine similar to Peg's, soothing the nightmares that had haunted Enid since Jack had passed.

They would need me at first, but then what? Would they both go to San Diego? My movement stilled over the pan until a glop of batter smacked into the hot oil and spattered at me. Served me right for grasping after things that weren't mine to hold. It seemed God had brought Lennie full circle in my life for a reason. But maybe the reason was just to help for the moment and then release her.

God help me, I didn't know if I could do it again.

CHAPTER EIGHT

Lennie

EVERYTHING IN ME wanted to skip church, not because I had anything against it or Peg's favorite preacher, Pastor Dursma. But my family would be there, and I wasn't sure I wanted to face any of them individually, let alone in a horde led by Bitsy and her government-cover-up husband. Unfortunately, the tongues were already wagging about Gideon being in collusion with me. If we didn't attend, the congregation would pin Enid and Gideon on the prayer board right alongside me—the town heathen.

I'd nearly forgotten that I'd told Enid to dress herself . . . and me. Fortunately, my sister had impeccable taste in children's clothing, and Enid chose an adorable red velvet dress for herself. Then my niece took one appalled look at my meager possessions and declared "no" with all the force of an editor asked to publish a libelous article.

"It's all I have," I said, setting forth the unequivocal evidence.

She lifted her brow, stalked across the room, and swung open the closet. "This one." She pointed at a pale-pink confection of lace and silk. It was exactly Peg's style, which is to say, nothing like mine.

"That might be a bit much for church."

Enid ruminated as though I was trying to pull one over on her. But really the dress belonged at a prom, not church.

Just as I was wondering if that was indeed where Peg had worn it, Enid yanked out a pale bluish-green shirt dress with contrasting buttons. I ran my hand across the chiffon overlay, and colors flickered like the tide moving in and out of the clear water of La Jolla Cove.

Peg's eyes would have morphed to match.

A choke settled in my throat, but there was nothing about this dress I could reasonably object to. Even the matching hat Enid pointed to was perfectly respectable.

The dress slid over my curves, gapping only a little in the chest.

"I can tie it tight." Enid pointed to the ribbons hanging from the side of the dress. "That's what Mama did after Daddy . . ." Her blue eyes filled.

No. No. No. Tears gathered in my own eyes. I spun so she could tie me in and tried not to think about all the things I wished I'd done and all the things I wished I could still do. I couldn't tell Enid everything would be all right when both her parents were dead and gone. I couldn't tell her I'd figure everything out. I couldn't promise her anything when I didn't know the answers myself.

Refusing to see myself in the mirror and catch any hint of Peg, I smoothed my blond waves into a simple chignon, pinning the flyaways by feel and memory.

Enid studied me, an assessing frown growing. Her face cleared, and she rummaged through the top drawer of the dresser. When she drew back, Peg's cross necklace dangled from her fingers. "Mama always wore it to church."

I swallowed hard. Twelve years ago, I'd left the necklace with her—the faithful sister.

"Someday," she had said. "Someday you'll come back, and I'll return it to you because you've found your place. Until then, I'll have enough faith for both of us."

I latched the clasp behind my neck and smoothed the cross against my chest bone. *God, if you're there, please help.*

Gideon

I'd lost all thoughts when Lennie had emerged from the bedroom. The simple dress smoothed over her curves and turned the somber brown hazel of her eyes into a variable landscape of Black Mill Pond at sparkling dusk. But she didn't want me, and so I knelt in front of Enid and folded her into a hug. I would safeguard them both, hold on, until it was no longer an option. Some time was better than no time at all.

Or at least that's what I tried to tell myself.

Despite the chill in the air, Lennie suggested we walk to church. She said she was used to walking miles every day, but I suspected it had more to do with the nerves revealed by the shake in her hands.

As we approached the white clapboard church, Lennie's grasp clamped down on my bicep, but she smiled assuredly, politely, and entirely fakely at the butcher's wife, a few of the farmers, and Pastor Dursma. But when Lennie caught sight of the trio we'd met at Russ', her smile settled into a real greeting, staying even when Judy threw an arm around Lennie and half hugged her before dragging her into a pew . . . right behind Bitsy.

Lennie contained herself until Radcliffe strode down the aisle, the organ growing quiet enough to hear the man's prideful steps echoing through the room. One could nearly hear all the ladies sigh—a man in uniform. As if the rest of us menfolk were cod liver oil—useful, but rather distasteful.

Beside me, Lennie's fingers strangled her pocketbook.

The man had the audacity to turn, innocent as you please, and ask if we had found all we needed at the site.

"In fact, we did." Lennie's smile told the world that she was untroubled and getting along just fine, but her quiet voice swarmed with warning. "But you won't find the evidence I have by breaking into Peg's home. In fact, if I catch either of you nearby, I will call the sheriff, and I will write the story, and my editor will publish it. I dare you to try." She relaxed into the pew as if pleased with herself.

But she'd set the timer on a different kind of bomb. I had already failed Peg. I would not allow a second explosion to destroy another Sweers sister.

--------><-------

Lennie

Goodness, it felt good to ruffle Bitsy's perfectly laid feathers. I knew I'd made Gideon more nervous than a seaman facing a hurricane, but I didn't care. Radcliffe, Bitsy, and all the powerful people like them were going to learn a thing or two about taking on Lennie Sweers. Unlike little quaking Eleanor, Lennie fought back, and she won.

I barely heard the pastor's sermon—something about Jesus coming into the world quietly in the dark of the night while all of us mortals slept.

There'd been a time I truly believed that God was as unendingly powerful as he was kind. When I was a kid, I won the part of the angel that announced the birth of the baby. Bitsy said it was because I was the only kid with blond hair, but I practiced my lines as if my life depended on it. *"For unto us is born this day the Savior of the world."* When I said the lines, I felt hairs raise on my arms. I was sure that if I turned, I would see a host of angels behind me in support. I'd said every word perfectly, earning a nod from Mrs. Jelsma in the front row. Even Jonah Seiler, famous for once *being* baby Jesus, smiled sagely behind his shepherd beard. But now?

Where are your angels, Lord? Where are the ones who fight for what is right?

The organist played the opening chords to "O Little Town of Bethlehem," causing Gideon to stir, clearing his throat, and little Enid stretched on my other side, arm reaching across me to tap Gideon ever so playfully. Some dilapidated army we were. But maybe this time, the mortals wouldn't sleep and a wrong might be righted.

We stood and sang the carol, Gideon's baritone mixing in harmony. "Praises sing to God the King and peace to all the earth." If only it were so simple.

The amen of the pastor's prayer hadn't even finished echoing through the wood structure when Bitsy turned on me. "I see you took no time at all to raid our sister's belongings. Don't get too comfortable. I won't rest until the world sees you for what you are." She shoved past her husband, who hesitated as the rest of the congregants shuffled past.

I stood square to the man and, though he towered over me, I refused to budge.

"I'm sorry," Radcliffe said, attention drifting to Gideon with seemingly heartfelt commiseration.

"Are you apologizing for trying to cover up Peg's death?" I snapped, not falling for his pitying words. "Or for your wife's lifelong vendetta against me?"

He drew back like I'd slapped him, mouth pulling down at the edges. But it was anger that sparked in the tightening of his shoulders, not disappointment. "I'm not sure what you mean."

"Of course not." Rage shook my body. "You need to know that I have a reputation in San Diego for unearthing the rotten things that powerful people bury. You best keep that in mind while you're digging a hole for yourself." I pivoted and pushed through the crowd meandering toward the exit.

"I don't know what's going on, Radcliffe." Gideon's voice echoed behind me, and I stormed back up the aisle, silently praying that Gideon wouldn't let his sweet nature overcome his good judgment. "But we found things that can't be explained. It doesn't look good."

"Gideon. We need to go." The pieces of metal and rope burned in my bag, and if that man knew Peg had left me a message . . .

"I have to go potty." Enid and her potty dance to the rescue.

Gideon opened his mouth and snapped it closed, then lifted Enid into his arms, and strode away with me in tow. The bathroom was blissfully out of the normal flow of traffic, and Enid made quick work of using the toilet before we slid out into the blustery cold.

On the sidewalk, a blanket of frigid air muted all conversation, sparing me an argument with Gideon about the wisdom of being rude. It was an inherent difference between us. Gideon always saw the good, whereas I flipped the metaphorical stone over to reveal the mold underneath.

Single flakes of snow drifted through the air, hard pressed from the doleful sky. Glacial air breathed over the relatively warmer Lake Michigan, gulping up moisture. Even though I left Michigan a long time ago, I recognized a brewing lake-effect storm when I saw it. Soon the sky wouldn't be able to hold more. We'd wake to a heavy blanket of snow tomorrow.

I was so absorbed by my to-do list of storm preparations that I nearly missed the man dressed in a black trench coat step off the main sidewalk and trot across the street behind us into the long, deserted street leading to Peg's home.

"Gideon," I whispered, trying not to let the alarm sound in my voice.

"I know. I saw him." Gideon's nonchalant tone belied his serious expression. "He was at church. I thought he was one of Radcliffe's men, but they didn't so much as acknowledge one another. We'll call the sheriff as soon as we get to Peg's."

I'd never been so glad to see Peg's cheery walkway. Inside, I sent Enid to change out of her Sunday dress while I secured the house and Gideon called the sheriff.

"The sheriff is sending a car past. Since he's on foot, there's a chance the sheriff might catch up." Gideon peeked out the window. "I don't see anyone out there now. He was probably a drifter moving through."

I lifted an eyebrow at his dubious reasoning. "Well, we can't send Enid to school if they're following us. What if they snatch her to get to us? And you can't leave now." My words tumbled over one another, the panic in them obvious even to me.

What had happened to the calm, cool, and collected reporter poking at the government man? Pompous, flamboyant, in-your-face Radcliffe I could handle. I could see him coming. But this menacing shadow was an entirely different threat.

Chapter Nine

Gideon

THE THREE OF us spent the next week hunkered in the living room, combing through encyclopedias, writing out underlined letters in painstaking order. Enid hadn't questioned missing another week of school and, given the loss of her parents, neither had the principal.

My sister, the saint, promised to check on our invalid mother before and after school, and also brought Enid's schoolwork every night. As for Enid, the brilliant little scamp sensed our urgency and tension, internalized it, and spewed it out in concentration on the pages during the days and torturous nightmares through the night.

Despite a blurring lack of sleep, by the next Monday afternoon, we had fifteen pages of letters spread across the wood floor in the living room and no idea what any of it meant. Enid was beginning to bore of the game. Why would Peg have sent us on this wild goose chase? Had we imagined it all?

"*Ventojenla*. It makes no sense." Lennie slapped a page on the floor. "It's not English. It isn't French. It looks like Spanish, but it isn't. What confounded language is it? Enid, did you and your mom make up a language?"

Enid glanced up from the worn book of Hans Christian Andersen tales she'd taken refuge in. She squinted in confusion, as though the transition from fairy tales to an imaginary language was too jarring for her young mind.

"How about I make some hot cocoa?" I groaned to my feet. My

spine ached from hovering over the pages and sleeping on the couch. We'd forgone any concern about what the neighbors thought about me sleeping here. There were too many actually harmful things to worry about. And since Lennie planned to return to San Diego, she'd shrugged off the concern of a ruined reputation.

If I added a bit of coffee to my chocolate, maybe that would shake me from my morose thoughts.

I heated milk and water while I dug out the sugar and cocoa and shook the nearly empty canisters. Tomorrow we'd have to go to the grocery store, if nothing else. How long could we stay holed up? What would happen if we never figured out what happened?

Maybe Peg really had died in a freak fire.

But that didn't explain the pieces of a bomb and filling in the crater, and Radcliffe's acting as if we were on the verge of committing treason.

The coffee bubbled in the percolator bulb, and I poured steaming milk over the cocoa and sugar, adding a dash of precious cinnamon. We were lucky to have so much available in our farm town. I knew how bad it was in Britain and the Netherlands, where so many of our neighbors originally hailed from.

I gathered the mugs on a wooden tray and added a few slices of apple for a snack. I slid cheerful red napkins under the plate and carried it into the living room.

Enid was no longer on the couch but bent over the first page of our notes, mumbling like an old professor poring over first-year student papers. "Winds in the upper . . ." Enid sat back, her hair a sleep-induced tangle on top of her head. "But I don't know this." She pointed to the page.

I nearly dropped the tray. "What did you say, Sunshine?"

"Mama and I didn't have our own language, but she taught me one that someone else made up. It was Esperan—" Enid slapped a hand over her mouth. "Mama said it was our secret, and I shouldn't tell anyone. Does that mean I shouldn't tell you?"

Lennie closed her gaping mouth. "Esperanto? You know Esperanto?"

Enid glanced at me, for guidance maybe, but I must have given the impression that I was as lost as I felt.

"Enid." Lennie pulled out the letter Peg had left for her with the will. "Look at what your mama left for me. You work out the code."

The little girl bent over the sheet, her bottom lip tucked under her teeth. "She told you to ask me. How come you didn't ask?"

"We didn't want you to worry," I answered for Lennie.

Enid studied the scars on her knees.

"Your mama told me she was teaching herself Esperanto," Lennie said. "She said that a man in Poland invented it and one of the immigrants she worked with taught her. Am I right?"

I set the tray down to study the page Enid clutched.

"She didn't teach me much. Just this." Her fingers trailed the letters she'd written carefully on a blank page—*Ventoj en la supra*. "It means 'winds in the upper.' But I can't remember this one." *Atmosfero*.

"Atmosphere." Lennie and I said in unison.

Winds in the upper atmosphere?

"What does that mean?" I sat cross-legged next to Lennie.

She picked up her own page of notes and her mug, then signaled me to the kitchen with a jerk of her head. "I told Peg about the balloon bombs dropping on the west coast. In my research, I uncovered theories that the Japanese launched them, but no one knows how they're getting across the Pacific." She glanced behind her, making sure Enid couldn't hear. "What if she found incriminating evidence, and the government tried to stop her from telling me? What if she knew they were coming for her? What if she was trying to tell us?"

"Why would they stop her from telling you? You already agreed to keep the news embargo."

She dropped onto a chair. "But what are the odds that she and I would talk about it and then a bomb would drop way out here?"

"Weird coincidence or not, you found the trigger, the rope, and all."

She stood and dug them from the freezer where she'd re-stashed them after church. She set the components on the table, and they rolled about, crashing into one another before settling in a heap of metal. "They're exactly like the pieces the bomb expert showed me."

"With that and everyone seeing that balloon and explosion, it all adds up to a bomb. Probably one attached to a balloon."

Lennie

I settled my forehead on my arms crossed on the table. My mind pinged through scenarios so quickly my head ached with the effort. What had Peg found out that put her in danger? How had a Japanese bomb floated this far? If only she were still here to tell me what she'd seen.

"I miss her so much." My words bounced against the table and slammed into my ears, the sorrow so obvious it hurt. I'd pushed it away, under the mystery, but I was cracking with the strain of it. My sister was dead. She had known someone was coming. She was depending on me to figure it out and to protect her daughter.

"I miss her too." Gideon's hand slid over mine—warm, inviting. "She was a good friend."

"The best." And I'd lost her. Was there anyone who wouldn't abandon me? I glanced behind me, checking on Enid. But she sat contentedly on the floor, book open and pencil flying. Was she drawing or had she found something?

"Eleanor?" His voice was even, not pleading, but carrying a level of insight that made me want to run. And as if sensing I was about to do just that, he sat back, giving me space. "Why won't you let us all the way in?"

I rolled the coin in my pocket. "If I do it myself and things go badly"—I shrugged—"at least I can predict when it's coming and I only have myself to blame."

"But does it hurt less?"

If I let myself feel it, I would fall apart. But I couldn't tell him that. Couldn't tell him that as much as I wanted to lean into him, I couldn't open the trunk or all the ghosts would burst out and push me into the yawning grave of my own making.

"Why are you afraid of loving us?"

"I can't live here, Gideon. I can't give up everything I've worked for—my independence, my job. People depend on me there."

"You were made to be a reporter. I'd never take that from you. But Enid has faith in you. Can you have faith that it might work out? Can you try?"

"How can I have faith like a child when my childhood was so . . ." So *what*? Bad? I had two living parents and, though they didn't spend time with me, Peg and Gideon had. And now Phil watched out for me in San Diego, and Gideon and Enid had made space for me here.

"Sometimes things don't work exactly like you expect, but you don't have to figure it out all on your own. That's not your job."

"Then whose job is it? God's? Look what's happened, Gideon." I swung my arms in a juvenile arc.

"I see it." The edge of his calm finally chipped away under my onslaught, and he loomed over me, voice raised. "It's impossible not to. I'm half-deaf and have a broken tongue, remember? I'm not blind. Look at what I've survived. And there are people who've survived far worse. God sees and cries with us. But I know Peg is happy where she is. And she'll be thrilled to see you and Enid someday."

He'd come out swinging and delivered an emotional punch to the gut. Heaven. Where good Christians go when they die. The hope of happy, future Christmases spreading into eternity. But according to my mother and older sister, I was a rebellious child doomed to the pits of hell. I could feel the grim Ghost of Christmas Future lurking behind me.

"If you keep pushing everything down, who you are will suffocate underneath all the pain you've stored inside you. A broken heart can't beat, Lennie."

The hot, laughing breath of the reaper sighed on my neck even as he shoveled dirt over my self-made grave. "How do you do this? How do you choose to see the good in everything? It's maddening." I shoved my chair back, smashing my knee into the sharp edge of the table leg, tears clawing at my eyes, my throat.

"Come here." Gideon threw my coat at me and waited for me to slip into it before stepping onto the back porch and into the purple light of the snowy December afternoon.

"You have to find the joy." His voice puffed a cloud of condensation. He held out a gloved hand and waited patiently for a single flake of snow to land on the black wool.

And all at once, I remembered. Remembered running away from Bitsy. I'd done something wrong yet again—dropped the sheets in the mud, allowed the oatmeal to boil over, or only heaven knew what. Gideon saw me sprint past his house and had caught up to me. He had a blanket for my shivering body in one hand and a sack lunch in the other. I let him throw the blanket over my shoulders and put an arm around me as we walked the trail from the school to Black Mill Pond, catching snowflakes on our tongues. We'd laughed at the squelch of snow underfoot, studied the perfect shapes of tiny flakes— each one unique. We'd shared a sandwich and apple on an enormous rock jutting into the half-frozen pond. It had been so quiet out there, everything so clear. And when he'd made a penny appear from behind my ear, I'd wanted to stay with him forever.

How naïve had I been? No one wanted to marry a grasping, uppity woman who worked a man's job. My Christmas Future was destined to be as lonely as my Christmas Past.

"Lennie." Gideon's breath warmed my cheek a moment before his thumb wiped a rebellious tear from my cheek, a subtle scratch from the callous at the corner of his nail trailing behind. "You are one of the most capable, intelligent people I know. Let me be the safe place where you can be yourself. Sometimes"—he reached behind my ear—"sometimes you can find miracles." In his fingers was a penny, worn from decades of my fingers holding it, wishing on it.

I plucked the coin from his fingers. It was the Indian Head he'd given me all those years ago—one with immense value that he'd found in his meager tips.

"How did you get that?" A laugh puffed from my lips as I flipped the coin then tucked it back into my pocket.

"I've learned a trick or two about distraction and magic. It entertains the children at the church fair at least." Gideon's smile was lopsided. "You kept it all these years."

"Of course I did. It reminds me of all that is good." Suddenly I was so tired, so tired of trying to do it all. If only I were fourteen again, sitting on that rock in the woods.

I laid my head against the breadth of Gideon's chest.

Heartbeat steady, predictable, he had always been the rock I could come back to, and he'd always insisted that it was God beneath him, holding him up.

Maybe, just maybe, I could trust the pair of them.

Gideon settled his cheek against my forehead, a smile quirking at the corners of his mouth. Settled. Calm. The satin light reflected in his eyes, and I recognized the soft place that he was. I had never wanted to nestle into a safe haven so much.

A snowflake alighted on his long lashes, and he blinked it away, staring up in undisguised wonder. The breeze teased the ends of my hair, and he smoothed the strands against my shoulders, his chin lowering, the vapor of our breaths kissing, hesitating. His hands spanned my hips, my waist, my shoulders, consuming my senses with the rightness of being held if even for a moment.

I let my anxious thoughts and questions float through the air with the falling snow. My fingers skimmed to his broad collar. His Adam's apple dipped, and I collected him, drew him to me, pressing to the tips of my toes, his lips warm on mine, as I prayed for the nearness to banish the churning.

Gideon chuckled, the vibrations rumbling against my chest, and I nearly toppled as he eased away, cradling my hands in his—a reassurance that he was staying. He bowed over our entwined hands, kissing the tips of each of my fingers.

In that moment, in the steadiness of his breath, the splay of his lashes across his cheek, I saw his devotion. He would love me well if it killed him.

Dear, sweet Gideon. My protector.

"Yes." My words lifted vaporous, thin, and as frail as a snowflake.

"Yes?" Gideon lifted his mischievous gaze to my lips before sliding to my eyes. "Yes what?"

Stubborn Gideon, he was going to make me say it. "Yes," I shouted. "I don't know how I can stay." My voice lowered. "But I trust you. Are you happ—?"

The sound of a door smashing open echoed across the snow-covered landscape.

It took a hair's breadth to register. "Enid."

Gideon was already up the stairs and through the kitchen door by the time I scrambled in behind him. Snow drifted through the wide-open front door, pages fluttered on the encyclopedia, a single sheet of paper drifted across the floor.

"Go," I said to Gideon. "I'll search for her here."

And he moved into the growing darkness of a coming storm.

Chapter Ten

Gideon

I SPRINTED DOWN the front walkway, pursuing the footprint trail as it curved into the thick ridge of trees lining the road. I was in loafers, hardly appropriate footwear for a skim of snow, let alone the four inches that had already collected. But someone had been in the house and may have taken Enid. All I could think of was my little Sunshine shivering in her thin dress, fingers slowly turning blue.

As I forced my body between the slender gaps in brush, the prickers snagged and pulled, and I struggled to ignore the biting cold in my toes. I ducked underneath a limb, and it caught on my collar, sending a deluge of snow plummeting onto my head and dripping down my neck. Cold bit at my skin.

Even as I extracted the last big chunks of fast-melting snow, I squinted into the band of woods. If anyone had come through holding a struggling Enid, wouldn't there be a larger path? And surely she wouldn't go with a stranger quietly. I stilled, listening to the thick silence of a world hunkered against the snow. Maybe Enid was still in the house, and I'd just imagined the footprints.

"Enid?" Lennie's voice lifted, plaintive, from the house, puncturing my balloon of hope.

Ripping through the last of the brambles, I searched the sheltered ground for signs of a trail in the scant snow. But with the uneven scramble of leaves and detritus marring the blanket of white, there was nothing to go on.

I turned a circle in the gloom. If only I had a flashlight.

At the sound of scuffling and heavy breathing, I spun to my left, scanning the ground for a weapon of any kind.

Lennie burst through the trees. She clutched a sheet of paper and, blessings of blessings, a lit flashlight. The arc of light flickered my way and her footsteps crashed across the distance, running to me rather than away. "Gideon." Breathless, she gripped a crumpled paper. "She's gone."

I would kill whoever had done this.

"There was only one page left behind." She held the paper to the light. "How did we miss this?"

It was Enid's scrawl, precise lettering only slightly marred by a childish hand. Most of the words we'd yet to decipher, but there was a clear word written above everything else—*Radcliffe*.

"Do you think they saw what she'd found?" I hauled my voice into submission. "Would Radcliffe have taken her?"

"It's worth checking." There was hope in her voice.

I nodded, praying that the sprite would be safe and sound with Bitsy. She wouldn't let anything happen to her . . . at least I didn't think so.

My prayers ran in echoing rhythm with our feet as we struggled back to Peg's through the gathering snow.

⸻ ❋ ⸻

Lennie

We burst through the back door, and I dialed my sister.

Radcliffe's voice crackled through the line.

"Where's Enid?" I said without preamble.

"Eleanor." From someone else, it might have been a greeting. From him, it was a cold reproach.

I leaned my aching head against the flowered wallpaper, crumpling beneath the history, the brittle pain of rejection.

"I'm here," Gideon whispered, holding my frantic gaze, as he gripped my arms. "Even the strongest people need support."

I swallowed the prickling in my throat.

"Am I to understand you've lost my niece?" Radcliffe's voice grew louder, and I held the receiver away from my ear. "Have you called the police?"

I sputtered, knuckles cracking around the receiver as I tried to restrain my creeping anger toward the imperious cretin. "She left a note with your name on it. We thought you might have heard from her."

"As a matter of fact, she called my wife just a moment ago and said she'd found something and was afraid. Elizabeth tried to calm the girl, but it seems you all poisoned her against me, so she hung up. Elizabeth is beside herself with worry. Naturally Elizabeth called the police, and we were about to head over. Enid was so distraught she'd become convinced that something nefarious had happened to her mother. But, as we all know, it was an accident. And accidents do happen."

"Peg's death wasn't an accident, Radcliffe. And you know it." The black-and-white tile under my feet shuddered, shifting, threatening to swallow me whole.

"I know you don't want my advice"—Radcliffe's voice was low, almost concerned—"but you need to restrain yourself. You've convinced a child that there's some kind of conspiracy, and by doing so, you've put her in danger. If you don't care enough about her to stop this madness, think about yourself. Breaking a news embargo put in place by the Office of Censorship could be considered treason."

Treason. Confounded spooks. I slammed the receiver onto the base, resisting the urge to pick it up and slam it again. "If he thinks he can stop me—"

"Let's focus on finding Enid." Gideon's words had enough snap that a flush rose to my cheeks.

"Radcliffe said she wasn't there." And somehow, I believed him. I sank to the kitchen chair tucked into an arc of windows, watching the gathering storm with no idea where to turn. My mind was a chaotic mess. It was cold and dark, and I was terrified for my niece. What had she discovered that had made her run from Gideon and me?

My fingers itched for a pencil and paper to lay it all out in black and white. Had Enid found a clue I'd missed? What did it have to do with Radcliffe? Back home, Phil would holler for me to stop letting people and assumptions cloud my perception. No one would listen if I went off half-cocked with guns blazing. Then I'd never figure out where Peg's little carbon copy had gone.

My breath glazed the window and dissipated. Enid, who had slipped into my life quiet as a ghost and reawakened memories of what life had been like with family. Where was she? And what would I do when I found her?

Half of me wanted to escape to San Diego and recruit Phil's help to bust open the press embargo on these balloon bombs, but the other half . . . I shoved the lonely thought away.

First, we needed to figure out where a child might go, where she might find hope of a small refuge. A place where she felt safe. A place where . . .

"I know where she is." I leaped to my feet, pounded down the hall, and cracked open Peg's room.

"Enid?" My voice ricocheted in the darkness.

The only light filtered through the crack in the door behind me, and it was too weak to even stretch my shadow across the floor.

"Enid?" I said again, taking slow, measured breaths so I could hear even the lightest of sounds.

Gideon hovered in the hallway, his breathing tight and rapid in counterpoint with mine.

The house siding moaned in the barren landscape. Then, from the closet, a rustle.

"Enid, honey. Come out so we can talk." I made my voice sweet as an iced cupcake, but there was no response.

What could I say that might make her trust me? What had gone wrong?

Radcliffe claimed my niece had been panicked when she called Bitsy. Why would she have reached out to my sister?

A shadow passed over the light, and Gideon appeared beside me, his presence settling the flaring fear. "Hey, Sunshine, Uncle Gideon's here too. Whatever you have to say, your aunt and I are listening. We won't be mad, no matter what."

"You're going to leave like everyone else did." Enid's petulant voice came muffled from the closet.

And what could I say? Could I promise I would stay?

"I won't ever leave you," Gideon said with all the confidence of someone who knew exactly what he was called to do.

"You will always be in my life, sweetheart." I softened my voice, praying she wouldn't parse out the words and see the careful distinction.

Gideon froze next to me, but I would deal with the ramifications later.

"Promise?" Her voice was already closer, the door cracking open.

"Promise," I said.

"Then why did you say you couldn't stay?"

She'd heard Gideon and me talking. I sighed. The girl had experienced too many losses, too many dark twists.

Enid's fingers appeared on the doorframe before her round face peeked moonlike around the corner, reminding me of the promise Peg had always invoked.

"If I break my promise," I said, solemn as the night, "the moon will see and tell God to make me pay."

After hearing her mother's favorite promise, Enid came out from the closet wrapped in a quilt and frowning. "And God will tell Mama you lied."

I swallowed at the childish theology. Why was it easier to think of shading truth to God than Peg?

"I promise." I held out my hand to the girl, who shed the blanket along with her doubts and leaped into my arms.

⸻ ❈ ⸻

Melting snow had plastered Gideon's shirt to his square body. But he refused to change until he talked to the police and then Radcliffe, ensuring them that Enid was safe while informing them that there *had* been someone outside the house. Enid, intent on running away, had encountered a shadowy figure and darted to the closet instead. By the time he hung up the receiver, Gideon was shivering so intensely he could barely stay on his feet.

"I'll t-t-" Gideon's tongue stuck until he slammed a fist on the doorframe. "Take a bath."

"How about I make us some tea?" I asked Enid as I wrapped her in a blanket and set her on a kitchen chair. At least, I was fairly sure I could manage that much. I filled the teapot and set it on the fancy stove with a million knobs. It was gas, and nothing like the woodstove I'd grown up with or the electric hot plate I had in San Diego. When I turned the knob, the burner clicked incessantly, and I switched it off. Tapping a finger on the stove, I wondered how to light the gas. With a match? I looked, but there weren't any matches in the drawers by the stove or in the junk drawer by the back door.

The stove clicked again, and I spun.

Enid had successfully lit the burner and made way for me, humor sparking in the sweep of her curtsy.

Smart aleck. "Thank you," I said. "Where does your mom keep the tea?"

"We only have coffee and cocoa." The girl slid the percolator onto the burner, then shinnied onto the counter, opened a narrow cabinet, and lifted out the jars of cocoa and sugar, as well as a tin of coffee. After setting her bounty on the counter, she wobbled backward and leaped off the counter, landing on her bounding toes like a gangly cat.

"I suppose you want cocoa?"

"With extra sugar . . . please." The last syllable came as a wheedling afterthought.

I'd never been able to say no to her mother's pleading either.

"Best get the milk, then."

The girl snatched the bottle and poured milk into a pan. She set it on the burner and made sure I was paying attention as she turned the second burner on. At least I'd be able to make coffee. Tomorrow maybe eggs, then what? A million mornings stretching forward if I were stuck here. But I'd promised Enid. And there was a magnetic draw to her, to Gideon begging me to consider, to find some way to

185

stay. Phil would say the good Lord was calling me. But Phil was a man. He could take his job to any place on earth. Me?

I measured coffee into the percolator, and cocoa and sugar into a mug. When the milk was warm, I poured some for Enid. Gideon and I could both use a bit of creamy comfort, so I added milk to our coffee as well. I lowered myself to a kitchen chair, cradling steaming ceramic, blowing absently over the surface.

"Aunt Lennie?" Enid studied me. "You said it wasn't an accident, what happened to Mama. Is that what the code is about?"

I sat back in the chair, the question crushing my lungs. How does one explain a bombing to a child?

"Mama always told me the truth. She told you to ask me."

Curse my sister for putting me in this position.

"I saw Uncle Radcliffe's name in the code, and you sounded mad at him. Did he hurt Mama?"

"No honey. He's just doing his job."

"His job is to hurt people?" Enid's voice was shrill.

"No. No. He's . . ." How could she understand that someone in another government was trying to hurt enough people to force our government to capitulate to their demands? "A different person is trying to hurt people with those balloons you saw, and your uncle's boss thinks it's best if people don't think about what might happen, in case they panic."

"I would rather have known, so I could've stopped Mama from going to see why the funny balloon was out in the fields at Grandpa's house."

And how could I or anyone else disagree with that?

The bathtub drain gurgled. If Gideon hurried, he could finish answering Enid's complicated questions.

"Aunt Bitsy said it was Mama's fault, not Uncle Radcliffe's." Enid traced a finger over the lip of her mug. "That Mama was being stubborn."

Wait. I set my mug on the table, careful not to startle my niece. "What was your mama being stubborn about?"

Enid shrugged, as if Peg's being stubborn was perfectly normal.

But it wasn't. Not really. While I was cold and hard as the winter ground, Peg was as sweet and full as early summer. What had caused her to dig in? If Bitsy's secretive husband was protected by the government, why did she think she needed to throw suspicion on Peg? For that matter . . . "Why did Aunt Bitsy think you were worried it was your uncle's fault?"

"His name is in Mama's papers, and I told her about it."

The tick of the cooling percolator pinged loud in the ongoing silence.

"You told Aunt Bitsy about the code?"

"No. Mama said not to tell anyone. I just said that Mama had left papers for you, and Uncle Radcliffe's name was in them. I wanted to know why."

So hearing that Radcliffe's name was in Peg's notes caused Bitsy to lash out and paint Peg as the bad guy? It didn't add up. If just knowing my brother-in-law's name was in Peg's notes caused this much backlash from Bitsy, we were in for a world of trouble. I stood, shoved a chair back under both doors, and ensured the drapes were tightly closed. Our only hope of protection was to gather enough evidence to go public. And we needed to start over with the code.

I stared at the blackout drapes hanging limp in the darkness. "We need a miracle."

Enid hopped from the chair, slippers flapping against the hard floor. Her enthusiasm was contagious enough that I trailed her as she ducked into the living room and extricated a basket from the bookcase.

All the pages we'd been working on were filed carefully under the girl's wooden blocks. The smart little fox.

She snatched the page I'd abandoned in the living room and fit it into the proper order. "Does this help?" Enid poked at the top of the fourth page and sure enough, the name Radcliffe swam up from the mishmash of letters.

Right next door were the words *responsible for the government cover-up*. Except the letters ran right to left, backward across the page. "It's right there!"

"What's right there?" Gideon leaned over the back of the couch, close enough I felt the heat of the bath emanating from his skin.

"Radcliffe was responsible for a government cover-up." My finger traced the line, confirming that I hadn't read it wrong. That my brother-in-law had, in fact, suppressed information about the balloon bombs. Of course I knew that they existed, but I'd been led to believe they were relatively harmless—akin to firecrackers attached to weather balloons . . . and I'd also been told that they were Japanese. The government line was that if we printed information about where the balloons fell, the Japanese could perfect their system. But this balloon had killed my sister . . . in Michigan, which was not only far from the west coast, but also conveniently timed to when she'd discovered all this about Radcliffe.

What if the bombs weren't Japanese at all? What if the government was experimenting with weapons, and Peg, with her knowledge of language, had accidentally decoded evidence that Radcliffe was trying to keep secret?

"We need to figure this out." I set the page on the coffee table. "Tonight."

CHAPTER ELEVEN

Gideon

IF I HADN'T seen Radcliffe's name in my own handwriting, I wouldn't have believed it. Not that I was naïve enough to think Radcliffe didn't have secrets. He was military intelligence. But that he was somehow involved with Peg's death was beyond comprehension.

Cocky and stiff? Yes. But a murderer?

As we teased apart Peg's code, it became more and more obvious that there was more here than the cover-up of Japanese balloon bombs.

Earlier in the night, Enid had declared a slumber party and Lennie, not wanting her niece out of sight again, had readily agreed. Fortunately, the scamp had eaten bits of the leftovers we'd pulled together and long ago succumbed to sleep in a pile of blankets and pillows worthy of the Princess and the Pea fairy tale.

Just as daylight tinged the sky lavender, I set down the page I had been scrutinizing. I was careful not to wake Lennie who had, somewhere along the line, drifted to sleep snuggled against my shoulder.

Lennie and I had dissected almost all the pages of Peg's work detailing how the Hope College librarian, knowing Peg was teaching herself Esperanto, had found a Japanese scientific paper about strong upper-atmospheric winds that could carry balloons across the Pacific Ocean. Some of the information Lennie already knew from her research, but other intelligence was new—bits and pieces about suspected numbers of bombs reaching the States; weapons the enemy had attached, like antipersonnel components; and Peg's persistent harassment of government officials, including Radcliffe, about the potential for catastrophic harm if the capacity of the plan was fully realized.

Lennie sighed in her sleep and curled her head into her arm like a napping kitten. At rest, she seemed so vulnerable, so reachable. If only I could erase the savage pain that gnawed on her, and yet I was powerless to do so.

Was this how the angels felt, hovering over mortals while they slept? An aching desire to protect, to heal? I tugged the edge of the blanket a little higher.

She shifted, her arm wrapping across my chest, tangling with the hair at the nape of my neck.

I held my breath.

As much as I wanted to hold her in my arms and claim her as mine, I knew better than to cage her wild self. She had to want to stay. *Please, God.*

I shifted her so she laid flat, then hoisted myself up and tiptoed across the floor. The coffee had long ago gone cold, but the bitter brew would brush away the cobwebs so I could decipher the last of Peg's code.

I had barely eased onto a chair when a *thump* at the front door made Lennie bolt upright. Her hair escaped the pins, springing like exclamations from her head.

"Get Enid to the bedroom." My voice hovered above a whisper. "I'll see who it is."

Lennie protested, but I brushed a hand on her arm to still her.

"I'm the supervisor, and that means I have the authority to get rid of whoever it is."

Lennie scooped up the notes and her niece, humming to the girl, who mumbled nonsense before drooping contentedly again.

I waited a beat, set my mug on the table, and smoothed my ruffled hair before peeking out the window.

Nathaniel Tolsma, the county sheriff, stood, flanked by two dour military men. All three had their hands on their service revolvers. They meant business.

Sliding the chair from under the handle, I breathed deeply. I needed to be a shark, not a stuttering teddy bear.

I swung the door open with a firm "Gentlemen, how can I help?"

Sheriff Tolsma fidgeted with the brim of his hat, unsure. His mission had obviously been to deal with a troublesome woman, not the town's supervisor.

"We're looking for"—one of the military men consulted a pad of paper—"Eleanor Sweers."

"I'm her lawyer. How may I assist you?"

"Now, Gideon." Nathaniel removed his brimmed cap as if he assumed I would welcome him inside, but I didn't budge. "We don't want to make a scene."

"You aren't coming in without a w-warrant. And Eleanor certainly doesn't need to speak to you without cause. It's hardly five o'clock in the morning, and there's a child here. Did you think about that when you chose the time of your arrival?"

Nathaniel's cheeks pinked beyond the wind-touched color. "That's not why we're here." His attention flicked to the dark car idling in the street.

Bitsy was halfway out of the car before Radcliffe reached across the seat and caught hold of her.

"Lovely. You've brought reinforcements." I shoved my hand toward the frowning lieutenant. "I'm Town Supervisor Gideon Braum. Eleanor was concerned about some break-ins and an apparent peeping Tom, and asked me to stay to protect her and her niece. I'm glad you took her seriously and are here to help."

"Sir." The lieutenant's frown grew. "We've been notified that Miss Sweers is in violation of a military gag order and stands accused of leaking classified information to the press."

"Interesting. When was this leak?"

"Last night an Eleanor Sweers placed a call to the *San Diego Times* with details regarding a story that the Office of Censorship has embargoed. This is Miss Sweers's second attempted violation of the same order."

"I'm afraid that isn't possible."

"And you know this because?"

"As I previously stated, I was here all night. The only phone in the house is hanging on the kitchen wall."

"And what were you doing here all night?" The sheriff burst into the conversation, then visibly paled at his accusation.

The two behind him chortled, no doubt thinking of the scandal. A single man, the supervisor no less, sleeping in the home of a single woman.

"Are you d-done?"

The men tried to control their smirks, but the effort was nearly too much for their pea-sized brains. Somehow I'd managed to make things worse.

***

Lennie

"Sheriff, what can I do for you?" My sudden appearance made Gideon jump and had all three other men scrambling for their weapons.

"Go b-back in the bedroom, Lennie," Gideon growled under his breath.

The younger man sniggered.

I clenched my fist, ignored Gideon's dismissal, and turned on the lawmen standing on the stoop. "I did call my editor yesterday, but it wasn't last night, and I certainly didn't call in a story about anything classified. Who was your source regarding the leak?"

The brick of a sheriff broke ranks, retreating and allowing the military men to step forward to brace their flagging attack.

"We're not at liberty to say." The lieutenant wore a mask of feigned concern.

"See, that's the difference between you military types and a journalist. I'm required to have several sources corroborate a story before I print it. You accuse someone based on the tiniest bit of hearsay. The fact is the evidence I've found seems to point to him"—I gestured to the car, where Radcliffe was now attempting to duck under the window—"hiding information that eventually led to my sister's death. Given the content of my sister's notes, along with the coroner's report due later today, I think we'll find that my sister didn't die of a freak fire in the middle of an empty field. I also expect we'll find significant evidence that a Japanese balloon bomb exploded and she was caught in it. Your counterparts on the West Coast have not only suppressed similar explosions in the past, but you continue to do so as well. If what I suspect is true, your persistence in neglecting to notify the American public will cost you more innocent lives. And that, gentlemen, will be a story my boss will fight your Office of Censorship for. So, if you have questions, you can call Phil McNamara at the *San Diego Times*, and he'll put you in touch with the lawyers on retainer."

"I thought you said you hadn't given your editor classified information."

"Oh boys. You'll have to listen better than that. I said I called my editor, but I didn't give him classified information. That doesn't mean he doesn't know that some government types are sniffing around trying to break the tenth amendment. He's already alerted the lawyers that you might call." I passed the scowling lieutenant my editor's card. "In the meantime, unless you have a warrant, I'll ask you to leave the property." Without waiting to be sure they were clear, I slammed the door.

Gideon stood, mouth agape. "That was impressive. You should have been a lawyer."

The awe in his voice wasn't at all what I expected and burst my bubble of irritation. "This isn't the first time I've run into a bunch of stuffed shirts who didn't want me to publish a story."

"But you said you weren't trying to break the embargo."

"I didn't say that. I said I didn't call Phil late last night. I have every intention of eventually telling the truth of what happened."

"See? A lawyer."

"But to push through the embargo, we need all the information."

"The pages?" Gideon rubbed his bloodshot eyes.

"And the answers to a lot of questions. Starting with, who called San Diego pretending to be me?"

"They had to have also contacted Radcliffe."

I pondered this, settling onto the couch with a paper and pen. *Radcliffe.* I wrote on the page. *Balloon. Cover-up. Peg.* I wrote out the information from the witnesses. Then I scratched arrows showing connections and realized every single one pointed the dagger tip at my brother-in-law. "What makes you think it wasn't Radcliffe himself fabricating everything?"

"He couldn't possibly sound like you."

"You're assuming that someone actually phoned the paper."

But when I called the receptionist, she confirmed that a woman claiming to be me had, indeed, rang the evening before. Phil hadn't been in, but the night clerk had taken a message. The night clerk's message was cryptic—that I'd called and had a story about a balloon bomb in Michigan all ready to go.

As I waited for the receptionist to patch me through to Phil, questions rattled in my mind. Would Bitsy have gone that far? I knew I'd been a thorn in her side—difficult, klutzy, emotional, prone to wander toward whatever took my fancy. I knew she didn't like me. But this? Would she have called the paper pretending to be me so that her husband could accuse me of treason?

"What is it?" My boss's booming voice filled my ear, his gruff answer, meant to ward off interruptions, had the opposite effect on me, settling my racing mind.

"Phil? Someone is—" A screech shattered the line, and I held the phone from my ear until it settled into silence. "Hello?" I tapped the hook switch, hoping to reestablish the connection. "Hello?" But Phil was gone, swallowed by a cut connection.

Fingers shaking, I settled the handset on the cradle.

"Lennie?" Gideon stood above me. Half of me wanted to rail against his solid, dependable form, and the other half wanted to dissolve into a mess. I shook my head to dislodge the clambering voices. Was I like Scrooge? Had I been so horrible of a person that I'd exorcised every right to expect decent treatment from my family?

"I'll make coffee." He set the last two pages of scrambled letters on the tabletop, then bustled about the kitchen. With the happy noises and warmth easing into my bones, I almost believed I belonged there.

I woke to the quiet clunk of a mug on the table next to me.

"Is it worth it?" Gideon's voice was apologetic, careful.

"Is what worth it?"

"The truth."

I bolted upright, electrified. "Truth is worth everything I can give it and more."

Gideon's grin sneaked up one side of his cheek, and he scratched at the bristles on his square chin. "Then you can't knuckle under, can you?"

The heat of the hunt buzzed through me.

Gideon leaned against the counter, awaiting orders. "What's the next step?"

"Figure out who accused me of trying to get around the embargo."

"And prove an explosion killed Peg. Not a fire. The doctor said he'd have results today, right?"

"If Radcliffe hasn't gotten to him first."

"Well, the township office does still have some pull in a small town." Gideon waggled his brows, and I giggled like a schoolgirl.

Boy Howdy, I could have kissed him.

CHAPTER TWELVE

Gideon

AFTER MAKING AN appointment with the coroner, we bundled up Enid and brought her to Mrs. Schmucker, my grandmotherly secretary. Though she was no longer the fastest with dictation or the most accurate typist, Mrs. Schmucker had photos of eight grandchildren lining her desk. She not only kept a "grandma bag" of toys, puzzles, and treats at her desk for the local kids, but she would also do anything for Enid . . . or me. And while Enid was a curious child and would love to visit a morgue, under the circumstances, Lennie refused to bring her.

Of course, that didn't mean Enid agreed with the plan. She whined about us leaving her at the township office even after I'd given her a few dimes to buy a hamburger lunch. She stood, fist clenched around the coins, teeth set, refusing to go to Mrs. Schmucker, who held a plate of cookies.

Lennie knelt in front of the scamp, her halo of blond leaning into the child's well-tamed braids. "Did you know I'm magic?" Lennie held her hand out, palm up, asking for a dime.

Enid, no doubt as curious as I, opened her fist.

There was a coin missing.

The girl gasped and spun a circle, searching for a flash of metal.

"I know where it is." Lennie stopped the girl's frantic search, and with a flip of her fingers, produced a coin from behind Enid's pint-sized ear.

Even though I was the one who'd taught Lennie the latter trick, I didn't know how she had lifted the dime from Enid's fist. There's an immense difference between picking a pocket and picking tight fingers.

"Now." Lennie held the coin between two fingers, pretending to listen to what it was saying with an occasional *uh-huh*. "You need to hold on to my magic coin for me. It doesn't enjoy going to visit doctors and asked to stay behind. Would that be all right with you?"

Enid was still gaping at her aunt.

Lennie tucked the dime into her niece's pocket and then gave a little gasp as if remembering. "Oh! I almost forgot. You can't spend that. You'll need a dime for your lunch." Lennie pointed at the lone dime. "And then"—she snapped her fingers and produced another coin from Enid's ear—"you can use this one to buy Mrs. Schmucker a hamburger as well. She looks mighty hungry."

Enid clenched her fist around the remaining coins, nodding vigorously.

Lennie kissed the crown of the girl's head, and Enid flung her arms around her aunt's neck, sealing a bond that would not easily break.

Lennie

Covering news on the San Diego docks meant I'd seen my share of death, but the thought of possibly seeing images of my dead sister had me swallowing back bile and praying I wouldn't have to pretend to be strong. That prayer was chased by one where I pleaded for enough evidence to find justice for Peg and Enid.

The drive to the hospital's morgue in Grand Rapids was blessedly short. Gideon, who seemed to sense that I couldn't form coherent words, hummed in a familiar, soothing baritone, lulling me into a drowsy state. I didn't recall parking in the lot or putting one foot in front of the other to carry my body down the cement stairs to the basement door. But I awoke to the lonely call of a hawk soaring above us in the winter-blue sky.

Powerful but alone, he dipped behind the brick building even as I followed Gideon through the yawning darkness of the door and was swallowed into the hospital.

The cloying smell of decay and embalming fluid would make anyone gasp. But I knew from experience that breathing through my mouth wasn't a good idea. If I did, I'd allow the smell to coat my tongue and claw down my throat. Better to clench my teeth and forbid the taste of death entry.

At Gideon's whispered query, a receptionist led us through a sterile hall festooned with glittered paper Christmas bells. Somewhere a tinny radio played Bing Crosby as he dreamed of a white Christmas.

Christmas would never again be like I had dreamed. And the overly cheery baubles failed to distract my mind from repeating, *Please don't let it be the autopsy room. Please don't let it be the autopsy room.*

Gideon wove my fingers through his dependable ones.

I flinched, but knew I needed his strength to propel myself through the door, and I'd told him I would trust him. *Please don't let it be the autopsy room.*

The woman tapped on the frame before flinging the door open to reveal a cramped space with a diminutive doctor perched behind an enormous desk that squatted like a pregnant rhinoceros over the lushly appointed room.

Though intimidating, it was not an autopsy room.

The man, dressed in a lab coat as white as his hair, enthusiastically greeted Gideon, who then introduced me as the deceased's sister, carefully avoiding the fact that I was also a newspaper reporter. The doctor waved at the seating, and Gideon wedged himself into a flimsy chair.

I settled onto the edge of the only other seat in the room. My knee brushed Gideon's, and he smiled half in reassurance, half in apology—there wasn't anywhere else to put both our legs unless he plunked his feet on the rhino-sized desk. The thought of Gideon so egregiously breaking protocol for me made me release my breath.

"You were right to call." The doctor scrutinized me over the flat tops of his reading glasses before flipping open a thick file on his desk.

"I've received a few directives asking me to seal the results, but there's no legal reason not to release this information to next of kin. Their claim of national security is suspect when a housewife is first shot, then mysteriously burned with an accelerant in the middle of a field."

I gasped, heart stopping for a moment. *Shot?*

He swiped off his glasses. "Oh dear. I made a mess of that entirely." He pressed the button for the intercom. "Joyce? Joyce, please bring Miss Sweers a cup of tea."

But I didn't need tea. My mind was sparking with questions smashing into each other until one emerged on my tongue. "She was shot? Who would shoot Peg?"

The doctor glanced at Gideon as if he were asking permission from the only other man available.

For the love . . . "I'm not some fainting debutante. I've seen as many dead bodies as an undertaker." My exclamation was a reminder to myself and realigned my thought process. I was a reporter, for heaven's sake! "What caliber was it?"

His enormous eyes flickered behind the thick lenses of the glasses now resettled on his nose. No doubt he was wondering what kind of monstrous woman had invaded his precise domain. Men over here, on the capable side. Women over there, needing to be coddled, protected, and most certainly not discussing the finer points of murder.

"The bullet, what kind of weapon fired it?"

The doctor consulted his notes. "It was a .45."

"Which is any army officer's sidearm. How spectacularly unhelpful."

The coroner flushed. "It isn't my job to find the who, only the how. But I will say it was at close range, from the front."

"Someone she knew?"

"Or," Gideon said, "anyone threatening all she loved to keep her quiet."

"The angle suggests the shooter was a hair taller than she, but"—he referenced the sterile photographs in front of him—"there were several hummocks in that area of the field. So I can't be sure. Especially given the . . . ah . . . the damage from the explosion."

It was my turn to blink in complete confusion. "I thought you said she was shot."

"She was."

Gideon's chair complained as he stirred.

I clenched my fist around the strap of my bag, pushing my frustration through my fingertips, away from my mouth. "But you said there was an explosion." I was pleased to hear only mild confusion in my voice.

"Indeed. It appears that she was shot and then a blast with an accelerant was set off nearby."

I lost all attempt at reasonableness as my spine smacked into the wooden back of the chair. "There is absolutely no way someone shot her, only for a Japanese balloon bomb to explode in the exact spot."

The medical examiner darted a frantic look at Gideon, as though I might detonate and derail his perfectly planned afternoon.

Of course the doctor didn't know about the balloons. Why would he? But why were there bomb components and a crater if the government had cleaned up the site of an attack? They wouldn't miss such obvious signs of it—the rope, the bomb fragments.

Howard, Judy, and Oliver had even seen a balloon. So had Peg.

Unless the pieces had been left on purpose. But why?

The doctor stood with a "well" that was near enough a *get out of my office* that I allowed Gideon to lead me into the long hall. A light flickered, blinking out and then on again, making my skull congeal into a thick headache.

Why would the military entice people to think my sister's death came from a fire, only to suggest that she'd instead been killed by a top secret bomb? Were they trying to distract folks from what had really taken place?

Which led me back to the questions we'd been asking since the beginning: What had happened to Peg? And why?

Chapter Thirteen

Gideon

As I NAVIGATED the drift-clogged roads, snow muffled all but the low hum of Henry's engine.

Lennie coiled into the door, forehead pressed against the window. Rare bright sunlight poured from the sky, casting her in a shadow hemmed by a ring of gold. By afternoon, much of the snow would melt only to freeze again overnight. A confusing state of weather, to be sure.

I tapped my fingers on the steering wheel, trying to dissolve the thoughts crystalizing in my mind. Lennie was right. There was no way a Japanese balloon bomb had exploded in the same place where Peg was shot. But why were there bomb parts and why had there been a balloon? A freak accident at the sight of a murder? It bent believability. But one thing was clear, Peg had been murdered. And from what I knew about the government, they wouldn't condone murdering the housewife of a war hero over a few questions about enemy balloon bombs.

So there had to be something else. Some*one* else. And that meant there were no state secrets to protect, and the government should leave Lennie and Enid in peace. At least the autopsy would close the government's concern and open a murder case under the sheriff's jurisdiction, out of Radcliffe's control. That said, there was still a murderer lurking out there somehow connected to Radcliffe, which meant there was no way I would leave Lennie alone, huddled against the storm.

Confusion radiated off her. But with no investigative prowess, I was as helpful as an ice salesman in the arctic.

Perhaps I could get Lennie access to the case files.

She would hate me for interfering, but what else could I do?

"I came home to square things away. I never expected this." Lennie didn't turn from the window, the planes of her face drawn.

"Sometimes we can't fix everything." It was a piece of Mom's advice as relevant to Lennie as me.

"I'm not trying to fix it. I . . . I just miss Peg."

"Do you regret leaving?" I slowed to take our exit off the highway.

"No." Lennie's voice carried more than a little regret.

"But . . ."

"I wish I'd found a different way, maybe. I thought that making it on my own might somehow prove to my parents, to Bitsy, that I wasn't a total loss. But look what happened."

"It wasn't your fault." I turned onto a lonely side street, one that meandered between miles of scraggly corn fields, bristling with broken stalks.

A dark Pontiac that had been trailing us from Grand Rapids turned with me.

I clenched my fists over the steering wheel, calmly swinging onto a narrow, barely used track.

The car followed.

We were still a good five miles from home. Five miles of desolate fields. A farm lane with two dirt tracks opened ahead, and I spun into it, sending Lennie skidding across the bench seat, slamming her hip into mine with a muffled exclamation.

The Pontiac bumped into the two-track, and I knew we might be in trouble.

Lennie

"Don't panic, but we're being followed." Gideon was placid, and it took me a moment to process what he had said.

Followed? Don't panic? "Don't panic? We're in the middle of nowhere being followed, and we just found out someone murdered my sister." I glanced behind us at the menacing vehicle. I would lay money on my hunch that it was the lieutenant who'd tried to arrest me. Why was he following us? The military had no jurisdiction to arrest civilians.

"But I know this field and the back roads." Gideon downshifted, a devious glint in his eye, and I may have screeched a bit as Gideon treated the bare field like the brickyard of the Indianapolis 500-Mile Race.

The Ford veered left, launching across the pitted rows, and I cartwheeled across the bench seat again, barely catching myself before crashing into Gideon at almost the same moment the truck bucked over a swell in the earth.

I latched onto Gideon's arm even as my legs scrambled to keep me upright.

Gideon whooped like a bull rider, praising Henry as we shot onto a tree-lined gravel road.

Somehow the black Pontiac was still coming—farther behind, granted, but still coming.

I was praying now, under my breath, nonsensical snatches of words. If God was all-knowing, he'd piece it together.

The Ford's tires spun, spitting ice chunks and gravel, and we barreled onto an actual road long enough to put some distance between us and the pursuing vehicle.

But once the Pontiac hit the road, it would overtake Henry in no time.

I leaned forward, talking to the Ford as if I might propel us faster, and Gideon grinned as though I'd finally seen the light.

"Hang on!" he shouted as he cranked the wheel right.

I slammed into Gideon again. "How about a little more warning next time?"

"You like being close, and you know it." Gideon gave me a cheeky grin, and I smacked his arm.

"You're enjoying this!" I'd known he tinkered with cars, even racing them from time to time, but this was entirely different. "This isn't some joyride on the back forty. They're trying to kill us."

"Those boys won't do any real harm. If we showed up in the coroner's office on a slab an hour after he told us your sister was murdered, red flags would fly so fast everybody would know the county had one colossal disaster to deal with."

"Well, that's comforting." My caustic words raised at the end in terror as Gideon slid Henry through a small gap in the evergreen trees and then whipped sideways, paralleling the previous road.

"Of course it is," he said, and winked like a fool.

It was quite clear he was making light of the fact that we were in the middle of nowhere fleeing a couple of ne'er-do-wells who probably had guns and murderous intent. We swung onto a main road and dipped back into the woods so quickly I didn't even identify where we were or take a breath of relief in the relatively smooth ride.

Before I properly formed a coherent, scathing sentence worthy of a newspaper reporter, we slid calmly onto Church Street, serene as Black Mill Pond in fall and minus the black Pontiac and the overzealous lieutenant.

"Lunch?" Gideon said as he seamlessly parallel parked in front of Russ' Restaurant.

Stunned, I watched the animation of the neon sign pour out a cup of coffee over and over.

"Are you okay?"

My attention snapped to Gideon, who was reaching across the seat. "Of course." I slapped on the nonplussed persona of a hardnosed reporter. "But shouldn't we hide Henry?"

Gideon preened. "You called him by his name."

I raised an eyebrow in my best imitation of Phil's editorial disapproval.

Gideon sobered. "We don't have anything to hide from the government boys. They'll find that out soon enough."

It was obvious Gideon had never been an investigator. "Someone still murdered Peg." I stilled, waiting for his mind to make the connection.

The moment he did, he put the Ford in gear and curved around the corner, coasting into a wedge of space between the butcher and a bank of enormous evergreens. The engine ticked happily in its makeshift garage even as my mind clambered for purchase.

What to do next? "We should talk with Judy again, and probably Howard and Oliver too."

"I'm already ahead of you. I called them before we left for the hospital. They'll be here in about forty-five minutes, which should be enough time for us to eat a late lunch."

Lunch. My stomach heaved with the thought.

"Eating will help."

"You don't say." Despite the sting in my retort, I knew Gideon was right. Food would help settle the spinning sensation in my head.

"Sorry. I thought . . ." Gideon studied me as though he feared I might go to pieces.

"Forget it. I'm just tired."

"You just found out your sister was murdered."

I blinked, sniffing at the burning behind my nose.

"If you don't want to go in, it's okay."

"No." I shoved open the door and stumbled onto the sidewalk. If nothing else, I needed to talk to the witnesses again. Somehow we had to reconcile the evidence of a bomb with the reality that my sister had been shot and then burned. Burned.

My sister—sweet, innocent Peg—had been murdered, and if I thought about it too long, I wouldn't be able to move. I shook my head, clearing the fog of grief, forcing myself to ask my original question. "Who would kill Peg? It usually comes down to money, pride, or fear."

"I think she found out someone's secret." Gideon led the way to Russ', opened the door, and waited for me to enter, but my feet stuck right along with my mind.

"Of course she did. We saw the research she did on Esperanto and the winds. She proved the Japanese could send, and probably are sending, balloon bombs into the States. But there have been more than a few that have landed out West, and no one has been murdered

205

over it. Plus, a bomb certainly wouldn't leave the telltale signs of a .45's close-contact bullet wound."

"We need to call the sheriff."

Talk about whiplash. "Why would we call the sheriff? He seemed awfully willing to arrest me for even questioning what was happening in his quiet little town."

"He's a good man." Gideon's voice was infuriatingly placating.

"Good men get swallowed by power and influence every day, and there's nothing more powerful or influential than the US government in wartime."

"Maybe. But, like you said, I don't think this has anything to do with balloon bombs, and that means the government isn't involved. This is a murder, not a possible breach of a press embargo."

He'd gone all lawyer on me, and I didn't see a way around his logic. "Fine. But we're not showing him my sister's notes. Not yet."

"Fair enough."

And with that I walked into the dim light of the diner, not at all sure what I'd agreed to.

⟶•⟵

Gideon

Seeing as it was just after three o'clock on a Tuesday afternoon, the restaurant was currently and blessedly unoccupied.

Mrs. Bouws, the gray-haired waitress and good friend of my grandmother's, waved me to my favorite corner booth and settled two glasses of water and a Coke on the table before Lennie and I had even shrugged out of our coats. "The usual for you?"

My mouth watered at the thought of the food her son, Russell, had grown up cooking.

"Yes, ma'am. But we also need some discretion and a bit of interference."

"Keep folks from bothering you and looking over your shoulder?"

At my nod, she turned to Lennie. "Absolutely. And you must be

Eleanor, she of San Diego fame, and the best aunt in the world to the little imp who graced my table a few hours ago."

Lennie stood mute, open-mouthed, a slight blush creeping up her cheeks. It made her appear as innocent as her elementary school self—before she learned to shut herself off from the rest of the world.

"Don't worry. I know how to keep secrets. I've been Gideon's vault of secrets for years. He and my Russell spent more than a few hours chatting over pie at my table. What'll it be for you?"

Lennie glanced at the homey American menu and unwittingly ordered the duplicate of my usual—Russ' Famous Fried Chicken, fries, coleslaw, and a Coke—which earned a sly wink from Mrs. Bouws. She and my grandmother were forever manipulating meet-ups with eligible women in the county.

The tips of my ears set to blazing, which only made Mrs. Bouws's smile grow into a blinding brilliance. "Coming right up."

"Can I use your phone?" I asked her retreating back.

"I'm sure you're capable of using a phone, young man," she snapped at me, and stood hand on hip in perfect imitation of Mom.

"*May* I use your phone?" I corrected myself.

"Of course." She slotted the order into the spinner and hollered at Russell, who was manning the kitchen, to let him know an order was coming in. Though the place was named for him, if a person didn't know better, one could assume she was the owner and not him.

Lennie smothered a grin and slid onto the seat that would allow me to sit next to her after I made the call and still have my good ear toward the rest of the diner rather than the wall.

I dialed the sheriff and told him what the doctor had said.

"I already got the report," Nathaniel said. "How anyone missed a bullet wound is a mystery to me. It's got me all kinds of sideways."

"The feeling is catching. Lennie's as jumpy as a fish out of water about talking with you."

"Well, she don't have much reason to. She's the only person who was in another state when someone shot her sister. I also had a chat with her editor, and he seems mighty keen on your Lennie's investigative prowess. If she's found evidence, I'd like to know what it is."

"Just treat her carefully, will you?"

"I'm not a hack, Gideon." The bristle in Nathaniel's voice scraped my conscience raw. He'd been nothing but good to me.

"Might as well come over to Russ'," I said, smoothing things over. "We're eating lunch, then talking with a few folks."

He agreed to head out from Vanderburgh Center in a bit, which gave us a few minutes to eat, and I hung up.

Lennie stared out the window as I slid in beside her.

Water dripped from the roof to the sidewalk, gathering in a widening puddle of slush.

I was exhausted, confused, and the gentle rhythm allowed my mind to settle into a lower gear. Lennie and I were dry, warm, and safe, and the sheriff was on our side.

"You must think I'm a mess." Lennie's assertion jerked my attention from the dreary afternoon.

"You're not a mess any more than anyone would be, given the circumstances."

"My circumstances never seem to—" She waved her hand in front of her, not looking at me, and obviously trying to find a word that didn't make her sound crazy or desperate or completely incapable of rational thought.

"Circumstances never seem to go in your favor?" It was mostly a statement, but I curled my voice up at the end, knowing Lennie didn't much appreciate someone seeing through her clear as glass all the way to the soggy middle.

Lennie gave a snort that I took as approval. "Bitsy wouldn't say it that way. She'd say I was born with Satan directing my steps."

No wonder she had a chip on her shoulder.

"I can't blame her." Lennie tore at the paper place mat, leaving little bits of confetti scattered on the table. "I always left a trail of mess behind me."

"And you learned to suck in your tears, raise your chin, and give as good as she got, hiding all that hurt under a solid layer of strong."

Lennie brushed the place mat shreds into a pile. "There's no reason to kowtow to a bully."

"Instead, you run away." I sucked in a breath, wishing I could drag the words back.

Lennie just kept piling the scraps. "It isn't running if you've done everything you can, and the other people won't listen. What should I have done differently?" Her voice rose a touch. "Settled down and been a content housewife? Pregnant and barefoot, with a noose of pearls around my neck."

"There are options between that and running."

She shook her head, the motion overflowing with frustrated weariness. "Maybe for a man, but not for me. Not here." Sadness hung heavy from her slumped shoulders.

"I would never want you in some box. You're too vibrant for that." I slid my hand over Lennie's.

She was icy, shaking, but she turned her hand over, connecting her fingers to mine, trusting me with her pain. "My family wouldn't use that word to describe me."

"Then they're the ones missing out. Even Enid sees the shimmering color in you."

A grin grew on Lennie's face. "That's because she's like me. Promise not to let Bitsy get to her."

"You're the one in charge of that, not me."

Lennie sobered and glanced away.

Mrs. Bouws strode across the tile floor, a tray balanced precariously on her shoulder, and I had more than an inkling that Lennie welcomed the interruption.

"Fried chicken, fries, slaw, Coke, and one of our famous apple dumplings to share, on the house." She winked at me, conspiracy rumbling under her expression. If only a dessert was capable of solving Peg's murder and keeping Lennie in Mapleview, while still letting Lennie be Lennie. The good Lord had plenty to figure out.

Lennie

By the time I'd choked down a bit of the chicken and a few fries, the ice cream surrounding the dumpling was completely melted—absolutely perfect in my book. Even better, we'd translated another page of Peg's code. She planned to talk to Radcliffe about what she'd found, but it was clear she was nervous.

"There's no way Radcliffe killed Peg over a news embargo." Gideon reiterated the sentiment for the third time in the last fifteen minutes.

Although I'd prayed for patience the other two times, my patience shattered under the barrage of insistence. "He tried to arrest me for treason."

"Sweetheart." Mrs. Bouws's voice at my shoulder made me jump. She set a fresh Coke in front of me, the ice clinking happily against the glass. "That boy is wound so tight he squeaks when he walks, but that also means he walks an awful straight line when it comes to the rules."

And we were back to that. I couldn't disagree—they both knew Radcliffe far better than I—but nothing else made sense. Why else would the lieutenant follow us if Radcliffe hadn't commanded him to do so? I flipped the coin in my pocket and focused on the penciled jumble of letters, pulling out random words and phrases. Darkness was already falling hard, and I was grateful for a place to work in the quiet. Though the restaurant wouldn't stay that way long. Headlights flashed, temporarily blinding me, and the sheriff's marked car slid into the parking spot on the other side of my window.

He levered himself out of the cruiser, and I waited until he moved past the window to slip the pages into my bag. Gideon trusted Sheriff Nathaniel Tolsma, but God hadn't made me any kind of fool. I didn't trust anyone without authenticating them myself.

The sheriff deposited his hat on the hook attached to the booth seat before sliding in across from us. "Eleanor, I am sorry for your loss."

His sympathy would've been more plausible if he'd said it the first time he'd seen me . . . instead, he'd tried to arrest me.

"I suppose," he said, hitching up his generous waistband, "I owe you an apology for the other night as well. Phil says you wouldn't go around him to break an embargo, and well, he has the ear of our Governor Kelly."

So it wasn't my feminine credibility he trusted, but two men's opinions.

"You boys can be so patronizing sometimes. You know that?" Judy, bless her, peered down from her full height, barely clearing the sheriff's head while he was sitting.

Still, the man ducked his chin, properly chastised, and I was reminded how much I liked her.

"Now, what's this about our sweet Peg being shot?" She pulled up a chair and plunked down at the head of the table, presiding over the assembly like a benevolent queen, her brother hovering behind her like a bodyguard. "I declare I nearly fainted at the word. Oliver thought I should stay home and rest. But there's more you all need to know. Sure as apples come from an apple tree, Peg was going out to look in on that balloon, but she was all hot and bothered earlier that day. She'd come over to tutor my daughter and said she'd seen something she didn't expect over at Radcliffe and Bitsy's. She wondered if we could reschedule."

Was Gideon ready to believe me yet? Radcliffe was a liar. If I could prove that, I'd be sure to set his pants on fire.

"What did she find?" Gideon frowned. "If she went to talk to Radcliffe about a balloon bomb and there was something unexpected . . ." He ticked his thoughts out on his fingers, the emphasis spurting water on my thoughts. "That means it definitely wasn't Radcliffe covering up a balloon. She saw or heard proof that pointed to someone other than Radcliffe." At this, he looked to me for confirmation, but all I heard was the rushing of a tsunami wave crashing over me.

Gideon was right. It wasn't a balloon bomb, but . . .

"But that doesn't mean it wasn't Radcliffe." The sheriff rallied to my side of things. "And how did you all know anything about these Japanese balloon bomb things, anyhow? The government was keeping that secret close to their chests."

And we were back to that. My potential treason.

"Knock it off, Nathaniel." The waitress smacked the back of the sheriff's head.

Seeing his eyes smart as he rubbed his head satiated my frustration, at least for the moment.

Mrs. Bouws set another pair of water glasses on the table, then planted a fist on her hip. "You can't sling a cat 'round here without hitting someone who saw that balloon, and everybody in town heard about the explosion. If Colonel High and Mighty wanted to keep the town from gossiping about it, he shouldn't have made such a show of telling everybody to keep quiet. And since we now know the bomb didn't kill our Peg, that means someone in town probably killed her. I mean, setting up the balloon and explosion to cover things up would take too much planning ahead for someone passing through. Right?"

The sheriff opened his mouth as if to object.

The waitress thumped her other fist on her hip in a clear imitation of a superhero getting ready for a smackdown. "There's no way you'd think that bit of news wouldn't get out. Folks loved that girl and her daughter as if they were their own. You best focus more on the fact that there's a killer on the loose in Mapleview than giving heed to the stuffed shirts down in Fort Custer or a few gossiping women at the drugstore."

Well, that sobered all of us right up. And the fact that everybody in town knew the news also meant the killer was fully aware we weren't chasing a bomb anymore. And that meant we were all in danger, including . . .

"Enid." The girl's name slid out of my mouth in a gasp. "If Peg uncovered a secret . . ." Fear clawed my throat closed, but Gideon leaped out of the booth so fast, his leg smacked the table, sending the plates rattling.

"We have to get her. Now." Gideon must have finished my thought in his own mind.

If Peg had discovered a secret worth her life, whoever killed her might think Enid might know the same thing.

CHAPTER FOURTEEN

Gideon

IT WASN'T FAR from the restaurant to the town hall, but taking Henry would be quicker than not. My body propelled my feet faster, out the door, *faster*, down the sidewalk, *faster*, around the diner.

Lennie's footsteps pounding behind mine, Nathaniel's voice trailing, "I'll call for reinforcements and meet you there."

Lord, if anything happened to Enid . . . I didn't let myself complete the thought. Surely God wouldn't let a little girl pay the price for whatever her mother had uncovered.

I manhandled my way through the evergreens, then yanked the truck door open and slid in. Henry's engine grumbled about starting in the cold—an ornery old man carping in the frosty winter light—but I had no time for patiently waiting for the engine to turn.

Lennie crashed into the passenger seat. "You're going to flood it."

I struck a fist into the steering wheel. Pain mingled with fear, and anger boiled to the surface. I was going to be too late again. *Please, God.* I turned the key.

The engine blessedly ground to life.

I shifted into reverse, scarcely checking for cars before swinging into the street and speeding to the old Visser school, my fingers going numb around the steering wheel, the chill of the coming night seeping into every surface of my body.

Above us, clouds roiled in from the big lake, consuming what light was left in the sky. Streetlights flickered on as I urged Henry across the ice-skimmed road. Behind me the sheriff's car lights flicked on, the slow spin of the red light flashing warning, danger.

Finally the town hall appeared crouched on the small hill, the windows arched in surprise at the Ford barreling toward it. I tobogganed into my reserved parking spot and bolted from the truck, through to the open reception area. A festive garland fluttered in the breeze. Otherwise the office was still and dark. Panting, I took the stairs two at a time and burst through the upstairs door, through the conference room into my office at the end.

The entire building was barren.

I spun.

Where was Enid?

Lennie

A piece of paper fluttered on Gideon's pressed wood door, tacked there with a shiny pin. I shook as I pulled the pin.

We have Enid. Come to the mill with all of Peg's notes. 5 o'clock. No police.

It was a missive from the devil written in the blood of my regrets.

I glanced at my watch. *4:45.* There was no time to go for the encyclopedias. Our bits and scribbles would have to be enough.

Gideon, reading over my shoulder, smashed a fist into the doorframe. "We should have taken her with us." He elbowed past me and stormed down the gloomy hall, his footsteps thundering away.

I knew better than to take the crackle of his words personally. But the fury in them blistered, and the sting lodged in my throat.

I shoved the note into my bag. Suddenly I knew more than anything I'd ever known that I didn't want to stand in the cold future alone. I wanted Enid. Alone would not be my epitaph. I would, like Ebenezer Scrooge, rewrite my future Christmases.

Gideon

Outside, bitter wind slapped my face, penance for snipping at Lennie. But it did nothing to cool my anger or confusion. Who had taken Enid and how had they known about Peg's notes?

I ran across the parking lot, breath billowing out in a thick, vision-obscuring vapor. We'd been in the town hall just long enough for the quickly dropping temperatures to create an ice crust over Henry's windshield. I jammed the keys into the ignition and pumped the gas, feathering the keys and clutch in a practiced prayer. *Please, start.*

Lennie dove into the seat next to me, digging in her bag for the precious pages. I waved off the sheriff, telling him some cockamamie story about Enid's being ill and Mrs. Schmucker leaving a note saying she took her home. Would he go check on her at my secretary's house?

As I negotiated the deteriorating road, Lennie pored over the pages, grumbling at herself for being so dull-witted. I clattered onto the mill road, clipping the sign hard enough that I slowed to navigate the rest of the twists.

Up ahead, headlights gleamed in the crimson shadow of coming night.

I braked to a stop, heart thundering in my ears even as my mind caught up with my actions. "Now what?"

Lennie lowered the pages, and her eyes narrowed as she dashed the paper to the floor. "Now what? Now I'm going to kill my sister."

CHAPTER FIFTEEN

Lennie

"Bitsy!" The blanket of falling snow smothered my voice. "Bitsy!" I shouted again, shaking off Gideon's restraint and stalking toward the idling car. Whatever Peg had seen, I'd gotten far enough in her notes to know it had to do with our holier-than-thou older sister.

A shadow levered itself from the driver's seat, and I stumbled to a stop. It was a man. A lieutenant, in fact.

"The frowning lieutenant?" Gideon muttered, as utterly confused as I was.

This was the man who had tried to arrest me. But he couldn't have taken Enid. The government wasn't involved.

"You two are a major pain in my backside. Where are the documents?" Light glinted off his service revolver, underscoring not only his decided involvement but also his willingness to silence two more witnesses.

"In the truck," Gideon said, his voice steady as a rock even as he stepped in front of me. "Where's Enid?"

"In the mill. She's safe. For now."

"You'll forgive me if I don't precisely trust you." My crankiness earned an elbow in the side from Gideon and a gritted "not now."

The lieutenant shrugged. "I don't see that you have a choice."

I edged toward the Ford, hands up, brain churning. Unlike many of the farmers' trucks in the area, Henry didn't sport a rifle rack, and

I doubted Gideon had a pistol in his glove box—that would smack too much of a Chicago mob boss. A tire iron?

I eased open the door. I had a decent throwing arm, but how did one accurately throw a tire iron?

Just as I gathered all the pages, a terrific screech came from the mill, followed by a string of curse words flowing from what had to have been Bitsy's mouth. A shot rang out, and I burst from the truck, pages flying, barreling toward the dark Pontiac and a writhing duo of bodies.

A small shadow broke from the mill door, Bitsy hobbling close behind.

The shadow flew behind me, latching onto my leg as I wound up and unleashed a terrific punch to Bitsy's nose.

She stumbled back, clutching at her face, blood already peeking from behind her fingers. "You broke my nose!"

She lunged at me, but I ducked, neatly sweeping Enid with me.

My little shadow stuck out her foot at the last moment, sending Bitsy sprawling to the ground, smacking her head on the frozen ground. The little girl promptly leaped on my sister and tied the unconscious woman's hands behind her back with a bright-pink hair ribbon.

Who had taught the little sprite such a thing?

The grunts and roars behind me didn't leave me much time to ponder.

"Get in the truck and lock the doors," I shouted as I leaped into the fray between Gideon and the lieutenant, delivering a swift kick to the nether regions of the man who'd accused me of treason.

His inhale of shock dropped him to his knees.

Gideon snatched the man's sidearm, then neatly avoided the lieutenant's sweeping arm.

A siren echoed in the distance and lights swirled as I sprinted to the truck to check Enid for cuts and bruises.

She swiped away my searching hands and secured her arms around my neck. "I knew you'd come." Enid sank into me.

"I won't ever leave you. Remember, I promised the moon."

The sheriff's car spun into the mill's drive and came to a sputtering halt, spraying gravel and ice across a stirring Bitsy.

The sheriff and a deputy burst from the car, shouting, guns drawn.

Gideon stepped away from the lieutenant, hands up, dangling the gun in front of him.

In no time, the two police officers had Bitsy and the lieutenant, as well as Gideon, trussed like Christmas turkeys. The officers kept shushing my complaints and shooing me back to the safety of the truck.

Finally, Enid climbed onto the hood of the Pontiac and snatched the sheriff's arm. "Aunt Bitsy lied to Mrs. Schmucker, then threw me in the car with Mr. Grumpy—"

"Grumpy?" The sheriff interjected, eyebrow quirked.

Enid scowled, pointing at the lieutenant. "And then she slobbered all over him." She pantomimed a very involved kiss. "And then dragged me here. And if you don't let Uncle Gideon go, you're going to be in trouble."

"Well, young lady, before I can—"

"Why are adults so stupid? Grumpy was mad because Aunt Bitsy dragged him into a big mess, and she said he couldn't stop because he'd stolen Uncle Radcliffe's balloon, and he said he wasn't going to kill anyone, and that's when we got here. I told them Auntie Lennie wouldn't let them get away because . . . because . . . Aunt Bitsy killed Mama." Enid sagged against the weight of the words, tumbling from the hood into my waiting arms. "She killed Mama." Enid's voice broke, her tears slicking my hair as I slumped to the ground and leaned against the tire for support.

How? How could Bitsy have done this? I didn't realize the deputy had released Gideon until his arms were around us, hemming us in, murmuring, his hands smoothing Enid's hair, his lips kissing my forehead, his all protecting us.

The military had missed out on a brave man, and I, for one, was grateful.

————— ❊ —————

Gideon

By the time Christmas rolled around the following week, Bitsy's lieutenant, a Bobby Fenton, had spilled everything. When Peg had dropped by to show Radcliffe the information about the upper-atmospheric winds, she'd stumbled on Bitsy with Fenton.

A few days later, when the two sisters were hanging laundry for their father, Peg drummed up enough gumption to confront her sister. Bitsy laughed it off but then told the lieutenant they'd both be ruined if the information got out. Despite the lieutenant telling her to let it be, Bitsy called her sister out to the field with some story about an injured dog and told Peg to keep her mouth shut.

But Peg was resolved—the affair needed to end. Bitsy pulled the gun she'd brought, and her sister went for the weapon just as it exploded. Horrified, Bitsy concocted the balloon bomb story, then convinced her boyfriend to steal the pieces and launch the balloon just above the site. The rope tied to the tree made sure that the balloon would land where they wanted it to, and the real explosion made everyone think it was the top secret bomb that killed her sister. The government would do anything to suppress news of a balloon bomb reaching Michigan . . . thereby disguising Bitsy's part in her own sister's murder.

Radcliffe's only charge was concealing the theft of material associated with a Japanese balloon that had actually dropped northeast of Mapleview in Dorr. He'd likely receive a slap on the wrist and be moved out of intelligence, but he was cooperating fully with investigators. The deputy had seen me driving Henry erratically, even clipping the mill sign, and had called the sheriff in to deal with what he suspected was a drunken town supervisor. But that tipped Sheriff Tolsma off to the fact that we'd sent him on a wild goose chase, and he came flying. And since I'd sent him in the wrong direction, he'd been concerned I was involved. Of course Enid had set him straight as only she could.

Which left Enid, Lennie, and me exhausted on Christmas evening, snuggling in front of the fire, still in our pajamas.

Though I tried not to think about what came next, Lennie's flight would whisk her away in three days. Three days.

I untangled myself from the blanket, using the excuse of picking up scraps of wrapping paper to lead me away from the two people I most wanted to spend the rest of my life with. I dropped the paper in the bin and collapsed against the cupboards, dragging in a breath, forcing myself to be steady, to be strong enough and love them enough to let them go.

"Gideon?" Lennie, dressed in plaid pajamas, stood in the doorway, her blond hair tied in a tangle of ribbons and pins courtesy of Enid. I'd never seen her look more beautiful.

"Just making coffee." My voice was tight at the edges, barely holding together.

"There's another present." She held a small box wrapped in brown paper and twine.

Whatever it was, Lennie's somber mood had me wanting to run barefoot through the snow all the way home. But Enid's voice called from the other room to "hurry up, already."

A moment later, I sank onto the arm of the couch behind Enid as she ripped away the paper and opened a box to find a little ticket. Enid looked at her aunt in utter confusion.

"It's a ticket." Lennie grinned.

Enid still didn't respond.

Lennie laughed. "How would you like to fly to California?"

My heart stopped. She was taking Enid and would making a new life for herself thousands of miles away. She was capable, smart, strong, and didn't need me. Enid was growing up fast, and I would miss it all.

"Not without Uncle Gideon."

"Well . . ." Lennie glanced shyly at me. "That would be up to Uncle Gideon." She held out a duplicate small box. "It will only take me a few days to pack the apartment and come back home, but he's welcome to see the ocean with us."

By now she was beaming, and I was utterly confused. "I don't understand."

"I'm moving to Michigan."

"You can't give up your job." I reeled from the package. I would not be a part of ruining her dreams. I would not—

"I can if I have an offer from United Press that stations me in West Michigan."

"West Michigan?" I sounded like a parrot, but I didn't care. "B-but—" I smacked the back of the couch. "Why would you want to stay here with a tongue-tied, half-deaf man?"

"Gideon Caleb Braum, you do realize that the king of England has a stammer, and no one thinks he's ill-equipped or stupid. He's a brilliant politician and, from all accounts, an attentive father. He sounds rather like you. So I think the question is more, 'who would be dumb enough *not* to love you?'"

I blinked, expecting Lennie to withdraw her question, to splutter some excuse. Instead, she stood stock-still, waiting, twirling a bit of mistletoe between her fingers.

The moon shimmered through a crack in the blackout curtains, highlighting the soft sparkle in Lennie's eyes.

"Uncle Gideon?" Enid tugged on my sleeve, breaking my dazed trance. "I think you're supposed to kiss her now."

And so, in the glow of Christmas lights and the promise of a future, Eleanor Sweers stepped into my arms and let me kiss her.

AUTHOR NOTES

THE BASIS BEHIND this story—that the Japanese launched bombs on the United States during WWII—is real. In 1944, the Japanese crafted enormous thirty-three-foot-wide balloons out of mulberry paper, then attached incendiary and antipersonnel bombs with hundreds of feet of line. The Fu-Go (Fire Balloon) attacks were launched into what we now call the jet stream, which had been discovered by a Japanese scientist and written about in an obscure language called Esperanto. Hundreds of balloons landed across the west coast of the United States and Canada, extending as far east as Michigan.

I've changed the timeline just a hair so my novella could take place during Christmas. In reality, the news embargo didn't begin until *Newsweek* and *Time* ran a story in January of 1945.

I also changed the timing of the balloons landing in Michigan. In fact, it was the spring of 1945 when one landed in a deserted lot in a suburb of Detroit, where the incendiary device burned most of the evidence. But another did really land in Dorr, Michigan—an area similar to Mapleview. The bombing mechanism for this one was no longer attached, and was discovered by schoolboys before being taken into custody by the government and kept quiet under the news embargo. I had Bitsy's lieutenant steal the balloon and create an explosion to cover up murder. But that, of course, is all a product of my wild imagination.

The Dorr balloon is at the Byron Center Historical Museum and is currently folded in an enormous wooden box waiting for funding in order to be displayed. Since I live just down the street from the museum, I was able to touch the box, but not the soft, kid-glove-like balloon itself. Perhaps some day. The most complete resource I've found about the Fu-Go balloons is Ross Coen's *Fu-Go: The Curious History of Japan's Balloon Bomb Attack on America*. For more information about the Dorr balloon or to lend your aid to the historical museum, contact the curator at the Byron Center Historical Museum in Byron Center, Michigan.

Until we meet again in the pages of a good book, happy reading and Merry Christmas.

The
Wondrous Gift

—◆—

DEBORAH RANEY

To our precious newest additions to the family,
Adler Truett Smith
and
Xander Blake Raney

And praise be to God, this *is the wondrous Gift that*
was given on that holy night:

For God so loved the world, that he gave his only Son,
that whoever believes in him should not perish but
have eternal life. For God did not send his Son into the
world to condemn the world, but in order that the world
might be saved through him.
—John 3:16–17

CHAPTER ONE

February

RACHEL HAMBLIN SPRINTED down the school's long corridor, slowing as she approached the teachers' lounge. A few students from sophomore study hall were working on a project in the music room after the last bell. She'd hesitated to leave them alone, but Howie, one of the janitors, said he'd keep an ear out from the hallway. The email had said this Tuesday faculty meeting was mandatory, so she didn't dare miss.

Taking slow breaths—a little dismayed at how out of shape she was—she composed herself and opened the door. The meeting hadn't started yet, but the lounge was abuzz with whispers. Most of the school board members were present, clustered in one corner of the small room. Judging by their sober expressions, it didn't appear as though they'd come bearing Valentine cookies and Starbucks cards the way they had last February.

A frisson of alarm rose inside her.

Caleb Janssen, math teacher and football coach, caught her eye across the room, and she threw him a questioning look. He answered with a shrug of his all-league-linebacker shoulders. Seriously, why did jocks insist on wearing clothes that were two sizes too small?

She made her way to the back of the room, where Mindy Laughlin sat twisting her long blond braid. Usually warm and talkative, her friend barely looked Rachel's way. *What* was going on?

But before she could ask, Headmaster Lockhardt entered the

room, rapping on the door. "Everyone, take a seat, please, and give me your attention." He rapped again, on the table this time, until the room grew silent.

Rachel slid into the chair beside Mindy.

Jerry Lockhardt cleared his throat and sighed deeply. "I'll get right to the point. As you've probably guessed, we have some . . . difficult news to deliver."

The twenty or so teachers and staff of the small, private Christian school exchanged worried glances, but they all looked as clueless as Rachel felt.

"Mr. Bronson, I'll give you the floor." Jerry stepped aside but remained at the front of the room while the school board president came forward.

Mr. Bronson took a folded slip of paper from the pocket of his suit coat. Without preamble, and without meeting anyone's gaze, he read from the page. "We, the school board, administrators, and advisors of Vanderburgh County Christian School, regret to inform you that as of the last day of the current term, Friday, the twenty-second of February, the school will close and all positions will be terminated."

Rachel gasped in unison with the other teachers. Vanderburgh was closing? And on the twenty-second? That was *next* Friday. Ten days! Could they even do that? And what about the students? Surely they weren't going to spring this on the kids—and their parents—with ten days' notice!

The school board president paused for a moment before returning to the paper in his hands—hands that trembled slightly now. "Any decision to close a school is distressing, of course. We understand that this profoundly affects you as teachers, but more importantly, our students, their parents, and in fact, the entire community of Mapleview and Vanderburgh County. However, after carefully—and prayerfully—reviewing all options, the board and our advisors have recommended that, due to declining enrollment and severe budget-ary restraints, it would be imprudent to continue operating at a sig-nificant loss with no options to recover in a timely manner . . ."

The man's voice droned on about economic necessity and the

process of transitioning for students, until all Rachel heard was *blah blah blah blah*. The bottom line: their school was closing and she would be without a job. Practically in the middle of a school year.

The teachers sitting here with her—her *friends*—were now her competition for whatever jobs might be available. She cringed at the thought. This time of year, in a little town like Mapleview, they'd be lucky to find substitute teaching positions or private tutoring jobs.

Or you could teach private music lessons.

She startled at the silent voice that didn't really sound like her own. But it was true. From the time she was a little girl, she'd "taught" countless stuffed bears and puppies and a floppy-eared bunny, who refused to sit up straight at the piano bench. She loved teaching music here at VCCS, but teaching private lessons had always been her ultimate goal—piano, flute, voice. She could even teach violin if she brushed up a little. Never mind that the neighbors in her small apartment complex had requested she refrain from playing her own piano between the hours of five p.m. and eight a.m. It didn't leave much leeway, and her beloved baby grand—a college graduation gift from her parents—was feeling the neglect.

Still, she couldn't blame her neighbors. Mozart wasn't everyone's cup of tea. Although, when the apartment manager had delivered the edict, she'd been tempted to request that in return the neighbors refrain from blaring their TVs at 150 decibels during the hours *she* was home.

Mr. Bronson distributed thick envelopes and quickly moved to severance packages. Rachel scrambled to do some quick math. She had a reasonably healthy savings account—enough for a down payment on a house that, thank the Lord, she hadn't bought yet. It would be foolish to eat up all her savings trying to make it through to the next school year, but maybe if she rented a place downtown to teach lessons . . .

No, she'd checked into that possibility before she started this teaching job three years ago. She couldn't *begin* to live on the meager profits she'd see after paying to lease a building. Besides, most of the places she'd checked into adjoined office space and would require her to soundproof the place if she was going to teach piano.

Then again, maybe this *was* the time to buy that house. It would be both an investment and a place to offer lessons. And play her piano to her heart's content. It'd been a while since she'd checked the real estate market, but she'd do that as soon as she got home tonight. She might have to give up the idea of the two-story, three-bedroom cottage she'd decorated a thousand times in her dreams, but at least she wouldn't be throwing away money on rent anymore. That would make her parents happy.

Her heart sank at the thought of telling Mom and Dad about losing her job. They would be devastated for her.

The screech of chairs on the old linoleum floor brought her reverie to a halt. She turned to Mindy. "Wait . . . what did I miss?"

Her friend's eyes were red-rimmed as she held a sheaf of papers in her hand. "You mean the part where we don't have jobs? Or the part where they will only entertain written questions?"

"They said that?"

"Rachel." Mindy shook her head and held up the envelope. "Did you read this?"

"No . . ." She stared at the unopened envelope in her own hands. "I don't know, I guess I'm kind of in shock."

"Same here." Mindy's tears started again. "I can't even believe this is happening. Were there rumors somewhere along the way? Something I missed?"

"If there were, I missed them too. You saw how shocked everybody was. What do you think you'll do, Mindy?"

"I have no idea. Substitute, I guess. But I can't think of any job I'd dread more, except maybe cleaning toilets at a bar."

Rachel laughed, remembering the journey her friend had taken to finally become a teacher. "You speak from experience."

"Oh, Rachel. This is horrible. I mean, at least we can finish the term and they're prorating for our summer pay, but—"

"That's only ten days away. I don't get why they couldn't get us through the rest of the school year."

Her friend nodded. "Then we'd be on even footing when it comes time to apply for teaching positions next year."

"Maybe this will actually give us a foot up." Caleb Janssen gave an apologetic wave and stepped closer. "For finding new teaching positions. Sorry. Didn't mean to butt in on your conversation, but I couldn't help but overhear."

"It's okay." Mindy brushed at her cheek with the back of her hand. "So what about you, Caleb? What will you do? Man! I just hate to think about losing all you guys. This is the best school I've ever taught in." Her gaze swept the room. "And we didn't even have time to plan a going-away party."

Caleb patted Mindy's back. "Hey, nothing says we can't still do that. We could even throw a party for the kids."

Why was he so chipper? Rachel shot him a look. Jocks could be so clueless. "I don't think any of us are going to be in the mood for a party. Especially not the kids. Not to mention, who could afford to party now?"

"Did I hear *party*?" Della Grandin, who'd taught English and Literature since VCCS's inception, joined their little group. "We need something to cheer us up."

Rachel's concern deepened at the worry on Della's face. "What will you do, Della?" This would likely be harder on Della than on any of them, especially since the woman had lost her husband a few months ago.

Della patted Rachel's shoulder. "You know what, honey? I'm sixty-seven years old. Maybe this is the good Lord's way of telling me it's time to retire."

"Way to think positively!" Caleb crowed. "Hey, I'm *twenty*-seven. You think the good Lord might be telling me the same?"

Della's frown said she worried he might be serious.

Caleb's good humor gnawed at Rachel. This was no time for jokes.

But he pulled the older teacher into a side hug. "Just kidding. I'll put in a hard forty and earn my retirement like you did."

"You kids will be fine." Della said it with such conviction Rachel could almost believe it. "And if you need a reference, you know I'll happily vouch for each one of you. It's the students I'm worried about.

What are they supposed to do with their last term? I've never heard of such a thing."

"The school must really be in deep financial trouble," Caleb said.

Mindy frowned. "Was enrollment really down that much from last year? That they'd close the school?"

"Oh, it was down." Della clucked her tongue. "What did they expect, raising tuition two terms in a row? That's not sustainable."

"Interesting, given that I haven't had a raise since I started here." Sarcasm tinged Caleb's voice.

Rachel glanced around the room to be sure they weren't being overheard. Another group of teachers whispered among themselves, but the school board members and administrators had disappeared. "I'm sure there were a lot of families that just couldn't afford to keep having the prices hiked. Especially those with several kids in the school, even with a discount." Now those families would probably either put their kids in public school or homeschool.

If so, some of them might now have the funds for private lessons. The possibility filled her with hope. Maybe unrealistic hope?

"Who wants to go out for drinks?" Caleb raised his voice including the rest of the teachers. "We can commiserate over coffee. Or something stronger—like root beer—if need be."

"I'm in," Rachel and Della said together, over the murmur of the other teachers. It would be good to unpack everything they'd learned today. Maybe find out if some of the others knew any more details. Surely someone had had an inkling this was coming.

"I'm going to bow out, but you guys have fun." Looking defeated, Mindy gathered up her things and left amid a chorus of goodbyes.

Rachel stared at the doorway after Mindy's departure. Not that this wasn't plenty serious, but Mindy was taking it extra hard. Rachel's heart went out to her friend.

"You two can ride with me." Caleb put an arm lightly around her and Della's shoulders, ushering them into the hallway. "Get your coats and I'll meet you in the parking lot."

"I need to grab some papers to grade too, but it won't take me long." Rachel swung by her classroom, which, thankfully, was empty, and shrugged into her coat. She grabbed her purse and travel mug, along with a stack of essays on the Renaissance composers, then hurried to the parking lot. But as she and Della walked toward Caleb's car, Della's phone rang.

After a short conversation, she hung up with a sigh. "You guys go on. My daughter needs a last-minute babysitter. I may just have found my next calling," she teased.

"See you tomorrow, Della." Caleb went around and opened the passenger door for Rachel.

She climbed in, feeling awkward now that it was just the two of them. Last she'd heard, Caleb had a girlfriend. She didn't want to start any rumors. Not that he was her type at all. He was a jock. A PE teacher. And a math nerd. Probably her two least favorite subjects from elementary school through college. The only thing they had in common—well, besides their faith—was Vanderburgh County Christian School.

And now they wouldn't even have that.

She pulled the seat belt over her waist. "Do the others know where we're meeting?"

"I assume the usual. Paddy's?"

She hadn't heard anyone say, and she didn't often go out with the handful of teachers who sometimes gathered at the Irish pub–style restaurant for coffee or pop after work. "I guess I didn't know there *was* a 'usual.'"

"That's where they still meet, from what I hear. We don't have to go there, though. Is there someplace you'd rather go? Are you hungry?"

"I've kind of lost my appetite. But I'm fine with Paddy's. If you still want to go . . ."

"Sure!" He turned his key in the ignition and the late-model Highlander purred.

"This is nice." She ran a hand over the leather upholstery.

"Yeah, well, don't spill anything on it. It will probably be going on the block after today's news."

"Really? You might sell your car?"

"The payments on this thing already stretch me a little thinner than I'd like." He grinned. "You want to buy it?"

"Ha ha." She couldn't manufacture a smile. She hadn't even thought about where she could cut back if she didn't find another job right away. Her car payment seemed like a good place to start. But the thought of selling her car and trying to find another one—older and potentially unreliable—sent a strange panic through her. She'd taken so much for granted. Maybe she should take a cue from Mindy and be even more worried than she felt right now.

They drove in silence the rest of the way to Paddy's and, by the time they arrived, she was regretting her decision to go out with the group. All she really wanted to do right now was go home and make a new budget—as if she'd ever really lived by any budget she'd come up with. But she had to explore whether buying a house was even a remote possibility. Because if it wasn't, teaching private lessons was out of the question.

A sudden thought stabbed at her. What made her think she'd be able to get a mortgage when she didn't even have a job? Yes, she had a nice chunk saved for a down payment, but she would still have to come up with the same amount of money she was paying in rent—if not more—for a house payment.

And what if she bought a house but couldn't get enough private students to pay the bills? Mapleview was no metropolis.

And if she bought a house in town, then she'd be stuck here, maybe with few teaching prospects and no way to—

She rubbed her temple, trying to stave off the anxious thoughts bombarding her.

"You okay?"

The way Caleb looked at her made her wonder if her mascara was smeared or something. "I'm fine. Just thinking."

"Well, let's go think over coffee, okay?"

Chapter Two

CALEB OPENED THE door to the downtown bar and grill and motioned for Rachel to enter first. He hadn't seen any familiar cars in the small parking lot, but the other teachers may have carpooled and parked on the street in front.

The restaurant was dark and noisy, the bar nearly empty.

"Two of you? For the bar?" The hostess grabbed silverware rolled in green napkins.

"No, we'd like a table." The school frowned on teachers being seen in a bar but didn't comment as long as no one actually sat *at* the bar. It wasn't as though Mapleview had a lot of choices for restaurants. "We might hold off a bit though," he told the hostess. "We're waiting for friends." Looking past the girl, he still didn't see anyone from the school.

"Oh, I can go ahead and seat you. We're not busy yet. How many in your party?"

"I'm not sure. Maybe six or eight?" He felt a touch at his elbow.

"Maybe we shouldn't take up a table until we see how many show up," Rachel suggested.

"Sure." Caleb turned back to the hostess. "We'll wait a bit." He motioned to a long L-shaped bench in the front window.

Rachel sat on one side, and he took a seat perpendicular to hers. She scanned the dining room. "Are you sure this is where they were coming?"

"I'm beginning to wonder." He pulled off his gloves, stuffed them in his pocket, and checked his phone. Almost four thirty. "Do you want to call somebody and see where they are?"

She chewed a corner of her bottom lip. "I'm starting to think I just want to go home and work on a budget."

He laughed. "Um . . . you kind of need to have an income to create a budget."

She rolled her eyes. "Let me rephrase that. I need to go home and start selling all my earthly goods on Craigslist. Or Facebook Marketplace. Or wherever you do stuff like that these days."

"Don't do anything rash. Not yet, anyway."

"Hey, you're the one who was spouting off about selling your car."

"True, but I was thinking about doing that before this ever happened. I had no business buying that car—which my dad tried to tell me."

She laughed. "Doesn't it tick you off when parents are right?"

"Except they usually are."

She nodded as if she actually understood, then her expression turned serious. "What will you do? I mean, what's the first thing we should all be doing?"

"Well, we do have a little time. Paychecks don't end until April, and they'll be a little higher with the summer payments figured in early. At least that's how I read it. Have you looked over the letter?"

She shook her head.

"We should be able to find something until positions open for next year."

"But what if we don't? It's not like Mapleview is teeming with schools."

She was right about that. With a population of four thousand, the town had two elementary schools, a middle school, and one public high school. And the coaches there had all held their positions for a hundred years. "Maybe we'll all end up in Grand Rapids. Or Kalamazoo. We could commute. It's not that far."

"It is if you don't have your car."

He caught the gentle sarcasm in her voice and smiled. If he had to be in this particular boat, he was glad she was in it with him.

She groaned. "Maybe if there was an opening in Dorr or Vanderburgh Center, but I just do not want to teach in the city."

"No, me neither. We've had it good here. Mapleview turns out great kids. Case in point." He pointed back to himself.

That eye roll again. "There are always exceptions. But you're right. These are good kids. I feel so sorry for them."

He briefly touched her coat sleeve. "Hey . . . It'll all work out, okay? I'm sure of it."

"How can you be so sure?"

"Well, first of all, I'm trusting that God must have a reason for this. And if he does, then it'll be a good one."

"And if he doesn't? We do live in a fallen world, you know."

"He has a reason, Rachel. It might feel like a Plan B to us, but it's not like this took him by surprise. Just have faith, okay?"

"Wow. Thanks for making me look like a worthless, untrusting heathen." A tiny spark flashed in her brown eyes.

He laughed. He'd never seen this side of Rachel Hamblin. And he kind of liked it.

She always came off as just a tiny bit stuck-up. The cultured city girl with her perfect diction and no-frills wardrobe. He'd always seen her as kind of a plain Jane, as his mom would have said.

"So . . ." He risked another question. "If money was no object and you could have any job you wanted, what would you do?"

The look she threw him held . . . was it suspicion?

He shrugged. "Hey, they say crisis always brings opportunity. Seems like as good a time as any to at least think about what your dream job would be."

She gave a wry smile. "At this point, I think my dream job is *a* job. Any job. Walmart greeter, hamburger flipper . . ."

"Come on. Humor me." He waited.

"Well, this one is out of the question, but I've always wanted to teach music. As in private lessons. Piano, flute, maybe voice."

"You sing? Oh, duh. Of course you do. You're the music teacher."

"Was. Past tense. I *was* the music teacher."

"You still are. For ten more days."

She acknowledged the comment with yet another eye roll, then absently slipped the elastic from her ponytail. For a split second, her dark hair fell across her shoulders in a wave. He hadn't realized her hair was so long. In fact, he wasn't sure he'd ever seen her hair down. But with a twist of her wrist, she swept the shiny mane into a neat coil that rested at the base of her long neck. "And yes, I sing. Just not in public."

"Not in class?"

"Well, of course. I have to sing in class. But I don't do solos."

"Got it. Okay, so you want to teach private lessons. Why would that be out of the question?"

"Because I live in an apartment building. I can't even play my own piano except between the hours of eight and five."

He did the math. "Doesn't give you many options, huh?"

"No. It does not."

"So, why don't you rent a place? To give lessons, I mean."

"I already checked into that a while back. I'd have to teach about twenty hours a week just to pay the rent. And I'd have to soundproof the place and . . . Just trust me. It's not really feasible."

"Would your church let you teach there?"

She shook her head. "My church houses a day care, and we have stuff going on there pretty much twenty-four seven."

"What about a different church? I could ask the deacons at mine for you."

She wrinkled her nose. "I wouldn't really feel right using a church I didn't attend."

"Why not? They'd probably be thrilled to have the building used that way, and I doubt they'd charge much, if anything. I'd be happy to vouch for you."

"No." She seemed surprised at the volume of her own voice. "Sorry. I didn't mean to . . . I just don't think it would work, okay? I'd need to teach full-time. There'd just be too many roadblocks."

"Of your own making," he muttered.

She ignored his comment, or else pretended not to hear. "Okay, your turn. What would you do if money were no object?"

"That's easy. I'd open a gym. Be a personal trainer."

The face she made said it all.

"Hey, now. Hang on. What do you have against personal trainers?"

She at least had the decency to blush. "I'm sorry. That was rude."

"Yes, it was. But it was apparently an honest reaction. So what's your beef with personal trainers?"

"Um . . . the beef?" The twinkle in her brown eyes took him by surprise. In twenty minutes of waiting for friends at a restaurant, he'd gotten to know more about her than he had in almost two years working together at the same school. Not that coaches and music teachers traveled in the same circles in academia, but Vanderburgh was a small school. And he would have considered her a friend. Would have told people he knew her well if her name came up among mutual acquaintances.

His laughter was delayed but genuine.

"Just now get the joke, did you?"

"Just now getting that you know *how* to joke."

"Talk about rude!"

"Not an insult. Just an observation." He grinned. "And quit changing the subject. Tell me what you don't like about personal trainers."

"Where do I even start?" She held up a finger. "Number one, they make you sweat. Number two, they're jocks, totally full of themselves. Three, they have a . . . reputation. Four, they—"

"What? Wait a minute. What are you even talking about? A reputation? I'm a jock and I am not full of myself. And when have I ever made you sweat?"

"You're doing a pretty good job of it right now."

He laughed, but he wasn't going to let her get away with not answering his question. "What kind of reputation are you talking about?"

"You know."

He cocked his head and studied her. "You mean the one where they help people get in shape and stay healthy? The one where they encourage and motivate people to be their best? Or are you talking about the one where they give people a reason to feel good about—"

"Okay, okay. Perhaps you make some good points. But sorry. When you say personal trainer, I see a fawning coed batting her eyelashes while said trainer flexes his muscles while pretending he's not flexing his muscles." She flexed her own jacket-clad bicep and gave it a comical squeeze.

"Pretty good imitation there. But some of us don't have to pretend." Her expression told him his joke had fallen flat, and he wished he'd kept his mouth shut. An awkward few seconds crawled by.

Thankfully the hostess chose that moment to check in with them. "Still waiting?"

Caleb panned the room again, then looked to Rachel. "I have a feeling we're in the wrong place." *No pun intended.*

The hostess motioned toward the back of the restaurant. "I have a table for two. I could seat you now."

He cocked his head. "Do you want to stay?"

Rachel looked conflicted.

"We've got some great specials tonight, and you can still order from the lunch menu if you like." The perky hostess was flirting, talking only to him, completely disregarding Rachel, which did not help his cause with Rachel Hamblin.

And suddenly, he *had* a cause with her.

Ignoring the hostess in return, he raised an eyebrow at Rachel. "Want to get out of here?"

She nodded a little too vigorously and turned toward the door, not even looking to see if he was following.

CHAPTER THREE

THE SKY WAS already streaked with sunset when they stepped out onto the sidewalk. Rachel pulled in a breath that soon released in a cloud of steam in front of her face. She wrapped her coat tighter around her and fished her mittens from her pocket, strangely glad to be out in the frigid February air. The streetlights flickered up and down Main Street, not quite full-on bright yet, but working on it. Apparently, the other teachers had gone somewhere else, and girl-friend or not, it had started to feel a little awkward being alone with Caleb. Especially when the flirty hostess tried to seat them at a table for two.

She'd been glad when he made an excuse to leave the restaurant, even if it stung a little bit that he seemed so eager to end the evening. It shouldn't have, though. She'd never seen Caleb Janssen as any-thing more than a fellow teacher. A decent guy—as jocks went. But that was all. No doubt, he felt the same about her—a fellow teacher, nothing more. So why was she suddenly so disappointed that their time together had come to an abrupt end?

"Do you want to try to find the others or . . . ?" His gloved hand rested lightly at the small of her back, steering her toward his car.

"If you don't mind too much, I'd rather you take me back to my car."

"Sure thing."

She fell into step beside him, his swift agreement confirming her earlier suspicions. "I've got essays to grade." Why did she think she owed him an excuse?

"Not that it matters."

"What do you mean?"

"Just that I don't think we owe the board anything after what they've done to all of us. I don't really feel like knocking myself out for them, you know?"

"But it does matter! These poor kids are already getting the shaft."

Caleb raked a hand through his hair. "No, no, that came out wrong. Of course I wouldn't take it out on the kids. I didn't mean that."

"I wonder what they'll do. Mapleview doesn't have that many options."

"I'm guessing most of them will be fine. The ones who were home-schooled will probably go back to that until next year. My players are going to have plenty to say about it, but at least they didn't have their seasons cut short like the basketball team did."

She nodded. "The whole thing stinks. Especially for the seniors."

"At least they get to graduate."

"They do?"

"Oh, that's right. You haven't read the letter yet." He punched the key fob and opened the passenger door for her. Before today, she'd never taken him for the chivalrous type.

"Guess I'd better go home and do that. Read the letter." She climbed in and he closed her door and ran around to slip behind the wheel.

"Yeah, I need to read it again. I just skimmed it during the meeting. But it did say that all our seniors had enough credits to graduate and that accommodations would be made so they could hold a graduation ceremony at"—he formed quotation marks in the air—"a place to be decided at a future date."

She frowned. "That sounds like it won't be at the school. Somebody else must have already leased the building."

"Wouldn't be surprised. If only it were another school that would hire us all back."

She gaped at him, hope sparking in her chest. "Do you think that's a possibility?"

He shook his head. "I doubt it. If that was the case, VCCS surely would have just consolidated with them. And they would have told us, so we could put in our applications with the new school."

She blew out a breath, deflated. "I guess it's back to square one."

"Back to our dream jobs. You don't need a personal trainer, do you?" He took his eyes off the road long enough to cast her a sideways smirk.

"Not unless you're wanting to take piano lessons."

"Oooh, um . . . I don't think so."

"Yeah, that's what I thought." Still, she couldn't help but laugh. "But hey, don't let me keep you from your fantasy. I'm sure you'll be the exception to the rule."

"And what rule is that?"

"We already discussed this. The one that decrees all personal trainers flex their muscles for attention. And generally have a sleazy reputation."

"Sleazy? Seriously? You're going there?"

She laughed again. "Okay, I might want to check a dictionary first. How about *questionable*? A questionable reputation. You buy that?"

"No, I don't buy that." Despite the huffiness in his tone, she could tell he was enjoying this conversation.

She was too, and she actually was beginning to regret that she'd asked him to take her back. They were almost to the school parking lot, and she didn't want to go home and spend the rest of the evening with the dark thoughts that would surely come as she read through the letter detailing her bleak future in stark black-and-white type.

Caleb slowed the car and pulled into the school parking lot, scrambling to think how he could continue this evening for a while longer. He might talk a good talk, but he wasn't ready to go home to his empty apartment—and no, Wayne the Wonder Cat didn't count. His feline companion wasn't nearly as good a listener as Rachel. "Do you . . . want to drive through for coffee somewhere?"

She made a face he couldn't quite read in the dim of the car's interior. "If you do."

He shrugged. "Up to you." Her enthusiasm was underwhelming.

"I'd probably better get home. Read the letter. Look over my budget."

"Okay. Me too. Look over the budget."

"And look into opening up that gym of yours?" That twinkle in her eyes again. Almost mischievous. Who knew?

"It might be a tad premature for that. I'll give it a couple of days."

She snickered, then quickly stifled it.

"No, it's okay. You can laugh."

"If that's what you want to do next, I hope it works out. I really mean that, Caleb."

"Thanks. I appreciate it. But before I make a complete hypocrite of myself, I probably should make a confession."

"Confession? Do I look like a priest?"

He snorted. "No, but I don't want you coming back and saying, 'Told you so.'"

She looked askance at him. "Okay . . . what's the confession?"

He feigned a serious expression and must have succeeded, judging by her sober countenance. "Well, you accused me—actually, you broad-brushed all personal trainers—of being womanizers and—"

"That is *not* what I said. I said—"

"Okay, okay, of having only beautiful women for clients."

She nodded.

"Well, true confession, my first client *was* a beautiful woman. She's the reason I got into it in the first place."

"See? I rest my case." She tipped her head and studied him. "So you have worked as a personal trainer before?"

"Sort of. It's—"

"How beautiful are we talking? Like supermodel gorgeous? Which, by the way, don't you have a girlfriend?"

"We broke up." He waved off her question. "Ancient history."

"How ancient?"

"April, I think it was. No, May. Right before the end of school last year. Why?" He could almost see her counting the months on her fingers.

Apparently satisfied, she met his gaze. "Just checking. I don't make a habit of hanging out with other women's boyfriends."

"That's a nice quality in a woman."

"It is, isn't it?" she gloated. "Now, back to the subject at hand. The subject you keep changing, I might add. Just how beautiful was this first client? Are we talking Miss Michigan runner-up? Miss Universe?"

He huffed, feigning scorn. "Nothing like that. But I can honestly say, she's the most beautiful woman I've ever known." That was true, although the one sitting in his passenger seat was starting to look like stiff competition. "It felt like I'd known her my whole life."

"And did you ask her out?" She hesitated. "Ahh, wait. Don't tell me: it was your girlfriend. Your ancient-history ex, I mean."

"Oh, no. I would never train a woman I was dating. Or date a woman I was training."

"Well, that's comforting. I guess?"

He groaned. He'd set himself up and he was getting in too deep. "If you must know, my first client was my mother."

"Oh." She seemed at a loss for words but finally sputtered. "Well, that's okay then."

He smirked. "Glad I have your permission."

"I didn't mean it that way."

"Sure sounded like you did."

She ignored that and glared at him. But that hint of mischief still danced in her gaze. "So, your beautiful mom was your first client? Next you're going to claim that's where you get your chiseled good looks."

"You should see my dad." He gave an exaggerated shrug. "I was just destined to be ruggedly handsome."

She rolled her eyes.

But didn't refute him. Hmm.

"How'd you end up being a teacher? Why aren't you still a personal trainer? If that's your dream job and all?"

"At the risk of lowering your opinion of me further, I mostly went into teaching so I could coach."

"You couldn't do that without a teaching degree? And be a trainer too?"

"Maybe. But to set the record straight, I never really was in business as a trainer. Not officially. I'd still need to get certified. But yeah, Mom was my first and only client. She . . . passed away. Cancer."

Rachel gave a little gasp and laid her hand over her heart. "I didn't know."

"Of course not. You wouldn't."

"How long ago?"

"It'll be four years in June."

"I'm so sorry." She looked genuinely stunned.

Her sympathy took him by surprise, and he swallowed back the lump that lodged in his throat. "It's not as if it happened yesterday." Even though it sometimes still felt that way.

"No, but I'm sure it's still hard."

"It was a tough few years. I'll say that much."

"Is your dad still living?"

And there it was. The million-dollar question. He blew out a breath. "If you could call it that."

She frowned. "I don't understand."

"He's alive. But he . . . Dad kind of quit actually living when my mom died."

"Oh wow. Caleb, I'm so sorry. I didn't know any of this."

He sighed and slouched against the seat. "I didn't mean to unload on you. It's not . . . your concern."

"But it matters."

Wow, she put it well. It *did* matter. A great deal. "It was kind of like a two for one. I lost them both when Mom died." His voice was getting rougher and the moisture gathering behind his eyelids made him desperate to change the subject.

She must have sensed that because she did it for him. "Why did your mom need a personal trainer? Because of the cancer? Or did you help her before that?"

"It was after her mastectomy. Double mastectomy. Mom ran track in high school, and she was a runner as long as I can remember. Dad says she had me in a jogging stroller when I was three days old. But the surgery threw her balance off. She went through physical therapy, but she was still struggling, so I went to the gym with her one day and I guess it made a difference." He shrugged, still not sure why he'd been able to help Mom so much. But he had. And those seven months—until the cancer came back—had been the sweetest time with her. He knew it was a big part of the reason he dreamed of being a personal trainer. A professional one. But this was the first time he'd ever told anyone.

"That is so cool. You must have a gift." She winced. "And I officially take back everything I said about personal trainers."

He narrowed his eyes and affected a glare. "Every rude thing."

"I was rude." She dipped her head. "I apologize."

"No problem. I know you were just kidding."

She cleared her throat. "Actually, I wasn't. But I *am* sorry now. No excuse. I made a rash judgment on something I know nothing about."

"Don't be too hard on yourself."

"Okay. I'm off the hook then." She winked, lightening the mood.

"Um, you could be a *little* hard on yourself."

"I will," she said with conviction. "I promise." She reached for the door handle. "I should go. I need to call my parents and tell them what happened."

"They're in Kansas City, right?"

She looked surprised. "Yes. How did you know that?"

"You've mentioned it before. When your mom sent cookies to the teachers last Christmas."

"Well, it's not like news of Podunk Mapleview, Michigan, ever makes it to Kansas City, but knowing my mom, she probably reads the *Mapleview Messenger* online on a regular basis, and I'd hate for her to see the news there before I have a chance to tell her."

"No. That wouldn't be good. And I'm guessing it will be in the paper Thursday."

She nodded. "Yes, I'd better call them tonight."

"Well, tell them not to worry. It'll all turn out okay."

"I wish I had your confidence."

"Hey, if you'd just embrace your dream job, you too could be as cocky and, er, I mean as *confident* and certain of your future as I am." He wished he wasn't just joking.

She opened her door and a gust of cold air blew in. "You're a nut. You know that, right?"

"Know it and own it." He threw her a smug look. "A health nut."

"Goodnight." Chuckling, she started to get out. Then she turned back to face him. "And Caleb? Thank you. I'm really glad you suggested going out for coffee. Earlier."

"Even though we never did have any coffee?"

She nodded, apparently not willing to let him push her thank-you aside with a joke. "Even though."

She slammed the car door and strode to her own car before he could think of a comeback.

Chapter Four

Rachel's apartment was cold and dim, and the offbeat syncopation of some awful heavy metal music upstairs rattled the windows. If whoever lived above her could've heard over the din, she'd have given them a heavy dose of Beethoven on her baby grand. Sadly, with all the racket, sweet Mrs. Cosine in the apartment below would be the only one who'd be able to hear the piano, and that wouldn't be very neighborly.

Rachel walked through the space, turning on lights and cranking up the thermostat until the furnace kicked on. She felt guilty even as she relished the warm air wafting up from the vent in the bathroom. Her electric bill was probably one place she could cut back, at least until she knew for sure she had another source of income.

She notched the thermostat down two degrees, grabbed a sweatshirt from her closet, and went to put the kettle on. While she waited for the water to boil, she read through the board's letter, which didn't have much information beyond what she'd already heard at the meeting and from Caleb. Mostly it detailed how the release from their teaching contracts would work, stating the dates of the last day of school and the workday following. It irritated her a little that the contract was so easy for the school to get out of. No doubt it would have been a black mark on her resumé if she'd tried to get out of her contract early.

Spirits sinking, she fixed a cup of hot tea and took it and her phone out to the living room to call her parents. Dad rarely had his phone with him, so she dialed Mom, even though it was her dad she'd really rather talk to. Mom would only feel sorry for her and try to coax her to come home.

But she couldn't even let herself think about leaving Mapleview. She'd grown to love this little town. She felt like she belonged here, and she'd been foolish enough to imagine that she might settle down, eventually get married, have some babies, and raise them in Mapleview, watch them graduate from VCCS . . .

Her mom's voice came through the phone, but it was only her voicemail. Rachel hung up without leaving a message and dialed Dad.

Voicemail again. She hoped they weren't working too much overtime. They were supposedly in the process of training their assistant manager to take over the music store they ran, so they could eventually retire. But last time they'd talked, Mom told her that Dad had been putting in fifty hours a week since Christmas.

She waited for Dad's voicemail to finish, then hesitated. Maybe she could just hang up. But they'd be worried if they saw she'd tried to call each of them. "Hey, Dad. I'm going to bed early, but if you get this in the next ten minutes or so, give me a call back, would you? I tried Mom, but no answer." She forced a brightness she didn't feel into her tone. "I hope you're out doing something fun and *not* working. Talk to you later. Love you."

She hung up and set her phone on the coffee table. At least she could tell them she'd tried. She grabbed her laptop and settled in on the sofa. After pulling up her favorite real estate website, she entered a new set of parameters. She'd been looking in a price range that assumed her current salary and a nice down payment for that three-bedroom, two-bath house. But the truth was she could get by with something smaller and just teach out of her living room. One or two bedrooms and one bath would give her as much space and twice the freedom that she had here. And she could hold back some of her savings to serve as a cushion until she had enough students.

Thirteen homes popped up and she scrolled through the selection.

A couple of expensive townhomes with monthly HOAs as high as her current rent. A handful of fixer-uppers that looked altogether *un*fixable. She didn't have time for that. She needed something that was essentially move-in ready.

She deleted seven properties from her watch list. And then another one, after realizing it was fifteen miles outside of town. She refreshed the page and checked again. That left her with five possibilities that fit her criteria. She looked at two ranch houses, neither of which had been updated since the eighties. But she wasn't giving up. She might have to live with something a little outdated until she could afford to—

A two-story brick beauty appeared on the screen. She double-checked her search fields. Either that house had popped up in error, or it was gutted inside.

She clicked quickly through the photos of the exterior and her mouth dropped when the first photo of the main floor loaded. *What?* There was no way this place was in her price range. But a quick scroll to the top of the page assured her it was. At her upper limit, but with her down payment and if she took out a thirty-year loan, her monthly payment wouldn't be that much more than she was paying now.

She clicked back to the interior images, her eyes growing wider with every flick of her thumb pad. Hardwood floors, exposed brick, open floor plan . . . She couldn't have imagined a house that fit her better.

The lone bedroom was on the second floor, but it was huge as bedrooms went, and it opened onto a lofted space that would make a fabulous home office or a place to watch movies when friends came over. The kitchen on the first floor was tiny, but she wasn't about to let that deter her. Besides, the only time she cooked was when her parents came to visit. And given that Kansas City was a nine-hour drive away, that didn't happen often.

She scrolled through the photos a second time and a third, then read the detailed description more carefully, growing more excited by the second. The building was even zoned for office space, so no one should have a problem if she had piano students coming and going, parking on the street out front. There had to be a catch, though. She forced herself to contain her enthusiasm. There had to be some huge issue the photos were hiding.

According to the listing, the building had served as a school for Mapleview until the 1960s. "Well, how cool is that?" she whispered. And that would explain the fact that a section of the living room was on a higher level—what had been a stage at the old school for plays and musicals, according to the listing. It would be the perfect place for her beloved baby grand. And for student recitals!

She scanned the information once more.

Ah, no wonder. The building had only been on the market for three days. She held her breath and refreshed the page, fully expecting to see the dreaded *Pending* label.

But nothing changed.

Feeling humbled, she shook her head. "Lord? Are you trying to tell me something?" Wouldn't that be just like God to see to it that the perfect house was waiting for her just when she needed it?

But there had to be a catch. This was way too good to be true. She didn't really remember seeing the building downtown. Surely she would have noticed this gem, with its arched windows and the Dutch-style brick pattern that was typical of this part of Michigan. Especially if there'd been a *For Sale* sign in front of it.

Feeling brave—or maybe desperate—she rummaged in her desk drawer for the business card of a real estate agent she'd found tacked to the bulletin board in the laundry room. She copied the email address into a new message and sent a short note expressing interest in the Visser School property. Whether she heard back from the woman or not, she would leave for school half an hour early in the morning and drive by the place. Hopefully that would tell her why it was on the market at such a reasonable price.

Maybe it needed all the plumbing and electrical replaced. Or the images were deceptive, and the place was actually the size of a postage stamp. Still, if it had once been a school, it couldn't be *too* small.

But would the bank give her a loan without a job? It would definitely help that she had almost thirty thousand dollars in savings.

She wasn't sure which step to take first. But she couldn't let this place get away.

An idea struck. If she ran an ad in the *Messenger* saying she was taking piano and voice students, say, beginning March 1, she might be able to get a decent lineup before she had to talk to the bank about a loan. Then she would have a forecasted income.

She frowned. March was less than two weeks away and closings weren't famous for going off without a hitch. Maybe if she said March 15, she could still fill a roster with guaranteed income but hold off on actually beginning lessons until April. If she wasn't in the house by then, she'd feel more comfortable asking her church if she could use their facility for a few weeks until she was moved into the new place. *Her* new place. A shiver went down her spine.

She opened a new document on her laptop and typed furiously, making notes as fast as they came into her head. Maybe she was crazy. But she had a good feeling about this. A really good feeling.

Losing her job just might be the best thing that had ever happened to her.

------------>◦<------------

Caleb popped a coffee pod in the machine and skimmed the newspaper, waiting for his coffee to brew.

"Looking at the 'Help Wanted' section?" Jed Palmer pointed to the paper spread out on the table in the teacher's lounge.

He scoffed. "Got to beat you to the good jobs, don't you know?" Jed taught history and was the high school basketball coach. And a good one, but Caleb didn't really see him as the football-coach type. Still, desperate times and all that.

Jed raised his hands in surrender. "I'm not your competition, bud."

"Actually . . ." Caleb hesitated. He hadn't really intended to tell anyone his plans until he had a better idea if they were even feasible. But Jed might be interested in doing some kind of partnership. "Let me run something by you. I'm still thinking on it, but hear me out, will you?"

Jed straddled a chair, his expression saying he was listening.

"Now, again, I'm just exploring the possibilities, so don't say anything to anybody else or—"

"Hey, your secret's safe with me."

"I'm looking into possibly taking on some clients. Becoming a personal trainer. Maybe open a small gym. Mostly strength and conditioning, but maybe even something with nutrition. I've still got a lot of research to do, but . . . that wouldn't be something you'd be interested in partnering on, would it?"

Jed started shaking his head before Caleb even finished talking. "Sorry, man. I've already got something lined up."

"You dog!" Caleb clapped the coach on the shoulder. "That was quick. Can you say where? Will you and Jody be moving?" Jed surely hadn't found a coaching job around here already. Unless he'd been talking to someone before they got yesterday's news. But Jody was a nurse. She could work anywhere.

"No, no, Jody would never leave her sisters. It's here in town."

"Coaching?" He swallowed back an unexpected surge of jealousy. They'd known about the school closing for barely twenty-four hours. How on earth had Jed landed a position already? Unless he'd been looking before the edict came down—or he had some insider knowledge.

"No. Actually, I'm going a whole different direction."

"Oh?"

Jed gave a small laugh. "Our church has been looking for a youth pastor for a while now. I talked to the elders last night, and they hired me on the spot."

Caleb felt a little guilty that relief was his first reaction. But it quickly turned to genuine celebration for Jed. "That's great, man! Wow! Pastor Palmer, huh?"

"Now don't go crazy. Pastor Jed will do." His laughter faded and he shook his head. "I'm taking a whale of a cut in pay, but Jody's really happy about it, so that's something."

"A cut in pay?" He rolled his eyes. "I didn't know it could go any lower. But you'll be great at that, Jed. I have no doubt."

"Thanks, man. I haven't been this nervous since the VCCS/ Kalamazoo game last year."

Caleb huffed. "Well, the stakes are considerably higher with your new job, I'd say."

"Yeah, tell me about it. Only eternity." He shook his head slowly. "All those kids' lives hanging in the balance."

"You're perfect for the job," Caleb said again. And Jed was. He was a good coach, but where he really shined was connecting with the kids. As a mentor and counselor. "Congrats, man."

"Yeah, hey, you too. Are you planning to open this gym here in Mapleview?"

"Ha! I'm not that far into the thought process yet. I may just try to work out of a local gym. Grand Rapids. Or maybe the YMCA here."

Jed looked skeptical. "You think you could live on that?"

"Well, I'd have to do some serious trimming of the budget. I'm already looking to trade in my car. Hey, you aren't looking for new wheels, are you?"

Jed wagged his head. "Which part of 'I'm taking a huge pay cut' did you not hear? We'll be doing some serious budget-trimming too."

"Sorry, man. I was halfway kidding. This whole thing really stinks, doesn't it?"

"More for the kids than for us."

"That's for sure. But I have a feeling they're a lot more resilient than us old guys."

Across the room, the Keurig spewed steam and Caleb retrieved his coffee. When he came back, Jed slid the newspaper closer to him. "You talked about a gym. Did you see that old school off Main is up for sale?"

"What old school?"

"Well, it hasn't been a school for a while, but Jody's grandma actually attended there when she was a kid. I'm sure you've driven by. You'd know it if you saw it. It's been empty for a few years, and I guess the owner finally decided to sell. Our insurance guy had an office in the building for a while, and I think there was a hair salon there at one time?"

"Oh, sure. That used to be the Visser School. The building's for sale?"

Jed nodded. "It's kind of overgrown right now, but you ought to take a look. Location-wise it'd be perfect, and from what I remember, it's basically one big open space. It looks like a two-story, but unless they've changed it since the insurance agency was there, half the building is lofted, so it's got at least some high ceilings. I think there's even a little apartment upstairs. You could kill two birds with one stone."

"Hmm . . . I'll have to check that out." He scanned the classifieds page.

"There's a little blurb, but I'm sure there's more information online. It's on Twenty-Fifth, I think. Just off Main, downtown."

"Yeah, I know where it is. Thanks, man. I'll check it out after school. And remember, I'd rather you not say anything to anyone about the . . . gym or anything. You know how people talk and—"

"My lips are sealed."

CHAPTER FIVE

RACHEL PARKED IN front of "her" house on Twenty-Fifth Street and stared up at the two-story brick structure. This made three times since seeing the listing online that she'd driven by to look at the house, and she could hardly wait to see the inside. Twice when she was here, there'd been other cars parked on the street and lights on in the building. What if someone bought the place before she could even get inside? She actually shuddered at the thought. But later today, she had an appointment to go through the house, and Bridgette, the real estate agent she'd emailed, had promised they were still taking bids.

"If you like it, make an offer," Bridgette had said.

Ha! *If* she liked it? She was in love and she hadn't even seen the place in real life. But was Bridgette warning that Rachel needed to make a competitive offer, or was she saying, "Shoot us a lowball offer and we'll deal"? Those were two very different interpretations of "make an offer." And she wasn't sure if Bridgette even had the power to do that, since she wasn't the listing agent.

Rachel had obviously never bought a house before, but she'd already decorated every room of this one in her mind. Picked out the paint colors for each area—rooms she'd only seen in the listing and through the windows, but the colors would be perfect. It was all working out so well, she could hardly believe it.

Not that there weren't a thousand things to do still. She felt a little guilty about taking a personal day when there were so few days of school left, but she kept hearing Caleb's voice playing over and over in her head, saying he didn't feel they owed the school board anything after the decision they'd made. Besides, she had the day coming. She hadn't taken so much as a sick day all year, and her principal had to understand that all the teachers were scrambling to get their lives in order after Tuesday's announcement.

Anyway, Valentine's Day seemed like a good day to skip school. The kids would be distracted by the parties and the treats the parents were bringing in. Plus, she'd have all next week to tie up loose ends at school and be sure her students were ready to move on—wherever that ended up being.

She dreaded the goodbyes—mostly because she was afraid she'd cry and embarrass herself. But the kids seemed to be taking it okay and were being super supportive of each other. They'd spent the entire class period yesterday talking over the changes they'd all be going through. She doubted most of her students really understood what a pivotal moment this might be in their lives. Truth was she could hardly fathom how pivotal it might be in her own life.

But looking at this house, imagining herself pulling under the little carport in back, turning the key in the lock and letting herself in . . . It was all so real, so close, she could almost hear the fireplace crackling and picture the cat she'd have. A big gray one with blue eyes. He'd meow to be fed and then he'd curl up on the piano bench beside her and lick his whiskers while she pounded out a Sousa march as loud as she liked.

Her own giggling yanked her from her reverie. *Get a grip, Hamblin. You have a lot of hoops to jump through before you can go cat shopping.*

She checked her watch and put her car in gear. She'd emailed her classified ad for piano and voice students to the newspaper office yesterday, so it would run in today's paper, but the paper was old-fashioned and wouldn't take a credit card as payment unless she presented it in person.

"We've had too much trouble with pranksters when it comes to running classifieds," the woman who'd answered the phone told her.

"We need you to sign and pay for the ad in person, so we know it's legitimate."

With that errand done, she stopped by the local furniture store that had moved her piano into the apartment. She didn't have a date to give the movers yet, but at least she could find out how much it would be and get that figured into her budget. Mom and Dad had helped her move to Mapleview after graduation and had insisted on paying to move the piano. She couldn't remember for sure how much it cost, but she did remember Dad grumbling about the price when he thought she was inside. Still, it had to be done.

Maybe she would ask Caleb if his football guys would help her move the rest of her furniture when the time came, but she wasn't going to trust her piano to a bunch of hulking, clumsy teenagers.

She'd been playing phone tag with her parents since Tuesday night, though they finally had a date to video chat after supper tonight. She was halfway hoping she could tell them she'd already bought a house when they talked. Wouldn't that blow their minds? And yet, how strange to even think about buying a house when she hadn't asked her dad's advice or even told him what she was up to.

But she was a grown woman. She'd lived on her own since the day she'd graduated from college, and it was probably time she made a few big decisions on her own.

Be honest, Hamblin.

That stupid voice of reason. But it made her admit the truth. She didn't really want to tell her parents about the house until the sale was a done deal, because she didn't need any voices of reason thwarting her plans.

She couldn't get a commitment from the piano movers since she didn't have a firm date, but she got a quote that about choked her. Four hundred dollars to move a piano from her apartment to Main Street. Maybe she'd give those big, strong football players a chance after all.

Back in her car again, she checked the time on her phone. She was a little early to meet Bridgette, but it wouldn't feel so awkward snooping around the outside of the building since she had an appointment.

Thinking about finally getting to go inside, she shivered as excitement rose in her. What if the reality didn't match her ideal? She needed to prepare herself. But it couldn't be too far off from the listing photos, could it? There were rules about that stuff. Integrity and ethics and such.

She parked in the same spot on Twenty-Fifth Street in front of the house. Some kind of thick, wild bush had grown up on the sagging wire fence around the property, hiding the gorgeous bricked edifice the photos showed. That was why she'd never noticed the place before finding the listing, plus the woods surrounding the property prevented much of it from being seen from the side street. But Rachel could take the whole border out and put up a white picket fence.

Down the road, of course. First things first. She had to buy the place before she could start working her magic on it.

She picked her way around to the back of the building and peered in through the high window in the door. She couldn't see beyond a tiny entry porch, where a broom and cans of paint sat in one corner. That was a good sign, wasn't it? Maybe she wouldn't have to paint after all. Unless there was some awful color in those cans. It was hard to tell from the listing photos.

Coming full circle around the other side of the house, she heard a car pull up.

Bridgette, the agent, got out with a folder in tow.

Rachel hurried to meet her. This was it. The moment of truth.

Bridgette met her on the sidewalk with an outstretched hand. "You must be Rachel."

"Yes. Nice to finally meet you." They'd only spoken twice on the phone, but the real estate agent looked exactly like her photo on the website, and already felt like a friend.

"Shall we?" Bridgette motioned for Rachel to precede her up the front walk.

"Are a lot of people looking at it?" Rachel worked to sound nonchalant. She'd never bought a house before, but she did remember that the number one rule was not to appear overly interested.

Bridgette gave a little grimace. "This listing has received more interest than I expected, honestly. I'm afraid it's going to be competitive, but there are always some who're only looking out of curiosity."

Rachel walked through the door and waited for her eyes to adjust to the light. She took in a shallow breath, and something she'd never felt before clicked inside of her. *This is my house.* Somehow she just knew it in her heart. It *felt* like home.

The whole first floor—one glorious, open space—had classic caramel-colored hardwood floors, crown molding, and wide windowsills that had all been freshly painted in a perfect shade of white. A shade that glowed with just a hint of pink. Three arched windows cast curvy patches of saffron light on the floors, and the high ceilings made the room feel spacious and welcoming. The low stage beneath the loft would be perfect for her baby grand, and not too difficult for the movers to get it up there either.

Excitement built inside her and she turned a full circle, speechless, taking it all in.

"It's lovely, isn't it?" Bridgette's knowing smile told Rachel that her attempts to appear only mildly interested hadn't fooled anyone.

"It's very pretty," she said, still trying not to wear her offer on her sleeve. With her phone, she took a few quick pictures.

"Do you want to look at the rest of it?"

"Sure. I mean, as long as I'm here."

Bridgette's heels clicked on the hardwood floors as she led Rachel down a short hallway to the back of the building.

The kitchen wasn't much bigger than her bedroom in the apartment, but it did look efficient—like those galley kitchens in fancy New York apartments. It got good light from the tall window at the end of the galley. At least all the appliances were included, and they appeared to be fairly new. A few houseplants and some pretty dishes on the open shelving would add character to the kitchen. But she probably wouldn't be cooking a Thanksgiving dinner in here any time soon.

Bridgette pointed out the tiny back porch she'd seen through the window, and opened a small broom closet across from the kitchen and another larger closet that was plumbed for a washer and dryer.

Those spaces were in desperate need of paint, but Rachel wasn't going to let that ruin her growing excitement.

"Let's go upstairs to the loft, shall we?"

She followed the real estate agent back down the hallway and up the narrow open staircase in the corner of the building.

At the top of the stairs, Bridgette waited as Rachel looked the space over. "This could be a small office or sitting room. The bedroom is here." The agent crossed the loft and opened a set of double doors, revealing a small bedroom with one brick wall that would make a stunning "headboard."

Rachel entered the room and found the hot water heater space and another tiny closet that looked as though it had been added recently. A larger door on the opposite wall opened to a little powder room.

"Now that's the only bathroom," Bridgette said from the other side of the loft. "And I'll warn you, it's tiny. But for one person, it should be enough . . ."

Rachel's excitement dimmed ever so slightly. The antique claw-foot bathtub she'd imagined was actually a postage-stamp-sized walk-in shower, and the pedestal sink offered no storage underneath. But a tall window overlooked the wooded back yard, and dappled light played off the cream-colored walls. Again, some greenery and pretty linens would add the character that was missing.

The actual square footage was only slightly larger than her apartment, but the difference was that now her monthly payments would be an investment in something she owned. Not to mention, she could play her piano any time of the day or night and work from home teaching lessons without worrying about bothering the neighbors.

"Go ahead and look around, and then I'll take you down to the basement."

"Oh? There's a basement?" Had that been mentioned in the listing? She really didn't want a basement looming underneath her cozy house, collecting spiders—or worse.

"It's mostly unfinished. And the only entrance is outside, but it does add some extra space for storage."

Rachel walked through the loft once more, then followed the agent downstairs and out through the back door.

Bridgette opened one side of a set of double cellar doors that revealed wide steps leading down.

Rachel stepped back. "Is it just a cellar?"

"The school had a Michigan basement, which is just a crawl space under the original building. But at some point"—she consulted the sheaf of paperwork on her clipboard—"looks like sometime in the sixties, it was excavated to make room for a laundry. But you saw the closet across from the kitchen? Apparently, they closed off the entrance from the inside. Of course, that could be knocked out again—"

"No," she said too quickly. "I'm fine with the laundry in the house." The tiny closet was still better than the apartment complex laundry where half of the dryers didn't work and the other half took forever to dry anything. "I'm just not a huge fan of basements. Snakes and spiders . . ." She gave an involuntary shudder.

Bridgette laughed and flipped on a light switch. "Snakes and spiders would have no way to get up from this basement. I promise."

Rachel followed the agent down the stairs, her gaze searching every corner. If she was going to buy the place—and she was!—she needed to see exactly what she was getting. And if she didn't look, her imagination would create a vision far creepier than reality.

Though the dank and musty air was the opposite of appealing, the space turned out to be nothing more than a large concrete box that had been spray-painted white. The ceiling was surprisingly high for a basement, and there were no hidden corners for critters—or bogeymen—to lurk in. Plus, the ledge that ran along three walls would be nice for storage, if she ever needed it.

She snapped a few photos with her phone to add to the ones she'd taken of the main house.

When they emerged from the cellar a few minutes later, Bridgette turned. "So, what do you think?"

"I think I'd like to make an offer."

The agent's eyebrows rose. "Wonderful. Let's go back to my office and we'll get the paperwork started."

"Well, I haven't been approved by the bank yet. They're working on it, but I don't have the preapproval letter yet. But I am interested. *Very* interested."

"I'm sure there won't be any problem. We can go ahead and at least get started, so you're ready to jump on the offer as soon as you are approved."

Rachel followed Bridgette back inside, feeling a little like a fraud and desperately hoping she wasn't wasting the poor agent's time.

But, oh, this house had her name all over it! It just had to be hers.

CHAPTER SIX

CALEB HEFTED THE cardboard box onto one shoulder and headed down the quiet school hallway. He hadn't realized how much junk—mostly books and training videos—he'd collected in his classroom over the time he'd taught at VCCS. He'd decided it would be easier, physically and emotionally, to take one small box home each day rather than waiting and making a big production of moving two years of his life out of the building all at once.

The principal had declared the Friday afternoon after the final day of school to be a workday. They had to have the building cleaned out for the next tenant—a medical billing business, rumor had it. What a waste. Sadness dogged his every step as the last day crept closer, which surprised him. But maybe he'd feel better once his future was settled.

He'd wavered back and forth about what to do, but finally Jed had talked him into making an appointment to look at that old school downtown.

Caleb made a quick stop at the teacher's lounge. *Yes!* There were sugar cookies left on the fancy heart-shaped tray. The school board had, not surprisingly, ignored Valentine's Day, but the parent association had come through with a huge Valentine cake and homemade sugar cookies for the teachers. At least somebody still appreciated them. He tucked a cookie carefully in his coat pocket and stuffed another one in his mouth before hefting the box back onto his shoulders. *Mmm . . .* He needed to get this recipe.

And a wife to make it for him.

He chuckled to himself, imagining Rachel laughing and rolling her eyes at his admittedly sexist joke.

Or maybe she wouldn't laugh. She hadn't been at school today, and it actually worried him a little. Which was crazy, given that a week ago he wouldn't have given one thought to the woman's whereabouts at any time. But Rachel Hamblin had taken up an uncanny amount of real estate in his thoughts since two days ago, after they'd talked in the parking lot.

He'd come *this* close to asking her for a date that night. Not to his credit, what made him change his mind was the fact that it was the week of Valentine's Day. The holiday was awkward enough without trying to navigate it in a brand-new relationship. If memory served him right, Valentine's Day last year had been the beginning of the end for Liz and him.

Not that he was sorry. He was almost ashamed to admit that he hadn't missed Liz even one day since they'd broken up. They'd never really been good together. Why hadn't he recognized that before they'd wasted almost two years of their lives in a relationship that was going nowhere?

He wasn't blaming Liz. Although it *had* been a profound relief to be done with her constant obsessing about her calorie intake, her carb count, her glycemic levels, her *blah, blah, blah.* He appreciated a woman who took care of herself, but he didn't exactly need a play-by-play. Sometimes it would have been nice to go out for a romantic dinner and simply enjoy the food together without tracking every bite in an app.

Still, he was at fault too. He'd let his physical attraction to Liz override far more essential things. He wasn't even sure Liz had shared his faith, though she'd claimed to when they'd first met. Of course, he was to blame for that also. He hadn't made his belief in God a priority in their relationship. And if he'd learned nothing else, it was that a shared faith was essential if a relationship was to last. If he was ever ready to seek out a relationship again, he needed to remember that. For now, he'd been enjoying his unattached status.

So why he was suddenly looking at Rachel as prospective girl-friend material, he had no idea. But the music teacher he'd barely noticed before last Tuesday had invaded almost every waking moment since—and what dreams he could remember too. Maybe it was just that he'd never looked at her that way before. Partly because until May, he'd been attached, and partly because he'd always operated by an unspoken rule that he didn't date coworkers.

But with everything happening now, it was a low-risk proposition. If he asked her out and things didn't work out, no biggie. They were going their separate ways anyway, so there wouldn't be any awkward meetings in the school hallways or students razzing him about his girlfriend.

Maybe he'd call Rachel tonight with the excuse that he was just checking to be sure everything was all right—since she hadn't been in school and all. Never mind that he could have just asked someone. No doubt the secretary and Headmaster Lockhardt both knew why Rachel had been absent. But his asking about her would have raised all kinds of suspicion. And after his conversation with Rachel Tuesday, he'd surely earned the right to call her himself and make sure she was okay. As a friend.

Then, if the conversation went well, maybe he could ease into asking her to dinner. As friends.

Once off the phone with her parents, Rachel heated up some canned soup, then carried a hot bowl and her laptop to the sofa. She curled up cross-legged in the corner and pulled up the now familiar real estate website. She checked the property stats. Ugh. The listing had over four hundred views after being on the market only four days. Of course, probably three hundred and fifty of those were hers.

She opened her photo app and scrolled through the photos she'd snapped during the walk-through with Bridgette.

There were a few disappointments with the house, to be sure, but the music room—as she'd dubbed the main living space—made up for them all. She was obsessed with the house and already knew exactly where every piece of her furniture would go.

As she clicked through the photos once more, ideas came fast and furious. She texted a few of the pictures to her parents. Mom and Dad were upset about the school closing, but they hadn't balked at the idea of her buying a house in Mapleview.

Dad had warned she probably wouldn't be able to get a loan until she could prove a steady income, but he didn't tell her not to try. In fact, he'd given her some good tips about negotiating the contract.

She finished her soup, then found a fresh notebook and started a list of everything she needed to accomplish before she could move.

The ring of her phone interrupted her. She peeked at the screen. A number she didn't recognize.

Her finger hovered over *ignore*, but what if the call was about "her" house? Or maybe a parent calling about the ad she'd placed? People would be getting home from work and reading the paper about now. She couldn't afford *not* to answer.

She clicked Accept. "Hello?"

"Hey, Rachel. It's Caleb. Janssen."

"Hi, Caleb." She hesitated for a beat. Caleb? Calling her? "How are you?"

"Doing good. Thanks. Is everything okay with you? I noticed you weren't at school today and just wanted . . . to make sure you're not . . . sick or anything."

Since when did he call her to see why she wasn't at work? "No, I'm fine. I had some appointments I needed to take care of. Figured this would be a good day to miss, what with all the Valentine's Day parties."

"Okay. That's good."

She closed her laptop and put it aside. "Did something happen at school today?"

"No, no. Everything's fine. The kids seem to be in pretty good spirits. Of course, they were all hyped up on sugar today."

She laughed. "Yes, that's exactly why I figured today would be a good time to take a personal day." She was tempted to tell him that she'd met her true love on this Valentine's Day: her house. But she didn't want to jinx the deal.

"Don't worry. I took care of the last of the cookies in the teachers' lounge."

"Oh, we did get cookies? Man." The one downfall of taking the day off. "I hope you didn't take care of my Starbucks card too."

"Sorry, no gift cards this year. It wasn't the board that brought treats. It was the parents."

"That was nice of them."

"Yeah. I guess it was."

"Nothing new on the school closing?"

"There's a rumor that a medical billing company is going to put their offices in the building."

"Really? That seems like such a waste." Apparently this conversation wasn't ending any time soon. She pulled the plush throw blanket from the back of the couch and tucked it around her legs.

"I know. It makes me sad to picture my classroom with a bunch of cubicles in it. But it's only a rumor. Mostly it seems like business as usual. Even the kids are acting like nothing out of the ordinary happened."

"They're probably still in shock."

"I know I am. But at least—" His voice was muffled for a minute, then back, clear as before. "Get off of me, you idiot—"

She leaned forward. "Excuse me?" *What on earth?* "Caleb? What—?"

"Sorry about that." His laughter came through the phone. "I wasn't talking to you. My stupid cat thinks I'm a scratching post."

"You have a cat?" She never figured him for a feline lover. *Never.*

"Doesn't quite fit your image of a jock, huh?"

She settled back against the couch. "Not. At. All. What kind of cat is it?"

"I don't know . . . A boy?"

She grinned. "And what breed is this boy?"

"He's gray. He's a great big manly gray tomcat. Is that better?"

A gray cat—just like she had always dreamed of. "For you, I was actually picturing a fluffy white cat with blue eyes and a pink bow around her neck."

"Nope. Wayne is gray. Kind of a smoky gray. And his eyes are— Hang on. Let me check. I've never had to describe his eyes before." Another commotion came through the connection, then, "Come here, you dumb cat. Rachel wants to know what color your eyes are." A pause. "I guess his eyes are . . . gray too? I don't know. They kind of blend in with the rest of him."

She giggled, picturing Caleb Janssen with a cat on his lap.

"What's so funny?"

"I'm just having trouble picturing this side of you. And seriously? Wayne? You named your cat Wayne?"

"Let's just call it self-preservation."

She shook her head. "I don't get it."

"Wayne was Mom's cat. Dad didn't want a cat after she passed, so I got him by default. He had a different name when I adopted him. It, um, needed changing."

"Oh, do tell. What was it?" Even if she still had no idea why Caleb had called her, she was loving this banter.

"Promise you won't laugh?"

She sucked in a dramatic breath through her teeth. "I'm not sure I can keep a promise like that, given the way the rest of this conversation has gone."

"Fine. You can laugh, but what you cannot do is tell anyone else."

"I promise. Scout's honor."

"His name was . . . Puffy." The word came out in a whisper.

And it was that whisper that cracked her up even more than the name. Although *Puffy* was funny enough. When she managed to stop giggling, she said, "I'm sure that was a very good name . . . for your mom."

"No, my mom's name was Teresa."

"I meant for your mom to *call* him, silly."

"No, she didn't call him Silly," he deadpanned. "She called him Puffy."

"Caleb, cut it out. Are you even for real?" She was still smiling, but also wondering if she'd said that last part out loud. Because seriously, *was* this man for real? And if he was, sign her up.

"Oh, I'm for real. And there's more where that came from."

Apparently she *had* said it out loud. "Well, you're cracking me up."

"Maybe you need to meet Wayne."

"Puffy, you mean?"

"Hey, you promised."

"Don't worry. Your secret is safe with me."

"It'd better be."

She was suddenly without a comeback and an awkward silence stretched between them.

"Well," he said, "I probably should let you go. But hey, I was wondering. You wouldn't want to go out to dinner this weekend, would you?"

An actual date? Was he seriously going there?

"Maybe Saturday night?"

He *was* going there. And to her surprise, she wanted to go right along with him. "I'd like that. What time?"

"I could pick you up about six?"

"Okay. Sure. That'd be great. Do you know where I live?"

"It's that apartment complex on the south end of town, right?"

Not for long, she wanted to say. But Bridgette had said they were taking offers on the property until February 22. The whole thing could still fall apart. "That's right. I'm in 132B on the second floor. But if you'll text me when you get here, I'll just come down."

"You sure? I don't want to have to put up with any jock-bashing because I didn't come to your door like a proper gentleman."

"I promise I won't hold it against you."

"Okay, and I'll hold you to that."

She could just imagine the smug grin on his face.

He cleared his throat. "Again, glad everything is okay. I'll see you tomorrow at school."

"Okay. See you then."

"Um, this isn't going to be awkward, is it? At work tomorrow?"

"Why would it be?" It wasn't really fair to him for her to be so disingenuous, but she needed to be sure he saw this as a date. Or else confirm that he didn't.

"Just the whole dating someone from work thing."

So he did consider this a date. "I think it'll be okay. We're adults, right?"

"That's the rumor. And I figure, since we're not going to be working together after next week, if you decide you really just can't stand personal trainers under any circumstances, then you'll only have to deal with running into me for another week or so."

"Stop. You're not ever going to let me live that down, are you?"

"We'll see. Depends on how Saturday night goes."

"I'll be on my best behavior."

"Bye, Rachel."

"Bye, Caleb."

"Oh, and . . . happy Valentine's Day."

"Yeah, you too." Rachel ended the call, a happy tune dancing through her mind.

Best Valentine's Day *ever*.

Chapter Seven

Rachel lifted her fingers from the piano keys and listened. Were those footsteps coming up the stairs outside her apartment? But all was quiet, so she resumed playing through the first movement of the Schumann concerto she'd been working on. It was a piece she'd challenged herself with all winter, and she wasn't making much progress.

A minute later, her doorbell rang.

She checked her phone. If that was Caleb, he was early. She hadn't talked to him at all at school yesterday and had only seen him across the parking lot after the last bell. She wasn't sure whether he'd purposely made himself scarce or if maybe it was just by chance.

She rose from the piano bench and went to the door. It was probably one of her neighbors coming to complain because she was playing the piano after five p.m. She peered through the peephole in her front door.

Caleb stood there, smiling. Thank goodness she'd gotten ready a few minutes ahead of time.

She opened the door and a gust of cold air came in. "Hi."

"Sorry, I'm a little early."

"It's okay. I'm just surprised you came up, but I'm ready. Let me grab my coat and I'll be right there." She left the door open a crack and reached into the tiny coat closet.

"You might want a scarf too. It's really cold out tonight. And according to Channel Three, we're supposed to get more snow this weekend."

"Good. If it's going to be cold, it may as well snow."

"Speak for yourself."

"You don't like snow? Then what in the world are you doing in Michigan?"

The cadence of his laughter captivated her.

He shrugged. "I only like snow at Christmas. And speaking of Christmas, what was that music you were listening to? When I knocked on your door?"

She grinned, feeling as jittery as she'd been at her first recital. "I was playing the piano. But it wasn't Christmas music. It's a concerto I'm trying to learn."

"Whoa! That was you?" He blew out a low whistle. "I'm impressed. What was the song? Or concerto?" He pronounced the word with a fake Italian accent.

She gave a little bow from the hips as if she were about to take the piano bench. "Schumann's Piano Concerto in A Minor, Opus Fifty-Four. I'm trying to memorize it, but it's coming slow."

"Good grief. It'd take me a month just to memorize that title."

"Yeah, it's not an easy one. The concerto, I mean. But I like a challenge."

"'Chopsticks' would be a challenge for me."

"And catching a football would be a challenge for me."

"Well, there you go." After leading the way down the stairs to his car, he opened the door for her, then slid behind the wheel and started the ignition. "I actually did take piano lessons for a couple of years."

"Really?" She tried—and failed—to keep the surprise from her voice. "I wouldn't have guessed that."

"Because jocks don't play piano, right?" He held up a hand before she could protest. "But you would think I'm lying if you heard me play. Apparently, you're supposed to practice for more than fifteen minutes right before your lesson."

"An hour each morning and an hour after school. But I was an overachiever. I usually put in three hours a day."

"Sorry, but that sounds like pure torture."

"I loved it. My dad actually made me cut back to two and a half hours. He thought I was overdoing it."

"Yeah, duh."

"And how many hours do you make your football guys practice? I seem to remember something called two-a-days."

"Sure. But that's football. It's fun!"

"Plowing over each other and knocking your opponent flat? You have a strange idea of fun."

"To each his own." Smiling, he pulled out of the parking lot, and at the four-way stop, he turned to her. "Where would you like to eat?"

"I like everything. You decide."

"You're kind of dressed up. It seems like I should take you someplace fancy. You look very nice, by the way."

"This isn't dressed up." She shook her head. "I just tried to wear something I don't wear to school that often. Besides, we're both fixin' to be poor. Let's just do the café or something."

"You sure?"

"Positive. Casual is great."

He looked skeptical but turned left onto Church Street toward Black Mill Deli. The streetlights cast a warm glow over the shop awnings, and on each lamppost, twinkly Christmas wreaths added a festive touch. Rachel could almost see to the corner where her house sat. For a minute, she was tempted to tell him about it. To have him drive by and ask him what he thought about the property. Only the thought of how devastated she'd be if she didn't get the house kept her quiet. If things fell through, she wanted to bear that disappointment in private.

And even though Bridgette had told her there were several parties interested in the property, the agent seemed to think Rachel had a good chance of getting it. Assuming she was approved for the loan, she would initially offer three thousand over asking price, but

Bridgette said she'd get a chance to submit a higher offer if another party outbid her. She could only go about five thousand dollars beyond the asking price—and that would leave her savings account woefully low—but surely that would be enough to get the house.

"Don't you think so?" Caleb's voice jolted her.

Her cheeks heated. "What was that? Sorry, I was kind of off in la-la land."

"Wow. I'm boring you already?"

"No." She slanted an apologetic look his way. "Sorry, that street sign reminded me of something, and I—"

"Yeah, yeah, I can take a hint." He feigned a hangdog look. "I'm more boring than a lamppost."

She rested her hand on his forearm briefly. "What did you ask me, Caleb? I promise I'm listening now."

"I said I thought my kids seemed to be taking the news pretty well. I just wondered if you'd gotten the same from your students?"

She nodded, forcing herself to focus. "I'm not nearly as worried about my elementary students. They'll adjust just fine. But it'll be harder for the upper grades. I do think it helps a lot that they're all in this together. They've been able to support each other, and I know several of them are talking about going to public school."

"That's what my older kids were saying. I just worry about how they'll handle the local high school. They've lived pretty sheltered lives at VCCS."

"I know what you mean. There are a couple of my students that I worry about, whether they're strong enough to handle the peer pressure public school would bring." She wasn't so far out of high school that she didn't remember how brutal it could be.

"If they hang together, they'll do okay."

"I hope so."

"It still seems a little surreal that the school is closing."

"I know. Especially when I think about what life is going to look like a week from Monday morning. I did put an ad in the paper this week, though." Oops, now he might ask where she planned to teach those music lessons.

Instead, he looked clueless. "An ad?"

"Yes, to teach piano and flute lessons."

"Oh, of course. Chasing your dream job. Good. Have you gotten any responses yet?"

"I had a couple of inquiries. A lady actually took an appointment time, so that's one down. The other was a family with three kids, so it'd be nice to snag that client. Of course, I'll offer a discount for families with multiple students, so that's not as much money. But I'm grateful."

"I hope your students practice more than I did. Now that I know a human music teacher, I feel kind of sorry for Mrs. Culbertson."

She smirked. "Mrs. Culbertson wasn't human?"

"No. She was a saint."

"What? And I'm not?"

"You would be if you'd taught me and lived to tell the tale. Ten-year-old me, I mean."

"That bad, huh?"

"I once threw a football in her music studio and knocked over a bust of some famous composer—Who's that one with the wild hair?" He yanked his own blond hair into spikes to illustrate.

She laughed. "A lot of them had crazy hair, but that was probably Beethoven. Nice look on you, by the way."

Rolling his eyes, he quickly finger-combed his hair back in place.

"So, did you get in trouble?"

"The statue broke to smithereens. I had to sweep up the mess and pay to replace the dumb thing. At least I got out of my lesson that day. But what was really bad was she kept my football as collateral."

"Oooh, she was a meanie," she teased. "Why on earth did she let you bring a football to your lesson in the first place?"

He looked sheepish. "I may or may not have sneaked it in under my hoodie. Lessons were right after football practice. What was I supposed to do? Anyway, it wasn't long after that Dad talked Mom into letting me quit. Best day of my life."

"That's kind of sad. Just think how different your life would be if you knew how to read music and play an instrument."

"I don't mind *listening* to music. Whatever you were playing, that was nice. Sorry, but some people just weren't cut out to be musicians. Me, for instance."

"I'm not sure I believe that."

"Just think how different your life would be if you knew how to play football, huh?" He stared at her with a knowing grin.

"Well, now that's just silly."

"Hey!"

"Think about it, Caleb. How would my life be different? I'd probably be dead. Those big guys would crush me."

"Not if it was only flag football."

"I just don't see the point. And how many guys go on to play football after high school?"

"Counterpoint—before my cousins all moved away, we used to play every Sunday afternoon. It was good exercise, it was time spent together with family, and it was fun. Can you say any of that about playing the piano?" He leveled a smug look at her.

She started to answer, then clamped her mouth shut.

"See?"

"I refuse to debate you. But it is fun. And playing piano is very good exercise for your hands. Plus, my mom and I liked playing duets together, so there's your family time." She gave a decisive nod.

His eyes snapped with mischief. "That's weak sauce. You're reaching."

"No, those are all legitimate points. What are you—a lawyer or something? Oh, look, there's the café." She pointed up the street, but the café hadn't quite come into sight yet.

"Nice try." He laughed. "Maybe we should pick another subject to talk about."

"Ya think?"

"So, how are you coping with the whole job thing?" He flashed a genuine smile. "I'm being serious now, in case you couldn't tell."

"One never knows with you."

"I really do want to know. You feeling more settled?"

"I'm okay." She nodded and returned the smile, glad she'd said yes to this date. It struck her that while she'd had a few dates since moving to Mapleview, she'd never felt as comfortable with any of those guys as she did with Caleb. "I just really want my new business to work. Which means if I get any calls tonight, I probably should take them."

"Oh, sure. I don't blame you. Desperate times and all that."

Smiling, she gave a little huff. "Well, I'm not desperate yet, but I might be a week from now."

"You and me and a whole bunch of other people."

"Have you heard what anyone else is doing? Della sounded pretty happy about retiring."

"She did. And Jed took a youth pastor job."

"That's what Mindy said. He'll be really good at that."

Caleb nodded and pulled into the only empty parking space in front of the café. He started to open his door, then turned back to her. "It looks pretty crowded here. You sure you're ready for the whole town to see us together?"

"I don't know as many people as you do, but if you'd rather go someplace else . . ."

"No, I'm not ashamed."

"Wow, thanks. I think." She knew he was only kidding, but was he really ready for the whole town to see them as a potential "thing"? That was one of the downsides of living and working in a Podunk little town like Mapleview.

"Let me rephrase that. I would be proud to be seen with you. I was thinking more of you. The whole sophisticated music teacher stooping to date the local jock, you know? Could be really bad for your reputation."

"I'll just move if I have to."

"Oh, sure, take the easy way out." Laughing, he climbed out of the car and came around to open her door.

CHAPTER EIGHT

CALEB PUT HIS fork down and looked around the dining room, halfway disappointed that no one was paying any attention to Rachel and him. She looked completely beautiful tonight, with her hair down over her shoulders and wearing a little more makeup than usual. If any of his players had been here, he would never hear the end of it. And he wouldn't even mind. But the other diners were mostly retired couples and families with little kids at this time of night. The high schoolers would come in later for pop and ice cream. For Rachel's sake, he might try to steer her out of here before then. No sense asking for trouble.

Not that he was anxious for the night to be over. They'd had a great time, joking like longtime friends. But talking seriously too. He was still keeping his plans close to his vest for now. Not that he cared if Rachel knew, but he wanted to wait and make sure things worked out before he blabbed too much about what he hoped was going to happen.

But he could share about his car.

"I talked to a dealer over in Grand Rapids last night that might be interested in the Highlander. If we can agree on a price for this older Toyota they've got on the lot, I'll be out from under my car payment and have a pretty decent vehicle besides."

"Oh, that's great, Caleb. But I'm sorry you have to sell your car."

He waved her off. "It's just transportation. And like I told you, I probably shouldn't have bought it in the first place."

"At least it sounds like you have another good option."

"We'll see. But it feels like a step in the right direction."

Their server appeared again. "Can I get you any dessert?"

The girl had hovered a little too much to suit Caleb, but he looked to Rachel for an answer to the dessert question.

She shook her head. "Not for me, thank you. But you order something for yourself, Caleb."

He patted his belly. "No, I'm good to go."

"I'll leave your check here, then. You can pay at the table."

He took the folder and slipped two twenties inside. "I don't need any change."

"Thank you." The server tossed him an appreciative smile.

When she left, he asked Rachel, "Do you want to go get coffee somewhere maybe?"

Her eyebrows went up, but she didn't hesitate with her *yes*.

Half an hour later, they were settled in a corner booth at Paddy's. Back to where this surprising—and a bit perplexing—thing that was happening between them had all started. They ordered a round of mochas and settled in while they waited, talking and laughing like old friends.

No, it was more than that. They were very definitely flirting. And it emboldened him. During a rare pause in the conversation, he motioned between them. "Does this whole thing kind of, I don't know, *surprise* you?"

"This?" She mimicked his motions. "Are you talking about this mild-mannered music teacher and the airhead jock actually becoming friends? Is that the *this* of which you speak?"

"That's the *this*. But could you please remember that I also teach highly complex mathematics too?"

Her grin warmed him.

But he didn't want to joke his way through this conversation. Because it wasn't only friendship. Something more was at work here. "Don't take this wrong, but we've worked together for two years. Why is this just now happening? Why didn't we notice each other before?"

"It's not like we haven't spoken before, Caleb. You've always been very civil—in a jock-ish sort of way."

"But how did I not notice this fascinating, gorgeous woman I've worked with for two whole years?" He was pushing it for a first date, but he was pretty sure she was feeling the same way he was.

"Aww, that's sweet. But don't forget, Caleb, you had a girlfriend for at least some of that time. I appreciate that you didn't see me then. Not that I was looking your direction either. No offense."

He grinned. "None taken. But why was that? Did you have a policy against dating a jock mathematician or something?"

"Let's just say I wouldn't have considered you my type." She tilted her head as if deciding whether or not to say more. "Maybe the timing just wasn't right."

He shrugged. If she meant that God hadn't allowed them to see each other this way until now because of their work situation, he was beginning to agree. But things were moving fast. And if God did have something to do with this, Caleb didn't want to mess it up. "I'm not sure. But whatever the reason, I'm glad we finally . . . opened our eyes."

"Me too." She held his gaze, a nuance to her smile that he'd never seen before. Or maybe he'd been blind to that too.

It was all he could do to refrain from reaching out to stroke her cheek with the back of his hand. To see if that peaches-and-cream skin was as soft as it looked in the candlelit restaurant.

She cast a downward glance, looking suddenly shy. "I've been thinking that maybe we didn't notice each other because we—"

Her phone trilled from her purse on the bench beside her.

She gave a little growl. "I'm so sorry, Caleb, but I probably should answer. In case it's about the lessons."

"No, of course." He motioned for her to take the call.

Shooting him another apologetic smile, she looked at the screen, frowning as she answered. "Hello?" She lowered her voice and turned slightly to the side. "Yes . . . Oh, hi. No, that's okay. I can talk for a minute."

Caleb scooted his chair back from the table and made a production of creasing his napkin, trying not to listen in on her conversation though he couldn't help it. From what he could hear, it didn't sound like it was about piano lessons. And she seemed to be answering in a purposely vague manner. Maybe he should leave the table for a minute, give her some privacy. But just when he was about to get up, it sounded as if the call might be winding down.

"Yes, I could do that." She lowered her voice further. "Does it need to be in writing, or should I just let you know how much?" She listened, nodding at intervals. "I'll get it to you as soon as I can. The same email I've been using for you, right? You're sure that'll be soon enough? . . . Okay. Thanks."

She hung up and slipped her phone back into the side pocket of her purse. It seemed to take a minute for her to regain her composure.

"Everything okay?"

"Yes. Yes, fine. I'm sorry about the interruption. But I do need to take care of some paperwork." She pointed to her purse as if that explained her urgency. "Maybe you could take me home now?"

"Oh. Okay, no problem. Whatever you want." Though disappointment hit his gut hard, he rose and helped her with her coat.

On the ride back to her apartment, she seemed to be trying to recapture the lighthearted mood they'd enjoyed until that phone call had ruined everything. But he couldn't shake the feeling that something had changed her mind about what she'd been about to say.

And it drove him nuts that he couldn't fathom what it might be.

The door closed behind Rachel, and she leaned against it. Talk about the worst timing ever. Had that ill-timed phone call ruined the connection that had been building between her and Caleb? She wanted to cry.

Except, that made no sense. If there was anything between them that could be ruined by a two-minute phone call, then it was certainly nothing worth building a relationship on. But she'd felt so wonderfully close to him the whole evening. As if their friendship

283

was growing into something truly special. And so much more than mere friendship.

Chill, Hamblin. If God was behind what seemed to be happening between Caleb and her, it couldn't be so easily thwarted. It seemed crazy that this guy she'd known for two years—and had never once had a romantic thought about—had suddenly turned into someone she couldn't wait to see again. Did he think she'd made an excuse to end the evening?

She hoped not. They were finally having a serious conversation. About them.

And then that phone call had interrupted the beautiful crescendo of her conversation with Caleb.

She should have just told him what was going on. He would have understood, and at least she wouldn't have had to wonder if she'd ruined everything.

She sighed, hung up her coat, and grabbed her laptop. As disappointed as she was to have the evening with Caleb end, she was even more upset about the fact that she'd been outbid on her house. And after talking to Bridgette and learning that there were two other offers on the property that were currently higher than hers, and a fourth bidder who would also have a chance to raise their price, she felt she needed to offer the absolute most she could afford when she submitted what Bridgette called a "best and final" offer. She wouldn't get another chance to bid again. It was all or nothing.

And at a time when her finances were more uncertain than they'd ever been.

Still, the house was worth it and would be a good investment. She had no doubt about that. And it was a hopeful sign that she'd had two more inquiries about music lessons when she checked her email. Both for piano, which was fine with her. Those bookings were a sign she would get the students she needed.

She filled out the bid form Bridgette had emailed, took a deep breath, and hit *Send*. The loan officer she was working with had drawn up the preapproval letter, to be signed when she had at least fifteen confirmed clients. But Bridgette warned her she needed that letter in hand by next Friday for the bid to be official. "God, it's in your hands now," she whispered as her computer made a whooshing sound that said the email had been sent.

Exhaustion sucked all her energy, and she lay back against the couch. Her phone rang and she answered without looking, assuming it would be Bridgette letting her know she'd received the bid.

"Hey, I'll make this really quick." Caleb's voice perked her back to life.

"Caleb." Why did merely speaking his name bring her such joy?

"Totally understand if you don't want to, but I wondered if you'd like to go skating tomorrow. You have ice skates, right?"

"Ice-skating? Sure. My skates are sitting right where I left them last winter." He didn't need to know that the last time she'd skated had been on a date. With a guy she liked quite a bit, but who apparently hadn't liked her enough to ask her out again.

"Jed and Jody have a pond out on their place just past Black Mill Pond. They're out of town until late tomorrow, but he offered the use of it any time I wanted to skate there. It's supposed to be a full moon and . . . I just thought it sounded like fun."

"A full moon? So you're talking at night?"

"Have you ever skated at night?"

"Well, in a rink, yeah."

"Totally different. You're gonna love it."

"Okay. Sure. What time?"

"Maybe we can do drive-through for dinner on the way out there. How about I'll pick you up at five thirty?"

"Sure. That does sound like fun. How about if I bring hot chocolate?"

"Awesome. Okay. That's all. I know you have stuff to do tonight."

"No, it's fine. I got it taken care of."

"Already?"

"Yes." He was fishing. She could hear the unspoken questions in his modulated tone. And really, there wasn't any reason not to tell him—except that he might think she was being a little premature. Here he was, selling his car and getting his finances pared down while she was going out on a huge limb and putting an offer on a house. No. Even though Bridgette seemed certain that she'd be approved for the loan, she didn't want to take it for granted. She'd have a paycheck from the school until the end of April, but until she had enough lessons lined up to pay the bills, she wasn't ready to tell anyone. She cleared her throat. "I just had to fill out some forms."

"Oh. Okay. Well, I'll see you tomorrow. Dress warm. You might get that snow you've been hoping for."

"Can't wait." She clicked off her phone and tried to calm her breathing. But the thought of gliding over the ice under a winter moon, maybe even holding hands with Caleb . . . How could one man make everything better with a thirty-second phone call?

CHAPTER NINE

CALEB'S HIGHLANDER WAS toasty warm, but outside the city limits, the countryside was still blanketed in last week's snow. A few new snowflakes floated in front of the headlights. They'd grabbed Butter-Burgers at Culver's before heading out of town. Now, Rachel held tightly to the thermos of hot chocolate she'd brought as the wheels rolled almost soundlessly, the engine muffled by the cushion of gathering snow.

Caleb peered over the steering wheel into the night sky. "I think we're almost there. I've been to Jed's a couple of times, but everything looks so different in the dark."

Rachel squinted. "I see a mailbox ahead."

"Yep, that'll be it." He pulled into the long driveway, shifted the car into low gear, and drove slowly until a farmhouse came into view. There were no lights on inside the house, but a tall yard light illuminated the small farmstead.

"The pond is behind the barn down there." Caleb rolled past the barn, and the smooth frozen surface came into view. No footprints marred the ground around the oval pond, and a small platoon of maple trees stood sentinel, their upraised arms outlined against an almost full moon.

He parked near the edge of the pond, cut the engine, and opened his car door.

Rachel tucked the thermos of hot chocolate on the floor in front of her seat, along with the mugs she'd thought to bring at the last minute. Not waiting for Caleb to open her door as he usually did, she climbed out.

He pulled up the hood on his parka and she did the same with hers after quickly wrapping the thick wool scarf she'd brought around her neck. They tugged on gloves, then grabbed their skates from the back seat and carried them over to a snow-dusted bench near the edge of the ice.

Caleb brushed one end of the bench clean. "Here. Sit. I'll help you lace up."

"Thank you, because I've almost forgotten how." She slipped off her right boot as he knelt in front of her, their breaths fogging and mingling in the night air. He finished lacing one skate and gave her ankle a pat. "Is that too tight?"

She put her foot down, testing. "Feels fine."

He slapped his knee lightly. "Other foot."

She wriggled out of her left boot.

When he'd finished lacing that one, she stood on wobbly ankles and clutched the arm of the bench while Caleb laced his own skates.

When he finished, he offered his elbow. "Ready?"

She nodded. "Ready as I'll ever be." She held onto his arm as they clomped to the pond's bank.

Caleb slid her hand from its death grip on the crook of his elbow and tugged her out onto the ice.

Immediately, her skates wanted to go in two different directions. Flailing to regain her balance, she laughed. "Did I mention I haven't been on skates in over a year?"

He let her hand slide from his and skated a figure eight around her. "It's easy. Just follow my lead." His skates sliced through the dusting of snow on the ice like a knife blade through powdered sugar.

She put her hands out in front of her and shuffled her feet, feeling like a clumsy marionette.

Why had she ever thought this was a good idea? She was a klutz and he was athletic and graceful.

Caleb laughed, spun a full circle, and skated back to her. "Give me your hands."

She let him take her by the hands and guide her to the middle of the pond.

"Try to relax."

"I am. Remember, I didn't grow up on skates like you did."

"If you fall, you just get back up. How hard is that?"

"Easy for you to say. Oh—!" Her right foot veered way off to the side, taking her leg with it.

He sped up, tightening his grip and holding her gaze. "You're doing great. Just relax, Rachel. Bend your knees and lean forward a little bit." He tugged gently, pulling her closer to him.

She sucked in an icy breath, forcing her muscles to relax.

"That's better. See there, you're doing it. You've got this!"

Gradually, she found her stride, and soon they were gliding across the ice, matching each other's gait step for step. Only the intermittent scrape of their skates broke the silence of the winter night.

After a few minutes, he patted her gloved hand with his own. "See? Look at you."

"You make it look so easy." As they circled the outer edge of the pond again, her breaths came more evenly, matching the rhythm he set. "Last year my church had a skating party, and I finally figured it out by the end of the night."

"It'll come even quicker this time. You'll see." He picked up the pace a little, and she held tighter. They went around the pond again, and when they passed the bench on the shore, he turned to her. "Want to try it on your own?"

She didn't. She was quite content beside him. But maybe he was hinting. She looked up at him with a sheepish smile. "Am I cramping your style?"

"Not at all. I just thought you might want to test yourself."

"Maybe for a minute." She loosened the grip she had on his arm and took a tentative glide away from him.

"That's it. Don't try to lift your feet. Just let them feel the ice, find your rhythm."

She felt his eyes on her as she skated beyond him, but instead of feeling self-conscious, she felt safe, protected.

She skated a wide figure eight, confidence building with every glide of her blades. She counted out the time in her head, letting her natural rhythm take over. Despite the freezing temperatures, it was a glorious evening. The countryside looked enchanting with the moon reflected through the maple branches and the whole world hovering in a misty fog.

As she sailed back toward Caleb, she couldn't keep from smiling. "I may not be the most graceful thing on blades, but this has to be the next best thing to flying!"

Caleb grinned back at her, looking pleased. He reached out and, in one smooth motion, glided alongside her, placing his hand at her waist. The warmth of his arm around her, his weight against her, made her feel invincible. He took her hand again and, even through their thick wool gloves, his strength warmed her.

They skated in silence, but Tchaikovsky's "Dance of the Sugar Plum Fairy" plucked its merry way through her mind. What would Caleb say if she told him that? Did he even know who Tchaikovsky was? And if he didn't, was that a problem for her?

Would it be a problem for him that she didn't know the first thing about football? But maybe they could learn, each of them. Because there could be so many good things about her and Caleb together. *So many.*

"Are you warm enough?"

She nodded, not wanting to lie. The truth was her toes were starting to go numb and her cheeks stung with the biting air. But she didn't care. She wanted this night to go on forever.

"Let's go around one more time," he said, "and then we'll warm up with some of that hot chocolate you brought."

She smiled, leaned into him, and let *The Nutcracker Suite* continue to provide the soundtrack for the evening.

Caleb pushed the driver's seat back and leaned his head against the leather headrest. A chunky mug Rachel had brought warmed his hands, the hot chocolate warmed his belly, and the woman beside him warmed his heart.

Good grief, Janssen. What has gotten into you? He was turning into a sappy poet. And he blamed Rachel Hamblin completely.

Had he felt this way about Liz? Even in the beginning? He didn't think so. Liz had been . . . high-maintenance. Rachel was anything but. She was easy to be with, she seemed to think more often of him than she did of herself, and she not only laughed at his corny jokes, but she made him laugh in return.

This was crazy. Utterly crazy. They didn't even have that much in common. And yet, being with her made him want to learn more about the things that were important to her. Like music and composers. He wasn't going to start taking piano lessons or anything crazy like that, but he wanted to know what made her tick simply because if she cared about it, it was important.

He drained his mug and sighed contentedly. After changing out of their skates and getting the car warmed up, they'd talked and laughed for almost an hour until the windows fogged up all around them, enclosing them in a cozy cocoon that only the moonlight breached.

She unscrewed the lid from the thermos and held it out. "There's a little left. You want it?"

"You go ahead."

"I'm good. I still have some." She lifted her mug and took a sip as if giving proof, then looked at him over the rim. "Thank you for tonight. It was really special."

"You were getting pretty good on those skates. We'll turn you into a Michigander yet," he teased.

But her answer held no humor. "I really don't want to leave Mapleview, Caleb. I can't believe I'm saying this, but I think I'm a small-town girl at heart. I'd run the cash register at Family Fare before I'd take a teaching job in the city."

"Wow. That's pretty serious."

She shrugged. "Well, I can't actually see myself working in a grocery store, but I can picture that sooner than I can picture moving away from Mapleview." She met his gaze. "Especially now."

"Now?"

"You're not exactly making it easy to think about leaving town."

"You've come a long way, city girl." He nudged her playfully, afraid to take her comment too seriously. "I do hope you'll stay, though." He reached for her hand.

"I hope I can." She squeezed his hand and intertwined her fingers with his.

"But you wouldn't waste your teaching degree just to stay? I mean, you still want to teach, right?"

"I don't know anything else, Caleb. I just wish everything was settled. That I knew where I'd be a year from now. Or even a month from now."

"I know what you mean." He lifted their hands and kissed the back of hers. "Would I be presumptuous to say that I hope you'll still be here a year from now?"

"Here, as in Mapleview?"

"Here, as in with me. Like this." He kissed her hand again.

"Not presumptuous at all." Her words came out in a whisper.

He wanted to kiss more than her hand, but he needed to state the obvious first. "You do realize that you could be dating an unemployed loser, right?"

"You do know you could be dating the same, right?"

He laughed. "At least we'll have something in common."

"For a change."

He smirked, then turned serious. "You're getting some students though, right? You've had a good response to your ad? From people here in town."

"Do you know how happy it makes me to see you look so worried at the thought that I might move away?"

"Is it that obvious?"

She nodded. "And to answer your question, I have four spots filled and six other inquiries. It's a start."

"How many would you need? To make a living doing that?"

"I'd like to have thirty-five students. At least in the summertime when kids are out of school. But I could probably pay the mortgage—*rent*," she amended quickly, "with twenty-five or thirty."

"Mortgage? Are you looking for a house?"

She hesitated. "I can't teach in my apartment, so yes, if I get enough students, I'd like to buy a house here."

"I'm looking too, for someplace to open a gym. So you know I'm not going anywhere either." He inched closer, wanting to kiss her so bad he could taste it. "I'm kind of getting to like a certain girl I've met here."

Rachel smiled softly and met his gaze. "She might be kind of getting to like you too," she whispered.

"Do you think she'd mind if I kissed her?"

"I think she'd be really disappointed if you didn't."

He cradled her head in his hands and pulled her close, matching his lips to hers, careful to keep their first kiss tender and sweet despite the fire she lit inside him.

She caressed his cheek and tangled her fingers in his hair, pulling him closer, deepening their kiss. Far too soon, she pulled away, then moved close again for another kiss, shorter but even sweeter, if that were possible.

"You don't know how long I've been wanting to do that."

She giggled. "Caleb Janssen, it couldn't be too long. You never gave me a second look until a week ago."

"Yes, and I've been wanting to kiss you ever since I gave you that second look."

"Well, you got your wish."

He leaned in for another kiss, and when he came up for air, he noticed movement outside the car windows. He reached behind her and rubbed a spot clear from the fogged window. "It's really snowing hard now."

She extricated herself from his grasp and turned to look out the window. "Oh! How pretty! It's like 'The Waltz of the Snowflakes.' You know, from *The Nutcracker Suite*?"

"Ah, Tchaikovsky."

"Oooh, I'm impressed. You even pronounced his name right."

He shot her a sheepish grin. "Just don't ask me to spell it. And the snow *is* really pretty, but I don't want to get stuck out here."

"Would that be so terrible?" She tilted her head at him, wearing an expression that sparked an uptick in his pulse.

"Aside from the fact that we'd freeze to death as soon as my car ran out of gas, I'm not sure I trust myself alone with you in close quarters." He put a hand lightly on her cheek, wanting her to understand. "I don't want us to have any regrets, Rachel."

"Then you'd better take me home." Her voice turned husky. "Because that makes two of us."

Chapter Ten

Rachel stared at the phone, unable to help the grin that came. She'd been approved for the loan! Even with only a dozen confirmed piano students lined up, her down payment, combined with her credit score, meant the loan was hers.

Everything was falling into place better than she could have imagined. Once she heard from Bridgette, she would breathe a huge sigh of relief. But Bridgette had warned that three agents were bringing offers and they were meeting at five to review the bids. She'd said Rachel's was the only offer she was bringing to the table, but those multiple offers made Rachel uneasy.

Bridgette had tried to soothe her nerves. "Some of those may have contingencies—which would give you an advantage—but it may take a while to go through them too. It could be six o'clock or after before you hear anything. But I promise, I'll let you know as soon as I possibly can. I know you're anxious."

Oddly, Bridgette had also told her about another house that had just come on the market. Rachel had already seen that listing online and it wasn't even close to what she was looking for. There wasn't another house in town that would excite her now that she'd put an offer on the Visser School.

"Is there a reason you're mentioning this new property, Bridgette?" she'd asked, terrified the agent knew something she couldn't say.

But Bridgette had laughed and waved her off. "No, of course not.

I just didn't want you to win the bid on the school and then come back and chew me out for not telling you there was a new property to choose from."

———— ❧ ————

"Well, this is it." Caleb frowned and swallowed hard.

Rachel looked around the teachers' lounge at these friends she'd worked with for three years now. The official speeches were over, the students gone, and the building mostly cleared out. She'd been doing so well—hadn't cried once this week—but the emotion in Caleb's voice threatened to do her in now.

Mindy wept openly, and Caleb put an arm around her. "Gonna miss you. All of you."

"I'll miss you too, Coach." Mindy gave him a wavering smile.

Rachel swallowed the lump in her own throat but lost it when Caleb winked at her across the room, as if to say he didn't plan to get a chance to miss *her*.

They'd barely seen each other the whole week, with all the school activities that had been clumped together in an effort to give the students a sense of closure and the feeling that they'd actually had a full school year. Caleb had caught her on the way to her car last night and, after checking to be sure no one was watching, he'd wrapped his arms around her and kissed her good. "Just wanted to be sure you didn't forget about me."

"How could I forget you?" she teased. "We have a date Saturday."

"Okay. Just checking." He kissed her again, then jogged to his car without another word.

She'd stood there smiling like a fool for five minutes until Mindy came out to her own car parked beside Rachel's and asked if everything was okay.

Now Rachel sobered at the memory. She hated that she'd neglected her friendship with Mindy because of Caleb. She'd been on the other end of that situation when friends from Kansas City had found boyfriends and drifted away one by one, most eventually getting married.

She understood, but that didn't make it any easier to have a friendship fade. She made a mental note not to do that to her friend. She pulled Mindy aside and draped an arm over her shoulder. "How are you doing?"

"Hanging in there. I decided it's not worth getting depressed over. I'm sure things will turn out fine. Eventually."

"That's the spirit, girlfriend."

She needed to tell herself the same. But things wouldn't really be okay until she got the call about the property. She hugged Mindy and they promised to stay in touch, then she checked her phone for the dozenth time in an hour. She'd already planned how she would tell Caleb when she finally got the call from Bridgette. And she was pretty sure it would earn her another kiss.

Smiling to herself, she helped Della gather up leftovers from the tray of cookies and brownies the older teacher had brought for this afternoon's workday.

"I'm telling you, kids," Della said. "It seems like just yesterday we were in this room with our mouths hanging open at the announcement the school was closing. Now here we are, and it's all over. A done deal."

"I don't know." Jed shook his head. "Seems more like a lifetime ago." He inched toward the door. "You guys don't be strangers, okay?"

"You come here, Jed Palmer." Della opened her arms wide, crossing the room. "You're not getting out of here without a hug."

Laughing, Jed returned Della's embrace. "You enjoy those grandkids, okay?"

"Oh, you don't have to tell me twice."

Again, Rachel teared up. She hated emotional goodbyes, even though it would have been far worse to pretend this was just another Friday afternoon.

After all the goodbyes had been said, it was almost anticlimactic walking out the door for the last time. But it was close to five o'clock now, and she wanted to be home when Bridgette's call came.

She walked through her classroom—*former* classroom—one last time, whispering a prayer of thanks for all the learning she'd done in this room, this school. She snapped a couple of photos, then deleted them just as quickly because the room looked so empty and sad. She didn't want to remember it that way.

She crossed the room and untacked a tattered poster from the wall—a glossary of music terms done in artsy fonts. She'd bought it for her college dorm, dreaming of someday having it in her classroom—what had turned out to be *this* classroom. Maybe she would have it framed to hang in her music studio.

She sighed, gave the room a final lingering look, and headed to her car.

The clock above her baby grand ticked past seven p.m. Rachel checked her phone for the dozenth time in as many minutes. Still no call from Bridgette. Did that mean good news or the worst possible?

One hopeful thing—she'd gotten two new students, middle school brothers, just since she got home. That made fourteen for-sure clients—all piano students—for her new business venture. She was almost halfway to being able to pay the bills.

The phone made her jump. But when she turned it over, the screen showed Caleb's name. She hesitated. As eager as she was to talk to him, she didn't want to miss Bridgette's call, or cut Caleb off in the middle of a conversation if Bridgette called while they were talking.

But she didn't want him to think she was ignoring him either.

She clicked *Accept*. "Hey, Caleb. Before you say anything, I just want to warn you I'm expecting a call any minute that I need to take."

"No problem. I'll make this quick. I know we have a real date tomorrow night, but would you want to go out for coffee tonight? I just got some kind of amazing news that I want to tell you in person."

"News?"

"I don't mean to sound so mysterious, but it'd just be easier to show you."

"Well, you really have me curious now." She checked the time. "I need to wait on this call, but I'll text you when I'm off. That sound okay?"

"Sure. I'll text you when I'm outside."

She gave an exaggerated sigh. "I knew the rude jock would eventually kick in."

He laughed. "Fine, I'll come to the door."

"I'm kidding, Caleb. I'll text you as soon as I'm ready." She clicked off, smiling.

She carried her phone into the bathroom, quickly brushed her hair, and put a little lip gloss on, praying Bridgette didn't wait too long to call. Rachel didn't want to upstage whatever Caleb's announcement was, but she just might have her own "kind of amazing news" to share by the time she saw him.

The minutes dragged past. At 6:45 she was about to call Caleb and apologize when the phone rang.

Bridgette's name lit up her screen.

Rachel attacked the *Accept* button with three staccato taps. "Hi, Bridgette."

There was an ever-so-brief hesitation and somehow, in that moment, Rachel knew the news wasn't good.

"I'm so sorry, Rachel, but you didn't get it. The bidding was really super close, and you were right there in the running, but a couple of other offers came in just a little higher."

Rachel almost couldn't breathe, but she managed to squeak out, "Can I make a higher offer?" Maybe her parents would loan her enough money to up her bid another five thousand.

"No, I'm sorry. With best and final offers, the bid you place is the last chance."

Bridgette had already told her that, but Rachel was left grasping at straws.

"I really thought you had a good chance to get this, Rachel. And you will definitely be the first to know if the deal falls through for some reason . . ." Her voice trailed off.

"But they'd both have to fall through, right? Both of the higher bidders?"

"Yes, that's true. Though stranger things have happened."

The happy tune that had been playing in her head before the phone rang transposed to a minor key and became a dirge. "Sure. Thank you for letting me know."

"Would you like to take a look at that listing I sent you earlier?"

"No, I don't think so. But thank you."

"I'm really sorry, Rachel."

Rachel struggled to keep her voice even. "It's okay."

"We'll keep looking. I know there's a home just perfect out there for you."

"Thank you, Bridgette. Bye." She hung up and, despite telling herself that this wasn't the worst thing that could happen by far, the tears came. A flood of them. She couldn't remember when she'd last felt a disappointment so deep. Why hadn't she offered just a thousand dollars more? Bridgette had said the bids were close. And she'd seemed so confident Rachel would be the highest bidder.

But how could anyone know that? She shouldn't have trusted the agent. She should have—

Her phone dinged with a text. Caleb.

Just checking . . . :)

The smiley face didn't help. She didn't really want to see him now. And she'd probably just cry on his shoulder the whole night. Actually, that didn't sound like such a bad thing. She sniffed and texted back.

Just off the phone. Ready in five. It would be good to talk to someone. And being with Caleb would get her mind off the crushing blow she'd just received.

Be right there.

Bridgette had said there was still a chance if the other deals fell through. She wouldn't have said that if there wasn't at least a faint possibility of that happening, right? A spark of hope flared. Of course, Bridgette had also implied that she believed Rachel would get the property.

She blew out a breath. It was irrational to blame the real estate agent for what had happened, but she wanted to blame somebody.

She hurried back to the bathroom to repair the damage her tears had done to her makeup. *Lord, help me be excited for his news.*

Her phone chimed.

I'm here.

She pasted on a preemptive smile and texted back. *On my way.*

Caleb was beaming when she opened the passenger side door. "Hi. You look happy."

He reached to squeeze her hand briefly. "I'm with you, aren't I?"

She swallowed hard. If he was going to be sweet with her, she wasn't sure she could control her emotions. "So what's this cool news?"

He grinned, looking mysterious. "Just be patient. You notice the *show* in show-and-tell comes before the *tell*?"

"You're killing me." Her own ears told her it came out wooden.

He cocked his head and studied her. "Are you okay?"

She waved him off and forced back the tears that threatened. "I'm fine. So, where are we going? I need a hint."

Thankfully, he seemed to dismiss his earlier concern. "Not far. In fact, we won't even leave the city limits."

"Okay then, let's get this bus moving."

Caleb couldn't seem to quit smiling. He turned left on Church Street and drove down Twenty-Fifth. Was he heading out to Jed's pond again? No, that was outside the city limits. He drove past the turnoff. In another block, they would be driving right by "her" house. She looked out the window, purposely turning to the other side of the street. If she had to look at that beautiful brick house that was not hers, she would definitely break down.

She bit her bottom lip, watching street signs so she'd know when they'd passed the property. But the car slowed and she felt it turning. Turning toward the house.

She looked through the windshield at the house, the lights glowing from inside as if mocking her. "What . . . ? What are we doing?"

Caleb had turned into the driveway of the Visser School, and now he sat there grinning like Alice's Cheshire cat. "Welcome to Janssen's Gym. Come on, I'll show you!" He climbed out of the car and waited for her to follow.

Her legs felt as though they were made of wood, but she managed to get out and stand on the sidewalk in front of her dream house.

"Janssen's Gym." He held an imaginary sign up in the direction of the door. "But I'm thinking about spelling it J-Y-M . . . you know, for alliteration. What do you think?"

Mind reeling, she stared at him. "What do you mean this is your gym?"

"I bought it. This property. Put an offer on it last week and just got the call tonight that it's mine!" That stupid grin grew wider. "You should see inside. I haven't closed on it, of course, so I don't have the keys, but wait till you get a look inside. It is perfect for a gym. The main floor needs a little bit of paint. What's there now is a little too pink for my taste, but the building is exactly what I need. It's got hardwood floors and great light, and there's even living quarters up—"

"*You* bought this house?"

He nodded, looking so proud of himself. "It was an office most recently, but originally a school. It was called Visser Sch—"

"I know, Caleb. I know all about the history of this gorgeous home. And about the cozy loft and tiny bathroom. But *you* bought this?" Her brain finally put the horrible two and two together.

"I did." His smile faded. "But . . . how do you know so much about this place?"

"Because *I* tried to buy it." Her voice broke. "I bid on it, Caleb. Every penny I could possibly come up with."

"What? You mean . . . ?" He stood there with his mouth open. "You were one of the bidders?"

"One of the losers, you mean?"

"Oh, Rachel. I didn't know. I didn't—Why didn't you say something?"

"Why didn't you?" She had to work not to shout. "You knew I was looking for a place like this. You knew I needed a place to teach lessons."

"I knew you were looking for a house." His expression turned hard, but she heard the pain in his voice. "I never dreamed you had something like this in mind. I even looked at a couple of houses I thought would be perfect for you. With big living rooms that would have space for your piano."

"To soften the blow?" She hated the ugly sarcasm in her own voice.

"Rachel. I swear to you I didn't know. I had no idea you were looking at this place."

"Can't you see how perfect it would have been for my music studio?"

Their gazes locked for an uncomfortable second before he looked at the sidewalk, scuffing the toe of his boot along a jagged crack in the cement. "I'm sorry. It just never crossed my mind."

Was God really this cruel? It wasn't hard enough that she hadn't gotten the house? She had to lose it to *Caleb*?

She took a ragged breath. It wasn't Caleb's fault. She didn't think he was lying to her.

But maybe it said more about their relationship that it had never crossed his mind that it might be the perfect place for her lessons.

Did it cross your *mind that it might be perfect for his gym?*

Guilt washed over her. She was acting like a spoiled brat. He had every bit as much right to buy the property as she did. If only he'd told her before.

Did you tell him?

She had a feeling if the tables had been turned and she'd won the bid, he wouldn't be struggling so much to be gracious. To rejoice with her.

She should tell him she was happy for him. But that would be a lie.

"Caleb, it's a beautiful house." That much she could say honestly. "I'm so sorry, but I think I'd like to go home. I need some time alone right now. I . . . hope you understand."

The disappointment on his face made her feel awful. But she was disappointed too.

A troubling question pushed itself into her consciousness. How could she continue to see him, to consider sharing a life with him, while he was turning her dream home into a *gym*? Though she hadn't spoken it aloud, the word turned sour in her mouth.

But what did it matter? It was a nonissue. He'd gotten the house, not her. And without a place to teach lessons—if she ever even got enough students—there was nothing here for her.

Chapter Eleven

Caleb felt sick to his stomach. If he'd only known. But would he really have refrained from bidding on the property—for Rachel's sake? He was afraid to examine the answer to his own question too closely. At least he wouldn't have rubbed her face in it. Wouldn't have treated her disappointment like a cause for celebration.

He risked reaching out to put a hand on Rachel's arm.

At least she didn't flinch.

"I'm sorry, Rachel," he said again. He didn't know what else to say. Why hadn't she told him she was trying to buy the old Visser School? Of course, he hadn't told her either. They were only just getting to know each other, and he'd tempered his expectation because there had been a good chance he might not end up the highest bidder. It had seemed premature to share until he knew something for sure. "I promise I didn't know." The words felt lame.

"I understand that, but it doesn't make it any easier."

"I'll take you home."

Looking numb, she nodded, walked to the car, and climbed in.

They rode in silence back to her apartment. He parked in front of the stairway to her second-floor unit. "I'll walk you up."

He started to open his door, but she touched his arm. "No, it's okay. You don't need to. I'm fine."

"You don't sound fine."

With a weak smile, she opened the car door but didn't get out.

"Rachel? About tomorrow night . . . ?" The cold air that blasted around them seemed fitting.

"I don't think I'd be much fun. Maybe we shouldn't."

"I'd like to see you. You don't always have to be 'fun.' We should talk this out. I don't want to leave things hanging."

"I just need some time, Caleb." She shut the car door quietly, closing herself back in with him to continue the conversation. "I'm trying to process things."

"Fine. I'll give you space, but please don't shut me out. This isn't my fault, you know."

"Then whose fault is it?"

"Does it have to be somebody's fault? Sometimes things just happen."

"Seriously? What happened to the guy who was all, 'God has a reason' and 'just have faith'?" she mimicked.

The words stung. Deeply. He stared at her. What had happened to the woman he'd been so busy falling in love with? "I do still believe that—that God has a reason for all of this. But I don't know what it is. And it doesn't seem like you're quite ready to hear that anyway."

"I'm . . . I'm glad things are working out for you. Really." Chagrin colored her tone. "It just hurts that they seem to be working out for you at my expense."

He opened his mouth to reason further, then sighed, giving up. "Goodnight, Rachel. I'll call you." He started to add that he'd be praying for her—and he would—but somehow that didn't seem like the right thing to say under the circumstances. In her current state of mind, she would see it more like him throwing fuel on the fire.

She gave him a tight-lipped nod and got out of the car. "Goodnight."

He watched until she'd gotten into her apartment safely. Then he drove away.

Would he ever see her again? Suddenly all the hopes and ideas he'd had for the property, the excitement of starting this business he'd dreamed about most of his adult life, were crushed. All of them. Under Rachel's disappointment.

Because he did know how she must be feeling. He would have felt the same if she'd been the one to win the bid.

The truth was, despite all his lofty claims to Rachel, he didn't know why God had let this happen. And it might unravel every wonderful thing he thought God had been doing.

Boom! Boom! Boom!

Rachel stopped playing. Immediately, the pounding overhead came again—her upstairs neighbor letting her know in no uncertain terms that they did not appreciate her evening concert.

Knowing she shouldn't, she finished the third movement of Mozart's Piano Sonata No. 11 in A Major with a flourish, striking the final keys with defiance. She waited for more pounding, but none came. Either they'd enjoyed the conclusion or were on their way down to complain. She carefully closed the lid over the piano keys and put her head in her hands, emotions a jumble.

Not only had she lost the house to Caleb, but she couldn't even do the one thing she found comforting and therapeutic without getting reprimanded from neighbors.

She slid from the piano bench and walked through her apartment. Panic rose in her throat as she considered her options. She had promised piano lessons to fourteen students beginning on April 1. Not even six weeks from now. And she could not teach in this apartment. Nor could she afford to rent a building. Maybe she did need to take a look at the new property Bridgette had told her about.

She pulled it up on her laptop and wanted to cry. The listing called the property "move-in ready" but to her eyes, it was anything but. She would want to rip out the carpet and put in hardwood floors, and paint the builder's-beige walls a lovely shade of pink-tinged white. And build a stage at one end of the living room for her piano.

She gave a humorless laugh. It didn't take a psychiatrist to point out what games her mind was playing.

Get over it, Hamblin. You lost. Still, to think of how long she'd scrimped every month, saving the money for a down payment on a house, and then to settle for something like this pathetic listing? Talk about depressing. Especially when the absolutely perfect place was right across town.

Maybe she could find a house to rent. It didn't have to be large. But at least she could teach lessons if she got out of the apartment. And it would buy her some time until another dream house came on the market. She searched the rental website she'd used to find her current place, but everything in her price range was in an apartment complex.

Her phone rang from the kitchen where she'd left it, and her thoughts immediately went to Caleb. She wasn't sure she was ready to talk to him, yet she felt sick about the way she'd reacted. She'd been so thoughtless. Even cruel. Could he ever forgive her?

She went to answer, but it was her mom's photo lighting up the screen. She picked up without enabling her phone's camera. "Hi, Mom."

"Hi, honey. Oops, I must have done something wrong. I can't see you."

Rachel forced a laugh. "I didn't turn my camera on. I just got home and I'm a mess." It wasn't exactly a lie.

"Oh, stop it. I don't care what you look like."

Rachel ran to the hall mirror and checked to see how red her eyes were. Maybe if she didn't turn on any lights, her mom wouldn't notice. She returned to the living room and dimmed the lamp by the sofa before enabling her camera.

"There you are!"

She waved and gave a cheesy smile.

"How was your last day?" Mom's voice was thick with sympathy. "Dad and I have been praying for you."

"Thanks, Mom. It was hard, but it's kind of a relief to be done too."

"I'm sure."

"Where is Dad?"

Mom clucked her tongue. "That man. He's still at work. I don't know why he thinks we have to keep the store open until all hours of the night. It's not as if somebody is going to buy a grand piano at eight o'clock in the evening."

"Can you let him know I have fourteen students now?"

"You do? Oh, honey, that's wonderful."

"Yes. Now I just need somewhere to give lessons."

"Are you still thinking about buying that property you told us about?"

"Actually . . ." She willed her voice not to waver. "I did put an offer on it. But I didn't get it. I was outbid."

"Oh, Rachel. I'm sorry. Well, there must be a reason. I'm sure there are other nice houses there."

"Not really. But I'll keep looking."

"You know, there are a couple of cute places that just came on the market in Overland Park. Dad's been keeping an eye out for you. I can send you the links if you want."

"Tell him thanks, but I really don't want to leave Mapleview. My friends are here." She hadn't told her parents about Caleb. Not that there was anything to tell now.

"You have friends here too, you know."

"Not really anyone I'm close to anymore. And besides, I really like my church here." That much was true, but she'd only said it because that would make her mom stop pushing for her to move.

They talked for a few more minutes before a beep came through on the line. "Sorry, Mom, but I've got another call. It might be somebody about lessons." And it was a good excuse to end the call.

"Oh, of course, sweetie. Good luck. Love you."

"Love you too. Tell Dad hi." She clicked over and answered the other call. And when she hung up fifteen minutes later, she had confirmed a forty-five-year-old woman for both piano and voice lessons. She had fifteen students with sixteen hours of lessons now.

Okay, God. You must want me to do this. Please show me where I'm supposed to teach all these students. Though she still felt heavyhearted, at least it looked as though her dream job just might become a reality. Too bad it couldn't have happened in her dream house.

Chapter Twelve

Caleb put the key in the door of his new house, feeling strangely disappointed. His real estate agent, Mac McPherson, had met him at the house to do one last walk-through before the closing. Which wasn't for another week, but the house had passed inspection, and the owner had agreed to turn over the keys early. One of the perks of living in a small town. Caleb was thankful he could get started early on some of the projects he needed to get done before signing up his first clients.

As he followed Mac from room to room, Caleb struggled to stay focused, and when the walk-through was finished, they stood on the front porch looking out to the street.

Caleb took a deep breath and broached an idea he'd been toying with since last night. "Mac, let me throw something out here."

"Sure, shoot."

"Would I lose my earnest money if I decided to give up the property and let the second highest bidder have it?"

"Whoa." Mac shot him a questioning look. "Are you having buyer's remorse?"

"Not exactly. It's complicated. I just wanted to ask if that was even a possibility."

"Well, I guess you could approach the bidder and see if he's still interested. If he is, he might be willing to make up the difference with the earnest money. You only put a thousand down, right?"

"Wait. 'He'? I thought the other bidder was a woman."

"Reinhold Bailey from over in Dorr was second in line. Wanted it for office space is what I heard. We can talk to him, see if he's still interested. If you're sure."

"No. No, I guess I misunderstood. I didn't know there were that many bids on the place." Well, that answered his most burning question. It wouldn't make any difference to Rachel's situation if he backed out now. And, deep down inside, he was glad to not have to make that decision.

But did *she* know she wasn't second in line? He needed to tell her. Maybe that information would help her accept what had happened. At least a little.

A green pickup pulled up to the curb, and Jed Palmer tooted his horn. Jed had agreed to help with some painting and repairs in exchange for an equal number of personal trainer hours. "I need some kind of incentive," he'd told Caleb, "since I won't be working out with the team anymore."

Caleb was thankful for a continued connection to his friend. He could use a listening ear about now.

Rachel had asked for some time, and he was determined to give it to her. But he'd told her he would call, and he'd meant that too. She may not be interested in seeing him again, but he refused to just let things fizzle out between them without at least talking things through. Too many misunderstandings festered into bitterness simply because people refused to talk about hard things.

And this was a hard one, for sure. He'd wracked his brain trying to think of something he could say that might comfort her. But he was drawing a blank.

"Looks like your work crew is here," Mac said. "You sure everything's good?"

"Yes. Everything's fine. Don't worry, I won't be backing out. It was just a random idea I was considering for various reasons."

"Okay then, I'll leave you to it. See you at closing."

Caleb shook his hand and waited for Jed to reach the door.

"You actually bought this place, huh?"

"Yep, I did it. Thanks for the tip, man. I think it'll be perfect."

"I'm anxious to see the place. Like I said, I haven't been in here since it was an insurance agency." Jed went inside and walked through the place, saying all the things Caleb had hoped Rachel would say.

The thought was painful. He missed her. And yet, their last exchange—her caustic words—kept running through his mind. He fought off the bitter retorts that came. He'd argued with her more in his imagination over these last three days than he'd talked with her altogether since that first night together at Paddy's. Even so, he missed her.

"As much as I'll miss you and everybody from VCCS, I'm kind of excited." Mindy sat across from Rachel in a cozy booth at the coffee-shop downtown. Mindy had taken a job filling in for a librarian on maternity leave at the elementary school in Vanderburgh Center, with the possibility of teaching there full-time next school year.

"I'm so happy for you, Mindy. It sounds like the perfect opportunity. At least it beats cleaning toilets at a bar." She winked, remembering her friend's comment the day they'd learned their school was closing.

"You should put in an application, Rachel. Seriously, you never know what might open up." Mindy waited for a noisy coffee grinder to finish before continuing. "I figured there was no way I could get on at another school this year, but now I'll even have a couple of months with double paychecks. I might even look into buying a house. Well, once I know for sure I have a job for next year."

"Yes, don't rush into anything." Taking a sip of the hot brew, she told Mindy about trying to buy the property. "My bid wasn't high enough, though." She forced brightness into her voice that she didn't feel. "Caleb Janssen actually bought it. He's going to open a gym there."

"He did? Well, good for him." She stirred her coffee and took a tentative sip.

Obviously, Mindy didn't understand how badly she'd wanted that property. And that was okay. Nobody needed to know. It was history. Water under the proverbial bridge. "And I've got quite a few students lined up for lessons."

"Rachel, that's wonderful. It looks like things are working out for all of us. God is good."

"He is, but would you mind praying that I can find someplace to teach my lessons? I can't do it in my apartment, so I need to either find a house to buy, like, tomorrow. Or maybe just rent one until I find what I want."

Mindy gave her a curious look. "I had no idea you were looking to move out of your apartment."

She shrugged and crumpled her paper napkin. "I can't do lessons there because the walls are paper thin and the neighbors complain when I play, never mind some third grader playing 'Chopsticks.'"

The reference brought a memory rushing back. That night she and Caleb had talked about him neglecting his childhood piano lessons, he'd talked about "Chopsticks" being a challenge. So many memories between them. How long would those memories dog her?

But Mindy's enigmatic chuckle drew Rachel back to the present.

Her friend set down her mug and leaned toward Rachel. "Honey, I can do more than just pray for you."

"What do you mean?"

Mindy's smile lit up the coffee shop. "How would you like to move into my house for the rest of the year?"

"I don't understand." It had been a while since she'd been in the tiny house Mindy rented, but if she remembered right, it was a one-bedroom, one-bath tract house. Not exactly roommate material.

"I've got a place to stay in Vanderburgh Center once I start teaching, but I was going to have to pay rent here too." Her smile grew wider. "Unless I could find someone to sublet the house until my contract is up in January. But, like I said, I didn't know you were looking for a place."

The cookie-cutter house wasn't a place Rachel could get too excited about, but it did fill a need. No. A check in her spirit corrected the thought. It answered a prayer. "Would there be room for my piano?"

"I'm sure there would. You've been there. The living room and dining room are one big space. And there's an area for a little table and two chairs in the kitchen, so you could use the dining room for your music studio. I'll warn you, though, the bedroom is tiny. But hey, the rent is cheap."

"That just might work, Mindy. What a blessing. Thank you." If she could sock away a few hundred extra dollars each month, she would have more options when she was finally ready to buy a house. "I'm so glad you told me."

"And I'm so glad I could help God answer that prayer."

"Well, let me come and measure and make sure the piano will fit before you take me off your prayer list, okay?" Rachel winked. But her mood lifted a little and shifted a notch closer to gratitude.

It was time. He'd waited a full week and hadn't heard so much as "boo" from Rachel. It was March 1, and he wasn't waiting another minute. Besides, he had an idea.

Caleb glanced at the lidded cardboard box beside him on the passenger seat. Wayne meowed from inside, his tail flicking in and out of the box's cut-out handle as if to say he understood the mission they were on.

Nothing like a cat to break the ice, right? Caleb parked in front of Rachel's apartment, his headlights casting a long shadow down the street, and dialed her number.

She picked up on the first ring. "Caleb. Hi."

"Hi, yourself. Are you still mad at me?"

A too-long pause. "I was never mad at you, Caleb. I'm just . . . hurt."

"And I'm still sorry."

"I know. And you don't have to keep saying it. If anything, I owe you an apology."

"Can you come down?" He looked up to where the lights were on in her front window.

"Down where?"

"Oh, sorry. I'm parked outside your apartment building." He watched to see if her apartment door would open.

"Actually, can you come up? I'm kind of in the middle of something."

"Okay, sure. Be up in a sec." He ended the call, grabbed the box with Wayne in it, and headed up the stairs. Was there a no-pet policy? He rushed up the steps, praying Wayne wouldn't meow. The last thing he needed was for her to get kicked out of her apartment because he brought in a cat.

She opened the door before he had a chance to ring the bell. "Come in."

She wore polka-dot pajama pants with a baggy sweatshirt, and her hair was in a messy bun on top of her head. She looked completely adorable.

He carried the box inside, only to find her apartment stacked with similar cardboard boxes.

"You came to help me pack?" She motioned toward his box.

"You're moving?" Another look around the room provided the obvious answer. A sick feeling swept over him. Was she going back to Kansas City?

She nodded and sighed. "I have to be out by tomorrow night. Well, except for the piano. They can't move it until Monday."

"Where are you going?" He leaned against the wall by her front door, his mood sinking. "You weren't going to tell me?"

"I was. It just all happened kind of fast, and I hadn't gotten a chance yet."

The box in his arms meowed.

Rachel jumped back a step. "What was that?"

He set the box on the only clear spot on the sofa and took off the lid.

Wayne's gray head popped up and he perused the room.

She took in a sharp breath. "That's Wayne!"

"Yep. Rachel, meet Wayne. Wayne, Rachel."

She scooped up the cat and cradled it in her arms, nuzzling the top of its head with her chin. "Ohhh, he *is* beautiful." She held Wayne out and looked him in the eye. "Sorry, buddy. *Handsome.* Handsome is what I meant to say." She curled the cat back into the circle of her arms and held it close.

Wayne's half-closed eyes and kneading paws said he didn't mind in the least. But Caleb did mind. Totally irrational to be jealous of a cat, but he would have happily traded places with Wayne at this moment.

Rachel baby-talked the cat into abject submission just the way his mom used to. Within two minutes, the crazy cat was purring so loudly Caleb half expected the neighbors to complain. But the only thought vibrating through his mind was that Rachel was moving. And he wasn't sure she'd ever intended to tell him.

She finally set Wayne down on the floor.

The cat made a beeline for the piano and, before Caleb could stop him, Wayne jumped up on the keys and played a not-half-bad melody with his paws, tripping from high to low and back again.

"He could use a lesson or two," Rachel deadpanned.

Caleb went to retrieve the cat. "He's going to owe you for a new keyboard if he keeps this up."

"He's not hurting anything."

Before Caleb could even get to him, Wayne jumped down and sauntered over to explore a stack of boxes piled by the kitchen.

"So . . ." He turned back. "You're moving?"

She nodded. "Nowhere exciting, but at least I'll get to teach lessons." She dipped her head, her expression contrite. "I don't mean to sound ungrateful either. God provided just what I needed. He really did."

He frowned, hoping he wasn't misunderstanding. "But you're staying. Here. In Mapleview?"

Understanding gradually deepened her expression, and a slow smile curved her lips.

Lips he sorely wanted to kiss at the moment.

"Yes," she said quietly. "I'm subletting the house Mindy was renting. Did you know she took a job in Vanderburgh Center?"

Relief shot through him. "No, I didn't. But that's about the best news I've heard all day. If it means you're staying." He had to be sure.

"Of course. I told you I didn't want to leave Mapleview."

"I know. But that was before." He looked at the floor. "I thought maybe you changed your mind."

"Caleb . . ." Moving an almost empty box off the sofa, she motioned for him to sit before she claimed the piano bench across from him.

Wayne jumped up on her lap, and she smiled and stroked his fur from head to tail. She came away with a handful of fuzz, and it billowed off her hand into the air. She turned to Caleb, her expression serious. "I wouldn't have moved out of town without telling you."

"I wasn't sure."

"Also, I really owe you a huge apology. I acted like a spoiled two-year-old and—"

"No." He held up a hand. "I totally get it. I would have felt the same way if things had gone differently."

"You might have *felt* the same, but I doubt you would have acted the same."

"Don't be so sure. Can we call a truce?" he risked. "I'll help you move these boxes."

Her smile gave him hope that all was not lost. Not yet.

Chapter Thirteen

April

Rachel hefted a box of books, took a deep breath, and steeled herself. She'd agreed to help Caleb move into his new place, which was only fair, given that he and Mindy and Jed had helped her move into Mindy's house almost six weeks ago. They'd even assembled a crew of football players to help move her piano, saving her hundreds of dollars—and without putting one scratch on the monstrous instrument.

But today would be the first time she'd been inside the perfect little house on Twenty-Fifth Street since the day she'd walked through with Bridgette, believing it would soon belong to her.

"You sure you're okay with this?" Caleb stopped, obviously sensing her trepidation.

"I'm fine. Really." She smiled, immediately grateful it felt genuine. "Where do these books go? And hurry, please, they're heavy."

He laughed and took the box from her. "Here, give me those. Can you bring in the vacuum from the back of my car?"

"Sure." Grateful for a tiny reprieve before she had to go inside, she went to get the vacuum out of the Toyota he'd traded his Highlander for. They'd both pared their expenses to the bone and, after one last paycheck from the school next week, they'd be on their own. But they were actually enjoying the challenge of living on the cheap. Their dates were picnics on her living room floor or drive-throughs with buy-one-get-one coupons, then back to her place to play board games. Or if she

317

could talk him into bringing Wayne, laughing at the cat's antics batting paper wads across the floor or chasing her feather duster.

Despite the disappointment she'd experienced, Rachel's days were full and she was blessed. Maybe not quite content yet, but she was working on that part.

She'd gained seven more students and had managed to tuck away most of her last paycheck into savings. She enjoyed one-on-one teaching from home immensely and was falling into a pleasant rhythm of piano lessons and spare time. Which she spent doing what she could—given her newly pared-down budget—to make the rental house a little homier.

She entered through the back door, trying not to think about what could have been. Jed and his wife, Jody, who were putting Caleb's desk back together, called out a greeting, which Rachel returned. She walked across the hardwood floors, cringing a little at the weight machines lined up on the stage where her piano should have gone. *Would* have gone. *If. . .*

But *if* hadn't happened. And it wasn't the end of the world. Not by far. She held up the vacuum cord. "Where do you want me to start?"

"Maybe in the kitchen?" Caleb came and put an arm around her, speaking softly enough that the others couldn't hear. "I appreciate your being here. Are you hanging in there?"

"It helps to see you getting settled in. I'm happy for you, Caleb. I really am." And it was true.

He pulled her closer and kissed the top of her head. "Thank you," he whispered.

"It's starting to look . . . like a gym in here." She wrinkled her nose, but it helped to joke about it. "At least it doesn't smell like one. Yet."

Chuckling, Caleb looked up at the high windows. "It'll look a lot better once we get stuff moved where it goes. And get rid of this pink paint. But that may be a while. First things first."

"Aww, this paint was one of my favorite things about the place." She affected a pout. "And it's not pink. It's white, with just the faintest blush of rose."

He shook his head. "Looks pretty stinkin' pink to me." He tipped her chin up for a kiss.

After kissing him back, she extricated herself from his arms, then plugged in the vacuum and went to work. She could do this. And it really wasn't as hard as she'd thought it might be. Still . . .

With a wistful smile, she looked around the space. It would have made the best piano studio.

Rachel blew a wayward strand of hair off her face and put the paint roller back in the tray, stretching and rubbing the small of her back. She checked the clock in the kitchen. Her next piano lesson would arrive in a little over an hour. She'd better clean up.

With her new landlord's permission, she was giving the main living areas a much-needed fresh coat of paint. In her favorite shade of white. One called Rosy Dawn. She was pretty sure her inspiration—the walls in the old Visser School—were probably some dingy shade of concrete gray by now. The thought made her a little sad. Yet she wasn't angry at Caleb. And right now, they were both so busy getting their businesses off the ground that there wasn't time to dwell on what was in the past.

She hadn't been back to his place since she'd helped him move two weeks ago. He seemed to understand that she wasn't quite ready yet to see her perfect piano studio transformed into a smelly gym.

Someday she would be. Maybe after she found her new dream property.

This rental was just a place to live. A place where at least she could teach lessons. And she was grateful for it. It was just that she'd had a little taste of what could have been, and it had spoiled all other properties. But she was saving enough money living in Mindy's apartment that she was determined to be content here until the perfect house finally came on the market. She continued to watch the market and had gone to a couple of open houses, but everything she liked was way over her price range, and anything in her price range simply didn't appeal.

She covered the paint so she could take up where she left off later and went back to the tiny bedroom to change.

The doorbell rang as she came back out to the living room, and she opened the door.

Caleb stood on the porch with an armful of flowers in a rainbow of colors.

"Caleb, what are you doing here?"

"Just delivering these to my favorite piano teacher." He thrust the flowers toward her. "I think you need to get them in water. Before they wilt."

"They're beautiful. But you shouldn't have. You're on a budget, remember?"

He shrugged. "Four ninety-nine a bunch at Meijer. I got two. You're worth it."

She tipped her chin to plant a kiss on his cheek.

"Get those in water and I'll give you a proper kiss."

Laughing, she went to the kitchen and ran water into a tall white pitcher that had belonged to her grandmother. While she arranged the flowers at the sink—or tried to—he smothered her hair and neck with kisses.

"You'd better cut that out." But she leaned into the kisses just the same. "My next lesson will be here in a few minutes."

"I guess they'll learn about more than playing the piano, then, won't they?"

"Caleb, stop!" She giggled. "Besides, it's a seventy-year-old grand-mother."

"Well then, she could probably teach us a thing or two." But he let go of her and stepped back into the dining room—what she now called the music room.

She finished arranging the flowers and made sure the vase was dry before setting it on the piano. "So pretty. I think I need a line item in my budget for flowers."

He sniffed the air. "What do I smell?"

"Flowers?"

"No, it smells like paint."

"It is paint."

He panned the room. "Oh, I see now. That looks nice."

"Not too pink for you?" She grinned.

"It's a little pink. But it looks good on you." He kissed her again. "I'd probably even live in a house with walls that pink as long as you were in it too."

Something about his expression made her heart beat faster. Those blue eyes of his spoke fathoms when he looked at her. But this was the closest he'd ever come to talking about a future together.

She tried to make light of his comment, afraid to read too much into it. "You're just saying that because you painted over those pretty pink walls at your place."

He took her hand and pulled her close, meeting her gaze, his expression anything but playful. "I'm just saying that because I love you." He cocked his head as if to gauge her reaction.

"Oh, Caleb." Suddenly nothing else mattered but this man. He loved her.

"I really intended to make this moment more special. Tell you over candlelight and Mozart. Something more romantic than cheap grocery store flowers."

"You know what? It's perfect. Absolutely perfect." She kissed him. "I love you too."

Epilogue

December

RACHEL FORCED HERSELF to set the cruise control at the speed limit. But the miles were crawling by like a metronome set at forty beats per minute. She still had four hours to go, and she could hardly wait to get home. To Mapleview. It had been a good Christmas with her parents. They were doing well and she'd truly enjoyed her time with them.

But something—or *someone*—had been missing from her Christmas. Except for a quick video call on Christmas Eve, she hadn't seen Caleb for almost a week, and she missed him so deeply it felt like a physical pain.

She and Caleb had decided to wait until spring to go back to Kansas City together so he could meet her parents in person. They'd done several video calls together with Mom and Dad, and even if her mother hadn't told her so a dozen times, it was clear Caleb Janssen had easily won them over. Which made Rachel love him all the more.

Caleb hadn't wanted to leave his dad alone for the holidays, and she understood that. She'd finally gotten to meet Peter Janssen, and—according to Caleb—the man had declared her "good medicine." Which was the highest compliment his dad ever doled out, again, per Caleb.

Her phone played his ringtone, the chorus from "How Sweet It Is (To Be Loved by You)." Keeping her eyes on the road, she smiled and picked up the phone. "Four more hours."

He groaned. "Babe! It's taking forever."

She warmed at the endearment he'd started using for her. "I know. I'm going as fast as I can."

"No. Take your time. I want you back in one piece. But I miss you. You have no idea."

"Oh, yes, I do." If she knew him, he'd be waiting at her house when she got there. Just to tell her goodnight.

"Hey, I know it'll be late when you get home, but will you come by and see me? Just for a few minutes?"

"To your place?" Since he'd opened the gym at the end of April, they always met at her house. He had people using the gym equipment at odd hours, and the loft didn't afford much privacy, except in his bedroom, which they wouldn't feel comfortable being alone in.

"Yes. Here. Come straight here, okay? First thing."

She laughed. "You must *really* miss me."

"I do."

"Okay. I'm on my way." Something was up. Or maybe he really did miss her as much as she missed him. The last eight months had been the best of her life and had flown by in nothing flat. Even now, she had a hard time remembering what life was like before Caleb Janssen, and heaven knew she didn't even want to entertain a future without him.

Just past Chicago it started to snow, and Rachel prayed she wouldn't have to find a hotel for the night. The snow fell for the next hour all along I-94, but the roads stayed clear. After Kalamazoo, the accumulation of snow formed deep banks along the edges of the road, and she ran her wipers to keep the windshield clean. Fighting fatigue, she held onto the thought of being home—and back to him—which kept her going.

By the time the *Welcome to Mapleview* sign came into view, it was nine thirty and two inches of snow blanketed the highway. Exhausted from almost ten hours of stressful driving, she voice-texted Caleb to tell him she was almost there.

Surely, knowing how long she'd been driving, he'd tell her to go on home.

Instead, he texted: *I'll see you in a few. Can't wait.*

Feeling freshly invigorated at the thought of seeing him, she turned onto Church Street. Christmas lights twinkled all up and down the street, and the freshly fallen snow added a layer of magic to the scene in the little town she'd grown to love. Driving past Paddy's, she couldn't stop smiling, remembering that fateful day when two people who'd known each other for two years finally discovered they actually liked each other. A lot.

She took a left onto Twenty-Fifth Street and slowed as she neared Caleb's place, excitement building at the thought of seeing his smile and those blue eyes she loved. Patches of light spilled from his front windows onto the street. Boy, the place was all lit up.

Hopefully there weren't a bunch of clients working out in the gym.

But only Caleb's Toyota was in the driveway. She parked behind his car and turned off the ignition. She tapped out a quick text: *I'm here!* Then she climbed out of the car and started up the sidewalk, picking her way through the soft powder cushioning her steps.

Before she reached the front door, it swung open and Caleb hurried toward her with open arms.

She fell into his embrace, fitting into his arms as if she'd been created to belong there.

Neither of them spoke for a long minute. Finally, with one arm still around her shoulders, he turned her toward the house. "It's cold! Come inside for a minute."

She glanced toward the windows, trying to see inside. "Promise me there are no smelly jocks in the gym?"

"Promise. Only this one, and I showered today."

She laughed, then pointed back to the golden glow of light falling from the windows onto the snow. "It's so bright."

"It is since you got here." He winked. "But come on in. I have something to show you." He tugged her inside.

She shrugged out of her coat in the entryway, inhaling the scent of Christmas. Pine needles and woodsmoke and tangy cranberries. It took a minute for her eyes to adjust, but when they did, she gasped.

"Caleb, everything looks so beautiful! Oh, you made a fire in the fireplace. What—"

She couldn't take it all in at once. Three Christmas trees decked in nothing but white lights sparkled in one corner. The front windows were draped in green garlands and dripping with more twinkle lights. "You surely didn't do all this decorating for your clients?"

Wait.

She turned her gaze, sweeping from window to window. "Where's all the equipment?"

Caleb beamed in lieu of an answer.

The room was empty. And the walls were still that lovely shade of white, with just a touch of rose. She looked over at him. "What's going on, Caleb?"

He placed his hands on her shoulders and turned her toward the stage where a piano—her baby grand!—sat at just the right angle, the bench waiting in front of it.

Candles flickered all over the room. "Caleb? What is this?"

"Okay, don't be mad." He pulled out the piano bench. "Here. Sit."

She was grateful to obey, because she was feeling a little weak in the knees right now.

"This is your new piano studio. The same football crew moved it, and we had a guy come and tune it. He said it made the move perfectly."

"It's . . . staying here? But—"

"It's staying here because this is your new home.'"

"I don't understand." Her thoughts spun, frenzied, *agitato*.

"I can't exactly explain it in a way that makes sense until . . ." He knelt on the floor in front of her.

And then she *did* understand. Everything.

He'd been so afraid this would all backfire. So afraid that after everything he'd orchestrated to make this happen, she would have had too much time to think while she was in Kansas City. And on the drive home.

But looking at her face now, at the tears streaming down her cheeks, he felt pretty confident in asking the question he'd been practicing for a week now. No, longer than that. Much longer.

He took her hand, knowing without a doubt that this was the beginning—God's beginning—of the very best of his life, his future. "Rachel Hamblin, I have never loved anyone the way I love you. You have turned my life upside down and somehow righted everything in the process. God has given me so many blessings in my life, but you are by far the best of them all. Will you marry me?"

At first, her mouth moved but no words came. "Oh, Caleb," she whispered. "I can't even believe this is happening!"

"Believe it. And please say yes." He feigned a look of distress.

She laughed and took his face in her hands. "Yes. I'll marry you. Yes! But what do you mean this is my new home? And where's the gym?"

He looked askance at her. "The gym is where it's always been."

She looked past him. "But where is it now?"

"Downstairs. Where it's always been," he repeated.

"In the cellar?"

"Well, I prefer to call it a basement, but yes. Down there. Where did you think it was?"

"Right here. Where all the equipment used to be." She pointed to the front windows.

"No." He cocked his head. Why would she have thought that? "The machines were there the day we moved in only while the paint dried downstairs."

"Wait . . . You intended all along to have the gym downstairs?"

"Early on I might have considered using the main floor, but it wouldn't give me any privacy up here." He looked up to where the loft was clearly visible, as if that proved his point. "And really, the basement is perfect, especially with the outside entrance."

"You never said anything about that." She looked incredulous.

"You'll recall that you weren't exactly eager to talk about the gym or any of that."

She sighed and cupped her cheeks with both hands. "I can't believe what a fool I've been. But where will you stay?"

"That's the part I have to ask you about." He pulled her gently down beside him and gave her a sidewise glance. "You did hear the part where I asked you to marry me, right?"

She giggled. "Got that. And if memory serves, I said yes."

"Okay. Good. So, I don't know what you might have in mind as far as a timeline, but whenever—"

"Tomorrow?"

He kissed her. "That might be pushing it a little. I'm guessing your parents will want to be here for it."

"But where—?"

He put a finger gently over her lips. "Would you be quiet for two seconds and let me explain?"

She pretended to zip her lips.

"I don't have all the details worked out yet, because I wasn't sure what you would want, but if you agree, we'll trade places. You'll move here and live in the loft, teach your lessons right here. The gym will stay open just like it is now. Jed and I already tested it out, and with the new ceiling we put in last summer, you can barely hear the piano from down there, and you can't hear anything up here from the gym, even with music going. The outside entrance means you won't ever be bothered by my clients and—"

She'd started to cry. Big gulping sobs.

"Rachel? What's wrong, babe? Is it because I don't have a ring? I plan to get you one. I do. It's just that after buying the—"

"No, Caleb. I don't give two hoots about a ring." Her voice broke. "It's just *so* much. I can't even take it all in. It's too good to be true. All the trouble you've gone to. For me." She looked around the room as if in awe, and the tears started again. "It's a wondrous gift, Caleb. Truly wondrous."

Laughing, he pulled her onto his lap on the floor. "I haven't even gotten to the good part yet."

She drew back a little and stared up at him.

"I just mean the part where, after we're married, we both live here."

"I'm serious." She slipped her arms around his neck. "Tomorrow. Let's get married tomorrow."

"We'll talk about it tomorrow. How about that?"

She nodded. "Oh, Caleb. It really is like a dream."

A plaintive meow made them both look down. Tail held high, Wayne sauntered over as if he owned the place. Nudging with his nose, the cat tried to insert itself between them. Rachel giggled and Caleb shooed him away.

"I'm pretty happy with the plan too." He affected a frown. "There's just one thing."

Her brow furrowed. "What's that?"

He blew out a sigh. "I really wish you hadn't painted my new apartment pink."

She snuggled against him, shoulders shaking with laughter. "I will paint over it—any color you choose."

"Tomorrow," he whispered. "There'll be time for that tomorrow."

Author Notes

I'VE OFTEN SAID that there's not enough room on any book cover for the names of all those who pour into my life as I work on a manuscript. These dear souls deserve so much more credit than I can possibly give on one page. Romans 5:5 speaks of God's love being poured into our hearts, and that is just what it feels like when these friends, family members, and industry pros support, encourage, and offer their own gifts to help each book become a reality.

My sincerest thanks and deepest appreciation go out to: my agent Steve Laube; the talented editors and publishing team at Kregel, and especially Christina Tarabochia whose suggestions were spot on; Tamera Alexander, my dearest friend, confidante, and writing critique partner of more than 20 years now; my daughter Tavia, who proofread and cheered me on between taking care of babies (my grandbabies!) and along with my daughter Tobi and her husband, Ryan, gave insight into the hearts and lives of teachers. Thank you to these and so many other precious people who bless me in more ways than I can express. Last, but most of all, my amazing husband, Ken Raney, who makes me laugh like no other—even when I'm on deadline—and who is the inspiration for every hero in every book.

What a joy it was to write Caleb and Rachel's story. I loved brainstorming with Janyre and Amanda to dream up the sweet town of Mapleview. We especially delighted in weaving our stories together through the decades and via the stanzas of one of the most beautiful Christmas carols ever written, "O Little Town of Bethlehem."

You probably noticed that each of our titles comes from a verse in the carol. The third stanza inspired my story, especially this line, where I found my title: "The Wondrous Gift is given!"

Of course, that capital G on the word Gift indicates that the songwriter is referring to the Christ Child. Oh, what an unspeakably magnificent gift that holy child was to our hurting world—and *is* to each one who receives Jesus into his or her heart. If you haven't already accepted the forgiveness and new life he offers, I hope you "will receive Him still" and allow the dear Christ to enter in.

Wishing you a glorious Christmas and "the blessings of His heaven."

> *How silently, how silently,*
> *The Wondrous Gift is given!*
> *So God imparts to human hearts*
> *The blessings of His heaven.*
> *No ear may hear His coming,*
> *But in this world of sin,*
> *Where meek souls will receive Him still,*
> *The dear Christ enters in.*

AMANDA WEN is an award-winning writer of inspirational romance and split-time women's fiction, including the critically acclaimed *Roots of Wood and Stone* and *The Songs That Could Have Been*, the first two books in the Sedgwick County Chronicles series. Wen currently lives in Wichita, Kansas, with her husband and three children. To find her blog and short stories, visit amandawen.com.

JANYRE TROMP is a developmental book editor who has worked in the publishing industry for more than twenty years, spending time in both marketing and editorial. She is author of the full-length novel, *Shadows in the Mind's Eye*, and a contributor to the novella collection *It's a Wonderful Christmas*. When she isn't writing, she's a Bible study leader, writers conference speaker, ACFW member, wife, and mom of two kids and a menagerie of slightly eccentric pets. Visit her at janyretromp.com.

DEBORAH RANEY's forty-plus books have garnered multiple industry awards, including the RITA® Award, Carol Award, HOLT Medallion, National Readers' Choice Award, and have three times been Christy Award finalists. Deborah served on the ACFW executive board for almost eighteen years before "retiring" last year. She and her husband are recent transplants to Missouri, having moved from their native Kansas to be closer to family. Visit Deb on the web at deborahraney.com.

More from AMANDA WEN

Don't miss the books *Foreword Reviews* called "satisfying, moving novels that combine ancestral stories with a new romance."

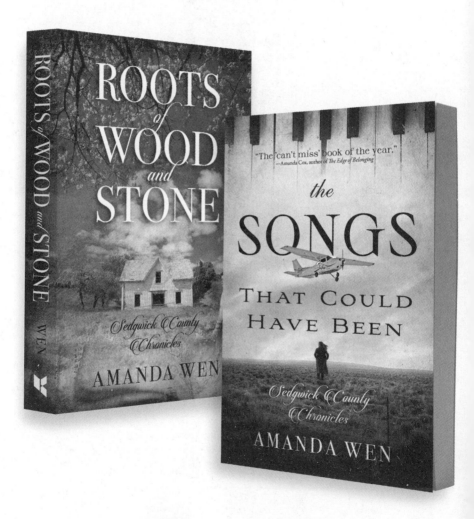

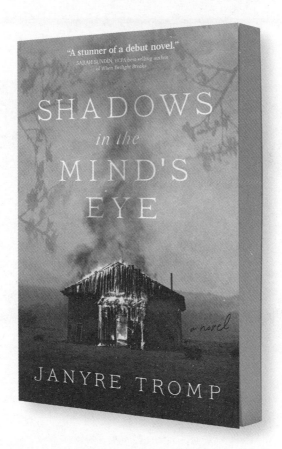

Meet the Chandler Sisters!

"Sweet romance wrapped around the life of sisters. Deb Raney captures the love of family like no other!"

—RACHEL HAUCK, *New York Times* best-selling author

"With her customary small-town charm and oh so memorable characters, Deborah Raney delivers big."

—TAMERA ALEXANDER, *USA Today* best-selling author of *With This Pledge*